Elaine

OBSESSION

Books by Jonathan Kellerman

FICTION

ALEX DELAWARE NOVELS

Obsession (2007)
Gone (2006)
Rage (2005)
Therapy (2004)
A Cold Heart (2003)
The Murder Book (2002)
Flesh and Blood (2001)
Dr. Death (2000)
Monster (1999)
Survival of the Fittest (1997)
The Clinic (1997)
The Web (1996)
Self-Defense (1995)
Bad Love (1994)
Devil's Waltz (1993)
Private Eyes (1992)
Time Bomb (1990)
Silent Partner (1989)
Over the Edge (1987)
Blood Test (1986)
When the Bough Breaks (1985)

OTHER NOVELS

Capital Crimes (with Faye Kellerman, 2006)
Twisted (2004)
Double Homicide (with Faye Kellerman, 2004)
The Conspiracy Club (2003)
Billy Straight (1998)
The Butcher's Theater (1988)

NONFICTION

Savage Spawn: Reflections on Violent Children (1999)
Helping the Fearful Child (1981)
Psychological Aspects of Childhood Cancer (1980)

FOR CHILDREN, WRITTEN AND ILLUSTRATED

Jonathan Kellerman's ABC of Weird Creatures (1995)
Daddy, Daddy, Can You Touch the Sky? (1994)

JONATHAN KELLERMAN

OBSESSION

AN ALEX DELAWARE NOVEL

MICHAEL JOSEPH
an imprint of
PENGUIN BOOKS

MICHAEL JOSEPH LTD

Published by the Penguin Group
Penguin Group (Australia)
250 Camberwell Road, Camberwell, Victoria 3124, Australia
(a division of Pearson Australia Group Pty Ltd)
Penguin Group (USA) Inc.
375 Hudson Street, New York, New York 10014, USA
Penguin Group (Canada)
90 Eglinton Avenue East, Suite 700, Toronto ON M4P 2Y3, Canada
(a division of Pearson Penguin Canada Inc.)
Penguin Books Ltd
80 Strand, London WC2R 0RL, England
Penguin Ireland
25 St Stephen's Green, Dublin 2, Ireland
(a division of Penguin Books Ltd)
Penguin Books India Pvt Ltd
11 Community Centre, Panchsheel Park, New Delhi – 110 017, India
Penguin Group (NZ)
67 Apollo Drive, Rosedale, North Shore 0632, New Zealand
(a division of Pearson New Zealand Ltd)
Penguin Books (South Africa) (Pty) Ltd
24 Sturdee Avenue, Rosebank, Johannesburg 2196, South Africa

Penguin Books Ltd, Registered Offices: 80 Strand, London, WC2R 0RL, England

Published in the United States by Ballantine Books,
a division of Random House, Inc., New York, 2007
Published in Great Britain by Michael Joseph Ltd, 2007
This edition published by the Penguin Group (Australia),
a division of Pearson Australia Group Pty Ltd, 2007

1 3 5 7 9 10 8 6 4 2

Printed and bound in Australia by McPherson's Printing Group, Maryborough, Victoria

ISBN: 978-0-7181-4824-9

www.penguin.com.au

To Faye

CHAPTER

1

Patty Bigelow hated surprises and did her best to avoid them. God had other ideas.

Patty's concept of a supreme being wavered between Ho-Ho-Ho Santa and a Fire-Eyed Odin thrusting thunderbolts.

Either way, a white-bearded guy bunking down in the clouds. Depending on his mood, dispensing goodies or playing marbles with the planets.

If pressed, Patty would've called herself an agnostic. But when life went haywire why not be like everyone else and blame A Greater Power?

The night Lydia surprised her, Patty had been home for a couple of hours, trying to wind down after a tough day in the E.R. Mellowing out with a beer, then another, and when that didn't work, giving in to The Urge.

First, she straightened the apartment, doing stuff that didn't need doing. She ended up using a toothbrush on the kitchen counter grout, cleaned the toothbrush with a wire brush that she washed under hot water and picked clean. Still tense, she saved the best for last: arranging her shoes—wiping each loafer, sneaker, and sandal clean with a chamois, sorting and re-sorting by color, making sure everything pointed outward at precisely the same angle.

Time for blouses and sweaters . . . the doorbell rang.

One twenty a.m. in Hollywood, who the heck would be dropping in?

Patty got irritated, then nervous. Should've bought that gun. She took a carving knife to the door, made sure to use the peephole.

Saw black sky, no one out there . . . oh, yes there was.

When she realized what Lydia had done, she stood there, too stunned to blame anyone.

Lydia Bigelow Nardulli Soames Biefenbach was Patty's baby sister but she'd crammed a lot more living into her thirty-five years than Patty wanted to think about.

Dropout years, groupie years, barmaid years, sitting-on-back-of-the-Harley years. Vegas, Miami, San Antonio, Fresno, Mexico, New Mexico, Wyoming, Montana. No time for postcards or sisterly calls, the only time Patty heard from Liddie had to do with money.

Lydia was quick to point out that the arrests were chickenshit, nothing that ever stuck. Responding to Patty's silence when she collect-called from some backcountry lockup and wheedled bail money.

She always paid the money back, Patty granted her that. Always the same schedule: six months later, to the day.

Liddie could be efficient when she wanted to, but not when it came to men. Before, in between, and after the three stupid marriages flowed an endless parade of pierced, inked, dirty-fingernailed, vacant-eyed losers who Liddie insisted on calling her "honeys."

All that fooling around, but miraculously only one kid.

Three years ago, Lydia taking twenty-three hours to push the baby out, alone in some osteopathic hospital outside of Missoula. Tanya Marie, five pounds, six ounces. Liddie sent Patty a newborn picture and Patty sent money. Most newborns were red and monkeylike but this kid looked pretty cute. Two years later, Lydia and Tanya showed up at Patty's door, dropping in on the way to Alaska.

No talk about why Juneau, were they meeting anyone, was Liddie clean. No hints about who the father was. Patty wondered if Lydia even knew.

Patty was no kid person and her neck got tight when she saw the toddler holding Liddie's hand. Expecting some wild little brat, given the circumstances. Her niece turned out to be sweet and quiet, kind of pretty with wispy white-blond hair, searching green eyes that would've fit a middle-aged woman, and restless hands.

"Drop-in" stretched to a ten-day stay. Patty ended up deciding Tanya was real cute, not much of a pain, if you didn't count the stink of dirty diapers.

Just as suddenly as she'd shown up, Liddie announced they were leaving.

Patty was relieved but also disappointed. "You did okay, Lid, she's a real little lady." Standing in her front door, watching as Lydia dragged the kid out with one hand, toted a battered suitcase with the other. A Yellow Cab idled at the curb, belching smog. Noise rose from down on the boulevard. Across the street a bum slouched past.

Lydia flipped her hair and grinned. Her once-gorgeous smile was insulted by two seriously chipped front teeth.

"A lady? Meaning not like *me,* Pats?"

"Oh, stop, take it for what it was," said Patty.

"Hey," said Lydia, "I'm a slut and proud of it." Shaking her chest and wiggling her butt. Laughing loud enough for the cabbie to turn his head.

Tanya was two but she must've known Mommy was being inappropriate because she winced. Patty was sure of it.

Patty wanted to protect her. "All I meant to say was she's great, you can bring her anytime." Smiling at Tanya but the kid was looking at the sidewalk.

Liddie laughed. "Even with all those shitty diapers?"

Now the kid stared off into the distance. Patty walked over to her and touched the top of her little head. Tanya started to recoil, then froze.

Patty bent a bit and talked softly. "You're a good girl, a real little lady."

Tanya laced her hands in front of her and mustered up the most painful little smile Patty had ever seen.

As if some inner voice was coaching her in the fine points of niece-to-aunt etiquette.

Lydia said, "Shitty diapers are okay? Cool, I'll remember that, Pats, on the off chance we ever roll around here again."

"What's in Juneau?"

"Snow." Lydia laughed and her boobs bounced, barely restrained by a hot-pink halter top. She had tattoos now, too many of them. Her hair looked dry and coarse, her eyes were getting grainy around the edges, and those long dancer's legs were getting jiggly around the inner thighs. All that and the broken teeth shouted Racing Over the Hill! Patty wondered what would happen when all of Lydia's looks went south.

"Stay warm," she said.

"Oh, yeah," said Lydia. "I got my ways for that." Taking hold of the little girl's wrist and pulling her toward the car.

Patty went after them. Bent to get eye-level with the kid as Lydia handed the suitcase off to the cabbie. "Nice to meet *you,* little Tanya."

That sounded awkward. What did she know about kids?

Tanya bit her lip, chewed hard.

Now here it was, thirteen months later, a hot night in June, the air stinking of Patty didn't know what, and the kid was back at her door, tiny as ever, wearing saggy jeans and a frayed white top, her hair curlier, more yellow than white.

Biting and gnawing exactly the same way. Holding a stuffed orca that was coming apart at the seams.

This time, she stared straight up at Patty.

A rumbling red Firebird was parked exactly where the cab had been. One of those souped-up numbers with a spoiler and fat tires and wire dealies clamping down the hood. The hood thumped like a fibrillating heart.

As Patty hurried toward the car the Firebird peeled out, Lydia's platinum shag barely visible through the tinted glass on the passenger side.

Patty thought her sister had waved, but she was never really sure.

The kid hadn't moved.

When Patty got back to her, Tanya reached in a pocket and held out a note.

Cheap white paper, red letterhead from the Crazy Eight Motor Hotel, Holcomb, Nevada.

Below that, Lydia's handwriting, way too pretty for someone with only junior high. Lydia had never put any effort into learning penmanship or anything else during those nine years but things came easy to her.

The kid started to whimper.

Patty took her hand—cold and teeny and soft—and read the note.

Dear Big Sis,
You said she was a lady.
Maybe with you she can really turn out to be one.
                                        Little Sis

CHAPTER

2

Not a whodunit," said Milo. "A did-it-even-happen?"

I said, "You think it's a waste of time."

"Don't you?"

I shrugged. We both drank.

"We're talking terminal illness, probably went to her brain," he said. "That's a mere layman's theory."

He pulled his glass closer, churned little viscous waves with his stirrer. We were at a steak house a couple miles west of downtown, facing up to massive T-bones, salads bigger than some people's lawns, icy Martinis.

One thirty p.m., a cool Wednesday afternoon, celebrating the end of a monthlong lust-murder trial. The defendant, a woman whose artistic pretensions led her to a killing partnership, had surprised everyone by pleading guilty.

When Milo slogged out of the courtroom, I asked him why she'd given up.

"No reason given. Maybe she's hoping for a shot at parole."

"Could that ever happen?"

"You'd think not, but if the zeitgeist gets mushy, who the hell knows?"

"Big words this early?" I said.

"Ethos, social ambience, take your pick. What I'm saying is for the last few years everyone's been big on wiping out crime. Then we do our job too well and John Q. gets complacent. The *Times* just ran one of their heartrending series about how a life sentence for murder actually means life and ain't that tragic. More of that and we're back to the sweet days of easy parole."

"That assumes people read the paper."

He huffed.

I'd been subpoenaed as prosecution witness, had spent four weeks on call, three days sitting on a wooden bench in a long, gray corridor of the Criminal Court Building on Temple.

At nine thirty a.m. I'd been working a crossword puzzle when Tanya Bigelow phoned to tell me her mother had died of cancer a month ago and she wanted a session.

It had been years since I'd seen her or her mother. "I'm so sorry, Tanya. I can see you today."

"Thank you, Dr. Delaware." Her voice caught.

"Is there anything you want to tell me now?"

"Not really—it's not about grief. It's something . . . I'm sure you'll think it's strange."

I waited. She told me some of it. "You probably think I'm obsessing."

"Not at all," I said. Lying in the service of therapy.

"I'm really not, Dr. Delaware. Mommy wouldn't have—sorry, I have to run to class. Can you see me later this afternoon?"

"How about five thirty?"

"Thank you so much, Dr. Delaware. Mom always respected you."

Milo sawed along the bone, held up a wedge of meat for inspection. The lighting made his face a gravel yard. "This look like prime to you?"

"Tastes fine," I said. "I probably shouldn't have told you about the call—confidentiality. But if it turns out to be anything serious, you know I'll be back."

The steak disappeared between his lips. His jaws worked and the acne pits on his cheeks became dancing commas. He used his free hand to push a lick of black hair off a mottled forehead. Swallowing, he said, "Sad about Patty."

"You knew her?"

"Used to see her in the E.R. when I dropped in on Rick. Hi, how's it going, have a nice day."

"Did you know she was sick?"

"Only way I'd know was if Rick told me and we've got a new rule: No business-talk after hours."

When cases are open, a homicide detective's hours never end. Rick Silverman works the E.R. at Cedars for long stretches. The two of them talk about boundaries all the time but their plans die young.

I said, "So you have no idea if she was still working with Rick?"

"Same answer. Confessing some 'terrible thing' that she did, huh? Makes no sense, Alex. Why would the kid want to dredge stuff up about her mother?"

Because the kid gets hold of something and doesn't let go. "Good question."

"When did you treat her?"

"First time was twelve years ago, she was seven."

"Twelve on the nose, not approximately," he said.

"Some cases you remember."

"Tough case?"

"She did fine."

"Super-shrink scores again."

"Lucky," I said.

He stared at me. Ate more steak. Put his fork down. "This ain't prime, at most it's choice."

We left the restaurant and he returned downtown for a paper-clearing meeting at the D.A.'s office. I took Sixth Street to its western terminus at San Vicente, where a red light gave me time to phone the Cedars-Sinai emergency room. I asked for Dr. Richard Silverman and was still on hold when the light turned green. Hanging up, I continued north to La Cienega, then west on Gracie Allen into the sprawl of the hospital grounds.

Patty Bigelow, dead at fifty-four. She'd always seemed so sturdy.

Parking in a visitors lot, I walked toward the E.R. entrance, trying to recall the last time I'd spoken to Rick professionally since he'd sent Patty and Tanya my way.

Never.

My best friend was a gay homicide detective but that didn't translate to frequent contact with the man he lived with. In the course of a year, I might chat with Rick half a dozen times when he picked up the phone at their house, the tone always light, neither of us wanting to prolong. Toss in a few dinners at celebratory times—Robin and I laughing and toasting with the two of them—and that was it.

When I reached the sliding glass doors, I put on my best doctor swagger. I'd dressed for court in a blue pin-striped suit, white shirt, yellow tie, shiny shoes. The receptionist barely looked up.

The E.R. was quiet, a few elderly patients languishing on gurneys, no electricity or tragedy in the air. As I approached the triage bay, I spotted Rick walking toward me, flanked by a couple of residents. All three of them wore blood-speckled scrubs, and Rick had on a long white coat. The residents wore badges. Rick didn't; everyone knows who he is.

When he saw me, he said something to the others that made them depart.

Detouring to a sink, he scrubbed with Betadine, dried off, extended a hand. "Alex."

I'm always careful not to exert too much pressure on fingers that suture blood vessels. Rick's grip was the usual combination of firm and tentative.

His long, lean face was capped by tight gray curls. His military mustache held on to some brown but the tips had faded. Smart enough to know better, he still frequents tanning salons. Today's bronze veneer looked fresh—maybe a noontime bake instead of lunch.

Milo stands between six two and three, depending on how his mood affects his posture. His weight fluctuates between two forty and way too high. Rick's six feet even but sometimes he appears just as tall as "the Big Guy" because his back's straight and he never tops one seventy.

Today, I noticed a stoop I'd never seen before.

He said, "What brings you here?"

"I dropped in to see you."

"Me? What's up?"

"Patty Bigelow."

"Patty," he said, eyeing the exit sign. "I could use some coffee."

◆

We poured from the doctors' urn and walked to an empty examining room that smelled of alcohol and methane. Rick sat in the doctor's chair and I perched on the table.

He noticed that the paper roll on the table needed changing, said, "Scoot up for a sec," and ripped it free. Wadding and tossing, he washed his hands again. "So Tanya did call you. The last time I saw her was a few days after Patty died. She needed some help getting hold of Patty's effects, was running into hospital bureaucracy, but even after I helped with that I got the feeling she wanted to talk about something. I asked her if there was anything else, she said no. Then about a week after that, she phoned, asked if you were still in practice or were you doing police work exclusively. I said from what I understood, you were always available to former patients. She thanked me but once again, I got the feeling she was holding back. I didn't say anything to you in case she didn't follow through. I'm glad she did. Poor kid."

I said, "What kind of cancer got Patty?"

"Pancreatic. By the time she was diagnosed, it had eaten her liver. A couple of weeks before, I noticed her looking worn down, but Patty on two cylinders was better than most people on full-burn."

He blinked. "When I saw she was jaundiced, I insisted she get it checked out. Three weeks later she was gone."

"Oh, man."

"Nazi war criminals make it to ninety, she dies." He massaged one hand with the other. "I always thought of Patty as one of those intrepid settler women who could hunt bison or whatever, skin, butcher, cook, turn the leftovers into useful objects."

He pulled at one eyelid. "All those years working with her and I couldn't do a damn thing to change the outcome. I got her the best oncologist I know and made sure Joe Michelle—our chief of anesthesiology—managed her pain personally."

"Did you spend much time with her at the end?"

"Not as much as I should've," he said. "I'd show up, we'd make a little small talk, she'd kick me out. I'd argue to make sure she meant it. She meant it."

He plucked at his mustache. "All those years she was my main RN, but apart from occasional coffee in the cafeteria, we never socialized, Alex. When I took over, I was an all-work, no-play jerk. My staff managed to show me the error of my ways and I got more socially oriented.

Holiday parties, keeping a list of people's birthdays, making sure there were cakes and flowers, all that morale-boosting stuff." He smiled. "One year, at the Christmas party, Big Guy agreed to be Santa."

"That's an image."

"Ho, ho, ho, grumble, grumble. Thank God there were no kids to sit in his lap. What I was getting at, Alex, is that Patty wasn't at that party or any other. Always straight home when she finished charting. When I tried to convince her otherwise it was 'I love you, Richard, but I am needed at home.'"

"Single-parent responsibilities?"

"Guess so. Tanya was the one person Patty tolerated in her hospital room. Kid seems sweet. Premed, she told me she's thinking psychiatry or neurology. Maybe you made a good impression."

He got up, stretched his arms over his head. Sat back down.

"Alex, the poor kid's not even twenty years old and she's alone." He reached for his coffee, stared into the cup, didn't drink. "Any particular reason you took the time to come over here?"

"I was wondering if there was anything about Patty I should know."

"She got sick, she died, it stinks," he said. "Why am I thinking that's not what you're after?"

I considered how much to tell him. Technically, he could be thought of as the referring physician. Or not.

I said, "Tanya's wanting to see me has nothing to do with grief. She wants to talk about a 'terrible thing' Patty confessed on her deathbed."

His head shot forward. "What?"

"That's as much as she'd say over the phone. Make any sense to you?"

"Sounds *ridiculous* to me. Patty was the most moral person I've met. Tanya's stressed out. People say all kinds of things when they're under pressure."

"That could be it."

He thought for a while. "Maybe this 'terrible thing' was Patty's guilt about leaving Tanya. Or she was just talking nonsense because of how sick she was."

"Did the disease affect her cognition?"

"Wouldn't surprise me, but it's not my field. Talk to her oncologist. Tziporah Ganz." His beeper sounded and he read the text message.

"Beverly Hills EMTs, infarc arriving momentarily . . . gotta go try to save someone, Alex."

He walked me through the glass doors, and I thanked him for his time.

"For what it was worth. I'm sure all this melodrama will fizzle to nothing." He rolled his shoulders. "Thought you and Big Guy were stuck in court for the rest of the century."

"The case closed this morning. Surprise guilty plea."

His beeper went off again. "Maybe that's Himself giving me the good news . . . nope, more data from the ambulance . . . eighty-six-year-old male with subterranean pulse . . . at least we're talking a full life span."

He stashed the beeper. "Not that anyone makes those value judgments, of course."

"Of course."

We shook hands again.

He said, "The primary 'terrible thing' is Patty's gone. I'm certain it'll all boil down to Tanya being stressed out. You'll help her come to grips with that."

As I turned to leave, he said, "Patty was a great nurse. She should have attended some of those parties."

CHAPTER

3

My house sits high above Beverly Glen, paper-white and sharp-edged, a pale wound in the green. Sometimes as I approach, it seems a foreign place, fashioned for someone with cold sensibilities. Inside, it's high walls, big windows, hard floors, soft furniture to gentle the edges. An assertive silence I can live with because Robin's back.

This week she was away, at a luthiers' convention up in Healdsburg, showing two guitars and a mandolin. But for the trial, I might've gone with her.

We're back together after two breakups, seem to be getting it right. When I start wondering about the future, I stop myself. If you want to get fancy, that's cognitive behavior therapy.

Along with her clothes and her books and her drawing pencils, she brought a ten-week-old, fawn-colored French bulldog pup and offered me naming honors. The dog flourished in the company of strangers so I christened her Blanche.

She's six months old now, a wrinkly, soft-bellied, flat-faced ball of serenity who spends most of her day sleeping. Her predecessor, a feisty brindle stud named Spike, had died peacefully at a mature age. I'd rescued him but he'd chosen Robin as his love object. So far, Blanche didn't discriminate.

The first time Milo saw her, he said, "This one you could think of as almost kinda pretty."

Blanche made a little purring sound, rubbed her knobby head against his shin, and turned up her lips.

"Is it smiling at me or is it gas?"

"Smiling," I said. "She does that."

He got down and took a closer look. Blanche licked his hand, moved in for the cuddle. "This is the same species as Spike?"

I said, "Think of you and Robin."

No welcoming bark as I passed through the kitchen and entered the laundry room. Blanche dozed in her crate, door open. My whispered "Good afternoon" caused her to open one huge brown eye. The natural stub that serves as a tail for Frenchies began bobbing frenetically but the rest of her remained inert.

"Hey, Sleeping Beauty."

She lifted the other eyelid, yawned, considered her options. Finally padded out and shook herself awake. I picked her up and carried her into the kitchen. The liver snap I offered would've sent Spike into a feeding frenzy. Blanche allowed me to hold it as she nibbled daintily. I toted her into the bedroom and placed her on a chair. She sighed and went back to sleep.

"That's because I'm such a fascinating guy."

I searched the storage closet for Tanya Bigelow's chart, found it at the bottom of a drawer, and skimmed. Initial treatment at age seven, one follow-up three years later.

Nothing relevant in my notes. No surprise.

At five twenty the bell rang.

A clear-skinned young blonde in a white oxford shirt and pressed jeans stood on the front landing. "You look exactly the same, Dr. Delaware."

Undersized child had morphed to petite young woman. I searched for memory jags, came up with a few: the same triangular face, square chin, pale green eyes. The tremulous lips.

I wondered if I'd have picked her out on the street.

I said, "You've changed a bit," and motioned her in.

"I sure hope so," she said. "Last time I was a baby."

Anthropologists say blond is attractive because so few towheads stay that way, it represents youth. Tanya's yellow curls had relaxed to honey waves. She wore it long, gathered in a high knot held in place by black chopsticks.

No resemblance to Patty at all.

Why should there be?

We headed up the hallway. As we neared the office, Blanche stepped out. Shook herself, yawned, padded forward. I scooped her up.

"Now, *this* is different," said Tanya. "The only livestock you had last time were those gorgeous fish."

"They're still here."

She reached out to pet the dog, changed her mind.

"Her name is Blanche. She's well beyond friendly and into gregarious."

Tanya extended a cautious finger. "Hi, cutie." A puppy shiver jelloed Blanche's rotund little body. A moist black nose sniffed in Tanya's direction. Meaty lips curled upward.

"Am I anthropomorphizing, Dr. Delaware, or is she smiling?"

"You're not, she is."

"*So* cute."

"I'll put her back in her crate and we can get started."

"A crate? Is that necessary?"

"It makes her feel more secure."

She looked doubtful.

I said, "Think of a baby in a crib as opposed to rolling around in open space."

"I guess," she said, "but don't banish her on my account. I love dogs." She rubbed the top of Blanche's head.

"Want to hold her?"

"I . . . if she's okay with it."

Blanche went along with the transfer with nary a twitch. Someone should study her brain chemistry and package it.

"She's so warm—hey, cutie. Is she a pug?"

"French bulldog. If she gets too heavy—"

"Don't worry, I'm stronger than I look."

We settled in facing chairs.

"Comfy leather," she said, stroking an arm. "That's the same . . ." Looking down at Blanche. "Am I holding her correctly?"

"Perfect."

She looked around the room. "Nothing in here has changed but the rest of the house is totally different. It used to be smaller. With wood sides, right? At first I didn't think I had the right address."

"We rebuilt a few years ago." A psychopath had made the decision for us, torching everything we owned.

Tanya said, "It came out extremely stylish."

"Thank you."

"So," she said. "Here I am."

"Good to see you, Tanya."

"Same here." She looked around. "You probably think I should talk about Mommy's death."

"If you want to."

"I really *don't,* Dr. Delaware. I'm not in denial, it's been a nightmare, I never thought I'd experience anything this horrifying. But I'm handling my grief as well as can be expected—does that sound like denial?"

"You're the best judge of that, Tanya."

"Well," she said, "I really feel I am. I don't bottle up my feelings. On the contrary, I cry. Oh, boy, I cry plenty. I still wake up every morning expecting to see her, but . . ."

Her eyes misted.

"It hasn't been long," I said.

"Sometimes it seems like *yesterday.* Sometimes, it's as if she's been gone forever . . . I suspected she was sick before she did."

"She wasn't feeling well?"

"She just wasn't herself for a couple of weeks."

Same thing Rick had said.

"Not that it stopped her from double-shifting or cooking or keeping up the house, but her appetite dropped and she started losing weight. When I pointed it out, she said don't complain, maybe she'd finally be skinny. But that was the point. Mommy could *never* lose weight, no matter how hard she tried. I'm premed, knew enough bio to wonder about diabetes. One night, when she'd barely touched her dinner, I pointed out what was happening. She said it was just menopause, no big deal. But she'd started going into menopause two years ago and women typically gain, they don't lose. I pointed that out but she brushed me off. Finally, a week later, she was forced to check it out."

"Forced by what?"

"Dr. Silverman noticed the yellow in her eyes and insisted. But even with that, before she agreed to see a doc, she had blood drawn in the E.R. When the results came back, Dr. Silverman ordered an emergency CAT scan. The tumor was sitting right in the middle of the pancreas and there were metastases in her liver and her stomach and her intestines. She went downhill fast. Sometimes I wonder if the shock of *knowing* took all the fight out of her. Or maybe it was just the natural course of the disease."

She sat straight-backed, dry-eyed. Petted Blanche slowly. Someone who didn't know her might judge her detached.

I said, "How long was she ill?"

"From the day of diagnosis, twenty-five days. Most of that was spent in the hospital; she became too weak to live at home. In the beginning, she did her best to be ornery—complaining her tray wasn't taken away promptly, griping that float nurses weren't like regular nurses, there was no continuity of care. Every shift, she insisted on reading her chart, double-checked that her vitals had been recorded accurately. I guess it made her feel in control. Mommy was always big on control. Did she ever tell you about her childhood?"

"A bit."

"Enough for you to know what happened to her in New Mexico?"

I nodded.

Small hands clenched. "It's a miracle she turned out so wonderful."

"She was a terrific person," I said.

"She was an *incredible* person." She studied an etching on the left wall. "That first week in the hospital, she was an absolute despot. Then she got too sick to fight, mostly slept and read fan rags—that's what she called celebrity magazines. That's when I knew it was really bad."

She turned her lips inward. "*Us, People, Star, OK!* Stuff she'd always made fun of when I brought it home for weekend reading. I'm no star-chaser but I do work-study at the U. library fifteen hours a week and between that and premed, why not enjoy a little guilty pleasure? Mommy loved to kid me. Her fun reading consisted of investment books, the financial pages, and nursing journals. At heart she was an intellectual. People tended to underestimate her."

"Serious error in judgment," I said.

She petted Blanche. "True, but the country-girl image could also work against her. She told me before she met Dr. Silverman she never got what she deserved from her bosses. He appreciated her, made sure she received her promotions . . . anyway, I think you can see that I'm working through the grief. I don't repress. Just the opposite, I *force* myself to remember everything I can. Like when you have a splinter and dig deep."

I nodded.

"Sometimes," she said, "I freak out, cry it out, get too tired to feel anything. Nights are the worst. I have nonstop dreams. That's normal, right?"

"Dreams in which she appears?"

"It's more than that. She's *there.* Talks to me. I see her lips move, hear sound but can't make out the words, it's frustrating . . . sometimes I can *smell* her—the way she always smelled at night, toothpaste and talcum powder, it's so vivid. Then I wake up and she's not there and there's a huge feeling of deflation. But I know that's typical. I read several books on grief."

She recited half a dozen titles. I knew four. Two were good.

"I found them on the Web, chose the ones with the best feedback." Wincing. "I'll just have to go through this. What I *do* need help with—and please forgive me but I'm not even sure you're the right person to talk to about it . . ." Her cheeks colored. "I thought of talking to Dr. Silverman . . . I turned to you because Mommy respected you. So do I, of course. You helped me . . ." She compressed her lips again. Plinked one thumbnail with the other.

Smiling at me. "You're not allowed to be angry, right?"

"What would I be angry about?"

"If I wasn't totally up front—okay, let me just get it out. The real reason I'm here is that you work with that detective—Dr. Silverman's significant other. I would've gone straight to Dr. Silverman but I really don't know him that well and you were my therapist so I can tell you anything." Deep breath. "Right?"

"You want me to put you in contact with Detective Sturgis."

"If you think he can help."

"With . . . ?"

"Investigating," she said. "Finding out exactly what happened."

"The 'terrible thing' your mother confessed."

"It wasn't a confession, more like . . . there was *drive* there, Dr.

Delaware. Drive and determination. Exactly the way Mommy got when a problem needed to be solved. You're thinking I'm being ridiculous, she was sick, her brain was impaired. But as sick as she was, she clearly wanted me to focus."

"On the terrible thing."

She blinked. "My eyes itch. May I have a tissue, please?"

Swiping her lids, she exhaled.

Blanche's flews billowed.

Tanya looked down at her. "Did she just *imitate* me?"

"Think of it as empathy."

"Whoa. She's the perfect *psychologist's* dog." Sudden smile. "When does she get her own Ph.D.?"

"*You* talk to her," I said. "She wants to be an attorney."

When she stopped laughing, she said, "What was that? Comic relief?"

"Think of it as a pause for air."

"Yes . . . so may I tell you exactly what happened?"

That's what they pay me for.

I said, "I'm listening."

4

T he second week was all about pain," she said. "That was everyone's focus except Mommy's."

"Hers was . . ."

"Getting stuff done. What she called putting her ducks in a row. At first, it upset me. I wanted to take care of her, tell her how much I loved her, but when I started to do that she'd cut me off. 'Let's talk about your future.' Saying it slowly, gasping, struggling, and I'm thinking it's a future without *her*."

"Maybe that distracted her from the pain."

The muscles around her eyes shivered. "Dr. Michelle—the anesthesiologist—had her hooked up to a morphine drip. The idea was to give her a constant flow, so she'd experience as little discomfort as possible. Most of the time she turned it off. I overheard Dr. Michelle tell a nurse she had to be suffering but there was nothing he could do. Do you remember how totally obstinate she could be?"

"She had definite opinions."

"Ducks in a row," she said. "She lectured and I had to take notes, there were so many details. It was like being in school."

"What kind of details?"

"Financial. Financial security was a big thing for her. She told me about a trust fund she'd set up for my education when I was four. She thought I had no idea but I used to hear her talking to her broker over the phone. I pretended to be amazed. There were two life insurance policies with me as the sole beneficiary. She was proud of paying off the house, having no debts, between my job and the investments I'd be able to pay the property taxes and all the routine bills. She ordered me to sell my car—actually quoted me the blue-book value—and to keep hers because it was newer, would require less maintenance. She spelled out exactly how much I could spend per month, told me to get by with less if I could help it but always to dress well, appearances counted. Then there were all the phone numbers: broker, lawyer, accountant, plumber, electrician. She'd already contacted everyone, they were expecting to hear from me. I had to be in charge of my own life, now, and she expected I'd be mature enough to handle it. When she got to the part about selling her clothes at a garage sale or on eBay, I started crying and begged her to stop."

"Did she?" I said.

"Tears always worked with Mommy. When I was little I took advantage of that."

"All that planning for your future had to be overwhelming."

"She's going on about property tax and I'm like, 'Soon, she's not going to *exist*.' It empowered her, Dr. Delaware, but it was tough. I had to recite back what I'd learned, like a pop quiz."

"Knowing you understood was a comfort for her."

"I hope so. I only wish we could've spent more time . . . that's selfish, the key is to focus on the person who's suffering, right?"

That sounded like a quote from a book.

"Of course."

She hugged herself with one hand, kept the other on Blanche. Blanche licked her hand. Tanya started crying.

Pulling her hair loose, she freed a blond mane that she shook violently before reknotting and jamming in the chopsticks.

"Okay," she said. "I'll get to the point. It was Friday night. I got to the hospital later than usual, because I had organic chem lab and a lot of studying. Mommy looked so weak, I couldn't believe the change since the morning. Her eyes were shut, her skin was greenish gray, her hands were like packages of twigs. The fan rags were piled up all around her, it looked like she was being swallowed by paper. I started straightening. She opened her eyes and whispered something I couldn't hear so I put my ear close to her mouth."

Twisting a chopstick. "At first I couldn't even feel her breath and I pulled away, panicked. But she was looking straight up at me, the light was still on inside. Do you remember her eyes? How sharp and dark they were? They were like that then, Dr. Delaware—focused, staring up at me, she was moving her lips but they were so dry she couldn't get the sound out. I wet a towel and she made a little kissy pucker and I bent and she touched her lips to my cheek. Then somehow she managed to push up with her head to get closer so I leaned down farther. She got one hand behind my neck and pressed. I could feel her I.V. tubing tickling the back of my ear." She looked away. "I need to walk around."

Placing Blanche on the floor, she stood. Blanche trotted over and settled in my lap.

Tanya crossed the room twice, then returned to her chair but remained on her feet. A hank of hair fell loose, blocking one eye. Her chest heaved.

"Her breath was like ice. She started talking again—gasping the words. What she said was, 'Did bad.' Then she repeated it. I said you could never do anything bad. She hissed so loud it hurt my ear, said, '*Terrible* thing, baby,' and I could feel her face tremble."

Stretching the corners of her eyes, she let go, took a deep breath. "This is the part I didn't tell you over the phone. She said, '*Killed* him. *Close* by. *Know* it. *Know*.' I'm still trying to figure it out. There were no men in her personal life, so it couldn't mean close as in a relationship. The only other thing I can think of is she was being literal. Someone who lived near us. I've been racking my brains to see if I can remember some neighbor dying in a weird way, and I can't. Just before I came to see you, we were living in Hollywood and I remember hearing sirens all the time and once in a while some drunk would knock on the door, but that's it. Not that I'd ever believe she could ever hurt someone deliberately."

She sat down.

I said, "You don't know what to believe."

"You think this is totally crazy. I did, too. I resisted dealing with it. But I can't let go of it. Not because of my tendencies. Because Mommy wanted me to learn the truth. That's what she meant by 'Know it.' It was important to her that I understand because the whole last week she was ordering my future and this was part of it."

I kept silent.

"Maybe it *is* crazy. But the least I can do is check it out. That's why I thought maybe Detective Sturgis could run a computer search on the places we lived to see if something happened nearby and we'd learn nothing and that would be it."

Child of the cyber-age. I said, "LAPD's computer system is pretty primitive, but I'll ask. Before we get into that, you might consider—"

"If I'm prepared to learn something horrible. The answer is no, not really, but I don't believe Mommy actually *killed* someone. That would be *totally* insane. What I'm thinking is at the worst she was involved in some kind of accident that she blamed herself for and she wanted to make sure it didn't come back on me. Like a legal claim. She wanted to make sure I was prepared."

She sat forward, played with her hair, used a long thick swatch to cover her eyes, let it drop.

I said, "After she told you all this, what did you say?"

"Nothing, because she fell asleep. It was like she'd unburdened herself and now she could rest. For the first time since she'd been hospitalized, she looked peaceful. I sat there for a while. Her nurse came in, checked her vitals, turned on the morphine drip, said she'd be out for at least six hours, I could leave and come back. I stuck around a little longer, finally went home because I had a test to study for."

One hand clawed a chair arm. "The call came at three a.m. Mommy had passed in her sleep."

"I'm so sorry, Tanya."

"They said she didn't suffer. I'd like to think that she went peacefully because she was able to express herself that last time. I need to honor her memory by following through. Since she died, I've been replaying it every day. 'Terrible thing.' 'Killed him, close by.' Sometimes it feels ridiculous, like one of those corny scenes you see in old movies: 'the killer was—' and then the person drops back and closes their eyes? But I *know* Mommy wouldn't have wasted the time and energy she had left if it wasn't important. Will you talk to Detective Sturgis?"

"Of course."

"Maybe if you tell him what Mommy was like, he won't think I'm totally whack. I'm so glad I came back to you. You understand why she was more than the best mother. I didn't come out of her womb and when Lydia ditched me, it would have been easy to send me off somewhere and go on living her life. Instead, she *gave* me a life."

"You brought meaning to her life, as well."

"I hope."

"Her pride in you was obvious, Tanya."

"It wasn't equal, Dr. Delaware. Without *her* I'd be *nothing*." She glanced at her watch.

"We've got time left," I said.

"That's really all I have to talk about." She stood again. Out of her purse came a white business-sized envelope that she'd brought to me. *P. L. Bigelow* embossed on the back flap, an address on Canfield Avenue. Inside was a sheet folded in perfect thirds. Typed list, centered.

Four other addresses, each accompanied by Tanya's handwritten notation.

Cherokee Avenue, Hollywood. *We lived here four years, from when I was three until I was seven.*

Hudson Avenue, Hancock Park. *Two years, seven until around nine or so.*

Fourth Street, the Wilshire district. *One year, nine to ten.*

Culver Boulevard, Culver City. *Two years, ten until twelve, then we bought the duplex.*

Constructing the timeline using her age. Playing adult but clinging to the self-centered world view of an adolescent.

I said, "Maybe whatever happened was relatively recent."

Pretending to be a believer.

"At Canfield? No, it's been peaceful there. And I was older when we moved, would know if something happened in the neighborhood. By the way, I relinquish all confidentiality so feel free to tell Detective Sturgis anything you want. Here, I've put it in writing."

Out of the purse came another razor-creased paper. Handwritten release note, composed in the stilted wording of amateur legalese. Then a check, made out to the discounted fee I'd billed her mother ten years ago. Twenty percent of what I got nowadays.

"Is that okay?"

"Absolutely."

She headed for the door. "Thank you, Dr. Delaware."

"Did your mother ever talk about any malpractice cases at the hospital?"

"No. Why?"

"The E.R.'s a high-risk unit. What if a patient she was involved with died and she felt responsible?"

"No way she'd ever mess someone up fatally, Dr. Delaware. She knew more than some of the doctors."

"Lawsuits don't always depend upon truth," I said. "In a hospital situation, lawyers sometimes go after anyone who blinked at the patient."

She leaned against the door. "Malpractice. Oh, my God, why didn't I think of that? There could be some huge lawsuit pending and she was worried someone would go after my trust fund. Or the duplex. She wanted to tell me more but ran out of steam—you're brilliant, Dr. Delaware!"

"It's just a suggestion—"

"But a great one. Scientific parsimony, right? Go for the simplest explanation. I can't *believe* I didn't think of it."

"You've had a lot on your mind. I'll call Dr. Silverman right now."

I reached the E.R. Rick was in surgery. "He'll call back. If there's something to tell you, I promise to let you know right away."

"Thank you so much, Dr. Delaware—no offense but can we be sure Dr. Silverman will be up front? Maybe his lawyers have told him not to discuss—okay, sorry, that's stupid, I'm being paranoid."

"Still want me to talk to Detective Sturgis?"

"Only if Dr. Silverman says there was no malpractice issue for Mommy, but something tells me you've figured it out. She always *said* you were brilliant."

Ten years ago my treatment of her had been anything but. I smiled and walked her out.

When we reached her van, I said, "Once we resolve this, would you consider a couple more sessions?"

"To accomplish what?"

"I'd like to know more about your living circumstances and who you have for support."

"My living circumstances haven't changed. The duplex is all paid off, and the downstairs tenants are a really nice young family, the Friedmans. Their rent covers expenses plus extras. They're in Israel for Dr. Friedman's sabbatical but they advanced me a year's worth and are planning to come back. Mommy's insurance and investments will take care of me until I finish at the U. If I end up at a private med school, I may have to take out some loans. But physicians do fine, I'll pay them off. My friends at school give me support, there's a group of us, all premed, they're very cool and understanding."

"Sounds good," I said, "but I'd still feel better if you were open to coming back."

"I will be, I promise, Dr. Delaware. Just as soon as my exams are over." She smiled. "Don't worry, I'm not having any of my old problems. I appreciate your caring. Mommy always said for you it was more than a job. She told me I should observe you, learn what caring for patients meant."

"How old were you when she told you that?"

"That was . . . right before the second time I saw you, we'd just moved to Culver, so . . . ten."

"At ten, you knew you wanted to be a physician?"

"I've always wanted to be a physician."

As we descended the stairs, she said, "Do you believe in the Hereafter?"

"It's a comforting concept."

"Meaning you don't?"

"Depends on what day you catch me." Images of my parents flashed in my head. Dad, red-nosed, in boozer's heaven. Were there celestial procedures in place for unpredictable behavior?

Maybe Mom could finally be happy, nestled in some heavenly duplicate bridge club.

"Well," she said, "that's honest. I guess it's the same for me. Mostly I think in terms of scientific logic, show me the data. But lately I find myself believing in the spirit world, because I sense her with me. It's not constant, just sometimes, when I'm alone. I'll be doing something and feel her. It could be just my emotional need but the day it stops may be when I show up for some *real* therapy."

CHAPTER

5

ick said, "No, nothing like that, current or past. In fact,
we're having a nice quiet spell, shyster-wise. And when the
vultures swoop, they avoid the nurses. No financial incentive."

"Did Patty moonlight?"

"Not since she's worked for me. When she wanted extra money,
she double-shifted."

"Where did she work before she came to Cedars?"

"Kaiser Sunset, but only for a year. Scratch the malpractice angle,
Alex."

"Okay, thanks."

"How's Tanya doing?"

"As well as can be expected."

"Good. Gotta run. Thanks for seeing her."

Straight to the point. Surgical. Just like his original referral.

*"I know you're not doing much therapy, Alex, but this sounds more
like a consultation."*

"Who's the consultee?"

*"Best nurse I ever worked with, a woman named Patty Bigelow. A
few years ago her sister dumped a kid on her, then left for parts
unknown. Sister died in a motorcycle accident and Patty adopted the*

girl, who's now seven. She's got some parenting questions. Can you see her?"

"Sure."

"I appreciate it . . ."

"Anything else I should know?"

"About what?" he said.

"Patty, the girl."

"I've only seen the girl in passing. Cute little thing. Patty's super-organized. Maybe a little too much for a kid."

"A perfectionist."

"You could say that. She fits in great in my E.R. It was hard for her to admit having a problem. I don't know why she chose me to tell."

"She trusts you."

"Could be that . . . I'll give her your number, gotta run."

An hour later, Patty Bigelow had called. "Hi, Doctor. I won't gab on the phone because you sell your time and I'm no mooch. When's your next opening?"

"I could see you today at six."

"Nope," she said, "on shift until seven and Tanya's out of day care at eight, so I'm in for the evening. Tomorrow I'm off."

"How about ten a.m.?"

"Great, thanks. Should I bring Tanya?"

"No, let's talk first."

"I was hoping you'd say that. What's your fee?"

I told her, said I'd be cutting it in half.

"That's seriously below average," she said. "Dr. Silverman assures me you're not."

We debated for a while. I prevailed.

Patty said, "I don't usually give in, Dr. Delaware. You might be just the right person for Tanya."

The next morning, at nine forty-two, I was out on the landing when a blue minivan pulled up in front of the house. The engine switched off but the vehicle stayed in place.

A woman with short brown hair sat behind the wheel, balancing a checkbook. As I approached she put it away.

"Ms. Bigelow?"

A hand shot out the window. Compact, nails cut square. "Patty. I'm early, didn't want to bother you."

"No bother, c'mon in."

She got out of the car, holding a black briefcase. "Tanya's medical records. Do you have a Xerox machine?"

"I do, but let's talk first."

"Whatever you say." She climbed the stairs just ahead of me. I put her at forty or so. Short and dark-eyed and round-faced, wearing a navy turtleneck over easy-fit jeans and spotless white tennies. The clothes made no attempt to streamline a broad, blocky body. Brown hair streaked with gray was cut in an anti-style as frivolous as a lug wrench. No makeup but good skin, ruddy with a faint underglow and no age lines. She smelled of shampoo.

When we reached the stairs to the front landing, she said, "Real pretty out here."

"It is."

No more conversation as we headed to the office. Midway there, she paused to straighten a picture with a fingertip. Hanging back a half step, as if to avoid notice. I noticed anyway and she grinned. "Sorry."

"Hey," I said, "I'll take all the help I can get."

"Be careful what you ask for, Doctor."

She scanned my diplomas and perched on the edge of a chair. "I see another couple more crooked ones."

"Earthquake country," I said. "The ground's always shifting."

"You've got that right, we're living in a jelly jar. Ever try museum wax? Little dab on the bottom center of the frame and if you need to get it off the wall you can peel it without leaving a mark."

"Thanks for the tip."

Positioning the briefcase so that its front end was flush with a chair leg, she said, "May I?" and got up before I could answer. When the prints were straight, she returned to her chair and folded her hands in her lap. A peachy blush coined the upper rims of her cheeks. High cheekbones, the only bits of definition in the wide, smooth face. "Sorry, again, but it really drives me nuts. Should I talk about Tanya or me?"

"How about both?"

"Any preference as to order?"

"Tell it the way you want," I said.

"Okay. In a really small nutshell here's my story, so you'll under-stand Tanya. My sister and I grew up on a ranch outside of Galisteo, New Mexico. Both our folks were drunks. My mother was the ranch cook, good in the kitchen but she didn't give a hoot about mothering. My father was the foreman and when he got plastered, he came into our bedroom and did ugly stuff to me and my sister—I don't need to go into details, do I?"

"Not unless you want to."

"I *don't* want to. It affected my sister and me differently. She turned wild and chased men and drank and took every drug she could get her hands on. She's gone, now, motorcycle crash." Short, deep breath. "I became a Goody Two-shoes. The two of us weren't very close. As it turned out, I have no interest in men. None. Or women, in case you're curious."

"I'm always curious, but that hadn't occurred to me."

"No?" she said. "Some folks think I'm pretty butch."

I said nothing.

"Also, seeing as how Richard—Dr. Silverman—was the one who re-ferred me and how people jump to conclusions, I could understand you thinking I was gay."

"I work hard at not jumping to conclusions."

"It wouldn't bother me if I was gay, but I'm not. I have no interest in anybody's anything below the waist. If you need a label, how about asexual? That make me crazy in your book?"

"Nope."

Another partial smile. "You're probably just saying that because you want to develop whatchamacallit rapport."

I said, "You're not interested in sex. That's your prerogative. So far I've heard nothing crazy."

"Society thinks it's weird."

"Then we won't let Society into the office."

She smiled. "Moving on: My sister—Lydia, she went by Liddie—couldn't keep her pants on. Maybe God played tricks, huh? Two girls dividing up one sex drive?"

"Hers on Monday, yours on Tuesday but she got greedy?"

She laughed. "Sense of humor's important in your business."

"Your business, too."

"You know much about my job?"

"Dr. Silverman told me you're the best nurse he's ever worked with."

"The man exaggerates," she said, but her eyes sparkled. "Okay, maybe just a slight exaggeration, 'cause off the bat I can't think of anyone better. Last night we had a guy, a gardener, mangled both hands in a lawn mower. Too much empathy and you find yourself depressed all the time . . . speaking of bad stuff, plenty happened to my sister, but nothing she didn't earn. She died on back of a Harley on the way to a big bike meet in South Dakota. No helmet, same for the genius driving. He took a turn wrong, they went flying off the road."

"Sorry to hear about that."

She squinted. "I cried some but—and this is going to sound cold—the way Liddie lived it was a miracle it didn't happen sooner. Anyway, the gist of all this is to explain how I came to have Tanya. She's Liddie's biologically but one day when she was three, Liddie decided she didn't want her anymore and dumped her on my doorstep. Literally, middle of the night, I hear the doorbell, go out, find Tanya clutching a stuffed toy, some killer whale souvenir she got in Alaska. Liddie's parked in a hotwheels at the curb and when I go to talk to her, the car peels out. That was four years ago and I never heard from her again, didn't even get the death notice until a year after the accident because Liddie was carrying fake I.D., it took the highway cops awhile to figure out who she was."

"How did Tanya react?"

"She cried for a few days, then she stopped. She'd ask about Liddie from time to time but nothing chronic. My answer was always Mommy loved her, had left her with me 'cause I could take better care of her. I bought a book on explaining death to kids, used the parts that made sense and discarded the parts that didn't. Overall, Tanya seemed to accept it pretty well. Asked the right questions. Then she went about her business. I kept telling her Mommy loved her, would always love her. After maybe the gazillionth time I said it, Tanya looks up at me and says, 'You're my mommy. You love me.' Next day I started the adoption process." Blinking and looking away. "This at all helpful, so far?"

"Perfect," I said.

"Maybe you'll find out something I missed but she really seemed to deal with it okay. She's a smart kid, her teacher has her at a half year ahead of the class. Got a grown-up way about her, which makes sense, given the years she spent traipsing around with Liddie. My influence, too, maybe. I'm no kid person, don't have a clue about 'em. So I treat her like she understands everything."

"Sounds like that's working."

"So how come I'm here, huh?" She looked down at her shoes, placed them together. Moved them a foot apart. "You probably noticed I'm a little strange in the neatness department. Need to have everything just so, nothing out of place, no surprises. Maybe because of the things my father did to me, but who cares why, the point is that's how I am and I like it. Keeps life organized and when you're busy, believe me, that's a big help."

"Making things predictable."

"Exactly. Like the way I hang my clothes. Everything's grouped by color, style, sleeve length. Blouses in one section, then jeans, then uniforms, et cetera. Why waste time looking in the morning? A couple of times, when I was working a shift that had me getting up when it was still dark, there were power outages. I'm talking a pitch-black house. I could get dressed, no problem, because I knew exactly where everything was hanging."

"It works for you."

"Sure does," she said. "But now I'm thinking maybe I should've kept some of that to myself, not revealed it to Tanya."

"She's doing the same things?"

"She's always been neat for a kid, which is fine by me. We clean house together, have fun doing it. But lately, it's more than that. She's got these little routines, won't go to sleep until she checks under her bed, first it was five times, then ten, now it's twenty-five, maybe even more. Top of that, she's got to straighten her drapes and kiss them, goes to the bathroom five times in a row, washes her hands until the soap's gone. I went in there once and she was polishing the spigots."

"How long has this been going on?"

"It started right around when she turned five."

"Two years ago."

"Give or take. But it wasn't a big deal until recently."

"Any recent changes?"

"We moved to a new place—got a sublease in a house in Hancock Park. No problems, there. Tanya's fine except for the routines."

"Do the routines always begin before bedtime?"

"That's the peak period," she said, "but it's moved into other times and it's starting to affect her schoolwork. Not in terms of neglecting her obligations—just the opposite. She'll tear up her work and redo it, over and over, unless I make her stop. Lately, she started getting real picky about her school lunch. If the sandwich isn't cut exactly on the right bias, she wants to make another one."

Reaching down, she touched the briefcase. "Want to see any of her records?"

"Has she had any unusual illnesses or injuries?"

"Nope."

"Then I'll read the records later. Do you have information about her birth?"

"Nothing. I had to run titers on her to make sure she'd been vaccinated. She had, I'll grant Liddie that." She leaned forward. "You need to understand, Doctor, the only time I met Tanya before Liddie dropped her off was once, when she was two. She and Liddie stayed with me a couple of weeks before heading up to Juneau, Alaska. Like I said, I'm no kid person. But I ended up liking her. Sweet, quiet, didn't get underfoot. She's still that way, I couldn't ask for a better daughter. It's just these new habits are making me wonder about my approach. I did some reading on OCD in kids and they say it could be genetic, in the brain, serotonin uptake, they're trying various meds as treatment."

"Nowadays, most everything is attributed to neurotransmitters."

"You don't recommend meds on scientific grounds? Or you don't like them because Ph.D.'s can't use them?"

"Meds have their place and if you're interested in that route, I'd be happy to refer you to a good child psychiatrist. I've found childhood OCD to respond well to nondrug treatments."

"Such as?"

"Cognitive behavior therapy, other anxiety-reduction techniques. Sometimes just finding out what's making the child tense and remedying it is enough."

"Tanya doesn't seem nervous, Doc. Just intensely focused."

"OCD's rooted in anxiety. Her habits are doing their job so the tension's masked, but you're describing a steadily expanding pattern."

She thought about that. "Guess so . . . listen, no offense meant by that remark about Ph.D.'s."

"None taken," I said. "You're an informed consumer who wants the best for her child."

"I'm a mother who feels bad because her kid seems to be losing control. And I blame myself because *I* need for everything to be predictable and everyone to be happy. And that's about as realistic as world peace."

"I'm a people-pleaser, too, Ms. Bigelow. If I wasn't, I could've been a lawyer and billed more per hour."

She laughed. "Now that I fixed your pictures, you do seem like a pretty organized guy. So you think you can help Tanya just by talking?"

"My approach would be to develop whatchamacallit rapport, see if there's anything on her mind that you're unaware of, find out if she's interested in changing, and help her change."

"What if she doesn't want to change?"

"My experience has been that kids aren't happy being bound by all those routines. They just don't see a way out. Have you talked to her about any of this?"

"I started to," she said. "Last week or so, when she got into the curtain-kissing. I guess I lost my patience and told her to stop being silly. She gave me a look that cut me right here." Touching her left breast. "Like I'd *wounded* her. I immediately felt like a truckful of manure and had to leave the room to do some breathing. When I gathered the gumption to go back in there and apologize, the lights were off and she was in bed. But when I leaned down to kiss her, her body was all tight and she was gripping the covers—with the fingernails, you know? I told myself whoa, Patty, you're screwing the kid up, time for professional advice. I talked to Richard—Dr. Silverman—and first thing out of his mouth is your name. He said you're the best. After meeting you, I'm feeling good. You don't judge, you listen. And those degrees ain't too shabby, either. So when can you see Tanya?"

"I've got an opening in a couple of days, but if it's urgent, I'll make time tonight."

"Naw," she said. "I think I can handle a couple of days. Got any advice beyond lay off and don't say anything stupid?"

"Explain to Tanya that you're bringing her to a doctor who doesn't give shots and won't hurt her in any way. Use the word 'psychologist' and tell her I help kids who are nervous or worried by talking to them, drawings, playing games. Tell her she won't be forced to do anything she doesn't want to."

She opened the briefcase, found a legal pad, scrawled notes. "I think I've got all that . . . sounds fine except for the games. Tanya doesn't like games, can't even get her to use a deck of cards."

"What does she like?"

"Drawing's okay, she's pretty good at that. Also, she does cutouts—paper dolls, she can handle a scissors like a pro. Maybe she'll be a surgeon."

"Like Rick."

"That would be okay with me. So what time in a couple of days?"

We set up the appointment. She said, "Fine, thanks much," and paid me in cash. Smiling. "You're sure you only want half?"

I smiled back, photocopied Tanya's medical records, and returned the originals to her. Five minutes to go, but she said, "We covered everything," and got up.

Then: "Just talking helps, even if it's genetic?"

I said, "There may be a genetic component. Most tendencies are a combination of nature and nurture. But tendencies aren't programmed like blood types."

"People can change."

"If they didn't, I'd be out of business."

That evening at five, she called me through my service. "Doc, if an appointment tonight's still an option, I'll take you up on it. Tanya started in on her homework, tore it up, redid it, then she got all hysterical. Crying that she could never do anything right. Saying I was ashamed of her, she was a bad girl, like Liddie. Nothing like that ever came out of my mouth but maybe I somehow communicated . . . Right now she's calm, but not a calm I like. *Way* too quiet, generally she chatters away. I haven't told her I made an appointment with you. If you say tonight's okay, I'll explain it to her in the car."

"C'mon over," I said.

"You're a saint."

◆

She showed up an hour later, with a little blond girl in hand. In her other hand was a small white jar.

"Museum wax," she said. "Long as I was coming here. This is Tanya Bigelow, my beautiful, smart daughter. Tanya, meet Dr. Delaware. He's going to help you."

CHAPTER

6

Milo touched a corner of the newspaper he'd slid across the booth. "Cute, huh?"

Ten a.m., North Hollywood. Hot Friday in the Valley, the Du-par's on Ventura east of Laurel Canyon.

I'd left a message for Tanya about no malpractice issue, told her I'd be contacting Detective Sturgis. An hour later I was watching him jab the front-page *Times* article with his fork.

Breathless coverage of the founding of a mental health program in Tahiti by a former film agent and a retired studio head. Diploma mill doctorate for her, deep pockets and May–December infatuation for him. The agenda was past-life regression, a Chinese menu of meditation games, all the therapy you could eat for two hundred grand a pop, no refunds. The projected client base was "people in the public eye."

I said, "What a scoop."

"Probably some kiss-ass reporter with a screenplay."

"That's networking, dude."

"Curse of the millennium. Hollywood sharks peddling mental health, what a concept. If you get in a tropical mood, maybe they're hiring."

I laughed and slid the paper back.

"Hey," he said, "you're not on the stand, volunteer an *opinion*."

"I get paid for opinions."

He grumbled something about "dogmatism."

I said, "How's this: Taking life advice from people like that is like learning the tango from gorillas."

"Eloquent. Now I might even listen to the further details of your little mystery."

We were putting away stacks of pancakes and drinking coffee strong enough to make my pulse race. With Milo, food smooths the process.

I'd driven out to Studio City because he'd been on the other side of the hill since midnight, cleaning up the details of a Mar Vista gang homicide whose tentacles had spread into Van Nuys and Panorama City. Another big one that would finally close. One more meeting with the D.A. and he'd be on a two-week vacation.

Rick was scheduled tight and couldn't travel. Too bad for Milo, lucky for me. I had designs on his leisure.

I told him everything Tanya had said.

He said, "First a 'terrible thing,' now it's a murder? Alex, I'm not prying into clinical details, but be brutally frank: Is this kid stable?"

"Nothing points otherwise."

"Meaning you're not sure."

"She's functioning well," I said. "All things considered."

"Mommy offed some neighbor? But she really *didn't*? What exactly does she want?"

"I'm not sure she knows. I figure we do a little searching, come up empty, I'll have more authority to ease her away from it. If I don't make an attempt, I lose her as a patient. She talks a good case about handling her grief, but there's a long way to go. If she falls I'd like to be around to catch her."

He played with the edge of the newspaper. "Sounds like you're a bit involved in this one."

"If it's too much of a hassle—"

"I'm not refusing, I'm *contextualizing*. Even if I wanted to say no, there are domestic issues at stake. Rick thinks Patty was some kind of saint. 'It's great you'll be free to help, Alex.'"

"Let's hear it for the zeitgeist," I said.

He threw money on the table that I returned to him.

"Fine, you're in a higher tax bracket." Hoisting his bulk out of the booth.

"When do we start?" I said.

"We?"

"You lead the way, I'll be your loyal assistant."

"Oh, sure," he said. "And I've got a life regression package to sell you."

I walked him to his unmarked as he studied the list of addresses.

He copied it into his notepad. "She moved around a bit, didn't she . . . so the kid's theory is Mommy was trying to protect her from some kind of revenge?"

"Less than a theory," I said. "She was tossing out possibilities."

"Here's one: Mommy was impaired and talked gibberish."

"Tanya's not ready to see that."

"I asked Rick about the whole brain damage thing," he said. "Unwilling to commit—all you doctor types are alike. Okay, let's be organized so we don't have to backtrack. You talk to Patty's oncologist and see if you can nail down some medical specifics. I'll hit the assessor's office and find out Patty's local residences before she took Tanya in. She from SoCal?"

"New Mexico."

"Where in New Mexico?"

"Outside Galisteo."

"If this terrible *thing* went down out of state, good luck." He snorted. "Listen to me. Like it really happened."

"I appreciate this—"

"I will file your gratitude under Things To Exploit At An Opportune Time. Another thing you can do is play computer games, see if Patty shows up anywhere in cyberspace. Plug in those four addresses. Anything else that strikes your fancy."

"Has the department database gotten any better?"

"Last coupla times I've able to boot up and not blow a fuse."

"Given an address, can you pull up crimes on neighboring streets?"

"Oh, sure, me and Bill Gates just did that yesterday. No, it's a mess. Recent cases have been entered but for the most part we're talking cardboard boxes in storage. Department's notion of pattern-tracing is the pin board and the board changes every year. Maybe we'll get lucky and it is something recent. 'Close by,' huh? That could be the same street but down the block, one street over, a quarter mile up to the cul-de-sac, turn left, toss salt over your left shoulder. For all we know, Alex, she meant something *un*geographical. Close by as in a friend."

"Tanya said she had no relationships with men."

"What about women? A bisexual triangle could get nasty, there was one a few years ago in Florida, woman had her girlfriend gut-shoot her old man for insurance money."

"Patty told me she was asexual."

"You asked her about her sexuality?"

"She brought it up during the intake."

"The intake was on the kid so why would Mama's sex life be relevant?"

I had no answer for that.

He said, "What was the context, Alex?"

"Letting me know she wasn't gay. But not in a defensive way. More matter-of-fact, this is who I am. Then she asked me if I thought she was abnormal."

"So she was uptight about being considered gay. Meaning she probably *was* gay. Meaning she coulda been doing stuff Tanya didn't know about."

"I guess it's possible."

"People with secrets parcel out what they want other people to know, right? If we're going to start excavating this woman's life, Tanya could learn things she doesn't want to. Is she psychologically ready for that?"

"If she runs off excavating by herself, it could be worse."

"She'd do that?"

"She's a determined young woman."

"Obsessive? Rick said Patty had tendencies in that direction. Did the kid start imitating her and that's why you treated her?"

I stared at him. "Very good, Sigmund."

"All these years absorbing your wisdom, something was bound to rub off."

He opened his car door. "Get ready for a whole new world of false starts and dead ends."

"Your optimism is touching."

"Optimism is denial for chumps with no life experience."

"What's pessimism?" I said.

"Religion without God."

He got in the car, started up the engine.

I said, "I just thought of something. What about Isaac Gomez? He was compiling some pretty good databases."

"Petra's boy genius . . . yeah, maybe he'll have some spare time. Hollywood went this whole year without a single murder. If it stays that quiet, the chatter has Stu Bishop vaulting to assistant chief."

"What's Petra been doing with herself?"

"My guess would be digging up cold cases."

"Patty and Tanya's first address was in Hollywood," I said. "Back then there were plenty of murders. Maybe Petra will want to hear about this."

"An unsolved she just happens to be working on? Wouldn't that be screenplay-cute. Sure, call her. Talk to Dr. Gomez, too, if Petra's cool with that."

"Will do, boss."

"Keep up that attitude, assistant, and you just might make the grade."

I took Laurel Canyon south to the city, used the red light at Crescent Heights and Sunset to call Hollywood Division and asked for Detective Connor.

"She's out," said the civilian clerk.

"Is Isaac Gomez still working there?"

"Who?"

"Graduate student intern," I said. "He was doing research on—"

"Not listed," said the clerk.

"Could you connect me to Detective Connor's voice mail?"

"Voice mail's down."

"Do you have another number for her?"

"No."

I drove east. At Fuller and Sunset, a group of Nordic-looking tourists risked a crosswalk sprint and nearly got pulverized by a Suburban. Naive Europeans, pretending L.A. was a real city and walking was legal. I could hear Milo laughing.

As I neared La Brea, development continued its encroachment:

big-box outlets and strip malls and chain restaurants sweeping through blocks that had once hosted by-the-hour motels and ptomaine palaces.

Some things never change: Hookers of both primary genders and a few that couldn't be determined were working the street with ebullience. My eyes must've been restless because a couple of them waved at me.

Heading north to Hollywood Boulevard and hooking a right, I cruised past the Chinese Theatre, the Kodak Theatre, the tourist traps attempting to feed off the overflow, continued to Cherokee Avenue. Just past the hustle of the boulevard sat a couple of padlocked clubs, mean and sad the way nightspots get during the daylight. Trash was piled at the curb and birdshit pollocked the sidewalk.

Farther north, the block had been rehabbed a bit, with relatively clean multiplex apartment buildings promising *Security* elbowing shabby prewar structures that offered no illusion of safety.

The first address on Tanya's list matched one of the old ones. A three-story, brick-colored stucco building a short walk below Franklin. Plain front, frizzy lawn, limp beds of overwatered succulents struggling to breathe. As tired-looking as the homeless guy pushing a shopping cart nowhere. He made split-second, paranoid eye contact, shook his head as if I were hopeless, and trudged on.

A cloudy glass door cut through the center of the brick-colored building, but two ground-floor units in front had entrance from the street. Tanya remembered drunks knocking on the door, so my bet was on one of those.

I got out and tried the handle on the glass door. Cold and unpleasantly crusty but unlocked.

Inside, a back-to-front hallway carpeted in gray poly smelled of mold and orange-scented air freshener. Twenty-three mail slots just inside the door. Liver-colored doors lined the murky space. Lots of interviews, if it ever came to that.

A door at the rear of the hall opened and a man stuck his head out, scratched the crook of one arm. Sixty or so, gray hair flying like dandelion fuzz, haloed by sickly light. Scrawny but potbellied, wearing a blue satin Dodger jacket over striped pajama bottoms.

He scratched again. Worked his jaws and lowered his head. "Yeah?"

I said, "Just leaving."

He stood there, watching until I made good on that promise.

South on Highland took me through two miles of film labs, tape-dupe services, costume warehouses, prop shops. All those people who'd never be thanked on Oscar night.

Between Melrose and Beverly a few dowager apartment buildings clung to twenties elegance. The rest didn't even try. A turn onto Beverly took me around the southern edge of the Wilshire Country Club and into Hancock Park.

Hudson Avenue is one of the district's grandest streets, and the second address on Tanya's list matched a massive, multigabled, slate-roofed, brick Tudor piled atop a sloping lawn that had been skinned as close as a putting green. Five-foot bronze urns flanking the front door hosted lemon trees studded with fruit. Double doors under a limestone arch were carved exuberantly. A black filigree gate offered a view of a long cobbled driveway. A white Mercedes convertible sat behind a green Bentley Flying Spur hand-fashioned in the fifties.

This was where Patty and Tanya had just moved when they first came to see me. Renting space in a house. The owners of this house didn't appear to need the extra income. Patty had been certain the move hadn't been stressful for Tanya. Face-slapping contrast with the sad building on Cherokee made me a believer, and I wondered now about the specifics of the transition.

I sat there and enjoyed the view. No one came out of the mansion or any of its stately neighbors. But for a couple of lusty squirrels in a sycamore tree, no movement at all. In L.A. luxury means pretending no one else inhabits the planet.

I put in a call to Patty's oncologist, Tziporah Ganz, left a message with her service.

One of the squirrels scampered over to the left-hand lemon tree, got hold of a juicy one, and tugged. Before it could complete the theft, one of the double doors opened and a short, dark-haired maid in a pink uniform charged out wielding a broom. The animal faced off, then thought better of it. The maid turned to reenter the mansion and noticed me.

Stared.

Another hostile reception.

I drove away.

Address three was a quick drive: Fourth Street off La Jolla. Tanya had returned to my office just after leaving there for Culver City.

The house turned out to be a Spanish Revival duplex on a pleasant leafy street of matching structures. The only distinguishing feature of the building where the Bigelows had lived was a concrete pad in lieu of a lawn. The only vehicle in sight was a deep red Austin Mini with vanity plates that read *PLOTGRL.*

Solidly middle-class, respectable, but a whole different planet after Hudson Avenue. Maybe Patty had wanted more room than rented mansion space afforded.

My final stop was a solid forty-minute drive in thick traffic to a grubby stretch of Culver Boulevard just west of Sepulveda and the 405 overpass.

The lot bore six identical gray-framed, tar-roofed boxes that ringed the crumbled remains of a plaster fountain. Two brown-skinned preschoolers played in the dirt, unattended.

Classic L.A. bungalow court. Classic refuge of transients, has-beens, almost-weres.

These bungalows weren't much bigger than sheds. The property had been neglected to the point of peeling paint and curling roof shingles and sagging foundations. Traffic roared by. Pothole–axle encounters lent a syncopated conga beat to the engine concerto.

Maybe it had been spiffier in Patty's day, but this part of town had never been fashionable.

Climbing the residential ladder, then down to this. Patty had come across solid and stable. Her housing pattern seemed anything but.

Perhaps it came down to thrift. Saving up cash for a down payment on her own place. Within two years, she'd pulled it off, snagging a duplex near Beverlywood on a nurse's salary.

Even so, there had to be better choices than moving Tanya to another "sketchy neighborhood."

Then another possibility hit me: That kind of jumping around was what you saw in habitual gamblers and others whose habits roller-coastered their finances.

Patty had achieved Westside homeownership, a trust fund, and two life insurance policies for Tanya on a nurse's salary.

Impressive.

Remarkable, really. Maybe she'd been a savvy stock-market player.

Or had acquired an additional source of revenue.

A hospital nurse with too much money led to an obvious what-if: drug pilferage and resale. Stealthy dope dealer didn't sync with what I knew about Patty but how well did I really know her?

But if she had a secret criminal life, why stir up the pot with a deathbed confession and chance Tanya finding out?

People with secrets parcel out what they want you to know.

Until something shattered their inhibitions. Had Patty's proclamation been the agonized product of a disease-addled mind? An illness-fueled stab at confession and expiation?

I sat in the car and tossed that around. No way, too ugly. It just didn't sit right.

Sounds like you're a bit involved in this one.

"So what," I said to no one.

A muscular guy in a ski cap pulled down to his eyebrows skulked by with an unleashed, pink-nosed white pit bull. The dog stopped, circled back, pressed its snout against my passenger window, created a little pink, pulsating rosebud. No smiling for this canine. A low-pitched growl thrummed the glass.

Ski-cap was staring, too.

My day for warm welcomes. I pulled away slowly enough so the dog wouldn't lose balance.

No one thanked me.

7

The encounter with the pit made me appreciate Blanche. As soon as I got home, I took her down to the garden for a puppy stroll, made sure her curiosity didn't land her in the fishpond.

One message at my service: Dr. Tziporah Ganz.

I called back, told her I was Tanya Bigelow's therapist and had some questions about Patty's mental status during her final days.

"Tanya's having psychological problems?" she said. Her voice was soft, slightly accented—Middle Europe.

"No," I said. "Just the typical adjustments, it's a tough situation."

"Tragic situation. Why is Tanya concerned about dementia?"

"She isn't, I am. Patty charged Tanya with taking care of lots of details that could turn burdensome. I'm wondering if Patty's intent needs to be taken literally."

"Details? I don't understand."

"Postmortem instructions that Patty thought would benefit Tanya. Tanya goes to school full-time, holds down a part-time job, and is faced with living alone. She was devoted to her mother and right now her personality won't allow her to deviate from Patty's wishes. Nor would I try to convince her otherwise. But I am looking for an out in case she gets overwhelmed."

"The dying person reaches out for one last burst of control," she said. "I've seen that. And Patty *was* an exacting person. Unfortunately, I can't give you a clear answer about her mental status. Strictly speaking, there were no clinical reasons for the disease to affect her thinking—no brain lesion, no obvious neuropathy. But any severe illness and its effects—dehydration, jaundice, electrolytic imbalance—can affect cognition, and Patty was a very sick woman. If you choose to tell Tanya that Patty was impaired, I wouldn't contradict you. However, I won't be comfortable being quoted as a primary source."

"I understand."

"Dr. Delaware, I don't want to tell you your business, but my experience has been that survivors don't want to give up responsibilities even when they *are* burdensome."

"Mine as well," I said. "In what way was Patty exacting?"

"She attempted to control every aspect of her hospitalization. Not that I blame her."

"Were there compliance issues?"

"No, because there was no treatment. Her decision."

"Did you agree?"

"It's always hard to stand back and watch someone die, but, honestly, there was nothing I could do for her. The goal became making her last days as comfortable as possible. Even there, she opted for less."

"Resisting the morphine drip, despite the anesthesiologist's best efforts."

"The anesthesiologist is my husband," she said. "Obviously I'm biased but there's no one better than Joseph. And yes, Patty resisted him. Still, I'm not judging. This was a relatively young woman who learned suddenly that she was going to die."

"Did she ever talk about that?"

"Infrequently and in a detached manner. As if she was describing a patient. I guess she needed to depersonalize a horrible situation. Is Tanya really doing okay? She seemed mature for her age, but that can be a problem, too."

"I'm keeping my eyes open. Is there anything else you can tell me?"

"About Patty? How about this: Last year my brother ended up in the E.R. Auto accident, pretty nasty. He's a dentist, was worried about a compression injury of one of his hands. Patty was on the night Gil came in and took care of him. Gil was sufficiently impressed enough to write a letter to Nursing Administration. He told me she was cool under pressure—absolutely unflappable, nothing got past her. When she was referred to me, I remembered her name, felt extremely sad. I wish I could've done more for her."

"You gave her what she needed," I said.

"That's kind of you to say." Small, edgy laugh. "Good luck with Tanya."

Petra answered her cell phone. "Detective Connor."

I filled her in.

She said, "Exactly where on Cherokee did this woman live?"

I gave her the address.

"I think I know it. Kind of raw sienna on the outside, not exactly posh?"

"That's the one."

"I've made busts pretty close to there but nothing in that building specifically. Back then, Cherokee was a tough hood. According to all the old-timers who delight in telling me The Way It Was. Not the best place to raise a daughter."

"Having a daughter wasn't in her plans." I explained how Tanya had come to live with Patty.

"Good Samaritan," she said. "A nurse, to boot. Doesn't sound like one of the bad guys."

"I doubt she is."

"Deathbed confession, huh? We love those. Sorry, Alex, nothing I've seen in the cold files matches that. Mostly, what I've been doing is compensating for other people's screwups. You read the murder books, everyone knows who the bad guy is but someone was too lazy or there just wasn't enough to prove it. But I'll have another look in the fridge."

"Thanks."

"A did-it-even-happen, huh? Milo came up with that all by his lone-some?"

"He's applying for copyright as we speak."

"He darn well should. Take all the credit and none of the blame—that's one of his, too."

"Words he doesn't live by," I said. "Is Isaac still working with you?"

"Isaac? Ah, the database. No, the boy wonder is no longer tagging along. Finished his Ph.D. in BioStatistics, starting med school in August."

"Double doctor," I said. "What is he, ten years old?"

"Just turned twenty-three, what a slacker. The obvious question is why I don't have a copy of his CD-ROM. The answer is he offered it to me but with all the static the department's been getting about privacy violations, he had to submit a formal application to Parker Center first."

"They made him apply to donate his own data?"

"In triplicate. After which the brass showed its gratitude by ignoring him for months, kept passing the forms to various committees, then Community Relations, legal counsel, the janitors, the catering truck drivers. We still haven't heard back. If the bosses don't get off their collectively spreading duff, I may just find myself a personal copy by accident. It's nuts. Here I am going through boxes and breaking fingernails and Isaac's got years worth of mayhem on a disk. Not that you just heard any of that."

"Heard what?" I said.

"Thank you, sir."

"What kind of static is the department getting about privacy?"

"Mario Fortuno," she said.

"Private eye to the stars," I said. "That was what, three years ago?"

"Three and a half is when they got him on the explosives charge but the larger issue is his wiretapping and what I hear is the fallout from that is just beginning."

"What do illegal taps have to do with Isaac's crime stats?"

"Fortuno gained access to personal data, had people stalked and harassed and generated some not-so-subtle threats to citizens who'd offended his honcho clients. One way he got the info—and once again you never heard it from me—is by bribing sources at DMV, the phone company, various banks. And the department."

"Oh," I said.

"Oh, indeed. If Fortuno ever opens up, there are Hollywood honchos and big-time criminal defense lawyers who could find themselves in the defendant's chair."

"Code of silence, so far?"

"In the beginning he put out the *omerta* line, guy loves the whole Mafia intrigue thing. But what I hear is he's got six more years on a nine-year sentence and prison life hasn't been fun. Whatever happens or doesn't, the brass hears 'computer disk,' there's a stampede to the little boys' room."

"Is there anything stopping me, as a concerned private citizen, from talking to Doctor-Doctor Gomez who is now a concerned private citizen?"

"Gee," she said, "that's an interesting question. Here's his phone number."

"Thanks, Petra. Good talking to you."

"Same here," she said. "I think I'll cut out early and get file dust out of my hair."

Isaac Gomez answered at his parents' Union district apartment.

"Hey, Dr. Delaware."

"Congratulations, Dr. Gomez."

"Dr. Gomez is some guy with gray hair and bifocals," he said. "Though if you ask my mother, I've already earned tenure and it's only a matter of time before the Nobel committee knocks at our door."

"Your mother's cooking might clinch the award," I said. "Getting ready for med school?"

"I'm not sure you can ever be ready. I sat in on a few classes last semester and after grad school it seemed regressive, everyone sitting in one room, no curriculum flexibility. One factor might make it more enjoyable. My girlfriend will be in the class."

"Congrats again."

"Yes, it's great."

Heather Salcido was a tiny, dark-haired beauty whom Isaac had saved from a killer. As good a foundation as any for romance.

"She'd already taken the premed courses studying for her RN. I convinced her to take the MCATS. She scored high, applied, got in. She's still a little apprehensive but I'm certain she'll excel. We're hoping seeing each other daily will help ease the process. So why are you calling?"

I told him.

He said, "Making you a copy of the disks—there are two—is no problem. But they're encrypted and fairly inaccessible unless you've had experience decoding."

"Not since I worked with the Navajos and unlocked secret Nazi transmissions."

"Ha. Why don't you give me the specific addresses on your list and I'll check for straightaway matches. If I don't find any, I'll program a search function that pulls up loci in a steadily widening concentric net where we can adjust for radius. Do you have any geographical criterion in mind?"

Close by.

I said, "Not yet."

"Okay, so we'll adopt an empirical approach. Swing the net—like a seine—and analyze which patterns emerge. I could do it in, say in a couple of days?"

"That would be great, Isaac. I really appreciate it."

"One complication, Dr. Delaware. Heather and I are taking a trip to Asia—last vacation before the grind. Once we're there, I won't be available because Myanmar—what used to be Burma—is part of our itinerary and the government there has been known to confiscate computers and refuse entry to anyone trying to bring one in."

"Maybe that'll be good for you," I said.

"How so?"

"Pure vacation, no encumbrances."

"That's what Heather says, but to me a computer's no encumbrance. The notion of traveling without one feels like leaving an arm or a leg at home. It'll be interesting to see how I adapt."

Talking about himself as a research subject. I thought of Patty's detachment. The partitions we all build.

He said, "Meanwhile, give me those streets and I'll play around."

Two hours of my own computer games produced no citation or image of Patty Bigelow, no crimes at any of the four addresses.

I made a grilled cheese sandwich that I shared with Blanche. When I poured coffee, she opened her mouth and panted. A coffee-coated fingertip placed on her tongue caused her to back away, shake her head, and spit.

"Everyone's a critic," I said. "Next time I'll brew espresso."

I tried Robin's cell, got her voice on message tape. After wondering some more about Patty's housing choices, I tried Tanya.

"No malpractice," she said. "Dr. Silverman's sure?"

"He is."

"Okay . . . have you been able to learn anything?"

"Detective Sturgis is going to do some introductory investigation."

"That's great," she said. Flat voice.

"Everything okay, Tanya?"

"I'm a little tired."

"When you have more energy, I'd like to talk to you again."

"Sure," she said. "Eventually."

"I don't mean therapy," I said. "I'd like to find out more about all the places you and your mother lived. For background."

"Oh," she said. "Sure, I can do that. I've some straightening up to do, then it's back to campus for study group. Summer school's supposed to be more mellow but the profs don't seem to realize that. And with the quarter system, you barely have time to buy books before midterms . . . could we do it late, say nine thirty? No forget that, I don't want to impose."

"It doesn't need to be tonight, Tanya."

"I hate having things pile up, Dr. Delaware. If you had time, so would I, but of course that's not right. You need your evenings—"

"Nine thirty's fine."

"You're sure?"

"Absolutely."

"Could we make it nine forty-five, just to be safe? I could come back to your office or you could come to my house—maybe you'd like to see the home Mommy made."

"I would."

"Great!" she said. "I'll make coffee."

At nine twenty, as I was crating Blanche, my private line rang. A welcome voice said, "I love you."

"Love you, too. Having fun?"

"I'm coming home a day early. The lectures were good but it's starting to feel like school. I sold that F5 replica, some dot-com guy kept upping the ante."

Robin had spent a year acquiring the aged fiddle-grain maple and red spruce billets for the elaborately carved mandolin, had worked on tapping and shaving and shaping for another twelve months, brought the finished product to Healdsburg for display only.

"Must've been a nice ante?" I said.

"Twenty-one thousand."

"Whoa. Congratulations."

"I hated to part with it, but a girl has her price. I guess . . . I figure to set out early Sunday morning, be back by evening. What's your schedule like?"

"Flexible."

"Has the little blonde moved in on my territory, yet?"

"The little blonde eats kibble and sleeps all day."

"The quiet ones," she said, "they always bear watching."

◆

I drove to Tanya's house, thinking back to the first time I'd met her.

Skinny little blond girl wearing a dress, anklet socks, and shiny sandals. Back pressed to the wall of my waiting area, as if the carpet was bottomless water.

When I'd stepped out of the office, Patty had touched Tanya's cheek gently. Tanya's nod was grave, a movement so brief it bordered on tic. Fingers as delicate as fettuccini gripped her mother's chunky hand. A shiny foot tapped. The other was planted on the imaginary shoreline.

I bent to child's eye level. "Nice to meet you, Tanya."

Murmured reply. All I could make out was "you."

Patty said, "Tanya chose her outfit. She likes to dress up, has excellent taste."

"Very pretty, Tanya."

Tanya mouth-breathed; I smelled hamburger and onion.

I said, "Let's go in there. Mom can come, too, if you'd like."

Patty said, "Or I don't have to." She hugged the little girl and stepped away. Tanya didn't move.

"I'll be right here, honey. You'll be okay, I super-promise."

Tanya looked up at her. Took a deep breath. Gave another grim little nod and stepped forward.

She surveyed the props on the play table. Open-sided dollhouse, family-member figurines, pencils, crayons, markers, a stack of paper. Prolonged eye contact with the paper.

"Do you like to draw?"

Nod.

"If you feel like drawing now, that's fine."

She picked up a pencil and drew a slow, wispy circle. Sat back, frowned. "It's bumpy."

"Is bumpy okay?"

Pale green eyes studied me. She put the pencil down. "I came here to break my habits."

"Mom told you that?"

"She said if I want to, I should tell you."

"Which habits bother you the most, Tanya?"

"Mommy told you all of them."

"She did. But I'd like to know what you think."

Puzzled look.

"They're your habits," I said. "You're in charge over them."

"I don't want to be in charge."

"You're ready to let go of the habits."

Mumble.

"What's that, Tanya?"

"They're bad."

"Bad like scary?"

Head shake. "They make me busy."

The pencil was an inch from where it had lain originally and she rolled it back. Adjusted the tip, then the eraser. Readjusted and tried, without success, to smooth a curling corner of paper.

"That bumpy circle," I said, "could be the start of a person's face."

"Can I throw it out?"

"Sure."

Folding and unfolding the sheet lengthwise, she ripped slowly along the crease. Repeated the process with each of the halves.

"Where, please?"

I pointed at the wastebasket. She dropped the pieces in, one by one, watched them drop, returned to the table.

"So you want to break your habits."

Nod.

"You and Mommy agree on that."

"Yup."

"You and Mommy are a team."

That seemed to puzzle her.

"You and Mommy agree most of the time."

"We love each other."

"Loving means agreeing."

"Yup."

She drew a pair of circles, one twice the diameter of the other. Squinted and hunched and added primitive features.

"Lumpy again," she pronounced. Another trip to the trash can.

"You really don't like lumpy," I said.

"I like it to be *good*."

Selecting a third piece of paper, she put the pencil down and traced circles with her finger. Looked up at the ceiling. Tapped the fingers of one hand, then the other.

"What kinds of things do you and Mommy do together?"

She retrieved the pencil. Twirled it. "There was a mother when I was a baby. She was too weak and Mommy wanted to take care of me . . . she was Mommy's sister."

"The other mother."

"She was called Lydia. She died in a accident. Mommy and I get sad when we think about her."

"Do you think about her a lot?"

Flicking the paper stack, she selected a female figurine, placed it in the house's living room. "We also have a fish."

"At home?"

"In the kitchen."

"In a tank?"

"Uh-uh a bowl."

"A goldfish?"

"Uh-uh goldfish are too dirty, the man said."

"What man is that?"

"From the fish store. Mr. Stan Park."

"What kind of fish did Mr. Park sell you?"

"A guppy. Real small."

"Does the guppy have a name?"

"We thought it was a girl but it got color on the tail."

"So it's a boy."

"We changed the name."

"From a girl name to a boy name?"

"He was Charlotte, now he's Charlie."

"How does Charlie feel about being a boy instead of a girl?"

"He's a *fish*. He doesn't *think*."

"He never thinks about anything? Like 'I wonder when Tanya will change my water?'"

"His brain is too little for words."

"So he just swims back and forth and doesn't worry about anything," I said.

Silence.

"Do you worry?"

"Fish also don't have stomachs," she said. "Food goes in and out so don't feed them too much."

"You know a lot about fish."

"I read a book." Tiny hands drifted to the stack of paper, squared the corners.

"I have some fish, too."

"Guppies?"

"No, they're called koi. Kind of like giant goldfish but all different colors."

Skeptical stare. "Where?"

"Outside in a pond. Want to see?"

"If Mommy lets me."

We walked out to the van. Patty looked up from her newspaper. "So soon?"

"He has giant fish, Mommy." Tanya's arms spread.

"Really."

"Outside in a giant pond."

"We're going to feed them," I said. "Want to come along?"

"Hmm," said Patty. "No, I'll just let the two of you get to know each other."

At Beverwil and Pico, less than a mile from Tanya's house, my service beeped in.

"It's Flora, Doctor. Detective Sturgis called. He'll be out for a while but you can try him in a couple of hours."

"Did he say what it was about?"

"No, Doctor. It was just him being him."

"Meaning?"

"You know," she said. "The way he always is, Mr. Jokey. He told me with my voice I should be on the radio selling beachfront condos in Colorado."

"You do have a nice voice, Flora."

"I used to," she said. "If only I could quit smoking. He sounds kind of cute. Is he?"

"Depends on your perspective."

Canfield Avenue was narrow and dark and quiet, but no sign of anything remotely ominous.

No reason for there to be. I'd slipped into thinking this was real.

Point me at a puzzle and aim.

Years ago, I'd been the perfect therapist for Patty and Tanya. They hadn't known the real reason why, never would.

Alexander is very bright but he seems to feel a need for absolute per-
fection that can lead to some emotion in the classroom. I rarely label
a child overly conscientious but that may apply, here.

Alexander needs to understand that not everyone in 3rd grade learns
as quickly as he does and that making mistakes is acceptable.

Alexander is doing well in junior high but he needs to work on ex-
hibiting more self-control when projects don't go as planned.

Alex is an excellent student, particularly in science, but he doesn't
seem to endorse the concept of group work. Hopefully high school
will teach him to accept himself as a member of a team . . .

Year after year of well-meaning teachers, leaving conferences with
my parents, convinced their insights were beneficial.

He's so hard on himself, Mr. and Mrs. Delaware.

Dad responding with the jovial, knowing grin. Mom at his side,
docile, silent, ladylike in a clean dress and the one pair of shoes with
heels.

How could any of those teachers have known that when Dad *wasn't*
feeling jovial, imperfection could result in rages as predictable as
snakebites.

That falling short meant a beefy workingman's belt scourging a
child's narrow back, next day's welts and bruises concealed by shirts
and sweaters and silence.

No way for the teachers to grasp that when too much discussion
filled the house, Mom had been known to lock herself in her bedroom
for days. Leaving Dad, banished, fuming, reeking of beer-and-shots,
lurching through the four remaining rooms of the house in search of
someone to blame.

My sister, Em, the sib I hadn't spoken to in years, had been quick to
sniff the air and get away, an ace escape artist. I'd thought her selfish because the rules made her safe: You didn't hit girls, at least not with a strap.

Boys were another matter . . .

Enough nostalgia, mawkish fellow, self-pity's a lousy aperitif.

Besides, I'd put it all behind me, courtesy of the training therapy required by my doctoral program.

A stroke of good luck: random assignment to a kind, wise woman. The mandatory six months stretching to a year, then two. Then three.

The changes I saw in myself reaffirmed my career choice: If you knew what you were doing, this psychotherapy stuff worked.

By my final year of grad school, the cognitive starbursts and compulsive corrections were gone. Farewell, also, to rituals, invisible or otherwise.

Death of the near-religious belief that symmetry was all.

Which wasn't to say vestiges didn't crop up from time to time.

The occasional bout of insomnia, the sudden stabs of inexplicable tension.

Preoccupation that led nowhere.

Therapy taught me to accept all that as proof of my humanness, and when I chatted with my parents over the phone I was able to hang up without fingernail crescents bloodying my palms.

The best tonic was taking care of other people. I started off hoping that no parent who stepped into my office saw me as anyone other than the amiable, calm, *understanding* fellow with whom they entrusted their children's psyches.

Several years of success made me believe I'd pulled it off.

Sometimes I allowed myself a bit of leeway. Like following through on Patty Bigelow's museum wax suggestion. Because that was a housekeeping issue, nothing wrong with a bit of geometry, right?

My patients' faith kept me up at night, devising treatment plans.

Patty Bigelow's faith had endured and I wasn't sure I'd earned it.

Now she was dead and her child was depending on me and I was making a house call.

A bit involved.

The duplex was Spanish Revival, not dissimilar from the building on Fourth Street. Peach-toned stucco, mullioned windows inset with stained-glass bluebirds, flat lawn instead of a car park; a young paper birch weeping dead center.

Alarm company sign staked to the left. Lights on in the second story. The stairs were whitened by high-voltage floodlights.

Tanya opened the door before I finished climbing. Loose hair shawled her shoulders. She looked exhausted.

"Thank God I'm not late," she said.

"Tough study session?"

"Tough, but it was all good. Please. Come in."

The living room was oak-floored, barrel-ceilinged, pale pink. Cream-colored tiles painted with lilies fronted the fireplace. A lilac chintz sofa faced the curtained picture window and two matching chairs. In between was a bleached wood coffee table with gilded rococo legs.

Patty had talked about being butch but she'd chosen delicate décor.

Above the couch, a dozen photographs were set low on the wall, framed identically in faux-driftwood.

The Story of Tanya from toddler to teen. Predictable shifts in hairstyle, clothing, and makeup as Cute Tyke grew to Pretty Girl, but stylewise no signs of adolescent rebellion.

Patty made no appearance until the final photo: Tanya in a crimson cap and gown, her mother in a navy jacket and white turtleneck, holding up a diploma and beaming.

Tanya said, "Here's one I just found," and pointed to the sole photo on the coffee table. Black-framed portrait of a broad-faced young woman in a white uniform.

Patty's upward gaze was solemn, so contrived it was almost comical. I pictured some hack photographer clicking away and uttering rote instructions. *Think of your new career, dear . . . chin higher—higher—even higher—there you go. Next!*

"She looks so hopeful," said Tanya. "Please make yourself comfortable, I'll get the coffee."

She returned bearing a black plastic tray silk-screened to look like lacquer. Five Oreos were stacked on a plate like a miniature silo. Between a pair of mugs bearing the U.'s insignia a ramekin held packets of nondairy creamer, sugar, and sweetener, wedged tightly, like tiny brochures.

"Cream and sugar?"

"Black's fine," I said.

I sat in one of the chairs and she chose the sofa. "I don't know anyone who drinks it black. My friends think coffee's dessert."

"Semi-blended soy mocha-java frappes with extra chocolate?"

She managed a tired smile, opened three sugars, dropped them into her cup. "Cookie?"

"No, thanks."

"Mostly, I drink tea, but coffee's good for long study nights." She scooted toward the front edge of the sofa. "Sure you don't want an Oreo?"

"Positive."

"I guess I'll have one. You hear a lot about prying them apart but lots of people like the sandwich effect and I'm one of them." Talking fast. Nibbling fast.

"So," she said.

"I drove by each of the addresses on your list. It's quite a mix."

"The mansion as opposed to all those apartments?" she said. "Actually, we only lived in one room of the mansion. I remember thinking it was strange, such a gigantic house but we had less space than in the apartment. I used to worry about rolling off in the middle of the night on top of Mommy."

"Did that ever happen?"

"No," she said. "Sometimes she'd hold me. It felt safe." She put the cookie down. "Sometimes she'd snore."

Her eyes got wet. "They let us use the pool when Mommy had spare time and the gardens were beautiful, lots of big trees. I'd find places to hide, pretend I was in a forest somewhere."

"Who owned the house?"

"The Bedard family," she said. "The only one living there was the grandfather—Colonel Bedard. The family came by once in a while, but they lived far away. They wanted Mommy there to take care of him at night, after the day nurse went home."

"An old man," I said.

"Ancient. All bent over, extremely thin. He had filmy eyes— probably blue originally but now they were milky gray. No hair on his head. There was a huge library in the house and that's where he sat all day. I remember him smelling of paper. Not gross, just a little stale, the way old people get."

"Was he nice to you?"

"He really didn't say or do much, just sat in that library with a blanket over his lap and a book in his hand. His face was kind of stiff—he must've had a stroke—so when he tried to smile nothing much happened. At first I was scared of him but then Mommy told me he was nice."

"Did she move there to make more money?"

"That's what I assume. Like I said, Dr. Delaware, financial security was important to her. Even in her spare time."

"Reading financial books."

"Want to see?"

A bedroom at the end of the hall had been converted to a no-nonsense office. U-build Swedish bookshelves and desk, black swivel chair, white file cabinets, desktop computer and printer.

"I've been through her files, it's all money stuff." She pointed to shelves stacked with back issues of *Forbes, Barron's, Money*. A collection of investment guides ranged from reasoned strategy to improbable hucksterism. The lowest shelf held a pile of thin, glossy magazines. The top issue featured a close-up head-shot of an actress who'd lost her husband to another actress.

Tormented eyes. Perfect hair and makeup.

"The fan rags," said Tanya. "The hospital boxed them up with her personal effects. Getting them back was a complete hassle. Some form I hadn't filled out. I could see the box, right there behind the counter, but the woman in charge was being a real beeyotch, said I had to go somewhere else to get the forms and they were closed. When I started crying, she got on the phone, made a personal call, gossiping away as if I didn't exist. I beeped Dr. Silverman and he just went behind the desk and got it. At the bottom of the box were Mommy's armband and her reading glasses and the clothes she had on when she was admitted and this."

She opened a desk drawer, held up a broken plastic band. "Should we go back and finish our coffee?"

Two sips later, I said, "So when you lived on Hudson, she was working two jobs."

"Yes, but looking after the colonel wasn't much trouble, he went to sleep at six and we were up early anyway so Mommy could drive me to school and make it to Cedars."

"How'd she find out about the position?"

"No idea—maybe a bulletin board at the hospital? She never got into those kinds of details with me, just announced one day that we were moving to a big beautiful house in a high-class neighborhood."

"How'd you feel about that?"

"I was used to moving around. From my days with Lydia. And it's not like I had a ton of friends on Cherokee."

"Hollywood could be a tough neighborhood back then."

"It didn't affect us."

"Except when drunks pounded on the door."

"That didn't happen often. Mommy took care of it."

"How?"

"She'd shout through the door for them to go away and if that didn't work, she'd threaten to call the cops. I don't remember her actually calling the cops, so it must've worked."

"Were you scared?"

"You're saying *that* could be it? Some drunk got dangerous and she had to *do* something to him?"

"Anything's possible but it's way too early to theorize. Why'd you move from the mansion?"

"Colonel Bedard died. One morning Mommy went up to his room to give him his meds and there he was."

"Was leaving such a beautiful place upsetting?"

"Not really, our room was pretty small." She reached for her coffee. "Mommy liked the colonel but not his family. The few times they'd show up, she'd say, 'Here *they* are.' They rarely visited him, it was sad. The night after he died, I couldn't sleep and found Mommy in the breakfast room sitting with the maid. Her name was . . . Cecilia—how did I remember that?—anyway, Mommy and Cecilia were just sitting there, looking down. Mommy led me back to bed, started talking about how money was important for security, but it should never get in the way of appreciation. I thought she meant that for me so I told her I appreciated her. She laughed and kissed me hard and said, 'Not you, baby. You're a lot smarter than some so-called grown-ups.'"

"The colonel's family didn't appreciate him."

"That's what I took it to mean."

"Did anything out of the ordinary happen while you were living in the mansion?"

"Just the colonel's death," she said. "I guess you couldn't call that out of the ordinary, seeing how old he was."

She chewed around the rim of her Oreo.

"Okay," I said, "let's move on to Fourth Street."

"That was a duplex, not as large as this one, but with a *lot* more space than we'd ever had. I was in my own room again with a great walk-in closet. The neighbors upstairs were Asian, quiet."

"You stayed there less than a year."

"Mommy said it was too expensive."

"The first time you came to see me was right after you moved to Hudson Avenue. The second time was right after you moved from Fourth Street to Culver City."

"You're thinking I got stressed about moving?"

"Did you?"

"I honestly don't think so, Dr. Delaware. Did I say anything back then about what was bothering me?"

"No," I said.

"I guess I'm a pretty closed-up person."

"You got better very quickly."

"Is that acceptable from a psychologist's standpoint? Changing behavior without going deep?"

"You're the best judge of what's okay for you."

She smiled. "You always say that."

She poured me another cup. Wiped droplets from the rim.

I said, "So Fourth Street was too expensive."

"The rent was way too high. Mommy wanted to put together a down payment so she could buy." She glanced at her mother's photo, looked down at the floor.

"Culver Boulevard was another sketchy neighborhood," I said.

"It wasn't that bad. I stayed in the same school, had the same friends."

"Saint Thomas. Even though you're not Catholic."

"You remember that?"

"Your mother felt it was important to tell me."

"That we weren't Catholic?"

"That she hadn't lied about being Catholic to get you in."

"That was Mommy," she said, smiling. "She was up front with the priest, said if he could convince me to be Catholic it wouldn't bother her, but not to get his hopes up."

"What was her take on religion?"

"Live a good life and be tolerant—Dr. Delaware, I don't want to be rude but I do need to study some more. Is there anything else I can tell you?"

"I think we've covered enough ground."

"Thanks so much for coming over, it made me feel as if . . . it's almost as if you were able to visit her. Now, I *insist* you take these Oreos—wait, I'll go get a bag."

She stood in the doorway as I descended the stairs. Waved before closing the door. Canfield Avenue had turned darker, barely limned by thinly spaced, anemic lamps.

As I walked to the Seville, something up at the second story caught my eye.

Back-and-forth movement, behind the drapes of Tanya's picture window.

A figure pacing. Vanishing for an instant, then reappearing only to reverse direction.

The circuit repeated.

I waited until the twentieth passage before driving away.

10

Iate an Oreo while phoning Milo.

He barked, "Yeah?"

"I woke you?"

"Oh, it's you—nah waking assumes I sleep. Up and festive—vacation, remember?"

"Congrats."

"Are you talking with your mouth full?"

I swallowed. "Not anymore."

"Late-night gourmet snack?"

"A cookie."

"Got milk? My bud at the phone company found Patty's old billing records. Cherokee was her first L.A. address. According to some vets Petra talked to the block was a big drug market back then. Interesting housing choice for a nice, respectable nurse, no? And she stayed six years."

Perfect time to let go of my dope suspicions, but I held back.

He said, "Rick says she was thrifty bordering on Scrooge, so maybe cheap rent attracted her. Still, bringing up a little kid in a tough part of Hollywood doesn't seem optimal."

"She never expected to be bringing up a little kid."

"True . . . I haven't had time to look for open homicide cases near any of her cribs except for Hancock Park. Only thing that went down there was on June Street, one block west and two blocks south. Victim was a diamond dealer named Wilfred Hong, three masked gunmen broke in at three a.m. after disabling the alarm, shot Hong as he sat up in bed, no warning, but they didn't shoot Mrs. Hong or two kids sleeping down the hall. After forcing her to pop the safe, they tied her up and made off with bags of loose stones and cash. Rumor had it Hong owed money and gems to lots of people. It stinks of pro talent and insider knowledge, so unless Patty was part of some high-level jewel heist gang, it ain't worth our time. If anything is. Any new thoughts about the bigger picture?"

"Nope. Isaac said he'd run some calculations."

"Beats hand-searches of old murder books. I've been thinking, Alex, before we spend any more time surmising, let's visit each address, see if we can locate any neighbors who knew Patty. If no one remembers anything remotely homicidal, I say we've got license to quit and you find a way to break it to Tanya."

"Okay," I said. "When?"

"Pick me up at my place tomorrow morning, say ten. Bring bright-colored clothing, piña colada mix, and a celebratory attitude."

"What are we celebrating?"

"I'm on *vacation,* remember? Or so they say."

"Who's 'they'?"

"The gods of false hope."

The small, neat house Milo shares with Rick sits on a West Hollywood side street shadowed by the green-blue bulk of the Design Center. Quiet during the week, sleepy-silent on Saturday.

The drought-resistant shrubs Rick had planted during a dry year were handling a wet year with mixed success. As I drove up, Milo was kneeling and pinching off dead branches. He straightened quickly, as if caught in a shameful act, patted the place where his gun bulged his jacket, and loped over to the car.

The jacket was a limp, brown, almost-tweed thing. His shirt was yellow wash-and-wear with a curling collar. Soot-gray trousers puddled over tan desert boots.

"That's vacation garb?" I said, driving away.

"Conceptually, it's a workday."

A block later: "With no pay, I might add."

"I'll buy lunch."

"We'll go somewhere expensive."

As I turned from Hollywood Boulevard onto Cherokee, he narrowed his eyes and lasered the block. When I pulled up in front of the brick-colored building, he said, "Definitely a dump. Any idea which apartment was hers?"

"One of those two in front."

"Not what I'd want, security-wise . . . okay, let's go bother someone."

Knocks on both ground-floor units were met by silence. As he pushed the glass door to the main entrance, I said, "When I was by here, an older guy stepped out and got kind of territorial. Maybe he's been around for a while."

"Territorial how?"

"Glaring, wanting me gone."

"Show me his door."

Music seeped from the other side of the brown wood panel. Janis Joplin offering a piece of her heart.

Milo rapped hard. The music died and the man I'd seen yesterday came to the door holding a can of Mountain Dew in one hand, a Kit Kat bar in the other.

Thin gray hair flew away from a high dome. His horsey face was all wrinkles and sags. Not the easy transition of nature—the muddiness of premature aging. I revised my estimate to early fifties.

He wore a light blue pajama top under the same Dodger jacket. Blue satin was grease-speckled and moth-eaten, bleached to pink in spots. Frayed red sweats exposed white, hairless ankles. Bare feet tapered to ragged yellow nails. Where stubble didn't sprout, his skin was pallid and flaky. Dull brown eyes struggled to stay open.

The room behind him was the color of congealed custard, strewn with food wrappers, take-out boxes, empty cups, dirty clothes. Warm, fetid air escaped to the hallway.

Milo's badge didn't do a thing for the man's wakefulness. Bracing himself against the doorjamb, he drank soda, gave no sign he remembered me.

"Sir, we're looking into a tenant who lived here a few years ago."

Nothing.

"Sir?"

A hoarse "Yeah?"

"We were wondering if you knew her."

Runny nose that he swiped with his sleeve. "Who?"

"A woman named Patricia Bigelow."

Silence.

"Sir?"

"What'd she do?" Clogged voice. Slurred enunciation.

"Why would you think she did anything?"

"You're not here . . . because you . . . like my cooking."

"You cook, huh?"

The man chomped the candy bar. The interior of his mouth was more gap than tooth.

Warm day but dressed for chill. Snarfing sugar, rotten dentition. No need to roll up his sleeves; I knew we wouldn't be invited inside.

Milo said, "So you remember Patty Bigelow."

No answer.

"Do you?

"Yeah?"

"She's dead."

The brown eyes blinked. "That's too bad."

"What can you tell us about her, sir?"

Ten-second delay, then a long, slow, laborious head shake as the old addict nudged the door with his knee. Milo placed a big hand on the knob.

"Hey."

"How well did you know Ms. Bigelow?"

Something changed in the brown eyes. New wariness. "I didn't."

"You were living here at the same time she was."

"So were other people."

"Any of them still around?"

"Doubt it."

"People come and go."

Silence.

"How long have you been living here, sir?"

"Twenty years." Glance down at his knee. "Gotta take a leak." He made another halfhearted try at closing the door. Milo held fast and the guy started to fidget and blink. "C'mo-on, I need to—"

"Friend, I'm a murder guy, don't care what magic potion gets you through the day."

The man's eyes closed. He swayed. Nodding off. Milo tapped his shoulder. "Trust me, pal, I'm not on speaking terms with any narcs."

The eyes opened and shot us a who-me? "I'm clean."

"And I'm Condoleezza Rice. Just tell us what you remember about Patty Bigelow and we'll be out of your life."

"Don't remember anything." We waited.

"She had a kid . . . okay?"

"What do you remember about the kid?"

"She . . . had one."

"Who'd Patty hang with?"

"Dunno."

"She have any friends?"

"Dunno."

"Nice lady?"

Shrug.

"You and she didn't hang out together?"

"Never."

"Never?"

"Not my type."

"Meaning?"

Another look at his knee. "Not my type."

"When she lived here did anything of a criminal nature go down near the building?"

"What?"

"Murder, rape, robbery, et cetera," said Milo. "Any of that happen here while Patty Bigelow lived here?"

"Nope."

"What's your name, sir?"

Hesitation. "Jordan."

"That a first or a last?"

"Les Jordan."

"Leslie?"

"Lester."

"Got a middle name?"

"Marlon."

"As in Brando."

Les Jordan shifted his weight. "Gotta piss."

From the stain spreading at his crotch, truth in advertising.

He stared at it. No embarrassment, just resignation. His eyelids fluttered. "Told you."

Milo said, "Have a nice day," and turned heel.

The door slammed shut.

Most of the other tenants were out. The few we found were too young to be relevant.

Back in the car, Milo phoned Detective Sean Binchy and asked him to run a criminal check on Lester Marlon Jordan.

While we waited, I said, "Sean's back on Homicide?"

"Nah, still wasting his time on armed robberies and other trivial matters. But the lad's grateful for my tutelage so he avails himself—yeah, Sean, hold on, lemme get a pen."

When he hung up, he said, "The charming Mr. Jordan has accumulated multiple arrests. Possession of heroin—big shock—and disorderlies. Five dismissals, three convictions, all bargained down to short stretches at County."

"Choosing the right lawyer," I said.

"Or he's too penny-ante to waste prison space on. Mister Rogers might love all his neighbors but you'd think Patty woulda been more discriminating."

"Maybe there's a reason for that."

"Such as?"

I took a deep breath, unloaded my dope suspicions.

"Respectable nurse dealing hospital junk on the side?" he said. "Rick considers her next to saintly and my impression was you concurred."

"I do. Just thought I should mention it."

"Dealing," he said. "Jordan did get a little edgy when I pushed him about knowing her . . . know what I find interesting? Here's Patty, an alleged solid citizen living in a dive, and once she moves from there, she's hopping around every coupla years. But a scuzzy junkie like Lester Jordan manages to stay at the same address twenty years."

"Maybe his family owns the building."

"Or he got a source of steady income that's managed to elude the justice system."

"Simple possession raps, but he deals," I said.

"He's made it this far without dying, Alex. Having some control over the product would help. Nice respectable hospital nurse moves in, you can see his digging that."

"For Tanya's sake I hope that stays a theory."

"Tanya's the one did the Pandora bit."

"Doesn't mean she's ready for what flies out of the box."

The two of us sat there for a while.

He said, "Why Patty would tell her anything is still beyond me. On the other hand, maybe she *was* pure and this is just us cogitating out of control. We've been known to spin some pretty good theories in our spare time."

I said, "Some of them have turned out to be real."

"Listen to you," he said. "I thought the key was to think positive. Whatever the hell that means."

I kept quiet.

"Any further wisdom at this juncture?" he said.

"Nope."

"Onward to Fourth Street."

Dappled shade from mature trees prettied the block. The same Mini Cooper was parked on the concrete pad. *PLOTGRL.*

Tanya had said Asians had lived above her so we headed for the duplex's ground floor. The door was answered by a slim, ponytailed brunette in her late twenties. A pencil was wedged behind one ear. A fuzzy pink sweater hung over black tights. Freckled nose, amber eyes, sharp chin. Soft curves molded the sweater.

Milo's badge made her giggle. "Cops? That is so weird. I'm right in the middle of a cop-show teleplay. Want to be my technical advisors?"

"What show?"

"A pilot," she said. "The main hook is a girl detective who's deaf because of a gunshot accident. She can't hear the bad guys coming so she has to develop her other senses to their utmost. Overcompensation, you know? She's an ace at sign language and that ends up being crucial in catching a serial killer."

"Sounds interesting," said Milo.

"Right now, it sounds sucko because what I'm really good at is comedy. But my agent says no one's buying. Hopefully when I finish *Hear No Evil* it'll suck less but not be too intelligent for the networks."

She stuck out a hand, shook energetically. "Lisa Bergman. What brings you guys around on a weekend?"

Milo smiled at her. "Background check. You're too young to help."

"I'm older than I look, but you made my day. Can you at least tell me what's going on—no names, just the basic story line? I can always use material."

"The story line," he said, "is we're inquiring about a woman who lived here nine, ten years ago."

"Nine, ten years ago," said Lisa Bergman, "I was a junior at Reed."

"There you go."

"You're saying something happened here?"

"A person of interest lived here. Who are your upstairs neighbors?"

"Four law students younger than me. What did this person of interest do?"

"She's deceased," said Milo.

"Deceased as in murdered?"

"Natural death, but we need to clear up some details about her life."

"How come?"

"Financial issues. Nothing juicy enough for TV."

"You're sure?"

"Do debentures and tax-free municipal bonds sound like a hook?"

"Ugh," said Lisa Bergman. Sliding the pencil from behind her ear, she touched the point to her lip, creating a tiny little temporary dimple. "You should go over and talk to Mary Whitbread. She's the landlady."

"Where can we find her?"

Stepping onto her porch, she pointed. "Five buildings down, the green one, first floor. She'll probably be there."

"Homebody?"

"No, she shops but mostly she's around." Nose-wrinkling frown. "Nosy?"

"Between you and me, she drops by more than she has to," said Bergman. "Supposedly to make sure the property's being maintained but really just to schmooze. Once, I made the mistake of inviting her in for coffee. An hour later, she was still here and all my ideas for that day's writing had floated away."

She grinned. "Maybe that was good."

Milo thanked her and wished her luck with her script.

She said, "From your mouth to God's ears. If this gig doesn't work out, I'll have to go back to being an event planner."

Mary Whitbread's duplex was painted mint green with teal trim, fronted by impeccable grass, shaded by a gorgeously contorted sycamore.

Freshly swept tile porch, pretty flowers in pretty vases. A cheerful, "One second!" preceded the opening of a black lacquer door.

From Lisa Bergman's description, I was expecting a mousy type in a housecoat. Mary Whitbread was fiftyish, tan, trim, and blond-coiffed, with huge blue eyes under eyebrows plucked to commas. Her white silk blouse was patterned with gold links and bugles and red orchids—Versace or trying to be—and tucked tight into tailored navy crepe slacks. Tiny waist, hard hips, sharp bosoms. Red spike-heeled sandals revealed nacreous toenail polish. Her fingernails were painted the crimson of the shoes.

"Hel-lo," she proclaimed. "If you're here about the vacancy, sorry, it's been rented, the service forgot to de-list."

Milo said, "Aw, shucks," and flashed the badge.

"Police? My goodness." Peering at us. "Now that I'm looking it's obvious you're not . . . in the market."

"Is it."

Mary Whitbread stepped out onto the porch and smiled. "What I meant was when I see two men looking for a place to rent together I assume—you know. Which isn't to say that bothers me. Actually, they're my favorite tenants. So meticulous, that great eye for proportion."

She patted her hair. Flashed teeth. "So how can I help the police?"

"We're inquiring about a former tenant."

"One of my people got in trouble? Who?"

"No one's in trouble, Ms. Whitbread—"

"Just call me Mary." She took another step forward, moved right into Milo's personal space.

"No one's in trouble, Mary. One of your former tenants is deceased and there are some corollary investigations going on into financial matters."

"Financial? White-collar crime?" she said. "Like Enron? Worldcom?"

"Nothing quite so monumental," said Milo. "I'm sorry but I can't discuss the details."

Mary Whitbread pouted. "*Meanie.* Now you've got me all curious."

Leaning forward, close enough to kiss. Milo retreated two steps. Mary Whitbread quickly claimed the space he'd vacated. "All right, Detective, I'll bite. Who's this mystery person?"

"Patricia Bigelow."

False lashes fluttered. "Patty? She died? How sad. How in the world did it happen?"

"Cancer."

"Cancer," she repeated. "That's terribly sad. She didn't smoke."

"You remember her."

"I'm a people person. My people stay for years, often we become friends."

"Patty Bigelow didn't stay long."

"No . . . I suppose she didn't . . . cancer? She couldn't have been too old." She frowned. "That little girl of hers . . . Tamara? Losing her mother . . . you're saying Patty became involved in some sort of *money-laundering* thing or whatever?"

Milo ran a finger across his lips.

"Sorry, Detective, I just find people so endlessly fascinating. Used to work as a casting agent in the industry and boy, that was a lesson in applied psychology. But your job, glimpsing the dark side, it must be endlessly fascinating."

"Endlessly. What can you tell us about Patty Bigelow?"

"Well," she said, "she paid her rent on time, kept the place up just fine. *I* certainly had no problems with her."

"Did anyone else?"

More lash calisthenics. "Not that I'd know. I'm just saying we got along dandy. Have you been over to the apartment she occupied?"

"The tenant sent us here."

"Lisa," said Mary Whitbread. "Pretty girl. Her father pays the rent.

Beverly Hills divorce lawyer, he's been financing Lisa's adventures for years. This month it's screenwriting."

I said, "Who lived above Patty?"

"A young couple from . . . Indonesia. Or Malaysia? Somewhere over there. They had Dutch names even though they were Oriental . . . Henry—no Hendrik. Hendrik and Astrid Van Dreesen. He was studying for a Ph.D., some scientific thing, she was . . . some sort of salesperson . . . electronics was his thing, I believe. They weren't as meticulous about upkeep as you'd think. Being Oriental. We always assume they'll be neat, right? But overall, good tenants. They stayed four years, then moved back to wherever they came from."

"During the time Ms. Bigelow lived here, did anything out of the ordinary occur in the neighborhood?"

"Out of the ordinary as in a swindle or a con job or laundering?"

"Anything you can think of," said Milo.

"Out of the ordinary . . . well . . . we don't have the kind of problems you'd see in a lower-income neighborhood. I do recall a purse-snatching, a poor old lady knocked to her feet by a Mexican—a busboy at a restaurant on Wilshire . . . but that was after Patty's time . . . there *were* a few burglaries, but the police caught whoever was behind them." She clucked her tongue. "Was it lung cancer? When she applied to rent she said she didn't smoke. And I never saw evidence that she did."

"She was here less than a year," I said. "Why'd she move?"

"The rent was beyond her budget," said Whitbread. "With a child in parochial school, it became a burden, though I don't know why you'd want that."

"Not a fan of parochial school?"

"Those priests? Every day a new headline. But that was Patty's choice. When she told me she was having difficulties I sensed she wanted me to reduce the rent but, of course, that was out of the question."

"Of course."

"In the real estate business, Detective, if one wants quality tenants, one must be fair but firm. Patty's unit was in terrific condition, tons of original features from the twenties. It didn't stay vacant long. Two gay guys, as a matter of fact, and they lived there for five years and the only reason they left was they bought a house up in the hills."

She frowned. "Where did Patty move? I was never contacted by anyone for a reference."

"Culver City," said Milo.

"Ouch," said Whitbread. "That's a bit of a comedown." Her eyes shifted to a spot over his shoulder.

A black Hummer had pulled up to the curb. Whitbread waved. Put her hand on my arm. "My son's here—is there anything else, Detective?"

"No, ma'am."

"Well then, nice talking to you." She nudged me, smiled at Milo. "If at some point you *are* allowed to give a civilian some juicy details, please remember me."

"Will do," he said. "Thanks for your time."

Clicking past us on red heels, she hurried to the Hummer and knocked on the passenger window. The glass had been tinted black. So had the grille and the rims.

As we pulled away, the driver's door opened and a huge young black man in copper-colored sweats and matching athletic shoes got out. Midtwenties, shaved head, razor-trimmed mustache and goatee.

"That's her kid?" said Milo. "I love this city."

"Always surprises," I said.

"Take a nap and your zip code's changed."

Mary Whitbread waved at us.

The giant did the same, but his heart wasn't in it.

11

This is different," said Milo.

We were standing near the dead fountain that centered the bungalow court on Culver Boulevard. The bowl was cracked, crusted with dead bugs, splotched with vaguely organic stains. A broken toy truck lay on its side. As we'd stepped onto the property, the children who'd been playing in the dirt had scattered like finches.

No bells on any of the units' warped doors. Milo's knocks had produced baffled stares, murmured denials in Spanish. What we could see of the units' interiors was dim and threadbare. A stale, morose uniformity shouted transience.

"I can try to find out who owned the property back then but it's not going to lead anywhere." His shoe nudged the fountain. "Patty didn't ask Chatty Mary for references because she didn't need any for this dump."

I said, "That could've been the point."

"What do you mean?"

"She moved to keep a low profile."

"Money wasn't the motive? Scared of something brought on by illicit commerce? I don't know, Alex. If she was running why stay in town and keep the same job?"

"I was thinking guilt, not fear," I said. "Running from herself."

"The alleged 'terrible thing'?"

"A step down the residential ladder might've seemed a bit of atonement."

"Punishing herself," he said. "Not caring if Tanya got punished in the process?"

"Tanya said she didn't care."

"Tanya sounds like a kid who'd say that."

"She does put on a good face," I said. "But kids are flexible. The main thing would've been the relationship between her and her mother."

"And now she's alone."

We walked to the car. I said, "Maybe the move here really was about saving money."

"Innocent till proven otherwise? Sure, why not. Now that we've had our useless geography lesson, what next?"

"Maybe we should narrow the geography down. If something had happened on Fourth Street, Chatty Mary would've remembered, so let's put that aside for the moment."

"Unless Chatty Mary didn't want the neighborhood besmirched by tales of violence."

"My guess is she'd still enjoy talking about a juicy crime. I agree that the murder on June Street is unlikely to be relevant and the only unusual thing that actually happened at the mansion—if you can call it that—was Colonel Bedard dying while under Patty's care."

"Not unusual—he was old." He rubbed his face, like washing without water.

"What?" I said.

"If you want me to be creative, I can be."

"Go for it."

"An old guy suffering, a compassionate person—could think they were doing him a favor by helping the process along."

"Euthanasia?"

"I told you it was creative."

"If Patty had a tendency to play God, wouldn't Rick know?"

"The E.R. is one thing, Alex. People come *in* to be saved. But watching some feeble old guy waste away? That could tug at the heartstrings—even a good person's heartstrings. Nothing premeditated, she wasn't a criminal. Something impulsive that she came to regret. Then she got sick, déjà-vued, and blurted it to Tanya. Maybe thinking about her own death got her obsessing on how she'd hastened the process for someone else. Or this whole deathbed confession thing is crap and you should concentrate on helping Tanya deal with being alone and *I* should spend my two weeks off watching TV."

"Deaf detectives?"

"Jesus," he said. "No, my concept of nirvana is TiVoing a month of Judge Judy, cooking up some microwave chili, and zoning out."

"Truth and justice," I said.

"Stupid people getting yelled at. If I were straight, I'd try to date that woman."

I laughed. Gazed out the car window. None of the children had returned to the fountain. "First Patty's a dope dealer, now she's a mercy killer."

"She said she killed a guy, Alex."

"That she did."

"I'll tell you one thing," he said. "No sense pursuing Colonel Bedard's death. Whatever happened, the certificate's going to say natural."

He tilted his head toward the bungalow court. "In terms of *this* Eden, there was bound to be plenty of street crime back then, let's see if Isaac pulls anything up. Not that I'm any more convinced something happened than I was yesterday. But if there was no euthanasia, my next bet would be something to do with the Cherokee drug market. Especially after meeting Lester Jordan. Let me sniff around some more, pay Jordan another social call."

He yawned, stretched, closed his eyes. "Enough for one day. Drive."

"TiVo time?" I said.

The eyes opened. "Not so fast, bucko. Expensive lunch on you."

"Sure," I said. "Afterward, we can revisit Jordan."

"Nope, too soon. I'll go it alone tomorrow."

"What do you need me to do?"

He lowered the window and breathed in smog. "Play it by ear. Which is a nice way of saying I don't have a damn idea."

I got home at three, belly full of Thai food, took Blanche for a puppy trot around the garden, freshened her water, heard about her day, toted her and her food bowl into my office.

She ate as I had another go at Tanya's file.

Starting at the beginning.

The tape-loop soundtrack of obsessive-compulsiveness is powered by anxiety. The noise can be switched off by SSRIs—drugs that increase the flow of serotonin to the brain. But not much is known about how psychoactive meds affect kids long-term, and when the patient stops taking the pills, the soundtrack cranks up again.

Cognitive behavior therapy takes longer and requires active participation by the patient, but it has no side effects and teaches self-help skills that can endure. By the time Tanya first came to see me, I'd successfully treated scores of kids with OCD, sampling from a grab bag of CBT methodologies.

I try to view every patient with a fresh eye, but after you've been in practice for a few years, preconceptions are inevitable, and when she arrived I had a plan in mind.

1. Build trust.
2. Find the anxious core.
3. When the time's right, use thought-stopping, guided exposure, desensitization, or some combination, to replace tension with relaxation.

By the fourth session, rapport seemed set and I was ready to work. Tanya marched into the office and sat at the play table and said, "They're gone."

"Who is?"

"My habits."

"Gone," I said.

"I don't do them anymore."

"That's great, Tanya."

Shrug.

"How'd you do that?"

"You said I was being nervous so when I got nervous I chased the habit feelings away."

"Chased them?"

"I said, 'Stop, that's stupid,' and put other feelings inside." Tapping her temple.

Would you like your clinical license to go, or will you eat it here?

"What other feelings did you put into your head?"

"Taking a walk with Mommy. Going to Disneyland."

"Disneyland's a favorite place?"

"Small World's boring," she said. "I like the Spinning Teacups." Rotating one hand. "I like the pink cup."

"Spinning Teacups is something you've done before with Mommy."

"No," she said, looking vexed. "We don't *really* do it, Mommy gets sick when she spins. We watch."

"You'd *like* to do it."

"I *pretend* to do it." Rotating both hands, now. Fast and choppy, like an agitated bus driver.

"You pretend to spin."

"Fast," she said.

"That makes the nervous feelings go away."

Doubt sharpened the pale green eyes. "You *said* the habits were being *nervous*."

"You're absolutely right, Tanya. You did a great job."

"I didn't do it all," she said.

"Someone helped you?"

Emphatic head shake. "I didn't do it all the first *time*."

"You did some of it."

She turned away from me. "I looked under the bed. A little. I washed my hands a bunch of times. The second time I didn't look under the bed and I only washed my hands once. I *had* to wash. To be clean, Mommy says to use soap and water before I go to sleep, and brush my teeth."

"Sounds like a good idea."

"Washing only once is a good idea," she said. "More is *stupid*."

"Mommy said it was stupid?"

"*No!* I say it to myself." She picked up a pencil, twirled, poked the playhouse.

"I'm really impressed, Tanya."

No response.

"You must be proud of yourself."

"Having habits made me tired," she said, airily.

"And now you can handle them."

"When I get nervous, I say 'You're being nervous, you don't need those habits.'"

I said, "Perfect. You could be a doctor."

She manipulated dolls. Worked hard at a poker face. Gave up and surrendered to a smile. "Mommy says no one's perfect but I'm close."

"Mommy would know."

Giggle. "Um . . . can I draw?"

The second time, three years later, I expected dejection due to relapse, was surprised to see her straight-backed and strutting as she entered the office. Still small for her age, she dressed older—pressed khakis, white shirt under a navy V-necked sweater, immaculate brown loafers. Her hair was combed out and straight. Suggestions of maturity had begun to firm the contours of her face.

The play table that had occupied her at age seven was dismissed with a glance. She settled in one of the leather armchairs, crossed her legs, and said, "Guess I'm here again."

"It's good to see you, Tanya."

"I'm sorry," she said. "I did it again."

"Your habits?"

"No. I mean they're *gone.*"

"You cured yourself again."

"Mommy said I should still come in."

"That's nothing to be sorry for."

"I was going to come in a few weeks ago but I had too many tests, so I . . ."

"In the meantime you did the job yourself."

"I don't want to waste your time. And Mommy's money. Mommy still wanted me to see you. She wants to make sure I'm okay."

"Do you feel okay?"

"Yup."

"Then I guess you're okay," I said. "Boy, you did it even quicker than the first time. I'm impressed."

"The first time *you* really did it," she said. "You explained that I was doing all those things because I was nervous. Now I understand." She sat up straighter. "I don't know why I *started* again. At least this time it wasn't as bad. I started washing and cleaning out my closet many times but I *didn't* do any checking."

"Were you nervous about anything?"

"Not really."

"Mommy told me you moved."

"I like it."

"Sometimes even good change can make someone nervous."

She thought about that. "I like it."

"How's school going?" I said.

"Pretty easy," she said. "Boring. I had a bad cold right before the habits started up again. Mommy thought maybe I got tired and that's why."

"Sometimes that happens."

"Every time I get a cold I need to be careful?"

"No," I said. "But anytime you get really upset about something it would be a good idea to practice relaxing—do you still use Disneyland as a favorite place?"

"No way," she said. "That's immature."

"You have a new place."

Her eyes shifted sideways. "I just tell myself to be relaxed."

"So school's easy."

"In some classes I have to work to get As."

"Getting As is important."

"Of *course.*"

"Are you feeling pressure?" I said.

"From Mommy?"

"From anyone."

"She says do my best, that's all. But . . ."

I waited.

"Sometimes," she said, "it's hard to study when it's so *boring,* but I *make* myself. I *don't* like writing papers and I *hate* social studies. Science and math are good, they make sense. I want to be a doctor. Helping people is useful."

"That's what your mother does."

"Mommy says doctors are always going to be in charge, not nurses. I don't like asking people for things."

Long pause. "I think Mommy's been a little nervous."

"About what?"

"She doesn't tell me."

"You asked her?"

Slow smile.

"What's funny, Tanya?"

"No way would I ask her.".

"Why not?"

"She'd say she's okay and start asking if I'm okay."

"You don't want to worry her."

"She's got a full plate."

Adult expression. I wondered how much time she spent with kids her age.

"How can you tell she's been nervous, Tanya?"

"Not sitting still a lot . . . straightening the pictures. Sometimes she looks worried." Fidgeting. "I'm really okay, I don't think I need to come in again."

"As long as you're here, is there anything else you want to talk about . . ."

"Like what?"

"Like Mommy being nervous, how that affects you."

"Please don't tell her I told you."

"Promise," I said. "Same rule we had the first time."

"You don't tell unless I want you to," she said. "She does it after I go to bed, thinks I don't hear it."

"Straightening up?"

"Mopping the floor even though it's clean. Taking out cans from the shelves in the kitchen and putting them back. I hear doors open and close and when she moves chairs sometimes they rub against the floor. She does it at night because she doesn't want me to know. Maybe she thinks I'll catch it."

"Like a cold."

"Can that happen?"

"There are no germs for habits but sometimes when we live with people we imitate them."

She gnawed her lip. "Should I try to help Mommy with her habits?"

"What do you think she'd say if you offered."

Big smile. " 'I'm *okay*, honey.' But I'd still like to help her."

"I think the best thing you can do for her is just what you're doing. Handle any problems that you can but ask for help when you can't."

She took a long time to digest that. "If it happens again, I'll come back."

"I always like hearing from you. It's okay to call when things are going well."

"Really?" she said. "Maybe I will."

She never did.

The next day Patty phoned me. "I don't know what you do but it's a miracle. She sees you and she's fine."

"She's gotten really good at understanding herself," I said.

"I'm sure she does but you're clearly guiding her. Thank you so much, Doctor. It's good to know you're around."

"Is there anything else I can help you with?"

"Nope, can't think of any."

"The move's been smooth?"

"Everything's just fine. Thank you, Doctor. Bye."

CHAPTER

12

I put the chart aside, wondered about a link between Tanya's childhood symptoms and the "terrible thing" that had occupied Patty's final hours.

Or was Milo right and it all boiled down to a final burst of obsessive thinking in a woman whose entire life had been about order, facing the ultimate disorder?

Tanya's initial visit had been shortly after the move to the Bedard mansion. Well before the colonel's death but maybe she'd picked up on Patty's tension about caring for the old man.

Killed him.

Milo had snatched the mercy-killing hypothesis out of the air, but his instincts were good. Had Patty, a decent person, struggled with the aftermath of an impulsive, crushingly permanent act?

How did I know Patty was decent?

Because everyone said so.

Because I *wanted* to believe it.

"Constricted thinking," I said out loud.

Blanche looked up, batted her lashes. Sank back down and resumed some sort of pleasant canine dream.

I tossed it around some more, realized Tanya's symptoms had

started two years *before* Patty brought her to me. Still living on Cherokee.

The second episode was after the move from Fourth Street to Culver City. So maybe Tanya's tension had been about transition, had no connection at all to anything criminal.

Blanche looked up again.

"You need to get out more, Blondie. Let's take a ride."

Hudson Avenue on Saturday was gloriously imposing, profoundly still.

The mansion's slate roof was silvered by afternoon light. The lawn was green marzipan; the half-timbers decorating the facade, fresh bars of chocolate. But for a sprinkle of lemons littering the stone landing, everything was spotless.

The vintage Bentley and Mercedes were just where they'd been yesterday.

The cars—the entire neighborhood—screamed old money but there was no reason to think Colonel Bedard's family had held on to the place. I scooped Blanche into my arms and walked to the double doors. The bell chimed Debussy or something like it. Rapid footsteps were followed by a click behind the peephole and one of the doors opened on the maid I'd seen chasing the squirrel.

Late forties, built low to the ground, skin the color of strong tea, black hair plaited into glossy coils. Wary black eyes. The pink uniform was spotless, edged with white lace. Legs in seamed stockings bowed as if clamping a cello. Her hand tightened around a chamois cloth stained with tarnish.

Blanche purred and did her smiley thing. The maid's expression softened and I produced my LAPD consultant badge.

It's a plasticized clip-on, long expired, and pretty much useless, but it impressed her enough to stifle a cluck of disapproval.

Tanya had mentioned the name of the housekeeper who'd worked with Patty . . . *Cecilia*. This woman was old enough to have been around twelve years ago.

"Are you Cecilia?"

"No."

"Are the owners home?"

"No."

"Mr. and Mrs. Bedard?"

"No home."

Blanche panted.

"But they do live here?"

"What kind dog?"

"French bulldog."

"Spensive?"

"Worth it."

She frowned.

I said, "Do you remember Colonel Bedard?"

No answer.

"The old man who—"

"I no work for him."

"But you knew him."

"Cecilia work for him."

"You know Cecilia?"

No answer. I flicked the I.D.

"My sister," she said.

"Where can I find your sister?"

Longer pause.

"She's not in trouble, just to ask a few questions."

"Zacapa."

"Where's that?"

"Guatemala."

Blanche purred some more.

"Nie dog," said the woman. "Lie a mownkey."

As she stepped back to close the door, a male voice said, "Who's there, America?"

Before she could answer, a young man swung the second door wide, exposing a limestone-and-marble entry big enough for skating. Wall niches housed busts of long-dead men. The rear wall was ruled by a portrait of a white-wigged George Washington look-alike. To the right of the painting, a walk-through was brightened by glass doors that showcased expansive gardens.

"Hey," said the young man. Medium height, midtwenties, frizzy dark hair, uncertain brown eyes. Indoor complexion, the haunted good looks of a teen idol softened by residual baby fat. He slumped a bit. Wore a wrinkled blue shirt, sleeves rolled to the elbows, olive cargo pants, yellow running shoes with loose laces. Pen marks stippled his fingers. The Timex on his left wrist had seen plenty of action. Milo would've approved.

"Police," said America, hazarding another touch of Blanche's forehead.

The young man watched, amused. "Cool dog. Police? What about?"

"I'm not a police officer but I am working with the police on an investigation into a woman who worked here around ten years ago."

"Working with how?"

I showed him the clip-on.

"Ph.D.? In what?"

"Psychology."

"Excellent," he said. "If all goes right, I'll have one of those. Not psych, physics. Ten years ago? What, one of those cold cases? Profiling?"

"Nothing glamorous. It's a financial investigation."

"Into someone who worked here—you mean Cecilia? Dad neglected to take out Social Security?"

America tensed up.

I said, "Not Cecilia, a woman named Patricia Bigelow. But if Cecilia remembers her it would be helpful."

He looked at America. She said, "I tell him Cecilia in Guatemala."

"I remember Patty," he said. "The nurse who took care of my grandfather." Extending a soft, ink-speckled hand. "Kyle Bedard. What'd she do?"

"She died but it's not about murder. I can't get into details."

"Hush-hush confidential," he said. "Sounds interesting. Want to come in?"

America said, "Meester Kyle, your father say—"

Kyle Bedard said, "Don't worry, it's cool."

She walked away, wringing the chamois, as he let me in.

All that stone lowered the temperature ten degrees. I took a closer look at the colonial painting and Kyle Bedard chuckled. "My parents overpaid for it at Sotheby's because some art consultant convinced them it was a family heirloom. My bet is some hack turned out dozens of them for Victorian social climbers."

A walnut door to the left topped by a limestone pedicle opened on a book-lined room. The décor was Rich Man's Library: enough leather binding to sacrifice a herd, gold-tasseled blue velvet drapes suspended from an etched brass rod that blocked out the day and spilled onto brass-inlaid parquet flooring, a massive blue-and-beige Sarouk covering most of the wood.

A carved partner's desk bore bronze Tiffany desk pieces. A dragonfly lamp emitted brandy-colored light. Leather armchairs sagged where bottoms had lingered. A few strategically placed paintings of hunting scenes completed the image.

The room Tanya had described, the old man sitting in his wheelchair, reading, dozing.

But warring elements had intruded: acid-green beanbag in the center of the rug, piles of textbooks and notebooks and loose papers, three empty fried chicken buckets, take-out pizza box, bags of chips in various flavors and hues, soda cans, beer cans, crumpled napkins, a dandruff of crumbs.

A sleek silver laptop rested on the beanbag, flashing eerie light as the screensaver shifted: A bug-eyed Albert Einstein morphed to sullen Jim Morrison then to the Three Stooges engaged in some spirited eyepoking then back to Albie. A charging iPod suckled through a well-kinked electric cord.

Rich man's library meets college dorm.

The room *smelled* like a dorm.

Kyle Bedard said, "I'm working on some calculations, the solitude's helpful."

"Who else lives here?"

"No one. Dad's somewhere in Europe and Mom lives in Deer Valley and Los Gatos."

"Ph.D. calculations?"

"An infinite array."

"Where do you go to grad school?"

"The U. Did my undergrad at Princeton, thought of staying back east. Realized I'd had enough ice and sleet and people who thought they were British."

"What area of physics are you working in?"

"Lasers as alternative energy sources. If my committee accepts my dissertation, my big wish is snagging a postdoc working with a genius doing cutting-edge research at Lawrence Livermore Lab. It would be cool to be part of something millennium-changing."

"Getting close to finishing?"

"My data's in and my writing should be finished by next year. But you've been through it, there are no guarantees. Show up for the orals, some committee member wants to screw you, you're screwed. I should practice my ass-kissing skills but the work keeps distracting me."

"That was my attitude," I said. "It turned out fine."

"Psych, huh? Clinical?"

I nodded.

"Thanks for that snippet of confidence-building therapy—here, sit?" Removing the laptop from the beanbag, he plopped down.

I positioned an armchair to face him, placed Blanche in my lap.

"That is one idiosyncratic dog—kind of a primate thing going on there," he said. "What is she, some kind of miniature bulldog?"

"French bulldog."

"Don't you mean Freedom bulldog?"

I laughed. He smiled.

"So you remember Patty Bigelow."

"I remember who she was. Grandfather was alive then and my parents were still together. We lived up in Atherton, didn't come down to see him very often. I always liked coming here—to this room, the smell of the books. The room my parents would never think of entering, God forbid they'd learn something. So I was able to get some peace and quiet. He's got some great stuff there, really rare editions." Pointing to the shelves. "How'd Patty die?"

"Cancer."

"That's a drag. What kind of financial investigation did that elicit and why?"

"All I can tell you is her death raised some questions and the police are going back and interviewing everyone she worked for."

"And they send *you* to interview the crazy people?"

I smiled.

He scratched his head. "Are you saying Patty embezzled? That would sure fit Mom's preconceptions."

"No, she's not suspected of anything."

"Hush-hush confidential? I can dig that. If I do get that fellowship at Lawrence it'll be lips-sutured-shut." He flexed his feet and the bean-bag squeaked. "Cancer . . . I don't remember her as being that old . . . I'm guessing she'd be in her fifties?"

"Fifty-four."

"That's way too young," he said. "One-third of deaths are due to cancer. A fact Mom keeps reminding me of because she confuses lasers with radiation and is convinced I'm going to fry myself . . . Patty had a daughter, younger than me, seven or eight. Each time we visited, she'd run away and hide, I thought it was a crackup. One time I got bored and wandered out to the backyard. She was sitting in the bushes, count-ing leaves or whatever, talking to herself. I thought she looked lonely but figured she'd freak out if I startled her, so I left her alone. It's got to be tough, losing her mom."

Squeak squeak. "Funny the things you remember."

"Do you remember anything else about Patricia Bigelow?"

"Let's see," he said. "She seemed to be taking decent care of Grandfather and by the end he was pretty much out of it. Dad appreci-ated her."

"Mom didn't?" I said.

"Mom has an exaggerated sense of social class."

"Embezzlement fits her preconceptions."

"She assumes the underclass will inevitably steal and the underclass is defined as anyone not as rich as her. When I was growing up, the maids had to open their purses for inspections every time they left the house. She's a suspicious person, by nature. I don't see her very often." Weak smile. "We're not exactly a cohesive social unit." His foot nudged a pizza box. "I should clean this place up but I probably won't. When Dad comes home and gets irate, my excuse will be that I was too busy. My real reason for noncompliance will be getting Dad irate. Im-mature, huh?" He threw back his head, poked at an eye. "Ouch, con-tact's rubbing—okay, now it's good."

I said, "When's your father returning?"

"A week, ten days, a month, a parsec. Basically, whenever he feels like it. He *doesn't* work. Lives off Grandfather's investments. Which I find a bit Edith Wharton. Even if you don't need to work, why not do something useful? The plan was for me to get a token brokerage job, marry a rich, dull girl, sire the requisite dull child or two, retire early to a life of calculated indolence. The physics thing *really* makes Mom irate. 'That's work for hire, good for Jews and Chinese.' She's convinced I'm going to sire two-headed progeny."

"Scholarship as rebellion," I said.

"I could've been a dangerous felon or a drug-addled loser or joined the Green Party, but developing a work ethic seemed more subversive . . . so what else do I remember about Patty Bigelow . . . attentive to Grandfather, moved fast—as in ambulation. That *definitely* sticks in my memory. Always rushing around, making sure he had everything he needed. Maybe that was just for Dad's benefit. If so, it failed. He believes any undue expenditure of energy is a vice. And he didn't give a shit about Grandfather. They loathed each other."

"Father-son issues?"

"Oh, boy," he said. "Compared to them, Dad and I are drinking buds. As to why, no one clued me in on all the dirty little family secrets. Grandfather *did* appreciate the value of work. He made it on his own, joined the army in '39—not a West Point deal, he started off as a technical noncom in Texas, ended up a lieutenant colonel designing communications systems in the ETO. After discharge, he got a job in television, switched to optics, then electronic components. He invented resistors and power cells and measurement equipment—oscillators, that kind of thing. Earned himself a slew of patents and made enough money for Mom and Dad to convince themselves we were *Mayflower* aristocracy."

His toe nudged the KFC box. "I don't know why I'm telling you all this. Maybe it's what you guys call a demand characteristic—you want me to talk, so I do."

"That's a pretty esoteric term."

"I took some psych as an undergrad. Found it interesting but I needed something less nebulous. Anyway, that's all I remember about Ms. Bigelow."

"How'd she come to work here."

"I was a kid. Why would I know?"

"Sounds as if you were a pretty attentive kid."

"Not really," he said. "Actually, I was mostly in my own world. Just like Patty's daughter, sitting in the bushes. I really need to get back to my calculations. World oil consumption depends on it. If you leave me your number, next time I talk to Dad I'll tell him to call you."

"Thanks." I placed Blanche on the floor and stood.

She trotted straight to him. He chuckled and rubbed her neck. She smiled up at him.

"Cool dog. She can definitely stay here."

"People keep making that offer."

"Charisma," he said. "From what I know of Grandfather he had it in spades."

"Self-made man."

"It's a nice ideal," he said. "I'll settle for accomplishing anything."

CHAPTER

13

Isaac Gomez had sent me an e-mail.

Dear Dr. D,

These are the open homicides with male victims that I was able to find for the time periods you specified, listed in chronological order. I used a geographical criterion of a quarter-mile radius. No cases were found on your exact streets. There'd obviously be a much higher frequency of closed cases.

    1. Cherokee Avenue Locus:

        A. Rigoberto Alfredo Martinez, 19, gunshot wound to the head

        B. Leland William Armbruster, 43, gunshot wound to the chest

        C. Gerardo Escobedo, 22, multiple stab wounds to the chest

        D. Christopher Blanding Stimple, 20, shotgun wounds to head and torso

    2. Hudson Avenue Locus:

        A. Wilfred Charles Hong, 43, multiple gunshot wounds to head and torso

    3. Fourth Street Locus: no open homicides

    4. Culver Boulevard Locus:

        A. D'Meetri Antoine Stover, 34, gunshot wound to the torso

B. *Thomas Anthony Beltran, 20, gunshot wounds to head and torso*
C. *Cesar Octavio Cruz, 21, gunshot wound to the head (Beltran and Cruz were murdered during the same incident)*

Best wishes and good luck,
Isaac

I forwarded the text to Milo, busied myself with paperwork for a couple of hours, got no callback.

Maybe he'd really gotten into a vacation mode.

Maybe I should, too. No more work over the weekend.

But Sunday morning I was up early, scanning cyberspace for the killings Isaac had found. Wilfred Hong's unsolved murder was noted on a diamond dealer's Web site. Gory details and warnings for his colleagues, but no new facts. None of the Hollywood cases were listed but the dual murder of Cesar Cruz and Thomas Beltran received notice in the *Times* archive. Cruz and Beltran were members of Westside Venice Boyzz with long police records, and their murders were termed "a possible gang retaliation slaying." I crossed them off, along with Hong.

I clicked away until noon, trying different approaches to the remaining cases, starting with those in the Cherokee Avenue zone. Nothing on three of them, but I unearthed notice of Christopher Blanding Stimple's death in a newspaper morgue at *The Philadelphia Inquirer.* Stimple, a Philly native and high school athlete, had been eulogized in a brief, paid-for obituary. His demise was listed as "accidental while Chris was visiting California."

The family sanitizing the details of a shotgun homicide? No reason to do that in a case of murder, but suicide could inspire shame. Maybe the coroner had closed the case as self-inflicted but that conclusion hadn't found its way into LAPD records. In any event, I couldn't see Patty Bigelow blasting a twenty-year-old man with two barrels and crossed off Stimple.

At four p.m., I took a punishing run, showered, made coffee, straightened the house. At six thirty, Robin's truck pulled up in front of the house.

She jumped out and hugged me hard. "Why do we ever stay apart?"

Moist cheek. Tears weren't often part of Robin's repertoire. I tried to draw her face away for a kiss. She hugged me tighter.

I'd made dinner reservations at the Hotel Bel-Air. She said, "I love that place but would you be disappointed if we just stayed in?"

"Shattered and ground to dust." I canceled and called out for Chinese from a place in Westwood Village.

As she unpacked, she said, "Where's Blondie?"

"Sleeping."

"Smart girl."

She bathed, towel-dried her hair, put on some makeup, and emerged wearing a white sleeveless shift and nothing else. We were kissing in the kitchen when the food arrived. I overpaid the delivery boy, let the food go cold.

By nine, we were sitting near the pond, tossing random bits of egg roll and noodles to the koi.

"They're Japanese," she said. "But they sure go for Mandarin."

"Diversity has made its mark everywhere."

"Ha . . . this is so wonderful." She winced, rubbed the side of her neck.

"Sore?"

"Stiff from all the driving." Crooked smile. "Also, that last position."

"New one on me, too," I said. "Creative."

"Nothing ventured."

I got up and massaged her upper shoulders.

"That feels good . . . a little lower—lower—*perfect* . . . I learned one thing over the weekend. The whole convention thing is getting old."

"Too much like school."

"Not just the lectures," she said. "The social scene, too—who's making money, who's sleeping with who."

"You made serious money on the F5," I said.

"Nice big check for a working girl but petty cash for Mr. Dot-Com." She rolled her head. "A little lower, still—*yes* . . . maybe he'll even learn to play."

"Not a note?"

"Not even a bad one. After he paid me, he wanted to have dinner. Discuss the historical roots of luthiery."

"Good line."

"Not good enough. I stayed in my room and watched movies."

Crooked smile. "Not much plot, but some interesting positions."

"So I've seen."

"Honey, you ain't seen nothing yet."

An hour later:

"It is *good* to be home."

"Alex," she said, "I'm the one who was gone."

"Whatever."

CHAPTER

14

Milo called back Monday, just after four.

"All the Culver City cases were gang hits. CC detectives have a pretty good idea who the shooters were on Cruz, Beltran, and Stover but no one talked. Moving down the list, Wilfred Hong. The consensus is that Mrs. Hong was in on it. She was tied up but not tightly. A month after the funeral, she sold the house, moved with the kids to Hong Kong."

"Maybe she was scared."

"Not scared enough to avoid a new boyfriend. Guess what he does for a living."

"Sells gems."

"Ding. Onward to Hollywood. Gerardo Escobedo and Rigoberto Martinez are both in Petra's fridge pile. Escobedo called himself Marilyn, wore hair and makeup to match. By nineteen he'd been hustling for three years, was known to get into anyone's car. He was stabbed somewhere else, probably a park from the leaves and twigs, and dumped in an alley near Selma. Mucho overkill, everyone sees it as a trick gone bad. Martinez worked as a gardener with a crew out in Lawndale and had two priors for solicitation. Big guy, nearly three hundred pounds. Once he'd get in a room with a girl, he'd try to bully her out of full payment. Probably annoyed the wrong pimp. Christopher Stimple also had a hustler history—four busts. He was found in a rented room with a shotgun lying nearby, possible suicide, but since no one had ever seen him with any firearm and the position of the weapon wasn't clear-cut, the coroner listed the COD as undetermined."

"I found his obit online," I said. "High school football hero, the family listed the COD as accidental."

"Easier for them. In any event, I don't see Patty blowing away some confused kid. Which brings me to Leland William Armbruster. White male, heroin addict, convicted felon, and generally annoying habitué of the Boulevard. His street name was Lowball. Forty-three years old when someone propelled three .22 slugs into his chest. Why am I not shocked to learn that one of his known associates was Lester Marion Jordan?"

"Interesting," I said.

"Could turn out to be fascinating. Armbruster's body was found on Las Palmas, a block west of Patty's apartment and three blocks north."

"Was Jordan a suspect in the shooting?"

"Nope, just a name that popped up in the file. The D on the case died a few years ago but he was thorough. Interviewed Jordan and several others in Lowball's social circle. The clear picture is that when Lowball wasn't high he had an abrasive personality. One informant described his voice as 'cat claws on glass.' Another opined that for Lowball heroin shoulda been court-ordered as a mood modifier. Another interesting tidbit is when the guy couldn't score smack, he took anything. Including fortified wine, which turned him ugly."

"Drunks used to knock on Patty's door," I said. "Tanya said shouting made most of them go away."

"And maybe the ones who didn't required more forceful handling?"

"According to Tanya, there was never a need to follow through."

"According to Tanya," he said. "A little kid sleeping in back. Alex, even if she tried to find out what was going on, Patty woulda shushed her and sent her to bed. Maybe Lowball and Patty got into a verbal altercation that heated up ugly. Here I was thinking no way would we find a damn thing and Armbruster pops up. His being a buddy of Jordan would explain Jordan getting antsy when we brought up Patty. It could also place him in the building. Maybe one of those times, Armbruster spots Patty, gets ideas. Comes back late at night, pounds the door. Patty yells for him to split, he does but he stews on it, decides his urges will not be denied. Next time she goes out, he's lying in wait and, as they say, a confrontation ensues."

"Be good to know if Patty had any registered guns."

"Or unregistered. If she wanted serious protection on the streets she'd have to break the law. You know the deal with carry permits."

"Movies stars, millionaires, and friends of the sheriff."

"For sure not a working nurse with no juice. This was a woman who grew up on a ranch, Alex. Got abused by her father, struck out by herself, and made a point of having her shit together. Rick says she reminded him of a pioneer woman. I can see her packing. A .22 wouldn't be too bulky for a woman's handbag. Armbruster attacks her, she's prepared. She mighta even felt good about it, at first."

He turned silent. No sense elaborating.

He'd killed several men in Vietnam, a few more in the line of duty. I'd ended one life. Self-defense, no question about the necessity. But at odd times it could chew at you. Thinking about the children my psychopath would never sire.

"She carries it around all these years," he went on. "Then she gets sick, her inhibitions drop, and she blurts it to Tanya. Anything that *doesn't* fit?"

"Not so far."

"Leland William Armbruster," he said, savoring the name. "Let me do a little more background and if nothing contradictory comes up, I say we settle on ol' Lowball as our dead guy and tell Tanya that Mommy operated with clear justification."

"Maybe it was more than self-protection," I said. "With Armbruster hanging around Patty's building, he could've spotted Tanya. Given Patty's personal history and her devotion as a mother, she'd have been vigilant about any threat to her child."

"Lowball's a kiddy-groping sleaze? Sure, I like that even better. Hell, even if it's not true, we spin it that way for Tanya, she's got yet another reason to feel good about Mommy . . . yeah, I like it enough to marry it. Big juicy happy ending and we all go out for pizza."

I called Tanya at six. She phoned back at eight. "Sorry it took so long, Dr. Delaware."

"Studying?"

"What else?"

"How've you been doing?"

"Reasonably well. Is there anything new?"

"I have a question for you. Do you know if your mother ever owned a gun?"

"She did and I still have it. Why, did you find out something about a shooting near where we lived?"

"All kinds of things have come up but nothing dramatic, so far. Detective Sturgis thought if she did have a weapon it would be useful to rule it out. What kind is it?"

"Smith and Wesson semi-automatic, .22 caliber, that dark metal finish—bluing—with a wooden grip."

"Sounds like you've handled it."

"Mommy took me to the range to teach me how to shoot when I was around fourteen. She learned as a girl, thought it was a skill I should have. I was pretty good but I didn't like it. Someplace out in the Valley, all these guys in camouflage. I said I didn't want to continue and she said fine but if I wasn't going to get proficient, she was going to separate the gun from the bullets for safety purposes. Are you saying Detective Sturgis actually wants to analyze it?"

"If you don't mind."

"Of course not," she said. "I know she never really hurt anyone. Anyway . . ."

"I was re-reading your chart and the second time you came to see me you talked about her being nervous."

"I did?" she said. "Did I give a reason?"

"No, but you described her straightening late at night, when she thought you were sleeping. You'd just moved from Fourth Street, so I wondered about some kind of stress related to the change. But both you and she said the move was a good one."

"I honestly don't remember any of that, Dr. Delaware . . . the mind sciences are ambiguous, aren't they?"

Echoes of Kyle Bedard. "They can be."

"I've been thinking about psychiatry as a specialty, wonder if I have the ability to deal with that level of ambiguity."

"It's a long way off before you need to decide," I said.

"I guess," she said. "But time passes quickly as you get older."

CHAPTER

15

Unless you're a heart-transplant surgeon waiting for an organ, you don't bring a phone or a beeper to the dining room at the Hotel Bel-Air.

Robin and I had decided tonight would be okay for a bit of glamour. We got a spot reservation, arrived at nine forty-five. She wore a sleeveless red sheath and black pearls I'd bought her years ago. Her auburn curls were combed soft and glossed with something that smelled good. I wore a black suit, a white shirt, and a red tie, figured I was doing a pretty good impression of someone who cared about haberdashery. The food was great, the wines were mellow, and when we left at eleven thirty, I felt flush.

We were in the bedroom, about to slip under the covers, when the phone rang.

"I woke you?" said Milo.

"That assumes I sleep."

"I wouldn't bug you but life just got complicated."

Hollywood Boulevard after midnight was grubby sidewalks, night-haze that turned neon to grease smears, retreat of the tourists, goblins, bats, and ghouls emerging from their hidey-holes.

Clubs shuttered during daylight drew clumps of hollow-eyed kids and those who preyed upon them. Adrenalized bouncers looked for trouble. Night types beyond categorization loitered at the fringes of the crowd.

I made it halfway up Cherokee before the LAPD sawhorses and the uniform charged with protecting them stopped me.

Milo's name coaxed a stare and a nod, then a muffled conversation with a two-way radio. "Park over by the side, sir, and proceed on foot."

I hurried to the brick-colored building. Petra had called it raw sienna. Artist's eye. Darkness shaded the stucco dull brown.

The uniform at the glass doors waved me in. Milo was up a ways, standing by an open door, talking to a skinny red-haired woman courageous enough to wear a mullet.

Coroner's badge on her lapel. Investigator Leticia Mopp. Milo introduced her anyway.

She said, "Nice to meet you," and turned back to him. "Rigor's come and gone. Want another look before we pack him up?"

"Why not?" said Milo. "Always been the sentimental type."

Mopp hung back and we crossed a toxic-dump living room. The few clean surfaces were pollened by fingerprint powder.

Petra Connor stood just outside a cramped gray bathroom at the rear. Stick-thin, ivory-skinned, and dark-eyed, she had on the usual black pantsuit. Hair that matched the suit was cropped in a glossy wedge. With her was another Hollywood detective I didn't recognize, even younger.

She said, "Hey, Alex. Looks like everything converges, after all. This is Raul Biro."

Biro was compact and broad-shouldered in a beige suit, brown shirt, and yellow tie. He smiled and nodded.

Petra said, "Love to chat, guys, but our job's done here for the time being. We'll talk tomorrow, Milo?"

"Count on it."

"First new case in thirteen months," she said. "I thought I missed the rush but now I'm not so sure. Raul doesn't mind, right?"

Biro said, "Need the experience."

The two of them left and Milo motioned me into the bathroom.

Lester Jordan sat hunched on his toilet wearing a periwinkle-blue terry robe that hung open on a pasty, ravaged body. His head hung low. The robe's lapel swathed his neck. A rubber-tubing tourniquet around his left arm popped veins as kinked as an old garden hose. A syringe flashed silver on the filthy tile floor to his right. Not some homemade spike; this was a medical-quality disposable syringe, bright and shiny and empty. On the back of the commode sat the spoon-lighter kit and an empty Baggie.

"All these years and now he O.D.'s?" I said.

Milo gloved up. Carefully, almost tenderly, he took hold of Jordan's chin and lifted the dead man's head.

Around Jordan's neck was another tourniquet. A white, braided cord, pulled so tight it nearly vanished in cold flesh. Triple-knotted in back, the hue blending in with Jordan's pallor. Jordan's eyes were half open, dry, alive as shirt buttons. His tongue drooped, black and distended, a Japanese eggplant.

Milo lowered the head just as gingerly. "I came here at ten thirty to talk to him about Leland Armbruster, found flashers and roadblocks, the full circus. Inside the apartment, Petra's on her cell punching numbers. My phone rings. It's me she's calling. She says, 'Beamed yourself up, Scotty?'"

"Karma," I said.

"Who did I offend in some former life?"

"When was Jordan killed?"

"The estimate is eight to fifteen hours ago. No one spotted any visitors and that's consistent with the scene. A window on the north side of the building was open and there's some disturbance of the dirt but no clear footprints. Jordan got discovered because he left his music running—loud, the way it was when we were here. Next-door neighbors say that was his usual thing, there were tons of complaints but the landlord ignored them. The routine was someone pounds Jordan's door long enough, he eventually stops. This time nothing worked and they called the cops."

"Who are the next-door neighbors?"

"Two girls," he said. "Dancers in a show at the Pantages."

He took a long look at Jordan's corpse. "Patrol officers show up half an hour later, bang the door, get no answer. They go around to the other side, see the open window, call for backup. Thank God they were smart enough not to touch anything, maybe we'll get some physical evidence."

Two crypt drivers arrived with a folded gurney. We slipped out of the bathroom, exited the building, walked to Milo's car. No unmarked tonight; he was driving Rick's white Porsche 928.

I said, "Jordan survives this long as an addict. We visit him to talk about Patty and a couple days later he's dead."

"High-risk lifestyle, anything can happen, but it does raise one's eyebrows." He demonstrated with his own shaggy hyphens. "No one remotely ominous knew we talked to Jordan—just that screenwriter, Bergman, and Chatty Mary Whitbread."

"Saturday I went over to Hudson and spoke to Colonel Bedard's grandson but Jordan's name never came up."

"Ominous fellow?"

"Hardly." I summarized my impression of Kyle Bedard.

He said, "But if it is related to Patty, Jordan told someone we'd been around and got hushed for his troubles."

"If someone cared that much about keeping the past buried, Tanya's safety could be an issue."

"If Patty hadn't brought the whole thing up, we'd never have talked to Jordan and there might *be* no safety issue."

"Maybe Patty knew something was going down whether or not she talked. In any event, I'm going to drive by Tanya's."

"Do that," he said. "I'll get some sleep and be bright and fresh for tomorrow's challenges."

But when I started up the Seville, the Porsche hummed behind me. I stuck my head out the driver's window and he pulled alongside.

"What the hell," he said, "let's do a convoy. Don't even think about saying 'Ten-four.'"

Canfield Avenue at one thirty-five a.m. was silent and peaceful. Milo and I parked and got out.

He eyed the alarm company sign on the lawn. "Good start. I'll sneak 'round back, make sure nothing's out of order."

"Tanya's got a gun."

"That so."

I told him about Patty's .22.

He said, "Same caliber as the one that did Lowball Armbruster." He slipped a penlight out of a pocket. "If she shoots me, you can have my Official Detective pencil box."

He returned three minutes later, gave a thumbs-up. "No sign of disturbance, she's got a security light at the back door and bars on all the rear windows. Toss in the alarm and I certify it as safe. Let's go home. Tomorrow I'll follow up with Petra."

I said, "We were wondering how Jordan managed to stay in the building so long. Now we find out the landlord never responded to the complaints about his music, even though that meant other tenants vacating."

"Connections," he said. "A family thing, like you said."

"I'd like to know who's got the deed to the building and if they owned it back in Patty's day."

"Petra got the landlord's name from the dancing girls, hold on." He pulled out his pad, used the penlight, flipped pages. "Deer Valley Properties in Utah, but it's managed by a downtown firm."

"Kyle Bedard's mother lives in Deer Valley."

He frowned, stared up the dark street. "My oh my."

The following morning at ten, we were standing on the front steps of the mansion on Hudson Avenue, listening to the chimes of the doorbell. An hour ago, Milo had talked to the company that managed the building on Cherokee, verified that Lester Jordan was Mrs. Iona Bedard's brother. Jordan was on their payroll as an "on-site inspector" but his duties were ambiguous and his three-hundred-dollar weekly paycheck traced back to Deer Valley.

"Company goes along with it in order to keep the building on their management list." He eyed the Bentley and the Mercedes. "What do these people do for cash?"

"Born into the Lucky Sperm Club."

The woman named America opened one of the double doors.

I smiled at her. She clutched her broom handle.

"Is Kyle here?"

"No."

"Do you have any idea where—"

"School."

My thank-you was cut short by the whoosh of solid walnut gliding into place.

Milo said, "Ah, the warmth of hearth and home."

The physics building at the U. is a sixties-era assemblage of glass, white brick, and mosaic murals that portray great moments in fusion. Across an inverted fountain looms the psych building, where I'd gotten my union card. I'd never paid much attention to the less ambiguous goings-on yards away.

Milo and I had come prepared to wrestle with department secretaries but Kyle Bedard was in plain view, sitting on the rim of the fountain eating a sandwich and drinking orange juice from a plastic carton. Talking, in between bites, to a young woman.

She was small, blond, preppy in pink and khaki. Kyle wore a gray sweatshirt, baggy jeans, antiquarian sneakers. He'd traded his contacts for black-framed eyeglasses.

As we approached, he righted the specs, as if trying to refocus.

The girl turned.

I said, "Hi, Tanya."

CHAPTER

16

Milo took Kyle by the elbow and ushered him halfway around the fountain. Tanya pressed a hand to her cheek and gaped. I sat down next to her. "What's going on, Dr. Delaware?"

"That's Lieutenat Sturgis. He needs to talk to Kyle."

"About what?"

"How'd you meet him, Tanya?"

The hand on her face pressed harder, created white spots. She turned to me. "Is he—are you going to tell me something *creepy* about him?"

Not yet. "No. How did—"

"He contacted me through Facebook, we had lunch yesterday, decided to do it again today. It wasn't some stranger-stalk, Dr. Delaware. He said a police psychologist had been by to talk to him about my mother and that reminded him of when we were kids and he used to visit. I told him I knew you and that I remembered him, too. Always reading a book. He seems like a good person and he's brilliant."

"I'm sure he is," I said.

"There *is* a problem?"

"Not with Kyle."

"Then why are you here?"

"A man living in the building on Cherokee was murdered yesterday.

The building's owned by Kyle's mother. She got it as part of a divorce settlement but back when you lived there it was owned by Colonel Bedard."

"It's all . . . connected?"

"It's possible your mother got the job at the mansion because someone from Cherokee recommended her."

"Who would do that?"

"That's what we're trying to find out."

She reached for a half-empty yogurt container and squeezed. "I still don't see why you're talking to Kyle. He was a kid back then."

"The man who was murdered was named Lester Jordan. Sound familiar?"

She shook her head.

"He was living there when you were. First-floor apartment, left side of the corridor, toward the back."

"I've never heard of him, Dr. Delaware. Mommy never let me go inside the building alone. Who killed him?"

"We don't know, yet."

"You think *Kyle* knows?"

"Lester Jordan was Kyle's mom's brother."

"And now he's—oh, my God, you're saying it's because of what I *started*?"

"No, there's no evidence of that, Tanya."

"But you think it's *possible*." She grabbed a handful of hair and twisted. "Oh, my *God,* I couldn't let go of it and now that man's dead."

"You are *not* to blame," I said. "*Zero* responsibility."

"This is horrible."

"Tanya, Lester Jordan was a heroin addict who led a high-risk lifestyle, it's a miracle he's survived this long. Unless your mother and he had some kind of relationship when he was alive, there's no reason to believe she's connected to his death."

"Of course they had no relationship, why would she hang out with someone like that?"

"It didn't need to be a social connection," I said. "An addict could require medical care from time to time."

"You're saying she helped him with overdoses?"

"Or with kicking his habit."

Or feeding it.

"I never saw or heard of anything like that," she said. "But I was so young."

"Even if your mother did help Jordan, it doesn't mean that had anything to do with his death. This was a man with an extensive criminal record. He associated with bad people. Lieutenant Sturgis is looking into Jordan's background. He needs to talk to Kyle's parents but they're both out of town. Kyle was the next best thing."

Letting go of her hair, she played with the yogurt cup. "I really can't see Mommy *knowing* someone like that. Her big thing was *protecting* me from bad influences."

"What about those drunks who knocked on the door?" I said. "That could've been an addict going through withdrawal."

"I guess. I never saw her open the door. That was the whole point, keeping that world outside."

"Sketchy neighborhood," I said. "But she lived there for six years."

"What are you saying?"

"Maybe she stayed that long because she was earning extra income caring for Lester Jordan. When Colonel Bedard needed nursing, his family remembered how effective she'd been and asked her to live in."

"She never told me anything like that."

"There'd be no reason to tell a seven-year-old."

A clapping sound drew our attention. Milo's hand landing on Kyle Bedard's shoulder. Kyle flinched, made eye contact with Tanya.

She stared past him and he turned back to Milo.

Milo spoke a bit longer, gave Kyle a half salute and a wolf-grin. Kyle chanced another glance at Tanya, headed for the physics building. Fooling with his glasses and hitching his pants, he stepped inside.

Tanya said, "He left his lunch."

Milo said, "His appetite may have waned."

A big padded hand shot out. "Milo Sturgis."

"Tanya."

He sat down next to her. "Sorry to interrupt."

"Lieutenant, I've never heard of that man, Jordan."

"Didn't expect you would, Tanya."

"Kyle's uncle," she said. "How'd Kyle take the news?"

"He's a little shaken," said Milo.

"Do *you* think this happened because of me?"

Milo eyed the murals. Promethean figures lofting test tubes, holding calipers, watching sparks fly. "That would be a quantum leap, Tanya. Jordan's lifestyle was what we call high-risk."

"Dr. Delaware told me all that, but how can you be sure it's *not* related?"

"We can't, that's why we're here. You told Dr. Delaware you thought your mother brought up the 'terrible thing' because she was trying to protect you."

"It was more a feeling than a rational thought, Lieutenant. I *sensed* it."

"Nothing she actually said led you to that?"

"No, just her intensity. As if it was really *important* for me to have the knowledge. She used to say 'Knowledge is power.' It just felt like this was another example—pointing me in a certain way. That's why I contacted Dr. Delaware." Looking down. "So he could direct me to you."

Milo scratched his nose. A pigeon swooped into the fountain's plume. Drank, showered, shook its feathers dry, and departed. "Are you pretty aware of personal safety issues?"

"Am I in danger, Lieutenant Sturgis?"

"I'm not ready to put you in the witness protection program but I would like you to be careful."

"About?"

"The basics. Keep your doors and windows locked, turn on your alarm when you get home, look around before you get out of your car, don't talk to strangers. Stuff you should be doing anyway."

"I am," she said. A trio of pigeons dive-bombed the fountain. "Is Kyle considered a stranger?"

"Not anymore, I guess—Tanya, I can't give you a cookbook. There's no problem hanging with him at a public place. In fact, that could be a positive if in the course of hanging you learn something useful."

"You want me to *spy* on him?"

"Sometimes things come out in the course of conversation."

"Like what?"

"Maybe Kyle will recall something about his uncle that will help close this murder."

"Did Kyle say he was close to him?" said Tanya.

"He said the two of them haven't had contact for years." Milo smiled. "Tanya, my bet's on Jordan's addiction and criminal history being the main factors in his death. But Dr. Delaware tells me you're mature and smart and you seem that way to me. So I'm being straight with you. At this point, nothing can be ruled out."

She thought about that. "Makes sense . . . I can see Kyle not wanting to hang with someone like that. Beer's the strongest thing he takes."

I said, "How'd that come up?"

She blushed. "We were discussing . . . values. I guess that sounds geeky."

Milo said, "Tanya, if more people paid attention to values, I'd have more leisure time."

I said, "You were talking about values and drugs came up?"

"Actually, I brought it up. I mentioned I was thinking of becoming a psychiatrist and that the whole biological revolution interested me. Kyle said he had a cousin who was on medication for all sorts of behavior problems and from what he'd seen, he wasn't sure that was the way to go. We ended up talking about where you draw the line between treatment and fostering chemical dependency. That's what we were discussing when you showed up."

Bouncing her knees. "Maybe Kyle has reservations about medication because of his uncle's problems."

"Could be," I said.

"If he's someone I shouldn't be hanging with, just tell me."

Milo said, "Keep your eyes open and trust your instincts."

Her eyes shifted to the entrance of the physics building. "Is inside Bergson Hall considered a public place?"

"For the time being, yes."

She stood, began collecting the food and depositing it in a bag.

He said, "Have you found your mother's gun?"

She stopped moving. "Do I need to learn how to use it?"

"I'd like to have it for a few days to run some tests."

"You think it was used to do something criminal?"

"I'm sure it wasn't but let's verify that. Do you know where it is?"

She nodded. "Should I bring it to your office?"

"How about I pick it up? When will you be home?"

"Today?"

"Sooner is better than later."

"Let's see . . . around five, five thirty. Six to be safe, if I end up doing some studying after work." Checking her watch. "I'm due at the library right now."

"Go ahead, see you at six," he said. "Nice to meet you."

"Nice to meet you, too," she said. "And thank you for taking the time to help me. I really appreciate it."

This time she held out a hand. Pumped Milo's mitt then gave me a quick hug. "I know I've made things complicated . . . I feel safe with you on my side. Say hello to Dr. Silverman, Lieutenant. Mommy *adored* him."

When she was gone, Milo said, "You lie to her, too?"

"You bet."

"Good man."

17

O ne thing *was* true," said Milo as we drove away from campus. "Can't protect her twenty-four seven, she needs to look both ways and be smart. Think she got the message?"

"Probably," I said. "All that gravitas you project. What did you learn from Kyle?"

"Uncle Lester was persona non grata, no one in the family had much contact with him. Last time Kyle remembers seeing him was after his parents divorced—shortly after the old man died. His mom and dad had been separated for a while and Kyle flew down from Atherton with her so she could get some art objects she considered hers. While she was scrounging, Jordan dropped by and Kyle answered the door. Jordan tried to make conversation, Mom saw who it was and told Kyle to go inside."

"Kyle have any idea why Jordan dropped by?"

"Nope. But seeing as Jordan was an addict and she was supporting him, my bet would be he was hitting on her for extra cash. What did you lie to Tanya about?"

"I suggested Patty might have been helping Jordan with his addiction but said nothing about her feeding his habit."

"All that medical-quality dope within reach and a junkie with a rich family. Yeah, it fits nicely, doesn't it?"

I said, "Patty stayed there six years, got paid by the family to keep the black sheep out of their lives. The old man turned ill and his needs took priority over Jordan's. When the colonel died, it was time for her to move on."

"Moving her around like a chess piece."

"Kyle's mother has definite ideas about social class." I told him about the daily purse inspection.

He said, "The wretched refuse. Still, if we're right about Patty being helpful with Jordan, why not send her back to Cherokee after the old man was gone?"

"Jordan was Mrs. Bedard's kin. I can see Mister not being thrilled about letting him live rent-free. Once he split from his wife, no more indulgence."

"Good riddance to you and your loser brother," he said. "Who just happened to be a pal of Lowball Leland Armbruster who just happened to get shot by a .22 while Patty was living a few blocks from the murder scene and just happened to own a .22. We handed Tanya a whole load of emotionally supportive bullshit, Alex. She was right to make the connection. Jordan survives twenty years shooting dope, we chat with him about Patty, and all of a sudden he's sitting dead on his toilet. If ballistics matches Patty's gun to the slug in Armbruster, we're talking major-league complications. The kind that could lead to eliminating witnesses."

"Jordan saw Patty shoot Armbruster? Who'd be threatened by that?"

"I'm saying Jordan knew something about the shooting that was worth killing for." His cell chirped some kind of Hawaiian music. "Sturgis . . . hey, how's it going . . . *did* you?" Big spreading smile. "Restores my faith in technology, kid. Yeah, let's do that, say half an hour? The doctor'll be there, too, maybe we'll gain some deep intrapsychic insights."

He hung up, still grinning.

I said, "Sean?"

"Petra. Jordan's john was wiped clean and so was the inner sill of the open window. But the techies got a partial palm print from the ledge outside. Palms are finally being cataloged on AFIS and there's a hit. Some naughty boy busted for assault last year. Ain't it nice when the bad guys don't learn?"

◆

We sat with Petra in an empty interview room at Hollywood Division. Raul Biro was out recanvassing Lester Jordan's building and its neighbors on Cherokee.

The room was windowless and hot and smelled of witch hazel. Petra had removed her black jacket. Underneath was a sleeveless gray silk shell. Her arms were white, smooth, sinewy, her nail polish a deep brown that fell just short of black. Lipstick of the same hue, a half tone lighter. She slid an arrest form across the table. Clipped to the top were full-face and profile mug shots.

"Gentlemen," she said, "meet Robert Bertram Fisk."

Fisk's picture screamed the virtues of cliché: bony off-center countenance, head shaved clean, close-set eyes devoid of feeling and dark with menace. A skimpy mouth was further reduced by a heavy black mustache, right-angled down to his chin like a croquet wicket.

Basic Bad Guy.

The taut, corded, tattoo-brocaded neck substantially wider than Fisk's jaws was overkill. But this was L.A., where subtlety could be a shuttle to obscurity.

Milo said, "You gotta be kidding. I'd take him for a social worker feeding the homeless." He ran his finger down to the stats.

Male Caucasian, twenty-eight, five seven, one forty. A gallery of skin art.

"Little guy," said Milo.

Petra said, "Didn't stop him from taking on a big guy—the assault victim was six one, two ninety. It happened last year, in a downtown club. Fisk was working as some kind of bodyguard, got into an argument with another hunk of hired muscle named Bassett Bowland."

She clawed her fingers. "First Fisk whipped off a few martial arts moves, then he pulled a one-handed move, got Bowland by the Adam's apple and started squeezing. He came pretty close to crushing the guy's neck before people pulled him off. Bowland lived but he suffered permanent vocal damage."

"Fisk does this a year ago and he's out?"

"It got pled down to misdemeanor battery, time served. The two weeks Fisk spent at County waiting to be arraigned was his entire sentence. According to the case file, Bowland didn't want to cooperate and witnesses disappeared."

"Any pressure for them to disappear?"

"Wouldn't surprise me, but the main obstacle was Bowland. Humiliated by having his butt kicked by a guy half his weight, he absolutely refused to talk."

"Fisk have any buddies?"

"No gang affiliation or felonious K.A.'s," said Petra. "He seems to be more of a freelance, hangs around the club scene, sometimes he gets up on stage and thinks he's dancing."

I studied the scowling face. "Bet he doesn't get too many bad reviews."

Petra laughed. "The only other thing I can tell you about him is he fought in some of those tough-guy contests—barbarians in a wire cage, testosterone running amok."

"You don't like competitive sports?" said Milo.

She stuck out her tongue. "Five brothers meant I had to fake liking competitive sports. Now I'm a big girl and can admit they suck."

I said, "Fisk uses a bare hand on a huge guy but slips a ligature around Jordan's neck."

"Maybe he didn't want to leave a handprint on Jordan's skin. Or a ligature was what he was instructed to use."

"Hired hit," said Milo.

"Fisk didn't do it for dope. He's got no narcotics history, just the opposite, and there was about a thousand bucks of heroin in Jordan's bedroom drawer. But no cash in evidence, so maybe he went for the money."

Milo flicked a corner of the arrest report. "What do you mean 'just the opposite'?"

"Fisk seems to be one of those health nuts. Irwin Gold—the Central D who handled the assault—listed three different gyms Fisk frequented, wrote down he was into martial arts, yoga, meditation. We went to get him this morning at three. Unfortunately, Fisk hasn't lived at his last known address for six months. Vacated soon after he got out of jail, no forwarding."

"No parole officer?"

"Clean release, no parole."

"Sounds more like a parking violation than choking someone out."

"Fisk had no priors, and given Bassett Bowland's size I suppose a case could be made for self-defense."

"No priors," said Milo. "A guy that aggressive stays clean for twenty-eight years?"

"Or doesn't get caught," I said.

Petra shadowboxed. "Maybe he channeled his aggressiveness."

Milo said, "He channels, then all of a sudden he's choking Bowland and a year later he's a murderer."

I said, "Maybe all it took was meeting the right person. Someone who needed a job done and was willing to pay."

Petra nodded. "I like that."

"From the way Jordan died—sitting there, no struggle—he was stoned or not alarmed seeing Fisk."

Milo said, "Fisk crawls through the window and Jordan's not alarmed?"

"Maybe someone else let Fisk in."

"The contractor," said Petra. "Maybe Jordan's dealer. He supplies Jordan, Jordan fixes up, zones out heavily. Would've been easy enough to go to the bedroom, crack the window. Fisk is waiting by the side of the building, climbs in, sneaks behind Jordan, and slips the cord."

No one spoke for a while.

Milo said, "Whose body did Fisk guard?"

"Gold's notes just say he described himself as a bodyguard. And Gold is retired, traveling somewhere in Southeast Asia. Guess it's time to start visiting gyms and yoga classes, what a drag."

"You don't like exercise, either?"

"All those automatons in spandex running nowhere fast, idiots thinking they're never going to die? Spare me."

"I'd take you for a runner, kid."

"What, because I'm bony? Genetics, sir. You should see my brothers, all rails. Except for Bruce, who's spreading a little, claims it's creative individualism."

Milo patted his gut. "Luck of the draw."

"That and anxiety," said Petra. "Getting too wound up to eat helps."

"You wound up over Fisk?"

"I'd like to have him in that chair." She slid the report back, placed it in a thin blue file. "Now it's your turn to show and tell, guys. What's the story on my victim and your nurse? Give me the long version."

When we finished, she said, "Your dredging up the past is threatening someone big-time? Something to do with the Bedards?"

"Rich folk pay others to do their dirty work," said Milo.

Petra traced the outline of one smooth, black eyebrow. "Maybe Fisk's easy plea-down was more than Bowland being too embarrassed to testify."

"Paid off to keep his mouth shut," said Milo.

"If the Bedards are behind this, they just had one of their own killed."

I said, "One of *Mrs.* Bedard's own. She and hubby are long divorced."

"Meaning Mister could be behind it," she said. "But Missus owns the building. How would her ex know you'd been there to talk to Jordan? And if Missus has been out of Mister's hair for a while, why would he care?"

Silence.

Milo said, "Maybe we're way off base. Jordan was no charmer. Guy like that could tick off lots of people."

"On the other hand," said Petra, "there's ticking off and there's setting yourself up as the target of a hit." She turned to me. "What bothers me is that with a junkie like Jordan, it would've been easy to fake a burglary gone bad. Open drawers, toss stuff around. Instead, Fisk cleans up nicely except for one palm print, leaves a grand's worth of heroin under Jordan's skivvies. Leaves *Jordan* sitting there with a curtain cord around his neck and the music blasting. Making sure Jordan's going to be discovered. This was a message hit."

She frowned. "Generic curtain cord, by the way. No forensic possibilities, there."

Opening the blue folder, she drew out a crime scene photo, studied it, pushed it across the table.

Lester Jordan, slumped on the toilet. I'd witnessed the reality but in some ways the snap was more brutal.

"Given Fisk's rabbit," she said, "I'm thinking we should talk to someone who's seen his dark side."

"Mr. Too-embarassed-to-testify," said Milo.

"Him I do have a current address on, North Hollywood. I tried his number. A male voice answered, kind of hoarse, and I hung up. How say we subject Mr. Bowland to additional humiliation?"

Milo said, "I could use some recreation."

Petra said, "As long as we don't have to wear sweats."

18

Bassett Bowland lived in a white, three-story apartment complex on Laurel Canyon, just south of Saticoy. That far north, Laurel ceases to be a leafy canyon and devolves to a noisy, smoggy mixture of low-rent commercial businesses and housing to match.

Sparkles embedded in the stucco gave the building the look of a Styrofoam cooler. A sign in front said units could be rented by the month. A ten-year-old brown Camaro in the rear carport matched Bowland's DMV registration. His single was on the top floor, just off an open stairwell.

Petra pushed his doorbell. The resulting buzz was barely audible over traffic noise.

Just as she was about to try again, the door opened, and the space filled with flesh.

A refrigerator with limbs whispered, "Huh?"

"Bassett Bowland?"

"Yuh."

"Detective Connor. This is Lieutenant Sturgis and Alex Delaware."

Bowland rubbed the front of his neck and curled his mouth. Puffy cheeks inflated to grapefruit size nearly blocked out his eyes.

Pink grapefruit; his skin tone was Permanent Sunburn. Limp, bleached-blond hair fringed his shoulders. Porcine features belonged on a much smaller man. He wore a black System of a Down T-shirt, frayed red shorts, no shoes.

Not much older than Kyle Bedard but he hunched like an old man. "May we come in?"

Bowland coughed, didn't bother to cover his mouth. His raspy "I guess" was overpowered by the traffic.

The apartment was the usual lonely-guy combo of cheap furniture and wide-screen TV. The set was on mute. ESPN Classic, the L.A. Rams getting walloped by Dallas. It's been a long time since Los Angeles has rooted for a home team.

Bowland glanced at the score, yawned, and dropped onto a black leatherette couch. A half-gallon carton of milk stood on the blue plastic counter of the kitchenette, spout open. A huge olive-green uniform hung from the knob of a kitchen cabinet. Military pockets, epaulets.

Petra said, "We'd like to talk to you about Robert Fisk."

Piggy eyes jumped. "Whu for?" Even with the door closed and the traffic noise dimmed, his voice lacked volume.

"He's a suspect in a crime and we're doing background."

"Little shit. Who'd he cold-cock this time?" Managing no more than a phlegmy whisper, each word taking effort.

"A guy in Hollywood," said Petra. "Fisk's a dirty fighter?"

"Cocksucker," said Bowland. "Motherfucking cocksucker dipshit." A melon fist pounded a catcher's-mitt palm. Bowland's arms and torso jiggled.

"What did the two of you fight about?"

"Nothing."

"Nothing?"

"He jumped me."

"Tell us about it."

Bowland breathed in through his nose, exhaled through his mouth. "I was working. Bouncer."

"At Rattlesnake," said Petra.

"That's what they called it that week." Another pause for breath. Bowland touched the front of his throat. "Still hurts. Mother*fucker*. Tell me where he's at and you don't need to waste no time."

Holding up a fist. Jumpy eyes tuned machismo down to pathetic.

"Don't blame you for feeling that way," said Petra, sitting next to him. He screwed up his lips, ran his tongue under one cheek. Each of his thighs was as broad as her body. "So you were working at Rattlesnake and then what happened?"

"Motherfucker comes in with some other motherfuckers, everything's cool. Then motherfucker thinks he's gonna get up and dance with the band. I tell him he ain't, he smiles and gets off the stage, like he's cool."

Bowland sighed. "I'm walking him away from the stage, he starts running his mouth. But being cool, he knows I'm just doing my job, he's been there, dude. I'm like you *been* there? You're a *toon,* man, know whum *saying?*"

"He is a little guy, Bassett—can I call you Bassett?"

"Bass. Like the ale." Bowland rubbed a thumb and forefinger together. "You do like this he could disappear, motherfucking toon."

"So he's cooperating with you, pretending to be friendly."

"We keep walking, I get him past the bar, go have a drink bro, chill, he's like I don't drink, keep it real. Holds out his hand like this."

He formed a power shake. "I wanna keep it cool so I do it know whum saying? Instead of shaking he gets me here." Touching a wrist. "My fucking arm goes dead then he kicks me in the knee then he grabs me."

"By the neck," said Petra.

"Fucking iron claw," said Bowland. "I'm hitting him upside the head, he's kicking me." Caressing a knee. "Dislocated the bone or something, I'm falling over and he's still doing the claw. They told me he stomped my back but I'm big, you know, he didn't break nothing."

Rasping out the words had exhausted him. He panted, sat back hard enough to budge the couch.

"Sneak attack," said Petra.

"Only way he coulda done it," said Bowland. "That's the whole story. Now I gotta sleep."

"Working hard?"

His reply was a yawn.

"What kind of work you do, Bass?"

"Security."

"Where?"

"Pawnshop on Van Nuys. Persians. Gotta wear that, pay to clean it."

"Who'd Fisk come to the club with that night?"

"Other cocksuckers. He's gonna get his." Lazy smile as he formed a finger gun.

"We sympathize, Bass, but we are the law, so be careful."

"I didn't mean that," said Bowland. "God's gonna pay him back."

"You're religious?"

Bowland reached inside his T-shirt and drew out a small gold crucifix. "Everyone pays."

"Fisk didn't pay because you didn't want to testify."

Bowland didn't answer.

"Guy did that to me, Bass, I'd want him to serve some jail time."

Bowland appraised her slender frame. "Guy did that to you, he should get the death penalty."

"As opposed to you?"

"I can handle myself."

"I'm sure you can, but still—"

"What?" said Bowland. "I go to court and cry and everyone's saying Bass is a pussy, needs the po-lice to do his game?"

He closed his eyes.

Petra said, "What else can you tell us about Fisk?"

"Nothin'."

"Ever see him before that night?"

"Coupla times."

"He always hang with the same people?"

"Yeah."

"How about some names?"

"One was Rosie," said Bowland. "The other was Blazer."

"Rosie his girl?"

"Black guy, he deejays sometimes."

"At Rattlesnake?"

"No."

"Where, then?"

"Dunno."

"How do you know he deejayed?"

"He told me."

"When?"

"Before."

"Before Fisk attacked you."

"Yeah."

"You and Rosie were having a conversation."

"We were by the stage and he was saying the band was okay but he could deejay more power by himself."

"Ever have problems with him?"

Head shake. "Always cool."

"What's his last name?"

"Dunno."

"What about Blazer?"

"Little guy, last name's something with Pain."

"Blazer Pain?"

"Something like that," said Bowland.

"Black or white?"

"White. Thinks he's a ceeleb."

"Wants the VIP room?"

"There weren't none at the Snake. Motherfucker just acts stupid."

"Stupid, how?"

"Walks around like he's all that."

"Blazer Pain," said Petra.

"Something like that."

"Robert Fisk hung with these two regularly."

"I guess."

"You don't know?"

"It was always crowded."

"You were at the door, you saw who came in."

Bowland shook his head. "Sometimes I was by the stage."

"The night Fisk attacked you, where were you stationed?"

"The stage."

"So you don't know if Fisk came in with Rosie and Blazer."

"I seen 'em inside. Rosie was with Blazer then Blazer walks away and Rosie stays by the stage. Fisk's like watching out for Blazer, then he comes back and says he's gonna dance."

"Watching out for Blazer how?"

"Standing close to the motherfucker, looking like, you know." He narrowed his eyes, bobbed his head.

"Fisk was Blazer's bodyguard?"

Shrug.

"Blazer needs a bodyguard?"

"Maybe he thinks so."

"Do you know of any reason for him to need a bodyguard?"

"Ask *him*."

"What I meant," said Petra, "was does he engage in illegal activities."

"Ask him."

"Where can we find him?"

Bowland laughed. "Maybe in toon-town." Yawning. "Gotta sleep."

"Why are you so tired?" she said. "Never heard of a pawnshop with a night shift."

"Gotta be there eight in the morning."

"Till when?"

"One," said Bowland.

"Part-time gig," said Petra.

"Feels like full-time. Standing around looking at the crazy shit those Persians buy."

She stood. "Bass, was not wanting to look like a wimp the only reason you didn't testify?"

"Yeah."

"No other reason?"

"Like what?"

"No one paid you to stay away?"

"Someone paid me, you think I'd be standing around looking at the crazy shit those Persians buy?"

Flipping on his back, he rested his hands on a mountain of belly and stared at the ceiling.

By the time we made it to the door, he was pretending to snore.

Loud, theatrical. More volume than he was able to produce by speaking.

Outside, standing next to her Accord, Petra said, "Rosie and Blazer Pain. Maybe the gang squad will have them on the moniker list."

I said, "Rosie's a deejay, Robert Fisk thinks he's a dancer, and Blazer has visions of celebrity. 'Pain' could be a stage name."

"Or an S and M angle."

"The club scene," said Milo. "You know what goes with that. Maybe Jordan will end up as just another dope hit."

Petra said, "Gyms, now clubs. Great. One place I *don't* have to go is Rattlesnake. I checked and it closed down three months after Fisk assaulted Bowland. Most of those dives are fly-by-night. This is not going to be simple."

I said, "There are a couple of places right on Cherokee, just off the boulevard. Walking distance to Jordan's place."

"Meaning it would've been easy for Jordan to walk over and sell or buy or whatever," she said. "Problem is I know those places, El Bandito and Baila Baila. They're reggaeton, a Latino crowd, white and black guys wouldn't make it past the door."

She checked her watch. "Got some time before the night crawlers are out, maybe Eric and I can have some dinner. What's on your schedule, guys?"

"Nothing too complicated," said Milo. "Gotta pick up a gun."

"The maybe match to Lowball Armbruster," she said. "I'm still trying to locate the slugs dug out of him. Coroner claims they have them, but all those years pass, you know how it goes."

"No casings on record?"

"Nope, either someone picked up after themselves or it was a revolver."

I said, "Patty's gun was a semi-auto."

"Would Patty be someone who'd pick up?"

I nodded.

"Well," she said, "it's probably nothing, tons of .22s floating around. Meanwhile, I search for Robert Fisk."

She crossed her fingers.

Milo said, "We could all use some luck."

19

At six fifteen we pulled up in front of Tanya's duplex. Over an hour of daylight left but the outdoor spots were on and the drapes were drawn.

The peephole on her door was covered by a tiny door. Before I knocked, it cracked an inch. A pale green eye inspected me.

"One second." A bolt turned, then another.

She wore a pink buttondown shirt and a khaki skirt and held a plate of cookies. Big Daliesque chocolate-chip inventions, the chocolate soft and runny.

"I just got these out of the oven."

Milo took one, finished it in two bites. "I like your style."

"How about some coffee?"

While she was gone, he helped himself to another cookie. "Playing grown-up makes her feel in charge. Only reason I'm eating this is to be supportive."

"That was my assumption from the beginning."

He walked around the living room, parted the drapes, looked down at the street, took in the space. "Roomy."

For a small girl.

Letting the curtains fall, he headed for the coffee table and examined Patty's graduation photo.

Tanya returned with a mug of coffee and a wooden box. "Here it is."

Milo wiped his hands and took the box. The interior was black foam with a gun-shaped cutout that cradled a small, blued pistol. He removed the clip. Empty. Dropped it into a Baggie and sniffed the weapon. "Oiled. Anyone use it recently?"

"Mommy took care of everything she owned, but I haven't seen it for years."

He shut the box, tucked it under his shoulder, reached for another cookie.

Tanya said, "You're really not trying to match it to a specific crime?"

Milo looked at me.

I said, "An unsolved murder came up in the files. Another drug addict, a man who'd known Lester Jordan. He was shot a few blocks from your apartment on Cherokee with a .22 back when you lived there. There's absolutely no reason to think your mom had anything to do with it. What's more likely is this man and Jordan were both involved in a dope war. But let's find out for sure so we can put your mind at ease."

"My mind at ease? This is just—my God, it's so *weird*!"

Milo said, "I don't have to check if you don't want me to."

"No," she said. "Do it, I want to know. Please."

"As long as we're here, does the name Robert Fisk mean anything to you?"

"No. Who is he?"

"An unpleasant fellow whose palm print was found on Lester Jordan's windowsill."

"You *got* him?" she said.

"No, we're looking for him. Identifying him should speed things up."

"Robert Fisk," she said. "Has he killed other people?"

"Not that we know about."

"Is there a good chance you'll find him?"

"We'll definitely get him."

She turned away.

Milo said, "This whole idea of your mother doing something terrible has to be pretty upsetting. I'm sure it'll come down to nothing."

She focused past him, stared at the fireplace tiles.

He said, "Tanya, coming forth in the first place was extremely courageous. But like I just said, if you don't want to continue, no harm, no foul."

"That wouldn't make you upset?"

"Not in the least. Officially, I'm on vacation. Give me the word and I go for the Hawaiian shirts."

Her smile was feeble.

"Lester Jordan's murder will be investigated fully by Hollywood Division, but anything to do with your mother has been and will continue to be unofficial."

Silence.

"Whatever you want, Tanya."

"I don't know what I—" She turned, faced us. "I'm so sorry, I thought I could handle anything that came up but now that someone—two people—have actually been killed . . ."

"That is a tough reality, but there's no reason to connect it to your mother."

Her eyes filled. He handed her a napkin, eyed the cookies.

She said, "But what if something did happen?"

"Everything I've heard about your mother tells me she was a terrific person. The chances of her doing anything that could be remotely considered criminal are pretty godda—they're darn low."

Tanya dabbed a tear, bounced the heels of her hands together, let her arms drop. "When she told me, I felt her reason was protecting me. I only wish I knew from what."

"Quite possibly nothing, she was sick," said Milo.

Silence.

"We're here to protect you now."

She hung her head.

I said, "Tanya?"

"I was thinking of myself as a self-sufficient person—I'm sorry, thank you. Thank you so much. Would you like a cookie, too?"

"Sure."

She passed the tray to me, then Milo. He began to refuse, changed his mind. The third cookie went down in one bite.

"Another?" said Tanya.

"No, but they're delish. Can I ask you a question about Kyle?"

She put the tray down. "What?"

"Did you end up talking to him again and if so, did he say anything about his uncle?"

"We spoke briefly. I had a class and he had an appointment with his dissertation chairman. He told me he couldn't honestly grieve because he barely knew Jordan. He felt his mother might take it hard because Jordan was her only sibling, but he wasn't sure, because she never mentioned Jordan. We talked some more about that—the whole sib thing—and then I had to go."

I said, "Some more?"

"That's what we discussed during our first lunch. Kyle's an only child, just like me. There were aspects we both liked, others we didn't. For me the bad part was not having someone to play with. Kyle feels he's at risk for being selfish so he makes an effort to be altruistic—feeding the homeless, giving a portion of his trust fund to charity each year."

"Nice guy," said Milo, gobbling a fourth cookie. "These are great."

"It's just a mix."

"Hey," he said, "take all the credit and none of the blame."

Her smile was weary.

"You okay here, by yourself?"

"I'm fine," she said, looking to me for support.

I said, "Tanya's good at asking for help when she needs it."

Milo said, "Smart thinking. But if you need help, just ask."

"Thank you, Lieutenant."

At the door: "You're a good person, Lieutenant Sturgis."

Color spread under Milo's ears.

Tanya said, "Is it still okay for me to talk to Kyle?"

"Unless he gives you a reason not to," said Milo.

"Like what?"

"If he gets weird. Has he asked you out?"

"No, nothing like that. You really think you'll find this Fisk pretty soon?"

"Everyone's looking for him. Speaking of which, here're a couple of other names: Rosie and Blazer Pain."

"Who are they?"

"Two guys Fisk hung out with."

"Blazer Pain? That sounds more like a band than a person."

I said, "Robert Fisk considers himself a dancer and his pal Rosie deejays, so maybe there is a music connection."

"A dancer?" she said. "But he killed someone?" Shuddering. "Once you've done something like that, how could you ever live with yourself?"

Milo reached for the doorknob. "I imagine it could be tough."

Placing the gun box in the trunk of the Seville, he slumped in the passenger seat.

"Dropping the whole Patty thing is like putting toothpaste back in the tube. What's the official shrink position on falsehood and perfidy?"

"Cops are allowed to lie."

"There's a direct answer for you."

I said, "No sense alarming her, what's the choice. Have you convinced yourself Jordan's death was related to Patty?"

"No, but the more I think about it, the more I lean that way. We get a match on that gun, it's gonna be harder to fib to the kid. Though I guess she doesn't need to know unless we turn up some sort of threat to her."

"Try keeping it from her," I said. "And what we don't tell her, Kyle might."

"Feeds the homeless—think that was a line?"

"Don't know."

"Tanya's got a crush on him, right? Go figure."

"You don't approve?"

"He's a slob, kind of nerdy, no? She's a good-looking girl."

I drove.

Two blocks later: "Ol' Kyle better be as righteous as he claims."

I said, "When are you planning to ease up on her curfew and let her wear makeup?"

He glared at me. "You can really be that hands-off?"

"One part of me wants to take her home and have Robin mother her."

"And the other?"

"The other reminds me of the value of boundaries."

"Must be nice to have those." He folded his arms across his gut. "That duplex is nice, but it's kind of eerie, she's like a kid playing house. At her age, I was living in a dorm. Total mess, psychologically, but at least there wasn't all that silence pounding my head. You're saying she can really be okay doing a solo act?"

"I'm keeping an eye out."

"I'm gonna talk to Kyle again. Just to let him know."

"Know what?"

"That I'm an interested party."

Robin was in the living room, curled on a couch, thumbing through Gruhn and Carter's *Acoustic Guitars.*

I sat down and kissed her. "Getting new ideas?"

She put the book down. "Appreciating why the old ones work so well. My day was good, how was yours?"

I gave her the basics.

She said, "Blazer Pain. Are you sure you don't mean Blaise De Paine?" Spelling it.

"You know him?"

"I've heard that name at recording sessions and not in a friendly context. He's a sampler—snips digital segments of other people's songs, patches together club mixes. First musicians had to deal with synthesizers, now this."

"Your basic techno-thievery."

"But tough to pin down. Samplers use tiny bits that can't be identified easily. Even if the sample can be documented, who says anyone can claim ownership over a combination of tones? And how would you arrive at a royalty fee? Guys like De Paine are everywhere but no one goes after them because they're a minor annoyance compared to the serious bootleggers."

"Maybe he sells other products," I said. "Ever hear of any dope connection?"

"No, but it wouldn't shock me. The whole club scene's all about X, oxycodone, the thrill of the week."

"Maybe a retro thrill. Lester Jordan was an old-fashioned junkie."

"I wouldn't call heroin retro. It never goes out of style completely."

"Blaise De Paine," I said. "No way that's on his birth certificate."

"I'd bet not, my dear. Want me to ask around?"

"That would be good."

She got up.

I said, "I didn't mean right now."

"No time like the present." She fluffed her hair, held up a fist. "Look at me, girl detective."

Blaise De Paine pulled up twenty-eight cyber-hits, twenty-five of them rants on a chat line called BitterMusician.com. The remaining three consisted of De Paine's name embedded in lists of partygoers.

Two club openings and the premiere of an indy film I'd never heard of.

The griping musicians grouped De Paine with "the usual cabal of digital scumbag thieves" but didn't single him out.

An image search produced four blurry photos of a slight young man with spiky, blond-tipped black hair and oversized teeth that drew your eyes away from a forgettable face. In each shot, Blaise De Paine favored long fitted coats over a bare chest and gold jewelry. He might've been wearing mascara. The group shots featured pretty young faces.

No sign of a scowling Robert Fisk or any black men. Combining *Robert Fisk* and *Rosie* with De Paine's name brought up nothing.

The images were still on screen when Robin came into the office. "That's him? Looks young, but that makes sense, it's a kid's business. I made more calls and from what I can gather De Paine's mixes are a small-time hustle, probably not his main source of income because he hasn't been seen lately around the clubs and someone thought he'd heard that De Paine had a high-priced house in the hills, above the Strip. Dope *could* be his other line of business."

"He dresses flamboyantly, so he loves attention. Wonder why he doesn't have a Web site."

"That is weird. Everyone has a Web site."

"You don't."

"I like my privacy and my clients know how to find me."

"Exactly," I said.

"Ah," she said. "This unearthing stuff gets interesting, doesn't it?"

20

The next morning I introduced Blanche to a lightweight leash. Twenty minutes of exercise was enough for her: When I carried her back to the house, she tucked her head under my chin.

The phone rang as I set out her water bowl.

Milo said, "The bad news is no sign yet of Robert Fisk, the other bad news is no one in any of the divisions has heard of Blazer Pain or Rosie."

"That's 'cause it's Blaise De Paine." I gave him the details.

"Music cheat, I'll pass it along to Petra. The final bad news is the evidence room is still having trouble locating the bullets used on Leland Armbruster. In the theoretically positive category, Iona Bedard—Kyle's mom—is in town to talk to Petra about Brother Lester. She's staying at the Beverly Hilton, we're invited to co-attend at ten a.m. If you're interested, meet me in front at five to. Dress nice. Class consciousness, and all that."

The lobby of the Beverly Hilton was a bright, vast amalgam of original fifties construction and postmodern, earth-toned upgrades.

Tourists waited to check in. Sharp-eyed executives and frightened minions wearing *Hi I'm . . .* badges hurried to meetings. Milo sat off to the side on a chocolate-brown sofa designed for someone thin, drinking coffee and watching people with the suspiciousness that never leaves him.

"Dressing nice" was a broad-shouldered suit one shade lighter than the couch. Some miracle fabric with a coarse weave that resembled shredded wheat. His shirt was barley yellow, his tie peacock blue. No desert boots; glossy brown oxfords I'd never seen before.

I said, "Nice spit shine."

"These are older than Tanya. Can't wear 'em anymore. Bunions."

He rubbed the offending bulge.

I said, "Nevertheless . . ."

"Protect and serve and suffer. Once a Catholic . . ."

A voice said, "Hey, guys."

Petra Connor strode toward us wearing a brown pantsuit one shade darker than the couch and carrying a big beige purse.

"Oh, boy," she said, eyeing Milo. "The Mud City twins."

"Except for Dr. Nonconformist," said Milo.

She touched the sleeve of my gray flannel jacket. "Thanks for rescuing us from gag-me, Alex. Thanks also for the Blaise De Paine info but if he owns a house in the hills, we can't find it, and there's no auto reg under that name. I'm not sure if I want to put too much time into him, the key is Robert Fisk. Lester Jordan's autopsy is scheduled in three days but the initial screen came through. Massive amounts of opiates plus three cocktails' worth of alcohol, no big surprise there, we found a nearly empty gin bottle in Jordan's fridge. And that's the longest speech I've delivered in a long time."

We shared an elevator with a stunned-looking Swedish family. Iona Bedard's suite was at the south end of the sixth floor. A black-haired woman shoved the door open, said, "You're on time," turned her back on us, and marched to an easy chair. Propping her feet on an ottoman, she reclaimed a smoldering pink cigarette from an ashtray.

The living room was bright, wide, and cold, with a long gray view of Century City. Furnished with the same ecru-to-topsoil formula as the lobby. Petra muttered, "Now I'll be invisible," and shut the door.

We stood around as Iona Bedard puffed and gazed at a chalky sky. An end table was piled with fashion magazines and glossy monthlies that pushed high-priced toys. Atop the stack was a sleek platinum lighter. A tray near her feet held a pitcher of iced tea and an empty glass. Iona Bedard didn't invite us to sit and we stayed on our feet.

Petra said, "Thanks for meeting with us, ma'am."

Bedard sucked in smoke and let it trail out of her nose. Midfifties, tall and leggy, she had wide, dark, heavily lined eyes that matched her ebony bouffant. Her black-and-pink houndstooth jacket and gray jeans were tailored to a bony frame that shouted self-denial. Her skin boasted of nicotine and sun exposure. The exception was a flat, glossy brow. That and the odd paralytic tilt along the outer edges of her eyelids screamed Botox.

She said, "I'm going to help you people. If you want to solve my brother's murder, take a good hard look into my ex-husband. Do you have something to write on?"

Petra produced her pad.

Iona Bedard said, "*Myron. Grant. Bedard.* Fifty-seven years old, six feet tall, two forty, though he lies and claims to be lighter. His addresses are—write this down: 752 Park Avenue, Apartment 13A, New York 10021, Crookback Ranch, Aspen Valley, Colorado 81611, and an apartment in London that he calls a *flat* because he's pretentious. Nine Carlos Place, Mayfair, W1, I don't recall the crazy English postal code but it should be easy enough to find. Do you have all that down?"

"I do, ma'am," said Petra. "Why should we be looking at Mr. Bedard?"

"Because he's always despised Lester."

"Personality conflict?"

"Baseless hatred," said Bedard, as if explaining to an idiot. "Lester wasn't the strongest person. Myron has no tolerance for weakness."

Petra wrote something down. "Could you be more specific as to a motive for murder, ma'am?"

"Hatred isn't sufficient?"

"Did Mr. Bedard and Mr. Jordan have any recent conflict?"

"It wouldn't surprise me."

"But you don't know of any specific—"

"I'm trying to *help* you, dear. If I *knew* more, I'd *tell* you."

"Where is Mr. Bedard at present?"

"I have no idea."

Milo said, "Your son said he was in Europe."

"If that's what Kyle said, then I'm sure it was true. At the time Kyle said it."

"Meaning?"

"Myron moves around. Locate a bevy of sluts and he won't be far."

Petra said, "He moves between his three residences?"

"And resorts and rented yachts and private jets and whatever whim of the moment seizes him."

"Who owns the house on Hudson Avenue?"

Iona Bedard's eyelids lowered. Her eye shadow was smoke-colored and glossy. She shifted her attention to Milo, then me, as if Petra had worn out the welcome mat. "That monstrosity is Myron's as well." Back to Petra: "I didn't mention it because I assumed you *knew* about it. *And* because you'll never find him there. He hates Los Angle-is. Fancies himself a waahrld *traahvelar.*"

"Anyone live there besides Kyle?"

"Kyle would prefer a small apartment appropriate for someone of his age. Myron refuses to pay for one."

"Not a generous man."

"When it comes to his own needs, he's *lavish.*"

"Are you saying Mr. Bedard murdered Mr. Jordan and flew off to Europe?"

Bedard's sigh was long, theatrical, world-weary. "People like Myron don't do for themselves."

"So we're talking a contract killing."

"I'm offering you insight, dear. Connect the dots."

"Any idea who Mr. Bedard would hire for something like that?"

"I don't consort with people like that."

"Mr. Bedard's motive would be resentment."

"Myron *despised* Lester. Throughout our marriage, Lester was an *issue* for Myron."

"In what way?"

"My helping Lester ate at Myron. What was I asking? Basic lodging for a family member who'd encountered more than his share of misfortune."

"The apartment on Cherokee," said Milo. "Lester lived there for free?"

Iona waved her cigarette. "Only one small apartment in a twenty-unit building. You'd have thought I was seeking to lease the Taj Mahal."

"Mr. Bedard objected but he gave in."

"It's not as if Myron ever earned a dime. What reason did he have to object? And Lester earned his keep. He managed the building."

"Mr. Bedard inherited his wealth," said Petra.

"My family was by *no* means middle-class, dear, but we know the value of work. My father was a top financial advisor for Merrill Lynch and my mother was a world-class beauty and gifted painter who never went out in the sun without a parasol. Culture was an *enormous* component of my upbringing."

No reason for her to smile, but she did. The movement created a network of facial creases in random spots, as if her head was tethered to invisible strings, manipulated by an unseen puppeteer. "Myron's family had the means to acquire culture but they lacked the motivation. Most of the objects of quality in my father-in-law's house were purchased at my suggestion. I have a degree in Art History from Weldon College. I'll say one thing for the old man, he was willing to listen. Obviously *not* a genetic trait."

Petra said, "Anything you could tell us about Mr. Jordan's history would be helpful."

"What do you mean by 'history'?"

"Who he was, his friends, his interests. How he got involved with drugs."

Iona Bedard flexed the pink cigarette, watched the smoke wiggle upward. Lifting her glass, she glanced at the pitcher.

Milo filled her glass. She drank, ground out her cigarette, pulled out a fresh smoke. Glanced at the platinum lighter.

Milo lit her up.

Three inhalations later, she said, "Lester's essence went beyond his illness."

"I'm sure it did," said Petra. "But it would still be helpful to know—"

"Lester's *history* is that he was a perfectly normal young man who had the misfortune of growing up in a family where normalcy wasn't sufficient. My father was Bertram Jordan."

Pausing to let the fact sink in.

She said, "Senior partner in Merrill's main San Francisco office? My mother was a Dougherty. Without her, the Palace of Fine Arts would be nothing. Lester's older than me. He wasn't the student that I was but his gift was music. All he wanted was to play music but that was an anathema to my parents. They meant well but their disapproval was hard for Lester."

"What instrument did he play?" said Petra.

"Clarinet, saxophone, oboe. He dabbled in trumpet, as well."

"We didn't find any instruments in his apartment."

"Lester hadn't played for years. His dreams were crushed."

"By your parents?"

"By life," said Iona Bedard. "Someone with a stronger constitution might've endured but Lester was artistic and sensitive and artistic people often lack backbone."

I thought back to Jordan's surly demeanor. Maybe dope and the passage of time had changed him. Or his sister was delusional.

She said, "Lester made one last stab at defying Father. Dropped out of college and joined up with a traveling jazz band. That's when he learned bad habits."

Petra said, "Heroin."

Bedard glared at her. "You seem to relish reminding me."

"Just trying to clarify the facts, Mrs. Bedard. What college did Mr. Jordan attend?"

"San Francisco State. During the turmoil. That Oriental fellow with the hat?"

"Pardon?" said Petra.

Bedard turned to us. "You're of that age, educate her."

I said, "Samuel Hayakawa was the chancellor of S.F. State during the sixties. It was a politicized campus."

Iona Bedard said, "Lester never participated in that nonsense. Nor did he become a hippie. Just the opposite, he had no use for politics."

"Just wanted to play music," said Petra.

"He was a clean-cut young man who fell in with the wrong crowd."

Placing her glass atop the fashion magazines, Bedard slashed the air. "End of story."

Petra said, "Who were his recent friends?"

"I wouldn't know."

"You own the building on Cherokee, now."

"A crumb tossed to me by Myron's attorneys. I rarely visit. It's all I received except for some moribund stocks and the house in Atherton that *I* insisted we purchase in the first place and *I* decorated from scratch."

I said, "Kyle mentioned a place in Deer Valley."

"*My* cabin," she said. "*I'm* the one who skis, Myron can barely handle a bunny slope, what use would he have with that? When may I retrieve Lester from wherever you people have him?"

"I'll give you all the details, ma'am," said Petra, "but first a few more questions. You have no knowledge of anyone your brother Jordan associated with recently?"

"Must I repeat myself?" Bedard puffed away, coughed roughly, covered her mouth with her hand belatedly.

"As the landlord—"

"I'm the landlord in title only, young lady. Checks are sent to me monthly, all of which I go over with a fine-tooth comb to make sure the management company I've hired doesn't steal more than their customary amount."

"What's the name of the company?"

"Embezzlers, Incorporated." Bedard chuckled at her own wit. "Brass Management. Arthur I. Brass. Jewish. When it comes to money, you might as well have them on your side. Now if you'll excu—"

"Did Lester ever try to kick the habit?"

"Several times."

"How?"

"By enrolling in so-called rehab programs."

"Who financed that?"

"I did. Another issue with Myron. As far as he was concerned, Lester could rot."

"Several years ago, ma'am, there was a nurse who lived in the Cherokee building—"

"The lesbian," said Iona Bedard. "Patricia something."

"Patricia Bigelow."

"That's the one."

"You know her to be a lesbian."

"She certainly *looked* like one. Hair like a man. Not that I held any prejudice against her. She did her job professionally, I'll grant her that."

"What was her job?"

"Looking out for Lester. That was my idea. The day Myron showed her the apartment, I was visiting Lester and came up with an inspired idea."

"Myron showed the apartments personally?"

"Back then, he did. At the insistence of his father, kicking and screaming all the way. When the old man had his stroke, Myron hired a management company. Not Brass, some Armenians who robbed him blind."

"But that day, when Ms. Bigelow was looking to rent—"

"Myron and I had just completed nine holes at Wilshire. I craved a light lunch but Myron said he had to show an apartment at Chero-kee. I said I might as well visit Lester. Patricia showed up. Afterward, Myron said he wasn't sure he'd rent to her, she'd just moved to town, didn't have much in the way of credit references or ready cash. Not that the tenants he chose were exemplary. But they had cash, much of which Myron pocketed unbeknownst to his father. On the other hand, he said, it was one of the front apartments on the street, which were harder to rent. And she was a nurse, so he supposed she'd be a steady worker. Then he waffled. That was Myron, unable to make decisions unless they pertained to his personal comfort. I said a nurse could come in handy. Thinking of Lester, immediately, because Lester had just been through a rough patch."

"Overdose?" said Petra.

Iona glared. "A *kind* person would have jumped at the opportunity to help a family member. But anything that smacked of helping Lester irked Myron."

"Ms. Bigelow did move in and she stayed for years."

"That, my dear, is because *I* exploited Myron's miserly nature by pointing out that hospitals and private nurses were expensive and we could have someone in-house."

"A barter," said Petra.

"Inspired," said Bedard.

"What did looking after Mr. Jordan consist of?"

"Checking in on him, making sure he had food, coffee. Patricia was mannish but she knew her job. There were at least three instances where Lester might have fallen more seriously ill but for her presence."

"What did she do?"

"Revived him, walked him around, whatever you do in those situations. One time she did have to call an ambulance but when they arrived, Lester was already on his feet and didn't need to be taken to the hospital. Don't get the wrong idea, dear. It wasn't only *those* kinds of problems. When Lester came down with a cold or a flu, she was there."

"Did she ever provide him with drugs?" said Milo.

"Of course not."

"Of course not?" said Petra.

"She told me she detested drugs. At first she didn't even want the job because of the nature of Lester's illness. Which I thought was a bit huffy, considering her own lifestyle issues."

"What convinced her?"

"Free rent and one thousand dollars a month in cash. Which I'm sure she didn't declare to the IRS. Why are you asking so many questions about her?"

"Her name comes up when we ask around about your brother."

"I don't see why it would. But if you want evidence of Myron's hateful nature, go ahead and talk to her. After the old man's stroke, Myron announced that his father's priorities outweighed Lester's and that Patricia was moving to Hudson. Needless to say, I was furious. She was an excellent caretaker and Lester had gotten used to having her around. You'd think *she* might have been loyal, but there was Myron, with his forty pieces of silver."

"He gave her a raise?"

"An additional thousand dollars a month and free use of the guest room. If you people have connections with the IRS, there's a tip for you."

Petra said, "You mentioned Mr. Bedard renting to disreputable types who paid cash. Anyone in particular?"

"Minorities," said Iona Bedard. "That kind of thing."

"Your brother didn't associate with any other tenants?"

Bedard ground out her second cigarette and placed her glass on the floor with exaggerated care. "You really don't understand, do you?"

"Understand what, ma'am?"

"Lester was *ill*. That doesn't make him one of *them*."

"How did he fare after Ms. Bigelow left?"

"Not well," said Iona Bedard. "Myron refused to pay for another nurse or for any additional treatment. One time, Lester had to be taken to the *county* hospital, which I understand is a snake pit. Myron *relished* the I-told-you-so. The names he'd call Lester I won't repeat."

"Lester had some legal problems, as well."

"All due to his illness." Iona Bedard flicked ashes in the general vicinity of the tray. Most of them landed on the carpet. "Shortly after the old man died, my marriage finally accomplished what it should have accomplished years ago. Disintegrated. Circumstances forced me to beg Myron to allow Lester to stay at Cherokee and I don't take well to begging. After the divorce I insisted on—and got—the building and that was that. Lester never beat his problem but his need for drugs did seem to be winding down a bit."

"That can happen with addicts, if they live long enough," said Petra. "Where did Lester's financial support come from?"

Iona Bedard poked her chest. Waved dismissively. "Go on, you people, I've done your work for you. All you have to do is find the bastard."

We didn't move.

"Please," said Bedard, making it sound like an order.

Petra said, "Does the name Robert Fisk mean anything to you?"

"There was a Bobby Fisk in my class at Atherton Prep. Flight surgeon in the navy."

"What about Rosie?"

"The Riveter?"

"Blaise De Paine?"

Iona Bedard patted her coiffure. Laughed.

Petra said, "Something funny, ma'am?"

"*That,* young lady, is *not* a real name. Now go on, do your *job.*"

CHAPTER

21

On the ride down, we had the elevator to ourselves. Petra fanned herself and laughed. "*That* must've been one lousy prenup."

Milo said, "If voodoo worked, ol' Myron would be frying in oil."

"She gives us no evidence he has anything to do with Lester, but on her say-so we're supposed to track him down in Europe."

"Hatred's a great motivator."

"I'm sure he adores her, too. After fifteen minutes, *I'm* ready to strangle her. But so what? For ten years Jordan's been out of his life."

I said, "As opposed to all those disreputable 'minority' types who shared Jordan's lifestyle but were nothing like him."

"Talk about denial," said Petra. "One thing she's probably right about. 'De Paine' is a moniker."

We crossed the lobby in silence. Milo and I had parked in the hotel lot but Petra had left her Acura on Walden Drive across Wilshire, and we walked her over.

She unlocked the car and tossed her purse onto the passenger seat. "Any parting thoughts, guys?"

"It was me, I'd keep it basic," said Milo.

"Concentrate on Fisk, anything else is a distraction. In terms of your Ms. Bigelow, I'm not seeing any stunning link. Even if she did channel hospital dope Jordan's way, that's also ancient history."

"Seems to be," said Milo.

"You have doubts?"

"The only sticking point is one day we're talking to Jordan about Patty and soon after he gets dead."

"The only possible connection would be he tipped someone off about some secret so big and bad he had to be silenced. Like what?"

Neither of us had an answer.

"Either way," she said, "the key is finding Fisk."

Milo said, "Dancing hit man. There's a network show for you."

I said, "Jordan was an ex–horn player. It keeps coming back to music."

Petra said, "Jordan hadn't played for years. The only music connection I can see is dope."

"Or an *anti*-dope thing. As in Jordan pushing product on the wrong person."

"Who's the wrong person?"

"How about a music-biz honcho's kid."

"Daddy puts the hit on Lester for supplying his prodge? Great, I'd love to haul in more suspects, maybe Fisk will fink once we have him in custody. I got DMV on his wheels, from the lapsed files. 'Ninety-nine Mustang, red at the time, registration fees six months overdue. I also put in a rush subpoena on his phone records, let's see what comes up. If I'm lucky maybe I can haul him in before Cruella phones the brass and trash-talks about us middle-class peons not following her *cultivated* instructions."

Milo said, "Gonna cover your butt and look for her ex?"

She swung her purse. "I'll sic Raul on it, give him some training in long-distance sleuthing."

"Smart guy?" said Milo.

"Smart but real new. Quiet, though. I like that. See you, guys."

We returned to the Hilton parking lot.

I said, "One thing meeting Iona was good for. Now we understand Patty's housing choices."

Milo said, "A thousand a month in cash for three years makes thirty-six K she didn't have to declare. Then ol' Myron moves her to Hudson and she's raised to two grand. How long did she stay there?"

"Around two years."

"Another forty-eight, for a grand total of eighty-four thou. Toss in her salary at the hospital, plus five years of free rent, and it's a nice six-figure haul. Talk about a sweet deal, Alex. The downside was no job security. The old man dies, sayonara."

"She moved to Fourth Street," I said. "Nicest place yet, but she stayed less than a year. Maybe paying full rent was jarring. Or she was determined to save her cash now that she had some. Eighty-four thousand even at a conservative rate of interest could double in ten years. If she participated in the stock-market boom, she could've done significantly better. Downshifting to Culver Boulevard meant living in a dump but it got her to homeownership. Without the windfall from Myron Bedard, she might never have pulled it off. Her portfolio's what started me wondering about dope, but maybe it'll boil down to savvy investing."

"Helped along by a little tax evasion."

"That, too."

Isaac Gomez's e-mail read:

Hi, Dr. D. We're in Bangkok and I'm writing this from an Internet café but the connection's tenuous and we're moving on so don't bother responding. I woke up thinking about that crime trace and realized I'd made a methodological error by limiting myself to cases classified as homicides, as opposed to manslaughter, aggravated assault, or anything else that could've developed into murder but wasn't reclassified. Unfortunately, there's nothing I can do about it right now but when I get back in a few weeks, I'll dig around the data a bit more and see what I can come up with. Hopefully, I haven't missed anything crucial. Heather says hi. Best, IG

I thought about that, decided Isaac was parsing too meticulously. Patty had said she'd killed a man. Everyone was dancing around that, but I couldn't forget it.

I was sitting on the couch, contemplating a warming shot of Chivas, when Blanche waddled into the office and nuzzled my shin. When I stood, she danced around a bit, then raced out the door.

I followed her down the hall, across the kitchen, to the back door. She sped with surprising agility down the stairs to the pond. Zeroed in on the locked bin that held the koi chow and began butting it with her flat nose.

"You're into seafood now?" I scooped out a few pellets and offered them to her. She turned her head in disdain.

Head-butted the bin some more. Stared up at me.

When I tossed food to the fish, she swiveled and watched. Panted. Gave a hoarse bark until I threw more pellets.

"Altruism?" I said.

I know the experts will label it anthropomorphism but she smiled with pure joy, I'll swear to it.

Robin found the two of us by the water. Blanche jumped off my lap and greeted her. The fish swarmed, as they do when footsteps sound on the stone pathway.

"They're starving," she said. "I'll go feed them."

I said, "They've already dined. Extensively, because Blanche has appointed herself Official Caterer."

"I know," she said. "She did it yesterday, too. Any progress finding Fisk?"

"Not yet."

"I networked some more on Blaise De Paine. The only thing I can add is that maybe possibly *could* be his house in the hills is on one of the bird streets. But don't put much faith in it, hon. The person who told me wasn't sure where he'd heard it or even if it was De Paine and not some other crook and he had no idea which bird. No one's heard of Fisk or Rosie, though there is a black guy named Mosey, does some dee-jay work."

"Last name?"

She shook her head. "He's probably not who you want. The person who met him said he was a nice guy."

"Where'd he meet him?"

"She. Some party, she was one of the dancers, hired by an agency in the Valley, she couldn't recall the name."

"Memory problems?"

"Maybe a bit blurred by recreational substances."

"The bird streets," I said. "Fog upon L.A., friends losing their way."

"Poor George. Remember when I met him?"

"Ten years ago, fixing the Rickenbacher."

"Sweet man," she said. "So gifted, so modest."

She sat down, rested her head on my shoulder. Blanche watched us kiss. Trotted back to the stairs and observed us with serenity.

An almost parental joy.

Robin said, "Let's go inside. Spread our wings."

By four p.m., Robin was sketching and I was at the computer running a search on *mosey deejay.*

One hit, no images.

Moses "Big Mosey" Grant was cited in a long list of people thanked for contributing to the success of a hospital fund-raiser.

Western Pediatric, where I'd trained and worked.

The party had been thrown a year ago by the Division of Endocrinology, the cause was juvenile diabetes, and the person offering thanks was the head, Dr. Elise Glass. Elise and I had worked together on several cases. I had her private number on file.

She said, "Hi, Alex. Are you back to seeing patients or is it still that police stuff?"

"As a matter of fact." I asked her about Moses Grant.

"Who?"

"The deejay at your benefit last year."

"Mosey? Please don't tell me *he's* in trouble."

"You know him personally?"

"No, but I remember him. Huge but gentle and really good with the kids. Am I going to be disillusioned?"

"He's not in trouble, but he's been seen with someone who is. I'm sure it'll turn out to be nothing."

"I hope so. First he cut his fees, then he insisted on working for free, stayed extra hours. He understood what we're about."

"Diabetic relative?"

"Diabetic himself. Unfortunately, he doesn't seem to be controlling it well. Toward the end of the evening, he was fading fast and I had to get him some juice."

"How'd you come to hire him?"

"The Development Office hired him. He really seemed like a teddy bear, Alex."

"I'm sure he is. Do you have a number for him?"

"That would be over in Development, too. Hold on, I'll have Janice connect you."

I waited as a recorded voice lectured me about nutrition and exercise.

"Development, this is Sue."

"This is Dr. Delaware. I'm planning an event and heard you use an excellent deejay named Moses Grant. Do you know how I can reach him?"

"Hmm, let me check that."

A new recorded message filled me in on the virtues of charitable giving. "We got him through a broker—The Party Line. Here's the number."

Valley exchange. Before I tried it, I plugged *Moses Grant* into the search engines and brought up a genealogy site and a lone reference to a miner who'd died in West Virginia a hundred and five years ago.

At The Party Line's number, a hoarse male voice answered, "Agency, Eli Romaine."

"I'm looking for a deejay you handle. Moses Grant."

"Don't handle him anymore," said Romaine. "I've got better people. What kind of party are you doing?"

"Sweet sixteen," I said. "I was told Grant's one of the best."

"It's not rocket science, he knows how to push buttons. What kind of sweet sixteen are we talking about? Kids acting their age or pretending to be twenty-one? I'm asking 'cause the music's different, depending."

"These are just normal kids."

Romaine's laugh was a nicotine bark. "Okay, I've got guys who can go either way. Girls, too, but sweet sixteens always want guys. Preferably hot guys. I got a couple who could be on soap operas and also know how to push buttons. I also got dancers, I recommend some blond girls, to get the action going. It's not that much more."

"Grant wasn't that good?" I said.

"Do you want someone who's going to show up or not?"

"He flaked out."

"Six months ago, so what kind of setup do you want?"

"Let me think about it."

"Oh, Jesus," he said. "This isn't about sweet sixteen. What, he owes you money? Don't waste my time."

Click.

I reached Petra's cell and gave her Moses Grant's name.

She said, "Thanks. I'm on my way to San Diego. Robert Fisk's Mustang showed up not far from the long-term parking lot at Lindbergh Field. I may have to go through the airlines one by one. This is handy, I can also search for Grant's name on the manifests."

"Good luck."

"If Fisk flew bye-bye, I'll need it. Bye."

I put that aside and thought about Grant dropping out of sight half a year ago. Same time Robert Fisk had left his apartment and turned invisible.

Had Grant stopped taking party jobs from Romaine because he'd found a better gig? Altruistic teddy bear or not, doing the club scene with Blaise De Paine or some other music-biz remora could be more enticing than spinning Raffi and Dan Crow for sick kids. Or dealing with sixteen-year-olds yearning for twenty-one.

Or maybe Grant's disappearance hadn't been voluntary. A diabetic who failed to monitor his blood sugar could face all sorts of complications.

I decided to start with hospitals and if that didn't pan out, move on to emergency rooms and long-term-care units. The information I was after was confidential and I'd have to lie my way through layers of medical bureaucracy. Blitheness and my title might help.

Grant's 818 number said the logical place to start was the Valley. Then I remembered a hospital where I could be truthful.

Rick said, "I'm walking to my computer as we speak. There's an overall billing file for inpatients. Outpatients I'm not sure about, they may be classed by department. So you think this Grant person might have something to do with Patty and that guy Jordan?"

"Grant was seen in the company of Jordan's murderer."

"The kickboxer who left the fingerprints."

"Milo's filled you in."

"I've been bugging him to keep me posted. I don't know if you've sensed it, Alex, but he's done a total turnaround on Patty. At first it was all I could do to get him to take Tanya's concerns seriously. Jordan's murder changed his mind, he's convinced it's tied to Patty. He's also convinced it's his fault because it happened right after he talked to Jordan."

"Didn't know it bothered him that way."

"Guilt's what Big Guy's all about . . . okay, I have entered the General Billing System . . . looks like I need a code . . . oh, would you look at *this*. The codes are listed right out in the open by department, talk about inane . . . okay, I'm typing in the E.R. code and . . . here we go: Grant, Moses Byron, male, twenty-six years old, 7502 Los Ojos, Woodland Hills . . . oh, boy."

"What?"

"Looks like he was one of ours. Came into the E.R. for hypoglycemia."

"When?"

"Two and a half months ago."

"Right before Patty got sick."

"The hairs on my neck are standing up, Alex."

"Did he come in alone?"

"That wouldn't be in the billing records unless someone else guaranteed payment . . . let's see . . . the account was settled in full, $869.23, no insurance co-pay or Medi-Cal. Either Grant's check was good or he paid cash. Let me go find his chart. That could take a bit, would you prefer bad music or silence?"

"I could use some quiet."

Moments later: "Mr. Grant arrived at our portals barely conscious at three fourteen a.m. on a Saturday night. I was off, the attending was Pete Berger. Let's check the nursing notes . . . oh, boy, they're Patty's. One of her double shifts."

"What did she write?"

"Basic intake material . . . okay, she does mention Grant being brought by 'friends,' no names . . . one of them had communicated to the triage nurse that Grant had taken an insulin shot shortly before feeling faint and nearly passing out. We got some sugar in him, monitored his vitals, found some funny stuff with the R waves of his EEG and recommended admission for further observation. Grant refused, checked himself out against medical advice, we never saw him again."

"Would Pete Berger remember?"

"With thousands of patients since? No way. And the resident was rotating through from Olive View. Let me try to reach both of them for you anyway, stay right there."

Ten minutes later: "Neither of them remember Grant, let alone his friends. I'm sure Patty would have total recall, her memory was astonishing."

"Which could be the point," I said. "She saw something while taking care of Grant that upset her. Soon after, she got sick, but it stuck in her mind."

"I guess so, but what could have bothered her that much . . . I told you she looked worn out two weeks before diagnosis. I've been assuming that was the disease taking its toll. You're saying it could've been emotional stress?"

"At this point it's theory, but it does establish another link between Patty and Lester Jordan. She took care of him and an associate of the guy who killed him."

"Speaking of which," he said, "Milo told me your suspicions about Patty pilfering drugs. I went back and checked our Class Three inventories for the last year and nothing looks funny. I've always run a really tight ship in that regard, Alex. I don't delude myself that anything's perfect and a twelve-month check says nothing about pilferage years ago but I have to believe that if anything significant was going on, I'd have known it. Beyond that, I just can't see Patty involved in anything like that."

"I can't either."

"Yet Tanya has a trust fund," he said. "That's been eating at me."

"Milo didn't tell you the new theory about that?"

"No. I've been on for the last two days, haven't seen him."

I told him about Myron Bedard's cash payments to Patty plus five years of free rent.

He said, "That makes me feel a little bit better. What I just said about running a tight ship? I might as well be up front. When I didn't check the dope cabinet personally, I had Patty do it."

"There's no evidence she stole drugs, Rick."

"I guess I just want to hear you say it. Anything else I can do for you?"

"No," I said. "Thanks for helping with Grant."

"Sure. Listen, maybe it's best if Big Guy doesn't know the extent of my involvement. He likes to shield me from the bad stuff."

CHAPTER

23

T he meeting took place the following night. Nine p.m. my house; Petra showed up first, at ten to the hour, though she'd driven from San Diego. "Big-rig overturn near Irvine, psycho traffic all the way to Newport and my cell phone battery died. Thank God I left early and changed into car clothes."

That meant a black cowl-necked top, charcoal velvet sweatpants, and white sneakers. After a bathroom break, she accepted the offer of a phone battery and coffee and began chatting with Robin. When I came back, they were talking handbags and Blanche was on Petra's lap.

"This one," she said, "is star material."

Robin said, "I know ostrich leg sounds gory but I like it better than straight ostrich."

Petra said, "Is that the one with a larger pattern instead of dots? A little like croc but softer around the edges?"

"Exactly."

"Oh, yeah, that's nice. Poor bird—but they say ostriches are mean, so if you want to rationalize, there's an out."

"Cows are nice," said Robin, "but I'm not limiting myself to hemp."

I left to pour my own cup.

Milo arrived with a corner of a pizza wedge in one hand and tomato sauce stains above his lip. The shoulders and back of his sport coat were coated with fine gray dust and random flecks of paper. His tweed slacks were seasons too heavy for the warm night.

Taking a half-gallon milk carton from the fridge, he ripped at the spout and guzzled.

Robin said, "Want a cookie?"

"Home-baked?"

"Mint Milanos."

"Kind of you, kid, but my standards are high."

Robin laughed and took Blanche to the bedroom.

Milo and Petra and I sat around the kitchen table.

She said, "So you found the bullets."

Milo said, "After two days of digging around. Some genius in the evidence room wrote down a 5 instead of a 3 and then another genius modified that to an 8 and added the wrong year code. They also had it clear on the wrong side of the room, with boxes from 'sixty-two."

"Maybe they were hoping you'd solve a few cold ones while you were there." She leaned over and flicked dust from his jacket.

"I got Bob Deal in Ballistics to agree to run comparison tests tomorrow. Anything happen with the airlines?"

"If only," she said. "Fisk's name doesn't show up on any outgoing flights since the day of Jordan's murder and neither does Moses Grant's. Plenty of prints in Fisk's Mustang but so far the only ones that pull up an AFIS match are his. Stu got San Diego to agree to work it over, in the interests of time. They've gone over the interior and the trunk, haven't found any body fluids. I've got a nice broad subpoena for all of Fisk's phone records but I can't find any evidence of a landline and if he uses a cell, it's a rental."

"Bad-guy habits," said Milo. "Any papers in the car?"

"Old reg, some PowerBar wrappers. It's neat but not freaky-clean, as if he did a recent wash. Back to our vic for a sec. Lester Jordan *had* only a landline, but it doesn't look like he had much of a social life, maybe twenty calls a month. The only long-distances were to Iona in Atherton and the last of those was seventy-four days ago."

Milo said, "Close-knit family."

"Regular Brady Bunch. The other numbers Jordan called were take-out restaurants and pay phones. The pay calls happened late at night, which fits with Jordan craving dope. Raul did a thorough recanvass of the building. Most of the tenants had no idea who Jordan was, it's not a touchy-feely place where they greet each other in the hallways. And no one had heard Jordan was the manager, so if Iona's palming him off as such for tax purposes, she's scamming. But a few people said they'd noticed lowlifes going in and out of Jordan's apartment in the wee hours. Still, the H left behind doesn't indicate Jordan got dead because he was dealing. Or maybe Fisk really can't stand drugs."

Milo said, "Even so, there'd be a profit motive."

"Maybe," she said, "Fisk and whoever let him in got careless. They did leave the window open. In terms of Moses Grant, there's absolutely no criminal record. Bassett Bowland saw Grant at Rattlesnake with Fisk and De Paine but he didn't observe any conspiratorial behavior. Barring new information, I don't think Grant merits much of my time."

I said, "Here's new information: A couple of weeks before she got sick, Patty Bigelow treated Grant at Cedars."

"For what?"

"Low blood sugar. He's diabetic."

"He's a sick guy, she's a nurse, and Cedars is the main E.R. on the Westside. Thousands of people move through there, Alex."

"Grant came in with friends."

She pushed hair behind one ear, rubbed a temple with her thumb. "Another layer of complication. Okay, what else do we know about Grant?"

Milo said, "According to his landlord in Woodland Hills, he was a model tenant, no noise, no guests, even played his music with earphones. Then six months ago, he cut out on the rent with no notice. Landlord sued him in small claims and won, but she hasn't collected because she can't find him."

I said, "Six months ago Robert Fisk skipped out on his rent."

"The two of them moved in together?" she said. "Fine, I'll keep Grant on the radar. Which so far has picked up nothing but noise."

She pulled out a sheet of paper and slid it across the table. San Diego PD fax sheet, an enlargement of Grant's driver's license in the center. "Real *big* teddy bear."

Milo peered at the photo. His neck muscles corded as he handed the paper to me.

Moses Grant had smiled for the DMV camera. Round dark face. Shaved head, barbered mustache, and goatee.

Six six, a wishful-thinking two fifty.

The giant who'd exited the Hummer at Mary Whitbread's place.

Oh, here's my son.

That's her kid? I love this city.

Milo told Petra.

She said, "Grant's mommy was Patty's landlord? Everywhere this woman moves has some kind of hidden *meaning*?"

I said, "We assumed Grant was Mary Whitbread's son because he was the only one who got out of the car. What if he was driving someone else who decided to stay out of sight? The Hummer's windows were tinted black, no way to know who was riding."

Milo said, "Lester Jordan was still alive then, but not for long. Mary Whitbread was the last person we spoke to about Patty. Soon after, Jordan's dead."

Petra took back the sheet. "Whitbread's son is Robert Fisk? Grant hangs with Fisk, doing the club scene, drives for him. Fisk's mommy tells him something about Patty that gets him worried so he takes care of business . . . meaning the second guy in the apartment could be Grant. Though why Jordan would let him in, I don't know. Unless Grant really wasn't a clean-living teddy bear."

She laughed. "Know a judge who'd sign a warrant based on that? Not that I've got a place to search."

I said, "There's another candidate for Mary's son. Blaise De Paine, the Music Sampler. Fisk and Grant were De Paine's sidemen. I found pictures of him on the Web. He's fair-haired like Whitbread. Dresses flamboyantly and parties with beautiful people, which makes him a good fit for flashy wheels."

"Let's have a look at this sweetheart," said Petra.

We headed to my office. I downloaded the images.

Petra said, "Looks like a kid playing dress-up . . . kind of a retro Sergeant Pepper thing going. Not that I'm old enough to remember . . . Mary Whitbread, huh? 'Pain' is 'bread' in French."

Silence.

Milo studied Blaise De Paine's poses. "Guy doesn't dress, he costumes . . . a poseur. Which is Gallic for 'bullshit artist.' "

"Pretentious and a thief," I said. "Wonder what else he's hiding."

24

Petra used her LAPD password to log onto NCIC.

The system bounced back two felons named Whitbread: Francis Arthur, male Caucasian, seventy-eight years old, paroled from a twenty-year bank-robbery sentence forty-nine months ago and living in Lawrence, Kansas. Jerry Lee, male American Indian, fifty-two, serving the second half of an eighteen-year armed-robbery stretch at North Dakota State Penitentiary.

An auto check pulled up Mary Whitbread's license and that of Peterson Ewan Whitbread, issued four years ago, living at the same address on Fourth Street. Peterson's DOB made him twenty-eight years old. Five seven, one thirty, blond and blue.

Four years ago, he'd worn his hair long and lank. Half-shut eyes shouted boredom. Minus mascara, the spike-do, and club duds, just another bland baby-face aiming at sullen.

Petra said, "Peterson Whitbread ain't too hip-hop a moniker, I can see why he'd reinvent. Still bunking with Mommy at twenty-four wouldn't be good for the image, either."

I said, "One of Robin's sources thinks he lives on one of the bird streets."

"Business must be good. Which bird?"

"Don't know."

"Who's the source?"

"No one reliable." I filled them in.

Petra leaned in closer to the screen. "He's got on mascara . . . looks like nail polish, too. The albino Michael Jackson." Sitting back. "A little showy guy like this would definitely use hired help for muscle. But if he did contract Lester Jordan's murder because of something related to Patty, the motive has to stretch back to when Patty was taking *care* of Jordan. That would make Bread-Head anywhere from ten to sixteen."

Milo said, "Adolescence is just temporary psychopathy, right?"

"Sometimes permanent," she said. "So what kind of link between a bad-boy teen and a solid-citizen nurse would be worth killing over?"

"The only thing I can see connecting a punk, a junkie, and a nurse is you-know-what."

She said, "If Patty did get involved with a felonious punk and peddled dope, why would she rent an apartment, years later, from the punk's mommy?"

I said, "Maybe the terrible thing happened after she moved to Fourth."

"Then what was *Jordan's* connection?"

"Just because she wasn't Jordan's neighbor doesn't mean she broke off contact with him."

"An enduring relationship? Okay, fine. But let's not forget that Isaac found no homicides on or near Fourth during the time Patty lived there."

"Isaac's having second thoughts." I switched to my mailbox and downloaded the e-mail from Bangkok.

She read the letter. "That's the high IQ talking, he's never satisfied. But let's go there for a sec, assume Patty's big iniquity went down on or near Fourth but fell short of murder. So what, she exaggerated to Tanya because she was terminal, and impaired? And how would knowledge of a noncapital crime lead to Jordan getting killed?"

I said, "Maybe what Patty meant by killing someone was she supplied him with dope that killed him."

"Her dealing wasn't limited to her private patient? Yeah, that would make her a bad girl."

She and Milo looked at me.

I said, "Take it wherever it goes."

Petra said, "Now I have to. Back to Bread-Head. This is a guy who steals music for a living and maybe peddles dope. He can't be too worried about some juvey misstep more than a decade ago."

"What if a murder *was* committed?" I said. "Something that was never reported and that's why Isaac didn't pick it up. Patty didn't participate directly but she conspired in a hush-up and it ate at her for years."

Milo said, "Before I'm willing to give her that pass, let's see if her gun matches the slugs dug out of Leland Armbruster."

Petra swiveled away from the screen. "Guys, this is starting to sound like a Pick One From Column A situation with nothing on the menu that looks fresh. What I need is concrete evidence of a link between the participants."

I said, "What if the friends who brought Moses Grant into the E.R. were Whitbread/De Paine and Robert Fisk? Patty recognized De Paine from her time on Fourth. That exhumed her guilt. Shortly after that, she became ill, started to obsess about the road not taken, was driven to stir things up. For all we know, De Paine recognized Patty, too. It shook him and he laid low. Then we came around talking about the past and his anxieties reignited."

"Mommy told him you were asking about Patty?" she said. "But how does Jordan figure in?"

"Maybe Jordan was a participant in whatever happened and she knew it. De Paine was worried he couldn't be counted on to keep his mouth shut."

Milo said, "All these years he kept it shut."

"Don't know," I said, "but if De Paine was doing business with Jordan, it explains the crime scene. Jordan let De Paine in and De Paine unlocked the rear window and let Fisk in. Or maybe De Paine did it himself and had Fisk along for support. Jordan nodding off heavily would've been an easy kill."

Petra crossed her legs, rubbed an ankle. "De Paine's that calculating but he doesn't take Jordan's dope?"

Milo said, "He's smart enough to be careful."

"Seems to me," she said, "*taking* the drugs would've been smart, Milo. Easy misdirect to a heroin robbery."

I said, "But that ran the risk of leading us back to Jordan's supplier. Who could be De Paine."

"So how does all this fit with Patty's housing pattern? I understand her going from Jordan's caretaker to the old man's live-in nurse with a double in salary. But the same question remains: If she knew De Paine had been involved in a serious felony, why would she be his mother's tenant? I realize she stayed less than a year but that's still a long time to expose your kid to a super-bad influence."

I had no answer.

Petra got up and fetched herself another cup of coffee. Milo phoned Rick and said, "Don't wait up."

When she returned, they settled next to each other on my leather couch.

Petra laughed.

He said, "What?"

"We look like patients—marital counseling or something." She pressed her knees together, put on an exaggerated scowl. "Doc, I've tried to make the relationship work but he just won't *communicate*."

Milo said, "Nag nag nag."

I said, "Time's up, I'll send a bill."

Their smiles didn't last long.

Milo said, "De Paine seems to be the glue in all this. He had to know Patty from when she lived on his block and he hangs with Robert Fisk."

I said, "Let's turn it another way. Patty *didn't* know De Paine before she lived on his block. Lester Jordan knew both of them, but Patty wasn't aware of it until later."

"Then how'd Patty get to be Mary Whitbread's tenant? Jordan referred her? Why would she take housing tips from a junkie?"

"Maybe she knew him as more than that."

"They were buds?"

"She was a compassionate nurse, saw Jordan's humanity," I said. "After she moved out, they maintained communication."

Petra said, "Or continued to do business."

"That, too," I admitted. "There's another way Patty might've learned about the rental on Fourth. What if Myron Bedard helped her find new lodgings?"

"Why would he do that?"

"She'd taken good care of his father."

"Benevolent Rich Guy?" she said. "What's his link to Whitbread? And how does that tie De Paine to Jordan?"

"The Bedards own property," I said. "Could be Myron owned Whitbread's duplex back then. Or some neighboring apartments. Or he was connected to Mary Whitbread in another way. Iona said he was a philanderer. Mary's an attractive woman. Ten years ago she wouldn't have looked any worse."

"Myron had a girlfriend," Petra singsonged. "Killed two birds by sending her a tenant and easing his own guilt about evicting a single mom and her cute little kid?"

She turned to Milo.

He said, "It's as good as anything else."

"Teenage punk hooks up with a junkie who just happens to be the brother-in-law of his mommy's sugar daddy?"

I said, "What do men talk to their mistresses about?"

She said, "My wife doesn't understand me."

"In Bedard's case, my wife doesn't understand me *and* she saddles me with a useless junkie brother-in-law. If Peterson Whitbread was a precocious teen criminal with a foot in the drug world, hearing that would've sparked his interest. He made contact with Jordan, the two of them ended up doing business. It's possible Patty didn't know about the connection when she moved to Mary's building. She thought she was stepping up in the world, to a nice spacious duplex. Instead, she somehow got involved in a crime that involved the landlady's son and Jordan."

Milo said, "Patty told Tanya she killed a neighbor. Nothing comes up on or near Fourth."

"What she actually said was a man 'close by.' Cherokee, Hudson, and Fourth span a wide range socioeconomically, but geographically, they're spaced pretty closely."

I pulled a Thomas Guide from my bookshelf, thumbed to a page, drew three red dots, passed the book to Petra.

She said, "Yeah, they are close . . . so we'd need to expand the geographical profile to what—all of Hollywood and Mid-Wilshire? Great."

"But if I'm right about the crime occurring when Patty lived on Fourth it narrows the time frame to less than one year. It would also explain why Patty didn't stay at Fourth very long. She'd done or seen something terrible and wanted out."

"If she was that freaked out, why didn't she leave town completely?"

"Maybe it wasn't a matter of personal safety, just guilt—wanting to get away psychologically."

The look that passed between them resonated. *Predictably shrinky.*

Milo said, "What if encountering Whitbread in the E.R. was more than bad reminiscence. Suppose he made a threatening remark to Patty."

"How's your little daughter doing, wink wink," said Petra. "But why wouldn't Patty report that immediately? Or use her little .22?" To Milo: "Find out yet when she registered it?"

"She didn't."

"By the time of the E.R. visit she was terminally ill," I said.

"Even better," she said. "She knows she's going to die. If she's nervous about Whitbread hurting Tanya, why not find him and go boom?"

I said, "You haven't been able to locate him. Why would she have better luck?"

"All those years of keeping mum and all of a sudden he's threatening her?"

"Maybe there was no overt threat, just a subtle remark that preyed on Patty's mind. She had a special kind of mind. Obsessive, a brain racing nonstop. She learned to control it, some people do. But the tendencies remain and stress brings them out. Add cognitive problems due to her disease and there's no telling how she'd process."

Petra chewed her lip. "*My* brain's ready for a pit stop . . . her place on Culver Boulevard isn't that far from the other three places—what, five miles southwest?"

I said, "It's a whole other page on the map. Literally and figuratively. More important, it had no link to the Bedards. She was out to disentangle herself."

She closed the Thomas Guide. "One easy thing I can do tomorrow is find out who owned Whitbread's building back then. Myron's name shows up on the deed, I'm a little more receptive." She grimaced. "*She's* going to love that."

"Who?"

"Cruella. Much as it pains me to admit it, she was right. Finding and talking to her ex is a must-do. But if she calls me *young lady* again in that tone, I bitch-slap her to Canada."

We played with the computer for another hour, trying with no success to learn more about Moses Grant and Peterson Whitbread aka Blaise De Paine.

Petra said, "Boys, my eyes are crossing, let's kick it in."

I said, "One question: Tanya's danger level."

"If you're right about Peterson threatening Patty because of some deep dark secret, it's significant. How's her home security situation?"

Milo said, "Decent. I gave her the lecture and she seemed to get it. I also did a few pass-throughs on her street. Nothing iffy, so far."

"Nineteen years old and living alone," said Petra. "Don't know how I'd handle that. What exactly does she know about all of this?"

I said, "We told her about Jordan's murder. She wanted to know if it was linked to her mother and we said there was no direct evidence of that."

"She bought it?"

"Maybe."

"Well," she said, "if what we've tossed around tonight is remotely right-on, you're not going to be able to sell that story too much longer . . . you're seeing her in therapy, Alex?"

"No regular sessions, on an as-needed basis. How much do I tell her?"

Petra looked at Milo.

He said, "It's your homicide, Detective Connor."

"Hmm," she said. "I wouldn't want her knowing every investigative detail but she needs to understand enough not to be careless. Is there some other place she can live if she has to?"

"She has no other family," I said. "Claims she has friends."

"Claims? You think she's lying?"

"She says she studies with other students but she's never talked about any purely social relationships. And there's nothing in her home that smacks of college life."

"Sounds old before her time. Losing a parent can do that to you. You're wondering if the dam's going to break?"

"I'm keeping an eye on the water level."

"She's got one relationship," said Milo. "Kyle Bedard tracked her down in Facebook, claimed he got curious after we talked to him about when Tanya and Patty lived in his grandfather's house. We warned her about getting too involved, but you know kids."

"Think he's stalking her for an unhealthy reason?"

"Probably not, but who knows? That a fair assessment, Alex?"

I nodded.

"Another Bedard entanglement," said Petra. "Alex, maybe you should guide her away from him. Somehow get it across that this family seems to wrap its tentacles around everything."

"But give her no investigative details."

She exhaled and fooled with her hair. "We do have a moral duty to protect her but scaring the hell out of her for nothing can't be good for her mental health. Can she be trusted not to leak to Kyle or anyone else?"

"I think so."

"Then follow your instincts."

Milo said, "While you're talking to her, maybe you can find out if she's got any memories of Blaise De Paine."

"Will do."

Petra stood and rotated her neck. "Walk me to my chariot, gents."

The next morning at nine, I left a message for Tanya to call.

By one p.m. I still hadn't heard back. At ten after Milo phoned.

"Finally a bingo. When Patty moved into the duplex on Fourth, Mary Whitbread owned it, along with Whitbread's own building and two others nearby. But two years before, all the properties had been owned by the Bedard family trust."

"Myron sold them to her?"

"The trust did. The trustees were the old man and Myron."

"Did she get a bargain price?"

"Sweet deal for the mistress? I'm no expert but the numbers don't seem deflated, maybe Mary had her own source of dough. Your guess about Myron sending Patty over there is looking better. The other monumental finding is that the bullets excised from Leland Armbruster's corpse did *not* match Patty's gun."

"Small blessing."

He said, "Raul and Petra got in early to track Myron down in Europe. So far, zippo. The final autopsy results on Lester Jordan aren't too profound: method of death, strangulation, mode of death, homicide. Robert Fisk still hasn't surfaced and Petra can't find current addresses on Blaise De Paine or Moses Grant. But, hey, if life was too easy, we'd start thinking we were more than apes with thin pelts."

"No intelligent design for you?"

"Not when I read the newspaper."

"Blaise De Paine is potentially accessible," I said. "We know his mom."

"Petra's view on that—and I agree—is that revisiting Mary Whitbread right now would sound too many alarms and raise the risk of another vanishing felon. What I came up with is back-tracing the Hummer to an address, it's not a common vehicle. There's no such beast registered to De Paine or Peterson Whitbread, but he could be using another aka. I'm waiting for DMV to fax me a list of all Hummer registrations. In the meantime, I've been calling around at dealers, no luck, yet. Seeing as De Paine likes to make an impression, I wondered if it could be a rental and started with the Budget lot in Beverly Hills because they do all sorts of thrills-for-a-day, a couple of birthdays ago I rented Rick a Lamborghini. Gave him a backache, but that's another story. Unfortunately, the only black Hummer on their lot has been on long-term loan to a film outfit. The other three are silver, red, and there's a yellow convertible, talk about tasteful. I'm about to call Hertz."

"The yellow one sounds right for your next birthday."

"Oh, sure," he said. "Rhino drives a Bumblebee."

When Tanya hadn't gotten back by three, I tried her again.

"Oh. Hi." Soft voice, tense.

"Bad time?"

"No . . . I was actually going to call you. Mr. Fineman—Mommy's accountant—asked me to look for some tax records and I found something in the bottom of the drawer."

"What?"

"Um—I'm not sure what it means. Can I show it to you?"

"Of course. One thing you should know: Your mother's gun doesn't match to any known crime and has been ruled out in the case we told you about."

"That's great," she said. All the emotion of a cyborg.

"Everything okay, Tanya?"

"Yes . . . I was planning to leave for campus at five. I could drop by before then. If you're not busy."

"I'll be waiting."

"Is four thirty okay?"

"Perfect."

She clicked off midway through my good-bye.

CHAPTER

25

She arrived five minutes early, clutching a padded envelope. Gray knit gloves sheathed her hands though the weather was mild.

In the office, she tore the envelope flap, pulling out a photo and a sheet of lined paper folded twice over.

The snapshot showed Patty and Lester Jordan standing next to each other in the dirty-custard space that was Jordan's living room. His hair was dark, wispy, and plastered to his skull. His eyes bagged, his legs bowed. A gray sweatshirt provided bulk that fooled no one.

Patty's stocky body tilted toward Jordan, as if she was ready to break his fall.

Tanya unfolded the lined paper and handed it to me. The creases were grubby and the edges were fuzzy. A note in blue ballpoint printing read:

To the alleged Florence nightingale: I'm giving this back to you because you don't give a damn. I don't know why you think it's professionally ok to do what you did. The old bastard's rich, he can get anyone to change his diapers but who's going to walk me around and wake-shake if I need that? I can understand others being manipulated by that a-hole's $$$$$ but why you, Pat? You always said $$$$$ wasn't a big

deal to you. You always said honesty was everything, Pat. Obviously, all
that talk about honesty was just the usual bullshit like what they shovel
in all those fucking rehabs. Don't get me wrong, Pat, I'm not p.o.'d, I'm
HURT. Capital H. And you know where that leads with me, Pat. What
else am I supposed to do, Pat? And whose fault will it be if I fall hard,
Pat?

Enjoy the rest of your life.
Les

Tanya said, "He says he's not mad but that's *rage.* Do you believe
his arrogance? 'Wake and shake'? She got him through an overdose,
probably saved his life, so instead of being *grateful,* he *guilt-*trips her?
And that last part—'You know where that leads with me.' He's threatening to O.D. again, right? Implying it'll be her fault. How does someone get so *entitled*!"

I said, "That's an addict focusing on his own needs."

"He probably *became* an addict because he was selfish. And weak.
All those people who can't hold it *together.*"

Her cheeks were ripe cherries. Her shoulders had bunched so
sharply that her lapel rode up around her ears. She shook loose a tor-
rent of hair, grabbed a handful, and twisted.

I sat down, motioned for her to do the same. She didn't move, finally plopped on the couch.

"She did take excellent care of him," I said. "That's the reason
Kyle's father wanted her to care for his father."

"The 'A-hole with money.' Wasn't it his right to spend his money
any way he wants? The colonel was dying, Dr. Delaware. Caring for
him was *good* use of Mommy's time."

"Jordan wasn't."

"Look how he treated her, Dr. Delaware. You can't call that rant *rational.* I don't care what his problems were, there was no excuse. It's
not like he and Mommy were best friends. After seeing the picture, I
vaguely remember seeing him—didn't even know his name. *Kyle* barely
knew him. Jordan lucked out by having a highly skilled nurse as a
neighbor. When it was time to move on, he should've *thanked* her, not
threatened to mess himself up."

She slapped her knees. "I'm just so *tired* of people not being fair."

I said, "You're right. He should've been grateful."

"After all she did for him, from the bottom of her heart."

"Your mother was one of the kindest people I've ever met but we have learned that she got paid to look after Jordan."

"How do you know that?"

"Kyle's mother told us."

"Her."

"You know her?"

"Kyle told me what an incredibly self-centered person she is, never had time for him. Maybe it runs on that side of the family."

More hair-pulling. "Okay, she got paid. Why not? But that doesn't change things. It was Mommy's right to move on."

"Of course it was," I said. "So you and Kyle have been talking regularly."

"We hung out on campus a couple of times and yesterday we went to Coffee Bean. And I did ask him about Jordan but like I said, he barely knew him."

"Has he seen the note and the photo?"

"No. Do I have to keep it a secret?"

"For the time being, that might be a good idea. How does Kyle feel about his father?"

"He's okay with him. Why?"

"The detective investigating Jordan's murder wants to talk to any extended family she can find. She's been looking for Myron Bedard but hasn't been able to locate him. Supposedly, he's in Europe."

"He is," she said. "Paris. He called Kyle yesterday, offered to fly Kyle over, but Kyle's too busy with his dissertation. Why does the detective want to speak to extended family?"

"That's often where an investigation starts."

"I thought this was a drug murder."

"No one's sure what it is, Tanya."

She let out a long breath. "So she got paid. Why should she donate her time?"

"I didn't want to upset you—"

"You didn't. I appreciate the honesty. It means you respect my intelligence."

She got up and paced the office. Tried to straighten a picture that was waxed in place, sat and jabbed a finger at the photo. "What I don't get is why would she keep it all these years?"

"Maybe it meant something to her."

"You're saying she *did* feel guilty?"

"No, but she was a compassionate person," I said. "Jordan's pain could've touched her."

"I guess . . . I'm so angry. It's not a feeling I'm used to. I don't like it."

She buried her face in her hands. Looked up. "They're coming back—my symptoms. I feel like I'm losing control. The house is so quiet at night, it's worse than noise, I can't sleep. Last night I fooled with my curtains for half an hour and then I washed my hands till they got like this."

Tearing off a glove, she showed me knuckles rubbed raw.

I said, "We can work on all that."

"Can or should?"

"Should."

How do you feel about hypnosis?"

"I've never really thought about it."

"It's basically deep relaxation and focused concentration. You'd be good at it."

"I would? Why?"

"You're intelligent."

"I'm suggestible?"

I said, "All hypnosis is self-hypnosis. Receptivity is a skill that gets better with practice. Smart, creative people do the best because they're comfortable being imaginative. I think it's a good choice for you right now because you can get some quick results and go back to the excellent progress you made when you were a kid."

No answer.

"Tanya?"

"If you say so."

I began with rhythmic, deep breathing. After the third exhalation, she opened her eyes. "Where's Blanche?"

"Sleeping in her crate."

"Oh."

"Hold on." I fetched the dog, placed her on the couch next to Tanya. Tanya stroked the top of her head. We resumed the breathing exercise. Within moments, Tanya's body had started to loosen and Blanche was asleep, flews puffing and fluttering.

I counted backward from a hundred, using my induction mono-tone. Matched the rhythm of my voice to Blanche's snorts. By seventy-four, Tanya's lips had parted and her hands were still. I began inserting suggestions. Framing cues for each breath as an opportunity to relax.

At twenty-six, the light on my phone blinked.

I said, "Go deeper and deeper."

Tanya slumped. With the tension gone, she looked like a child.

So far, so good. If I didn't think too hard about the larger issues.

When an hour had passed, I gave her posthypnotic instructions for practice and prolonged relaxation and brought her out.

It took several tries for her eyes to stay open. "I feel . . . amazing . . . thank you. Was I hypnotized?"

"You were."

"It didn't feel . . . that strange. I wasn't sure I could do it."

"You're a natural."

Tanya yawned. Blanche followed suit. Tanya laughed, stretched, got to her feet. "Maybe one day you can hypnotize me to study better."

"Having problems concentrating?"

"No," she said quickly. "Not at all. I was kidding."

"Actually," I said, "being relaxed would help with exams."

"Seriously?"

"Yup."

"Okay, I'll remember that." She reached into her bag. "I'll practice every day—you did say something about that, right?"

"I did."

"It's a little . . . odd. I'm looking right at you but you're . . . close and distant at the same time. And I can still hear your voice in the back of my head. What else did you tell me to do?"

"Nothing else," I said. "You're in control, not me."

She rummaged in her purse. "Hmm . . . I know I've got a check here . . ."

"When would you like to come back?"

"Can I call you?" Extracting a white envelope, she placed it on the desk. "Signed and ready to go." Her eyes shifted to Jordan's letter and the photo. "You can keep them, I don't want them."

"I'll pass them along to Lieutenant Sturgis."

She stiffened. "Mommy helped him with his addiction, I don't see how that would relate to his murder."

"I don't, either, but he might as well keep all the data. I would like to schedule another session, Tanya."

"You really think so?"

"If money's an issue—"

"No, not at all, I'm doing great in that department, have kept right on budget."

"But . . ."

"Dr. Delaware, I appreciate everything you've done—are still doing for me. I just don't want to be too dependent."

"I don't see you as dependent, at all."

"I'm here, again."

"Tanya, how many nineteen-year-olds could do what you're doing?"

"I'm almost *twenty*," she said. "Sorry, thanks for the compliment. It's just that . . . look at Jordan. All that rage because he couldn't shake his dependency. Mommy taught me the importance of taking care of myself. I am *not* going to be one of them."

"Them?"

"Weak, self-pitying people. I can't *afford* to be that way."

"I understand. But all I see is someone smart enough to ask for help when she needs it."

"Thank you . . . I really feel I'm okay, what we did today was amazingly helpful." She shook her arms to demonstrate. "Rubber girl. I'll practice. If I forget something, I'll get right in touch."

I didn't answer.

"I promise," she said. "Okay?"

"Okay."

At the front door, she said, "Thanks for trusting me, Dr. Delaware. No need to walk me down."

I watched her descend to her van. She never looked back.

Monday, the blinking light was a message from my service. Detective Sturgis had phoned.

I told Milo about Lester Jordan's angry missive.

He said, "So the guy was an asshole, we saw that in person."

"Maybe it clarifies things. From the note it's clear that Patty helped him through an O.D., but there was no hint she supplied him with anything other than TLC."

He said, "Great. Meanwhile, the hills are alive with the sound of suspects. I located a three-year-old black Hummer registered to Quick-Kut Music, address on the fourteen hundred block of Oriole Drive. I'm meeting Petra in an hour at Sunset and Doheny—near Gil Turner's liquor store. Come fly with us, if you're so inclined."

The bird streets worm their way into the hills above the Strip, just east of Trousdale Estates, skinny, sinuous, haphazardly paved feats of engineering.

Mockingbird, Warbler, Thrasher, Skylark, Tanager.

Blue Jay Way, where George Harrison sat alone in a rental house, waiting for a press agent who'd made a wrong turn, staring out at a vast table of city shrouded by night and fog.

Easy to lose your way up there. Random cul-de-sacs and no-warning dead ends say someone in the city planner's office had enjoyed playing darts. Grades are treacherous and jogging's a life-threatening procedure due to the lack of sidewalks, Porsches and Ferraris buzzing the curb. The houses, many of them hidden behind hedges and walls, range from Palladian palaces to no-style boxes. They butt up against each other like rush-hour straphangers, teeter over the street. Squint a certain way on the bird streets and the hills seem to be trembling even when the ground is still.

The good part is heart-stopping views, some of the best in L.A., and seven- to eight-figure property values.

A twenty-eight-year-old music thief would need a serious income supplement to swing it and the obvious answer was dope. Despite that, I meant what I'd told Milo about Patty not being involved in the dope trade. Jordan's note was personal—rage at losing an emotional safety net, not concern about being cut off from his supply.

Patty's sin had been doing her job too well.

Yet she'd committed another iniquity, something serious enough to haunt her for years. And Lester Jordan had probably died because of it.

When I got to the liquor store, Milo stepped out of his unmarked, unfolding a map and wondering out loud if the topography of Oriole

Drive allowed a decent vantage spot. Taking the padded envelope without comment, he dropped it onto the passenger seat and returned to the map.

Petra drove up in her Accord.

The two of them studied the street grid, decided to park at the bottom of Oriole and walk. Petra's car would be the transport vehicle because it was unobtrusive.

"Not cool enough to be a local," she said, tapping the hood, "but maybe they'll think I'm a personal assistant."

She drove north on Doheny Drive, used her stick shift to keep it smooth.

Milo said, "Nice gear-work, Detective Connor."

"Had to drive better than my brothers."

"For self-esteem?"

"Survival."

Every second property seemed to be under construction or renovation, and the side effects abounded: dust, din, workers darting across the road, gouges in the asphalt inflicted by heavy machinery.

As we climbed, the houses got smaller and plainer, some of the punier ones obviously subdivides of old estates. Oriole Drive began with the thirteen hundred block. We parked at the base and began a steep upward hike.

Petra's long, lean legs were made for climbing and my self-punishing runs made the grade no big challenge. But Milo was panting and trying hard to hide it.

Petra kept an eye on him. He forged ahead of us. Wheezed, "You . . . know . . . CPR?"

She said, "Took a refresher last year but don't you dare, Lieutenant."

Glancing at me. I threw up my hands.

The scrape-scrape of his desert boots became our marching cadence.

A *No Outlet* sign appeared at the advent of the fourteen hundred block.

Fourteen sixty-two meant the top of the hill or close to it.

Milo gasped, "Oh, great." Rubbed his lower back and trudged.

We passed a huge white contemporary house, then several plain-faced fifties boxes. What the Orwellian dialect known as Realtor-Speak would euphemize as "midcentury charmers."

The part about "drop-dead views" would be righteous.

Milo pressed forward. Mopping his face with a handkerchief, he sucked in air and pointed.

Empty space where 1462 should've been.

What remained was a flat patch of brown dirt not much bigger than a trailer pad and surrounded by chain link. The gate was open. A construction permit packet hung on the fence.

A man stood at the far end of the lot, a few feet from the precipice, staring out at smoggy panorama.

Milo and Petra checked nearby vehicles. The closest was a gold BMW 740, parked at the crown of the cul-de-sac.

"Car's not much bigger than the property," he said. "L.A. affluence."

Petra said, "That's why I don't paint landscapes."

Unmindful of us, the man lit a cigarette, gazed, and smoked.

Milo coughed.

The man turned.

Petra waved.

The man didn't return the gesture.

We walked onto the lot.

He lowered his cigarette and watched us.

Early forties, five eight or nine, with heavy shoulders, bulky arms and thighs, and a hard, round belly. A square, swarthy face was bottomed by an oversized chin. He wore a pale blue dress shirt with French cuffs, chunky gold cufflinks shaped like jet planes, sharply creased navy slacks, black croc loafers grayed by dust. The top button of the shirt was undone. Gray chest hair bristled and a gold chain nestled in the pelt. A thin red string circled his right wrist. A beeper and a cell phone hung from his waistband.

Wraparound Ray-Bans blocked the windows to his soul. The rest of his face was a tight mask of distrust.

"This is private property. If you want a free view, go to Mulholland."

Petra flashed the badge.

"Police? What, he's gone crazy?"

"Who, sir?"

"Him. Troupe, the lawyer." Cocking his head toward the house to the south. "I keep telling him, all the permits are in order, there's nothing you gonna *do* about it."

Some kind of accent—familiar but I couldn't place it.

"Now, what, he's again yelling about the noise? We graded a week ago, how can you grade without noise?"

"We're not here about that, Mr. . . ."

"Avi Benezra. Then what do you want?"

I got the accent. A few years ago, we'd worked with an Israeli police superintendent named Daniel Sharavi. Benezra's inflections were harsher, but similar.

Petra said, "We're looking for the residents of 1462."

Benezra removed his glasses, revealed soft, hazel eyes, squinting in amusement. "Ha, ha. Very funny."

"Wish we were trying to be, sir."

"The residents? Maybe worms and bugs." Benezra laughed. "Who's your intelligence source? The CIA?"

"How long has the house been gone, sir?"

"A year." Thumb curl toward the neighboring house. "Troupe had quiet for a year so he got spoiled."

"Fussy guy?"

"Fussy asshole," said Benezra. "A *lawyer.*"

"Is he home?"

Avi Benezra said, "Never home. That's why he's crazy to complain. Maybe you can tell him to stop bothering me. You know why he's mad? He wanted to buy it, put a pool on it. But he didn't want to pay what it's *worth.* Now I don't *wanna* sell. Gonna build for myself. Why not?" He waved at the view. "It's gonna be something, all glass, views to Palos Verdes."

"Gorgeous," said Petra.

"It's what I do," said Benezra. "I build, I'm a builder. Why not finally for me?"

"So you tore down the house a year ago?"

"No, no, no, a year ago is empty. I tore down five *months* ago and right away he's driving me nuts, that bastard, complain to the zoning board, the mayor." Spiraling a finger toward his temple. "Finally, I get the okay."

"How long have you owned the property, Mr. Benezra?"

Benezra grinned. "You interested in buying?"

"I wish."

"I buy five years ago, house was a piece of crap but *that*!" Another flourish at the view.

He smoked, shaded his eyes with his hand, gazed up at a jetliner climbing from Inglewood. "I'm gonna use as much glass as they let me with the new energy rules. I just finished building a gorgeous Mediterranean on Angelo Drive, nine thousand square feet, marble, granite, home theater, I'm ready to sell. Then my *wife* decides she wants to live in it. Okay, why not? *Then,* I get divorce and she gets the house. What, I should *fight*?"

"Have you ever rented to a man named Blaise De Paine?"

"Oh, boy," said Benezra. "That one. Yeah, he was the last."

"Problem tenant?"

"You call trashing every room and not paying a problem? To me, that's a problem. My fault. I broke the rules, got *clucked*."

Petra said, "Clucked?"

"I'm talking polite to a lady."

She laughed. "Which rules did you break?"

"Avi's rules. Two months in advance, plus damage deposit up front. Him I let go one month, no deposit. Stupid, I shoulda known better, the way he looked."

"How'd he look?"

"Rock and roll," said Benezra. "The hair, you know. But he was recommended."

"By who?"

Benezra put his shades back on. "A guy."

"Which guy, sir?"

"This is important?"

"It might be."

"What'd he do?"

"Who referred him?" said Petra.

"Listen," said Benezra, "I don't want no problems."

"If you haven't done anything—"

"I didn't do *nothing*. But this guy who referred him, he's a little famous, you know?"

"Who, sir?"

"I don't know nothing about his problems."

"Whose problems, sir?"

Benezra sniffed the air, smoked greedily. "What I hired him for was legal. What he did for other people, I don't wanna know."

"Sir," said Petra, "who are we *talking* about?"

"A guy I hired."

"To do what?"

"Watch the wife. She wants the house on Angelo, nine thousand square feet, she can roll around in it, fine, okay. She wants the jewelry, okay. But my boat? Properties I had before I met her? Very very very *not* okay. I knew what she was doing with you-know-who, maybe this guy can prove it, she don't get too pushy."

"We've got no-fault divorce in California."

"That's the official stuff," said Benezra. "But she got the fancy friends, the fund-raisers, lunch at Spago. Not gonna look good everyone knows she's not so perfect. I hired him to get the evidence."

"We're talking a private investigator."

"Yeah."

"Because your wife . . ."

"You're a woman. What do you think she did?"

"Slept around?"

"Not *around*. One *guy,* her *eye* doctor." Tapping a black lens. "I pay ten thousand for LASIK so she don't have to wear contact lenses, no more *itchy* itchy. She pay me back by getting another kinda treatment." Chuckling.

"It's good you can laugh about it," said Petra.

"What, I should get an ulcer?"

"What's the name of the private detective?"

"The famous one," said Benezra. "Fortuno."

"Mario Fortuno."

"Yeah. He still in jail?"

"As far as I've heard, sir."

"Good. He took my money, did nothing. The other stuff, I have no idea."

"Did Fortuno say how he knew Blaise De Paine?"

Benezra ticked a finger. "A friend of a friend of a friend of a friend. 'But he's okay, Avi, trust me.'" He laughed louder. "Maybe I missed one of the friends."

"What else did Fortuno tell you about De Paine?"

"Nothing else, I was stupid, but I figured a guy like that, he's working for me, why would he cluck me? I even gave discount rent because the place was crap, it was gonna get tear-down soon." Swiveling back toward the view. "Lookit that."

Petra showed him one of the party photos taken off the Internet. "Is this the person we're talking about?"

"That's him. What'd he do?"

Moses Grant's DMV shot produced a head shake. "Him I never seen. What, a gangster from Watts?"

Robert Fisk's mug shot evoked raised eyebrows. "*That* one was here, seen him at least a coupla times. Maybe living here, even though the deal was only one person, we're talking six hundred square feet, one bedroom, one bath. Used to be the garage of that bastard's place back in the fifties, he buys two years ago, thinks everything should go back together but don't wanna pay market. He drives me so crazy, I was going to leave green space but *forget* it, it's gonna go *inches* from the property line."

Petra waved Fisk's image. "What makes you think this person was living here?"

"One time, I come for the rent, he was the *only* one in the house. No shirt on, crazy tattoos, doing exercises in front of the window—on a mat, you know? Judo, karate, something like that, clothes and crap all around. I try to make chat. I learned krav maga—Israeli-style karate—in the army. He said yeah, he knows it, then he shuts his eyes and goes back to breathing in and out and stretching the arms. I say sorry to bother you but what's with the rent. He says he don't know nothing, just visiting. Those tattoos, all over here"—touching his own chest—"and up to the neck. He's a bad guy?"

"We'd like to talk to him. What else can you tell us about De Paine and Mario Fortuno?"

"That's it." Benezra looked at his watch. "I hire him to find out about her. He tells me she's clucking the eye doctor, thank you very much, big-shot detective. That I already know because she sees twenty–twenty and she keeps making appointments."

Shaking his head. "Thirteen thousand dollars for that, thank you very much. He should *rot* in jail."

Milo said, "So he never followed through?"

"Always excuses," said Benezra. "It takes *time,* Avi. We need to make sure it's gonna be bona fide *evidence,* Avi. The eye doctor's office is *locked,* Avi, maybe it's gonna cost a little *more,* Avi."

A wide smile nearly bisected his face. "I finally figure out I'm being clucked twice. Now I'm thinking maybe sue my divorce lawyer—he's the one sent me to Fortuno. I call him, he tells me Fortuno ripped him off, too."

"How?"

"Hired him to write some documents, didn't pay."

"The lawyer's name, please."

"Oy," said Benezra. "This is getting complicated. Okay, why not, I'm finished with him. Marvin Wallace, Roxbury and Wilshire."

Benezra took a last drag of his cigarette, pinched it out, flicked it across the lot. "Always excuses for not doing the job, Fortuno. Finally he's got a good one."

"What's that?" said Petra.

"The one you guys gave him. You put him in jail."

CHAPTER

27

We left Benezra worshipping his view and descended Oriole Drive.

Petra phoned Captain Stuart Bishop and filled him in, then clicked off. "He'll make calls, but wants a meeting."

"When?" said Milo.

"As soon as we get back to Hollywood."

"We?"

"You and me, Stu's big on interdivisional communication." She turned to me: "Your attendance is optional but certainly welcome. He said to thank you for helping his nephew."

Last year the preschool-aged son of Bishop's younger sister had been frightened by the evening news. Well-adjusted boy; a few sessions had been enough.

Confidentiality meant all I could do was smile.

Petra smiled back. "I thought you might say that."

The captain's office at Hollywood Division was a spare, white corner space livened by school art created by the six towheaded Bishop kids and masses of family photos. A white BYU Cougars mug shared a credenza with a case of Trader Joe's bottled water. A window cracked two inches blew in air and heat and street noise.

Stu was a slim, closely shaven man around forty with searching gold eyes and wavy blond hair gone gray at the temples. He wore braided leather suspenders over a tapered pink shirt, a turquoise silk tie, glen plaid suit pants, glossy wingtips. A matching suit jacket hung on a bentwood rack. He reached for a water, offered us our own bottles. Milo accepted.

The son of an affluent Flintridge Mormon family, Stu had left the department while still a D III, cutting short a fast-track career to care for a wife with cancer. Kathy Bishop recovered but Stu stayed with corporate security work and occasional film consulting until he was wooed back as a captain by the new chief.

The new chief was a new golf buddy of Stu's ophthalmologist father but few people carped. The amoral misanthrope Stu replaced had been shot to death by a jealous wife in a parking garage; three cops had attended the funeral, all out of obligation. Combine that with Stu's street experience, his rep for backing up his colleagues, and an ability to work the brass without wholesaling his soul, and the honeymoon seemed durable.

As Stu's former junior partner, Petra was in good shape for a promotion into administration. So far, she was sticking with detective work.

He filled his mug with water, sipped, and leaned back in his chair. "Your timing couldn't be better, in terms of leaning on Fortuno. He's become a person of exceptional interest to the federal government and no one wants a trivial matter like murder to get in the way. We're not talking public knowledge but I called San Luis Obispo where he's officially incarcerated, found out he was picked up a month ago by FBI agents and a U.S. Attorney and transferred to the downtown detention center. When I called *there,* I got a bunch of silence then a referral to the Feebie office at the Federal Building. A special agent I know played coy but finally let on that Fortuno's been spending the month in a hotel at taxpayer expense."

Milo said, "Spilling big-time."

"I can only imagine."

Petra said, "Thought Fortuno was into all that code of silence stuff."

Milo said, "A little cell time can adjust your attitude."

"You bet," said Stu. "Assistant warden at San Luis said he bumped up against some genuine bad guys."

Petra said, "I thought San Luis was a country club."

"They've got tennis courts and dorm rooms, but it's still prison. The idiots who kidnapped the Chowchilla school bus are up there and so's Charleton Jennings."

Milo said, "Cop killers get to play tennis?"

"They do after they work their way through the system for thirty years."

Cop silence, all around.

Petra said, "Did you get any idea about who Fortuno's going to spill on?"

"I got off-the-record semi-hints," said Stu. "If my religion allowed me to bet, my wager would be on master manipulators of the defense attorney and showbiz honcho species."

Milo whistled. "Straight to the top of the food chain."

Stu said, "It's definitely going to get interesting. Fortuno's baby-sitters aren't pleased about sharing him with us but they can't risk us derailing them by leaking to the press. The deal is you can see him tonight at seven, one hour, no extensions. I put all three of your names down, figuring you might want Dr. D to analyze the guy."

I said, "A hotel means a couch, why not."

Petra said, "Which hotel?"

"Don't know yet. Someone will call me at six and I'll call you."

She waved her hands. "Ooh, high intrigue."

Stu said, "Helps federal types forget that mostly what they do is push paper." Passing the flat of his hand over his own clean desk, he grinned. "As opposed to."

Petra said, "Anytime you miss the gore."

"Be careful what you ask for." Stu stood, shrugged into his suit jacket. Smooth drape. "Got a budget meeting downtown. Talk to you at six, Petra. Good to see *you* guys."

He held the door for us. As I passed through, he said, "I know you can't say anything, but thanks again for Chad."

Loews Beverly Hills was the usual case of Westside false advertising, located on Pico and Beverwil, half a mile south of the glitzy city. We took separate cars, parked with the valet, met in the lobby.

The same earth tones we'd seen at the Hilton.

Petra's artist eyes picked up on it right away. "Welcome to Beige World, check your imagination at the door."

No one paid us any attention as we crossed to the elevators. No sign of any special security, and when we were disgorged on the eleventh floor, the corridor was clear.

Petra's knock on the door of Suite 1112 was met by silence. Then, padded footsteps. A chain held the door less than an inch ajar. Barely wide enough to see the expanding pupil of a light brown eye.

"I.D.," said a boyish voice.

Petra showed her badge.

"Everyone's."

Milo flashed his credentials. My snap-on badge produced a "What's that?" but no comment on the expiration date.

"Dr. Delaware is our behavioral consultant," said Petra.

"This isn't a profile case," said the voice.

Another voice, from behind, shouted, "Let 'em in, I'm *lonely*."

The door slammed shut. Muffled voices rose in pitch, then silenced.

We stood in the hall.

Milo said, "Shoulda brought my Aston Martin with the ejection seat, shot myself right through the goddamn win—"

The door opened wide. A young sandy-haired man in a gray suit, white shirt, and blue tie said, "Special Agent Wesley Wanamaker." His face matched the boyish voice. He took another look at our I.D.'s, finally stepped back.

Two-bedroom suite, with nary a hue brighter than ecru. Ambiguous art dotted easy-care walls. Blackout drapes killed an eastern view Avi Benezra would've appreciated. The air was saturated with pizza and sweat. A greasy Domino box sat on an end table.

A pale, white-haired man waved from a stiff beige couch in the center of the living room. Sixty or so, narrow shoulders, widow's hump bristling the hairs on the back of his neck. He wore a black cashmere V-neck, cream slacks that looked new, black Gucci loafers without socks. In his hand was a glass of something orange. As we approached, he winked at Petra and the same voice that had urged our admission said, "Long time, guys. And gal."

Petra said, "Real long time, Mr. Fortuno. As in ever."

Mario Fortuno said, "When you're in love, everyone's your friend."

"Well then, since we're all buddies, I'm sure you'll be happy to tell us what we need to know about Peterson Whitbread aka—"

S.A. Wesley Wanamaker stepped between her and Fortuno. "Before we go any further, we need to get the rules straight. Mr. Fortuno is a convicted felon in custody of the FBI. As such, his movements and conversations are to be monitored at all times by the FBI. No inquiries regarding pending federal investigations will be allowed. You will have one hour to speak with Mr. Fortuno about approved topics . . ." Unbuttoning his coat, he drew out a pocket watch. ". . . three minutes of which have passed. Acknowledged?"

"Yessir," said Petra.

Behind Wanamaker's back, Milo mouthed, "Asshole."

When Wanamaker turned to face him, he said, "Ditto, Agent W."

"Doctor," said Wanamaker, "I need explicit acknowledgment from you, as well, seeing as you're serving in the service of local law enforcement."

"I acknowledge."

Mario Fortuno said, "Do you believe this guy? Like I'm important."

Wanamaker's hand drew back his coat and revealed his shoulder weapon. Another eye flick at his watch: "Four minutes gone."

Petra said, "May we start?"

Wanamaker stepped away. Fortuno picked his nose.

No chairs in sight, so we stood in front of him. His jaunty smile was dimmed by green-tinged jailhouse pallor. His white hair was thin, greased back, curling behind his ears. Puny, pocked chin, a bulb nose embroidered with gin blossoms. Squinty, hyperactive eyes the color of cigar ash were dragged down by pouches of skin. He fooled with his nose again, ground his index finger against his thumb.

Another lazy smile, off kilter and saurine. The offspring of a human-iguana mating.

Petra said, "Mr. Fortuno, we're here about Peterson Whitbread aka Blaise De Paine. Please tell us everything you know about him."

"Who says I'm cognizant of anything?" said Fortuno. Flat, midwestern inflection. Hint of emphasis on "cognizant." As if he'd just memorized the word.

"You recommended him for tenancy at a house on Oriole Drive."

"When was this?"

"Shortly before you went to jail."

"Boy, my mind must be slipping." Fortuno pointed at the pizza box. "Maybe too many carbs."

Petra turned to Wanamaker.

He said, "Nonfederal matters don't fall under compliance regulations."

"Meaning," Milo said, "he can jerk us around while you time us."

Fortuno said, "God forbid."

Petra said, "If you're going to be uncooperative, Mario, let us know right now and we're out of here."

Fortuno tensed. Forced a smile. "A feminist."

Petra turned heel. We followed.

When she reached the door, Fortuno said, "Ease up. There's no free lunch."

Milo said, "Spoken by someone getting federal babysitting at a four-star hotel."

Wesley Wanamaker frowned.

Fortuno said, "Don't fret, Ms. Pro-Choice. I don't want a meal, just an *amuse-bouche*—that's 'hors d'oeuvre' in French. And I'm not talking The Ivy or Le Dome or Hans Rockenwagner's place, I love that place."

Wanamaker said, "Food again? We've been through this. Our per diem budget is preset and no one but the FBI is authorized to—"

"I'm not talking cuisine, Mr. *Literal*." To us: "These guys have no clue about metaphors and similes."

"An English major," said Milo.

"Journalism," said Fortuno. "City College of Chicago, did a year until all the perfidy and falsehood got to me."

Petra touched the doorknob.

Fortuno said, "I'm crushed. You just got here."

She turned the knob and had a foot out in the hall when Fortuno said, "Let me talk to the shrink."

S.A. Wanamaker said, "The door must remain closed at all times."

Petra said, "No solo interviews, Mario."

"Oh boy, *another* literal one," said Fortuno. "What is it, all the TV and video games and microwaves in the brain, no one reads the classics anymore?" He waved. "Come back, honey, don't let me rile you, I'm really a sociable person."

"Plastique and machine guns in your office is sociable?"

S.A. Wanamaker said, "That topic is off limits, Officer."

Fortuno's arrest had been in the papers for weeks.

"Close the door, Officer."

Petra complied, shot Fortuno a long, dark look.

Fortuno said, "You've got gorgeous melting eyes. No offense, I'm avuncular not lecherous. What I'm trying to get across here is I can possibly offer you some satisfaction vis-à-vis your subject. But the shrink's the one who can make *me* happy."

Wanamaker said, "Nine minutes down."

Petra ignored him and moved closer to Fortuno. "You can *possibly* help us?"

"Let's upgrade to probably."

"What do you want from Dr. Delaware?"

"Come closer, dear," said Fortuno. "Conversing so far away makes my throat hurt. All the artificial coolants in the AC system, dries up the sinuses, they won't let me open the window. Or the curtains, I'm living like a gopher."

Wanamaker said, "It's dark, anyway. Stop complaining."

Petra said, "How do I know you can help us?"

Fortuno said, "How's this: The individual under question is a no-talent punk kid who purloins other people's songs and cobbles them together in what the popular parlance terms 'mixes.'"

The three of us returned to our former positions facing the couch.

Fortuno said, "Dr. Alexander Delaware, you've got street cred for helping kids. Anxieties, phobias—I like that paper you published on sleep problems. Could've used that with a few of mine, I have eight. From five wives, but that's another story. *Journal of Nervous and Mental Disease*—July, five years ago. Is my memory serving me well?"

My name had been given to the feds a few hours ago. Fortuno had managed to research me.

I said, "What can I do for you?"

"One of my progeny, the youngest, Philip, he's six. Quiet, a very quiet boy, know what I mean?"

"Shy?"

"That, too. Extremely *quiet*. Sits and draws, doesn't go outside to play, doesn't like sports. His mother's young, not too experienced in the parent department. With Philip, she's a pushover, spoils him completely. He used to go to private school but now he's in public school, due to the fact that I'm temporarily inconvenienced financially. Am I making myself lucid?"

"Philip's having problems in his new school."

"The other kids," said Fortuno, "do not appear to appreciate him. In public school, you've got some tough little rats. A tough kid—a resilient kid—could cope. Philip, being *quiet,* does not cope so well. If I was there, perhaps I could aid him, but I am not and that makes me feel regretful. His mother tells me Philip comes home crying. Sometimes he doesn't sleep well." Throat clear. "He has also started to have . . . accidents. Number one *and* number two. Which does not help his popularity with his peer group. I, being out of the picture, feel partially culpable for all this. Then I find out you will be visiting and lo and behold I experience epiphanization: Saint Agnes has sent me someone who can help the problem."

"I'll be happy to see Philip."

"As I said, my financial resources are limited. However, I do see that changing some time in the future and when that time comes you'll be recompensed ably."

"I understand."

Fortuno clapped his hands, as if summoning a servant. "Excellent. When will you see Philip?"

"Have his mom call me."

"She will do that. They live in Santa Barbara."

"That's ninety miles away. Maybe the best thing would be for me to find you a referral there."

Fortuno's mouth tightened and his eyes were black lines. "Maybe not."

"It's a long drive for a young chi—"

"*You* drive to *Philip,*" he said. "When I am in a position to do so, I will compensate you for your fuel and your time—portal-to-portal, like what lawyers get. Like what *I* used to get. I'm not talking long-term Freudian or Jungian psychoanalysis. One visit, maybe two, three four— a consultation. In one of those articles you wrote, you said a lot of child therapy can be done short-term. *Journal of Clinical and Consulting*—"

"I can't guarantee that in every case, Mr. Fortuno."

"I'm not asking for a guarantee, Dr. Delaware. Two sessions, maybe three, four. After that, if you feel Philip's needs are best served by a local expert, I will accept that. But *you* start the ball rolling, Dr. Delaware. Meet my son face-to-face and give me feedback. He's a very *quiet* boy."

"Okay," I said.

Another clap. "Excellent. When?"

"Have his mother call me."

"Give me something more specific." An order, not a request. He sat up straighter, buoyed by the shred of control.

"Have her call and I promise I'll drive up and meet with Philip as soon as I can," I said. "You've done what you can, the rest is up to her."

Fortuno breathed in sharply. "She will call you soon. Perhaps Philip can come visit you at that nice pretty white house. See those pretty fish in your pond."

My gut tightened. "Happy to show them to him."

Petra said, "Enough small talk."

28

Blaise De Paine," said Mario Fortuno. "Rotten kid."

"How so?"

"I do not approve of thievery. However . . ." Throat clear. ". . . in the course of my profession, I am forced to deal with individuals of dubious morality. Much the same as it is with you, Detectives." To me: "You, too, given your long association with law enforcement. My Philip will be a breath of fresh air."

Petra said, "What business did you do with De Paine?"

"His profession, such as it is, places him at various clubs and the like. Many of these nightspots feature so-called VIP lounges where inhibitions are relaxed, not to mention lavatories equipped surreptitiously with peepholes and hidden cameras by individuals of dubious ethics."

"He sold you incriminating pictures of celebrities."

Wanamaker said, "Be careful."

"Wesley, I owe these good people *something*."

"Be careful."

Fortuno sighed. "Skirting some paper-thin ice here, what I believe I can tell you within the bounds of Special Agent Wanamaker's approval is that Mr. De Paine found himself in possession of data concerning various individuals of interest to me for reasons I cannot and will not get into."

"Does he also sell drugs?" said Petra.

Fortuno glanced at Wanamaker. The agent was silent. "If he did, I would not be shocked. However, I have no firsthand knowledge of such transactions and, in fact, possess a strong aversion to toxic substances as they de-oxidify the body." Hoisting the orange juice. "Vitamin C."

"Which substances does De Paine peddle?"

"I'd term his activities . . . eclectic."

"Heroin?"

"It would not shock me."

"Cocaine?"

"Same answer."

"Ecstasy?"

"Detective Connor," said Fortuno, "the young man in question is enterprising. A type I'm sure we're both familiar with."

"What type is that?"

"The me generation. So many of them yearn for stardom but lack talent. Not to mention a moral core."

Petra said, "What did you give De Paine for his information?"

Wanamaker waved a finger. "Uh-uh."

"Did you trade him personal data for narcotics?"

Wanamaker said, "Change the subject, Detective."

Fortuno's cheeks quivered. "Wesley, throughout my relationship with you, your colleagues and your superiors, has anyone—*anyone*—come across a shred of evidence suggesting my active association with narcotics other than helping children of clients get clean and sober?"

Wanamaker looked at his watch.

Petra said, "How long were you and De Paine in business?"

"Awhile," said Fortuno.

"Months or years?"

"The latter."

"How many years?"

"I'd have to check my records."

"Take a wild guess."

"Five's a nice round number."

"What about Robert Fisk?"

"Who would that be, Detective?"

"A known associate of De Paine." Petra showed Fortuno the mug shot.

"He looks like an extremely resentful person. Bad eyes . . . is he De Paine's conduit for violence?"

"Why would you ask that?"

"Because De Paine is a sissy who avoids confrontation. Because you didn't take time out from your busy day to visit me due to a shoplifting violation."

"You don't know Fisk."

"Never heard of him, never laid eyes on him."

"What about Moses Grant?" Flashing the DMV shot.

Fortuno said, "This person I *have* witnessed in De Paine's company. I believe De Paine termed him his disk jockey. Another would-be music person. If you call that music."

"Call what?"

"In less enlightened times, what would've been termed jungle rhythms. Being a Chicago person, Sinatra is more to my taste."

"Sinatra was from New Jersey."

"His music is esteemed in Chicago."

"Tell me about Moses Grant."

"I have seen him in the company of Mr. De Paine several times—three or four times. He never spoke in my presence. My impression was he was a lackey. I believe I saw him driving Mr. De Paine's car."

"What kind of vehicle?"

"Two vehicles, to be precise. One of those gas-guzzling Hummers and a Lexus sedan. The Lexus belongs to Mr. De Paine's mother."

"Mary Whitbread."

Fortuno chuckled.

"What's funny?" said Petra.

"How she came to call herself that."

"You know her."

"That," said Fortuno, "is quite a story."

"We've got time."

Wanamaker said, "Forty-one minutes to be exact."

Fortuno removed a loafer, slipped a finger between his toes, dug and scratched, produced something that seemed to intrigue him.

Petra said, "Mary Whitbread."

"Her given name is Maria Baker. Her hometown is Chicago."

"Old neighbor?" said Petra.

"We grew up in different neighborhoods. I became acquainted with Maria through my activities in law enforcement."

"You were a cop?"

"I contemplated becoming one. Only briefly, all the perfidy and corruption . . . no offense, assorted gendarmes, but Chicago was quite a city back then and sometimes it was difficult to differentiate the good guys from the miscreants."

"What was your association with the cops?"

"I did some security consulting to various political figures. Occasionally that led me to interface with your Windy City counterparts. Because of my familiarity with various individuals of Italian ancestry—"

"Uh-uh, nope," said Wanamaker.

"Wesley," said Fortuno, "at some point you need to develop a sense of trust. I have no intention of breaching our agreement, if for no other reason than a breach would not be in my best interests. The events that interest Detective Connor predate any you'd be concerned with and I am simply providing context—"

"Provide it another way."

Fortuno drew back his lips, scratched pale, pink gum. "I met Maria Baker over thirty years ago."

"Where?" said Petra.

"If my recollection serves me well, the first time was at a club called The Hi Hat. Maria danced there, as well as at other nighteries." Lizard-smile. "Sans clothing. The Hat and the others were owned by various individuals of . . . a certain Mediterranean descent. From time to time, Maria became romantically entangled with some of these various individuals as well as with other individuals."

"Other?"

Fortuno smiled. "Comedians, drummers, assorted riffraff. Maria was rather . . . easy to please. Unfortunately, there came a time when one of the individuals—of a certain descent—became deceased in a highly non-natural manner and Maria Baker became concerned for her personal safety. I, having just moved to Los Angeles, and through my associations with law enforcement in both cities, was able to facilitate her passage here. Maria took well to the climate. Meteorologically and professionally."

"The profession being stripping."

"As well as other aspects of show business."

Milo said, "She became a casting agent."

Fortuno broke into laughter.

"What's funny?" said Petra.

"Who told you that?"

"She did."

"Maria, Maria," said Fortuno. Humming a few bars from the *West Side Story* tune. "*That* was music, Leonard Bernstein . . . Detectives, the primary aspect of casting that Maria Baker ever encountered was removing her clothing for gentlemen in Canoga Park."

"Porn actress?" said Petra.

"I'm sure none of us are devotees of the genre," said Fortuno. "However, we all know that the real Hollywood *is* Canoga Park."

"Mary Whitbread was her stage name? That doesn't sound too sexy."

"The genre relies upon clichés, Detective. Or used to, back when the product was shown in theaters and plots were believed essential. One common motif is the innocent maid debauched. One rather successful film was a full-length feature titled *Losing Her Innocence.* The story line was hackneyed but effective. A Victorian chambermaid travels to London and is seduced by lords and dukes and the like."

"The maid was Mary Whitbread."

"Thirty years ago," said Fortuno, "she had girl-next-door looks. The director thought she was so perfect that he used her real name as the basis for her *nom de film.*"

"Baker to Whitbread."

Fortuno closed his eyes. "The essence of wide-eyed Victorian purity. Even as her orifices were explored."

"Who was the director?"

"A gentleman named Salvatore Grasso. Deceased."

"In a highly unnatural manner?"

"If you consider a stroke unnatural."

"Wide-eyed purity," said Milo. "You're a fan of her work."

"On the contrary, Lieutenant Sturgis. It bores me." Half shutting his lids. "As I'm sure it does *you.*"

"Did your relationship with Mary ever turn personal?"

"With me," said Fortuno, "everything is personal." Turning away from Milo he faced Petra and leered. "Did I *fuck* her?"

She didn't budge.

"The answer is yes. I *fucked* her. I fucked her at will, every which way, on numerous occasions. That doesn't make me the member of an exclusive club. Nor was the relationship emotional."

"Casual sex."

"Your generation didn't invent it, dear."

"Tell us about the relationship."

"I just did."

"You helped her move to L.A., set her up in the porn business, and sampled the wares."

"I didn't set her up. I introduced her to various individuals. My sampling of the wares was by mutual consent."

"Blaise De Paine is twenty-eight. You've known him since he was born."

"I have."

"What can you tell us about him?"

"Nothing more than I already have."

"What's the relationship between De Paine and his mother like."

"Such as it is."

"They don't get along?"

"Mary probably thinks she's a wonderful mother."

"She isn't?"

"Actresses," said Fortuno. "It's all about *them.*"

"Who's his father?"

Fortuno held up his palms.

"There's something you *don't* know?" said Petra.

"There are many, many things I don't know, Detective Connor. In this case, paternity would be difficult to ascertain. As I said, Mary was eclectic."

"Was?"

"I haven't had contact with her in a while."

"Why's that?"

"She lost her interest in courtesanship and found a substitute passion."

"What's that?" said Petra.

"Real estate. She owns buildings, collects rent, believes that makes her nobility."

"How'd she get the money to buy buildings?"

"The old-fashioned way," said Fortuno. "She *fucked* for it."

"Any person in particular?"

"Quite the opposite."

"How about some names of her benefactors?"

Wanamaker said, "How about not."

Petra said, "We don't care about any of the creeps he's going to spill on, unless they've been involved in murder."

"Same answer," said Wanamaker.

"Whose murder?" said Fortuno.

"A man named Lester Jordan."

Fortuno didn't react, but holding still seemed to take effort. "Don't know him."

"You're sure about that."

"Couldn't be surer."

"Boy," said Petra, "here we were thinking you were the Human Rolodex and look at all these holes in the data bank."

Fortuno reached for his nose again. Picked with gusto.

"Life," he said, "can be disillusioning."

"Who else did De Paine hang out with?"

"I don't pay attention to who punks hang out with."

"You don't like him."

"He's got no—"

"Moral core, I know," said Petra. "As opposed to all your other vendors and clients."

"Knowledge is power, Detective. I provide a legitimate service."

"The federal government seems to feel otherwise."

Wanamaker cleared his throat.

Petra said, "De Paine trashed the place he rented from Mr. Benezra and he cut out on several months' rent."

"That does not surprise me."

"You knew he was a mope but you gave him references?"

"Mr. Benezra asked me to help find a short-term tenant at a run-down property he planned to demolish imminently. I happened to be speaking to Mary and she happened to mention that her son was looking for lodgings."

"Thought you hadn't seen her in a while?"

"She called me."

"Why?"

"To help find lodgings for her son."

"Where was he living at the time?"

"That she didn't say."

"Mary Whitbread owns properties," said Petra. "Why would her son need to look for lodgings?"

"You'd have to ask her that."

"She didn't want him close by?"

Fortuno said, "That's certainly possible."

"He's caused trouble for her."

"I'm not aware of any specifics, but once again, it wouldn't—"

"The notion of his being involved in murder doesn't shock you."

"I am *un*shockable, Detective."

"Where did De Paine live after he left the house on Oriole Drive?"

Long, slow head shake. White strands came loose and Fortuno tamped them back in place. "I've told you all I know."

Petra waited.

Fortuno drank orange juice.

Wanamaker reached for his pocket watch.

Petra said, "I know, the big hand's on bureaucracy and the little hand's on bureaucracy." To Fortuno: "Give us something else about Blaise De Paine."

Fortuno finished his juice, wiped his lips with the back of his sleeve. Wiped the sleeve on the couch and flicked pulp off a cushion.

"If you were us, Mario, where would you look for him?"

"Hmm," said Fortuno. "I'd say *Cherchez la femme*. That's French for 'women are slicker than men.' In this case, *la mamacita*."

"Multilingual," said Milo.

"Women love adroitness with language, Lieutenant. Not that such matters would concern *you*. Wesley, I do believe it's time for my supper. Dr. Delaware, when you see Philip, tell him Daddy loves him."

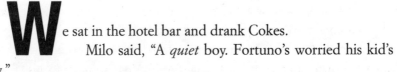 e sat in the hotel bar and drank Cokes.

Milo said, "A *quiet* boy. Fortuno's worried his kid's gay."

Petra said, "That's what he meant?"

His reply was half a smile.

She said, "Thanks for agreeing to see the kid, Alex."

"Santa Barbara's nice this time of year."

"Mr. Insider didn't end up telling us much other than De Paine's mommy was a wild girl who loves real estate. Which ain't exactly a rare L.A. bird. What's Ms. Whitbread like?"

Milo said, "Friendly, flirtatious, well put together."

I said, "Her son sells dirty pictures. She made them."

"So we're in Freud-World."

"De Paine came by to visit when we were there, so there's still some kind of relationship. Fortuno's right: Keep an eye on her and she might lead you to him."

"Day we met her, De Paine was right in front of us," said Milo, rubbing his face.

Petra put her glass down. "Everything we hear about this guy turns up nasty. But he's not a formal suspect on Jordan so no way I can get a tap on Mommy's line—where's Fortuno when we need him. In terms of surveillance, Fourth Street's quiet and respectable and relatively low-rise. Not the ideal situation for a stakeout. Any ideas?"

Milo said, "After dark it would be easier."

"True . . . okay, I'll talk to Raul."

I said, "Fortuno confirmed that Mary got into real estate with help from rich boyfriends. We know Myron Bedard sold her four buildings, including the two duplexes on Fourth. That confirms our guess about her being his mistress. It also strengthens our theory about De Paine meeting Lester Jordan through the Bedards. I'm convinced that whatever haunted Patty took place during the months she lived on Fourth."

Milo said, "Myron takes Mary and her kid along when he checks out his tenants on Cherokee. The kid just happens to run into Jordan and sees an opportunity?"

"Whatever the case," said Petra, "I've had no luck finding Myron Bedard. Or anyone else, for that matter. Why do I have this naggy little feeling that Fortuno played us?"

I said, "He played *me* to get therapy for his son. Maybe he really cares about the boy but mostly he needed to feel in control. What I find interesting is that he danced around every topic you brought up *except* Mary Whitbread."

"You're right, no problem laying out the details, there. Including how he did her. What was that, another power play?"

"He resents her. Or at the very least, he doesn't care what happens to her, or her son. If he knew more, he'd have told us."

"Dirty pictures for dope," said Petra. Thin music issued from her purse and she fished out a phone playing the first eight notes of "Time After Time." "Connor. Hey, Raul, what's . . . you're kidding. Give me the address. Be there in thirty to forty."

She clicked off and stood. "Moses Grant has surfaced."

"Excellent," said Milo.

"Not really."

The police own the crime scene but the coroner owns the body.

The three of us stood back from the scene, white-lit by night floods, as a coroner's investigator named Sally Johannon gloved up and labored to turn Moses Grant's massive corpse face-up. Two Central Division detectives named David Saunders and Kevin Bouleau stood nearby. Both were black, in their early thirties, dressed in well-cut dark suits.

A few feet away, Raul Biro, in a herringbone sport coat and gray slacks, scanned the crime scene.

For the third time, Johannon's attempt to get a frontal view failed.

Grant had been dumped near the 110 North, just above China-town, cars whizzing by a few feet away. The estimate was one or two days of decomposition and bloat. Despite the wide-open spot, the smell was unmistakable and it adhered to my sinuses, the way it always does.

Sally Johannon winced. "There goes my sacroiliac." She motioned for help. The two crypt drivers who'd come with the white van gloved up and the three of them completed the flip.

Grant's sage-green velour tracksuit blended with the shrubbery and the eucalyptus saplings. A bush-clearing crew of County Jail trustees had found him. They were gone, now, ushered back to the comfort of incarceration. The ramp was blocked by a squad car but the freeway remained open and the auto roar was constant.

"One here," said Johannon, pointing to a small, neat wound in Grant's forehead. Her hands moved down the swell of Grant's torso. "Two, three—four, five—and one here." Indicating a rip in the velour dead center of Grant's groin. "Someone didn't like this poor guy."

Petra said, "Any defense wounds?"

Johannon checked. "Nope, nothing."

Milo said, "The shooter was facing him when he let go."

David Saunders said, "Any shooter would probably be shorter than Grant. The crotch shot or one of the abdominals could've been the opener. Grant went down and the shooter kept pumping."

"A crotch shot makes me wonder about a grudge," said Kevin Bouleau. "Was he fooling with someone's marital situation?"

Petra said, "Not that we know."

"You've been looking for him for a while?"

"There's a whole long story."

"Can't wait," said Bouleau.

Sally Johannon said, "Let me double-check his legs . . . nope, that appears to be it, folks. From the size of the entry, I'd guess a .22, certainly not much bigger. No serious blood, so this wasn't the kill-spot. You're not going to find casings unless one lodged somewhere on his person and fell out."

Kneeling lower, she ran her eyes down the tracksuit. "Any pockets on this thing . . . ah yes, here we go."

Reaching inside the zip jacket, she turned a pocket inside out. "No I.D., sorry, people."

Raul Biro said, "We know who he is."

"Thanks to you," said Petra. "Good work."

Biro allowed himself a split-second smile. He'd been sitting at his desk working the phones while simultaneously monitoring incoming homicide calls on the scanner. Hearing about a downtown dump, he'd perked at the victim's race and size, gotten to the scene early, and helped secure it.

"Praise the Lord," said Saunders. "And His faithful servant, Detective Biro."

Everyone knew what he meant. Without victim identification, days could be lost.

Biro said, "What do you want me to do now?"

Petra said, "Up to these guys."

Saunders said, "Do you know if Mr. Grant has any local family?"

"We traced his residence a year back and he was living alone in the Valley. He was of interest to us as a K.A. of our suspect but nothing indicates he was a bad guy in his own right."

"Someone sure thought he was."

Johannon got to her feet. "Creak, creak, I'm getting too old for this."

I put her at thirty-five.

Fetching her camera, she circled the body, taking small steps, snapping lots of shots. "Okay, he's all yours. Where are your techies?"

Saunders said, "On the way."

Kevin Bouleau said, "We're ready to hear that story, Petra."

One of the crypt drivers said, "Any idea when we can get going?"

Petra summed up what she knew about Grant. Saunders and Bouleau listened until she was through, then Saunders said, "This guy Fisk is the obvious choice, seeing as he's already killed someone because of something the vic knew. Grant hung with these guys, probably also came to know too much. The only thing against that is Fisk strangled your vic."

Petra said, "That went down in an apartment building full of people, so noise could've been a factor. And Grant was even bigger than Bowland, maybe too big to strangle."

"So maybe he got shot somewhere secluded. No idea at all where he was living?"

"De Paine and Fisk were rooming together in the Hollywood Hills. No one saw Grant in the house, but it's possible he was there. But even if he was, that was months ago."

"Club dudes," said Bouleau. "There's lots of club activity on our turf. Abandoned buildings east of the Civic Center, it's basically industrial, dead at night. Club dudes break in, bootleg electricity, run raves, peddle dope, take the money and run. Once the party's over, it's nice and quiet."

Saunders said, "There're a few places we can check out, see if any copious body fluids show up."

Bouleau said, "That place on Santa Fe, for starts."

Saunders nodded. "Used to be a textile warehouse, amazing what you find in these places."

Petra said, "The one place the three of them were spotted together was the Rattlesnake."

"That one's long gone," said Saunders. "Looks like we're going to be up nights, Kev. You're doing that, anyway, but my social life's going to *die*."

"You don't deserve one," said Bouleau. "Be like the rest of us and suffer."

Saunders grinned. "Kev's wife just had a baby."

Milo said, "Congrats."

Petra said, "That's great, Kev. Boy or girl?"

Kevin Bouleau said, "Girl, Trina Louella. Best-looking baby in the known universe but she's not into sleep."

"If she can do thirty-six straight she can follow in her daddy's footsteps."

"Not going to happen," said Bouleau. "Trina's going to be a doctor."

The banter died and the Central detectives began walking around the dump site, looking for casings that wouldn't materialize. The LAPD Crime Scene van arrived and two techs got out carrying black cases.

As they began working, Petra corralled Raul Biro, asked him to watch Mary Whitbread's duplex.

He said, "I can do that."

"Are you free tonight?"

"I can be."

She turned to us. "All this bloodshed just to squelch information? Whatever memory Patty resuscitated must've been major-league. I'm away from the idea that it was anything less than murder. So maybe Isaac didn't pull anything up because it's unreported, like you said. Which is not hopeful."

She watched the techs crouch near the body. "Nothing for us to do here."

We returned to our cars.

I said, "I know .22s are common but you might want to check the slugs in Grant against those taken from Leland Armbruster."

Milo said, "De Paine shot Armbruster thirteen years ago and held on to his piece?"

"Thirteen years ago, De Paine was fifteen. If Armbruster was his first, the gun could be psychologically significant."

"Sentimental value."

Petra said, "Plus, he got away with it, so why ditch a lucky weapon? I agree, it's worth a try. Grant's autopsy won't be prioritized because six bullet holes is no whodunit. But let me go back to talk to Saunders and Bouleau and see if they can push a little. Once the slugs are fished out, I'll coordinate the ballistics. Raul, stick with me and let's talk about tonight. See you later, guys."

I got onto the 110 and sped south.

Milo said, "You can slow down now."

I said, "I'm heading over to Tanya's. Two people are dead in order to keep a secret. She's outside the loop but De Paine and Fisk have no way of knowing that."

"Did you talk to her about finding temporary lodgings?"

"Not yet."

"Timing wasn't right?"

"I should've made it right. Do me a favor and call her now."

He tried her landline and her cell. Voice mail on both. "She's probably studying."

"Hope so."

"One thing in her favor, Alex: With De Paine and Fisk doing the Osama bit, maybe they won't risk coming out in the open."

"They weren't too scared to shoot Grant. Want me to drop you at your car or go straight to her place?"

"Straight's always best," he said. "So to speak."

30

No van in Tanya's driveway. Lights ambered the living room drapes. The outdoor spots seemed to shine brighter and I said so.

Milo said, "She probably upped the wattage. Good girl, she's paying attention. She's likely still on campus, cramming for a test or something. But let me check the premises to make you feel better."

As he started to get out, a car across the street pulled away and drove toward Pico.

White Mercedes convertible. Classic model, conspicuous in this middle-class neighborhood.

I said, "Get back in."

Milo said, "What—"

"That Benz heading north. We've seen it before."

The convertible made a rolling stop and continued east on Pico without signaling. Moderate traffic made the tail easy. At La Cienega, the Mercedes hooked a left, picked up speed, sailed past La Cienega Park and the old Restaurant Row before pausing for a light at San Vicente. Then on to Third Street and a right turn.

Short ride past newer cafés and masses of valet-parked vehicles, then south on Orlando.

Milo said, "Hang at the corner."

We watched the convertible cover a few blocks then turn left onto Fourth Street. Again, no signal.

"At the least I can get him for traffic violations. Switch off your lights and move up a bit."

I pulled over just short of Orlando and Fourth and we watched as the Mercedes cruised up the block and paused in front of Mary Whitbread's duplex.

Sitting there, in the middle of the street. A full minute passed before the brake lights went off.

Milo said, "He's heading back to San Vicente, go, Alex."

The Benz sped east on Beverly. I stayed three car lengths behind, followed the sleek white chassis through the Fairfax district and into Hancock Park.

When the Benz turned onto Hudson Avenue, Milo had me hang back again. "Let's make sure any surprises are the ones we dish out."

The Benz turned exactly where we knew it would.

I raced onto Hudson, pulled to the east side of the street, positioned the Seville the wrong way, directly in front of the Bedard mansion.

The white Mercedes was behind the green Bentley. Lights off, no engine sound. A weathered plastic rear window killed any view of the occupants.

No one exited the vehicle.

Milo pulled his little Maglite from a jacket pocket, unholstered his gun, and got out. Standing just behind the Benz, he aimed a sharp, bright beam through the plastic.

"*Police!* Driver, open the door *slowly.*"

Nothing.

"*Do* it. Driver *out.*" His rumble echoed amid the silent elegance. Jarring, but nary a light went on in the neighboring houses. People slept well on Hudson Avenue. Or pretended to.

"*Out.*"

The driver's door opened partially. "Lieutenant? It's me. Kyle."

"Get out of the car, Kyle."

"I—this is my own house."

"*Do* it. *Now.*"

A voice from the passenger seat said, "This is absur—"

"Quiet, passenger. Kyle, out."

The door swung wider and Kyle Bedard stepped out squinting and blinking. He had on a fuzzy gray sweatshirt over olive cargo pants and the same yellow running shoes. The tips of his hair glinted in the flashlight beam like Fourth of July sparklers.

He said, "Can you please get that out of my eyes?"

Milo lowered the light.

"See, Lieutenant, it really is me. No one else wears shoes this ugly."

Milo said, "I'm going to frisk you, son. Turn around."

"You're kidding."

"Anything but." He patted Kyle down, had him sit on the curb. "You next, passenger."

The voice from the car said, "I don't believe this."

Kyle rubbed his eyes. Saw me and smiled. "In a surreal, kind of Jean-Luc Godard way, this is cool."

The passenger laughed.

"*Out!*"

Kyle jumped.

The passenger said, "My name's not Mohammed so why go to all the trouble?"

"For laughs," said Milo. "Careless people have been known to get shot."

"What's funny about that?"

"Exactly."

Kyle said, "That's—"

"Okay, okay," said the passenger. "I'm getting out. Don't shoot *me* for God's sake."

The man who emerged was taller than Kyle and fifty pounds heavier, with a commodious paunch. Late fifties, deep tan, clean dome. The remaining hair was dark and long enough to collect in a ponytail that drooped past his shoulder blades. Sideburns fuller than Milo's traveled toward a soft jawline. John Lennon glasses rode a beak nose. Both his chins were strong.

The overall image was Ben Franklin in Italian duds. A beautifully styled cream cashmere blazer was custom-tailored for a slimmer body. Chocolate slacks broke perfectly over caramel mesh loafers. The open collar of an electric-blue silk shirt was topped by a yellow-and-azure ascot. A wine-colored handkerchief tumbled from his breast pocket. I counted six gold rings on two hands, lots of glimmer.

A smile rich with scorn danced across thin lips. "Do I put my hands up? Say 'Uncle'? Recite the Pledge of Allegiance?"

"Just stand there and relax, sir."

"Due-diligence time, Lieutenant whatever-your-name-is. There's a fifteen-gizmo Swiss Army knife in my right front trouser pocket, don't nick yourself on the can opener. The only other potentially dangerous object on my person is my billfold. But seeing as there are no females in sight, I wouldn't worry."

His smile widened as Milo did the pat. "As long as we're tangoing, I might as well introduce myself. Myron Bedard."

Kyle said, "This is kind of cool, don't you think, Dad?"

Myron Bedard laughed. "Son, I guess I'll need some time to see it that way."

When Milo finished, he apologized to Myron and allowed Kyle to get up from the curb.

Kyle brushed off the seat of his pants and stood next to his father. "Think any neighbors saw this, Dad?"

"If they did," said Myron Bedard, "to hell with them." To Milo: "Was that really necessary?"

"Unfortunately, yes."

Bedard removed his glasses and wiped them with a corner of cashmere. "Doing your job . . . no hard feelings. Actually I *don't* get it. I mean I see your point about being cautious for your personal safety, but Kyle said you know him, so why the hell go through that?"

"I've met Kyle once, Mr. Bedard. Don't know him well enough to be sure of anything."

"Oh, that's—"

"We spotted you watching Tanya Bigelow's duplex."

"Spotted? We were just . . ." Sidelong glance at his son.

Kyle kept silent.

Milo said, "You were just what?"

Kyle looked down.

Myron Bedard said, "My son has a crush on the girl—is that okay to say, Kyle?"

Kyle cursed under his breath. "Guess it is now."

"He's concerned about her, wants to make sure she's okay, that's all. To show you the extent of his devotion, he picked me up from the airport and rather than head straight home, insisted we—"

"*Dad!*"

"These are the police, son. No sense dissembling."

Kyle faced us. "It was a dorky thing to do, I'm sorry."

Milo said, "Why are you worried about Tanya, son?"

Myron Bedard said, "I pay his tuition so only I get to call him that." Slapping Kyle's back. "Just kidding, go on, Lieutenant—I didn't catch your last name . . ."

"Sturgis."

Bedard extended his hand. He and Milo shook.

"Sturgis," he said, "as in the big Harley meet. Ever been there, Lieutenant?"

"Nope."

"You should, it's a blast. I've made it twelve years in a row. I alternate between a 95 Fatboy and a 2004 Speedster 883 Custom XL. There's absolutely nothing like the Black Mountains in August, you make a pit stop in Keystone, near Mount Rushmore. There's some serious partying going on." He nudged Kyle. "Next year, you've got to make good on that promise and go with me, son."

Kyle didn't answer.

"Noncommittal," said Myron Bedard. "He reverts to that when I'm being a pain in the ass. You should go, too, Lieutenant. I assume you bike."

"Why's that?"

"Don't all cops bike?"

"Not this one."

"Maybe it's the highway patrol I'm thinking of. What's Erik Estrada doing nowadays?"

Milo turned to Kyle. "Why are you worried about Tanya?"

"For the same reasons you are."

"Such as?"

"Such as Uncle Lester being murdered right after you talk to him about Tanya's mom. Such as Tanya living near Mary and Pete, such as the relationship between Mary and Uncle Lester."

"Pete as in Peterson Whitbread."

"He hated to be called that."

"You know him."

"We weren't friends."

"Same question," said Milo.

"I saw him from time to time."

"How long ago?"

"When we were kids."

"How'd that happen to be?"

Myron Bedard stepped in front of his son. "Could we continue this discussion inside, please? I don't want to be a spectacle."

CHAPTER

31

Bedard unlocked the mansion and disabled the alarm. *"Entrez-vous."*

We followed him through the limestone marble hall, past the George Washington look-alike and the library where Kyle had set up his research post. The clutter had grown; more crumpled paper than hardwood floor.

Myron stopped to take in the mess.

"I know, Dad."

"Eventually you will have to organize, Kyle."

"I'm organized cognitively."

"Different rules for geniuses?" Clapping his son's shoulder again.

Kyle winced. Myron marched ahead of him, ponytail swinging, switching on lights, pausing to scan a stack of mail on an onyx table and slapping it back down.

An arched limestone passage took us to a vast, hexagonal room backed by the glass doors that showcased subtly lit formal gardens. The trees where Tanya remembered hiding out were Chinese elms and sycamores, manicured but lush. A fifty-foot swimming pool, old enough to retain a diving board, reflected the waffled contours of a lattice gazebo. A wet bar on the west end of the room sported enough bottles to stock a cruise ship.

Myron Bedard went straight for the bar, pausing to fool with more lamps—on, off, dim, dimmer, brighter. Settling for a heavy orange ambience, he selected a crystal Old-Fashioned glass, held it up, and squinted.

Kyle had lingered near the entrance to the room, staring at his shoes. The first time I'd seen him he'd looked like a squatter. Two days of beard growth fed the image. Given the opulence, I wasn't sure Milo and I fit in much better.

The room was bigger than most homes, walled with Shantung silk the crimson of venous blood. The ceiling was a domed riot of plaster curlicues set off by yards of crown molding. Fruitwood stands hosted Chinese horses and camels and bewildered-looking deities, all glazed in the same green and gold. Gilded cases of glass and porcelain and silver boasted of exuberant acquisition.

Enough space for three large seating areas and a like number of Persian rugs. Damask couches, tapestry chairs, a few leather pieces thrown in for variety, inlaid tables strategically placed.

Myron Bedard uncapped a silver ice bucket. "Drink, anyone?"

"No, thanks."

"Ditto."

"Then, I'll drink alone." Mixing himself a bourbon Manhattan on the rocks, he ambled over while sipping, dropped into one of the sofas, kicked off his loafers, half reclined.

A longer swig of his cocktail evoked a thumbs-up and a sigh of pleasure. "Just discovered this stuff—Knob Creek, Jim Beam premium booze. The best they had on the plane was Wild Turkey, and we're talking a Gulfstream."

Licking his lips, he extricated the maraschino cherry, bit down, wiped scarlet juice from his chin, swallowed. "Why's everyone standing?"

Milo and I sat down as close to him as the layout allowed. Kyle hesitated for a moment before placing himself far from all of us.

Myron said, "Aw, c'mon, kiddo, it's been months," and motioned him closer. Kyle chewed his lip, found an armchair perpendicular to Myron's sofa.

Milo said, "For starts, let's hear about the relationship between Mary Whitbread and Lester Jordan."

Neither Bedard responded.

"All of a sudden, the plague of shyness?"

Myron said, "I suppose I should be the one to tackle that."

Kyle said, "Good *guess,* Dad."

"Son, maybe you should go calculate or something."

"The kids' table?"

"Kyle, I've never shielded you, but some things are best said in private."

"I'm aware of *everything,* Dad."

"Humor me, son."

Kyle didn't budge.

Myron said, "It's a matter of *propriety,* Kyle."

Kyle played with his shoe. The toe was cracked.

Myron said, "Is that the style, now? Affected poverty?"

"I don't *give* a shit about style, Dad." A trace of whine raised the young man's pitch. More moody adolescent than budding research scientist.

Being with a parent could do that.

Myron said, "And I never pressured you in that regard, did I, Kyle?"

Kyle didn't answer.

Milo said, "Why don't you take a breather, Kyle, but stick around."

Before Kyle could answer, Myron sprang up, drink sloshing, placed himself, once again, between us and his son. He touched Kyle's cheek. Kyle stiffened. Myron withdrew his hand but kissed the same spot.

Kyle's chin twitched.

"I'm sorry, son. For any iniquity you can think of at present and the multitude that haven't yet crossed your mind but are sure to. However, you might consider putting it in context. I'm fifty-seven, habitually overindulge in food and liquid refreshment, despise exercising, ignore my cholesterol. So my longevity is—"

"Dad!"

"—in serious question. Therefore, if I—"

Speaking quickly but with a mild slur. Wild Turkey hadn't been too rough for an in–flight appetizer.

Kyle said, "*Stop* it, Dad. I *hate* when you do that."

Myron crossed his heart. "Mea culpa. My eternal mantra."

He tousled Kyle's hair. "C'mon, bro, give me a little dignity and chill for a while."

Kyle shot to his feet and stomped away.

"We'll chat later, son. I want to tell you all about Venice."

With the young man gone, Myron said, "He's ambivalent about me, how could he not be? But I love *him* unconditionally. If I had to have only one kid, he'd be the one. Well behaved from day one—never had the imp in him. And, brilliant, I'm talking a whole different intellectual stratosphere. He's only twenty-four and a year away from a Ph.D. in plasma physics. I can't even comprehend what that *is*."

Paternal pride gave way to tension that halved the width of his mouth. "Must be a generation-skipping thing. As Father frequently told me. He was a scientific type, too. Self-taught but a bushel-peck of patents to his name. Kyle thinks he's anti-materialistic but he'll be loaded, despite himself, probably some high-tech invention. One day you'll open up *Forbes* there he'll be, on the big-list. When that happens, I hope he likes me a little. Do either of you have kids?"

"No, sir," said Milo.

"It's educational. There's a good chance that I've been a shitty father. Back then, of course, I thought I was a pretty good father."

"Back when, sir?"

"When Kyle was young. I was never controlling or dominating but I do have a tendency to be impulsive and I suppose that could be . . ." Hoisting his drink, he emptied the glass, returned to the bar, poured a double. By the time he got back to the couch, half was gone.

"Your impulsiveness affected Kyle?"

"It's complicated, Lieutenant." Bedard's eyes closed and his breathing slowed.

"How so?"

Bedard didn't move. Milo's head-cock told me to take over.

Mention of Peterson Whitbread had caused Bedard to seek the refuge of his house. Once inside, he'd wanted Kyle gone.

I said, "Impulsive as in taking Kyle along to see your mistress?"

Bedard's eyes fluttered open. "Mistress." The word amused him. "Mary was a nice stopover, nothing more."

Milo said, "You have a lot of those?"

"What can I say, I love women. Adore each and every one of them." Bedard drank and cracked ice with his teeth and used one hand to outline the guitar-contours of the female form. "I guess you could say I'm

enamored of half the world—what's that, three billion? Minus one—
my ex-wife. Lord, can you imagine working your way through that mass
of femininity? The concept's staggering."

Hoisting again, he said, "Here's to the X chromosome."

Milo said, "When did you start stopping over at Mary Whitbread's?"

"Let's see . . . way back—fifteen years or so."

"Are you still doing it?"

"She's over fifty. Far too mature for me."

"She was a stopover but you sold her four buildings."

"So I did."

"Quid pro quo?"

Bedard laughed. "Mary paid fair market value. The fact that no
agent's commission was involved gave me a bit more flexibility and she
didn't need to wait for financing."

"She paid cash?"

"A cashier's check to be exact."

"How much are we talking about?"

"Hmm," said Bedard. "That long ago, I'd say . . . a million, million
five."

"Where'd she get that kind of money?"

"I have no idea. What has she done to get you so interested in her?"

"Who initiated the sale?" said Milo.

"All questions, no answers, eh? The decision was mutual. Mary was
living in Carthay Circle, had sold some apartments in the Valley and
was looking to trade up, possibly go the owner-occupied route. We'd
owned the duplexes long enough to make a nice profit but as pure
rentals, the returns weren't optimal. I didn't want to waste time on
properties with less than a dozen units, so the timing was perfect."

Rocking his glass, he stared at the wave motion. "It's like playing
Monopoly, one trades houses for hotels. There's a school of thought
that says hold, never sell, but I find that uncomfortably static."

Another tightening of his lips.

I said, "Your father's school of thought?"

Little eyeglass lenses flashed as he focused on me. "You're playing
psychologist with me. But yes, you're correct. And no doubt Father
would insist *he* was right. Those four buildings have got to be worth
five, six mil. But I did fine on the ones I bought."

Adolescent strain in *his* voice. Kyle had told me his father and grandfather loathed each other. Cashmere and silk were nice, but they made for poor bandages.

He said, "I'm still intrigued by all the interest in Mary. Is it because Patty Bigelow lived in one of the duplexes? There's no mystery to that. I sent Patty to Mary after she had to leave here."

"After your father died."

"She was a terrific caretaker," said Bedard, "but there was no reason for her to stay."

"Let's get back to Peterson Whitbread," I said. "How did Kyle come to know him?"

"This is about *Pete?* What has *he* done?"

Milo said, "Did Kyle meet him during your stopovers?"

Bedard fondled his ascot. "I'm not obligated to talk to you."

"Any reason you wouldn't want to cooperate?"

"Jet lag, for one. Bedard orneriness for another." Capped smile. "No, I'm easy. Or so I've been told."

People like to talk about themselves. My profession banks on it. Sometimes, though, it's a means of avoiding substance.

I said, "What was the problem between Kyle and Pete?"

"Who said there was any?"

"You keep shying away from talking about it."

"Lord," said Myron Bedard. "And to think I've *supported* your profession."

Milo said, "Would it help if I asked the same question?"

"Ha . . . no, I'm not trying to be evasive. It's just that bringing up those days reminds me of . . . it's a rather jarring example of the impulsiveness I was talking about. Precisely why I didn't want Kyle here."

I said, "You took Kyle along when you saw Mary and he saw things he shouldn't have."

"At the very least he heard things. Mary could be . . . exuberant. Yes, I had poor judgment, but you need to understand, I was Kyle's primary parent, if I wasn't with him he didn't get any attention at all. You've met my ex-wife. Can you imagine her nurturing *anything*? So yes, I let him tag along everywhere. Now I realize there were some . . . inappropriate instances."

"How old was Kyle when he accompanied you to Mary's?"

"I'd say . . . nine, ten, who remembers? I thought it would be fun because Pete was a bit older. Kyle's an only child."

Drinking some more. "To my mind, it was better than leaving Kyle alone in *this* godforsaken place."

"Big house."

"Big cold *tomb*," said Bedard. "I *hated* growing up here. One day I'll sell it. I'm keeping an eye on the market."

I said, "How'd Kyle react to the visits?"

"What do you mean?"

"You said there were inappropriate instances."

"I was talking generally. Hearing Mary and I . . . for the most part, Kyle seemed fine."

"For the most part."

"One time—the last time—he seemed kind of moody. All I could get out of him was that he didn't like Pete, preferred not to go back. Those were probably his exact words—'Dad, I'd prefer not to go back.' He always talked like an adult, when he was really small, people would say, 'Where's the ventriloquist?'"

"Why didn't he like Pete?"

"He didn't elaborate."

"You didn't pursue it."

"I didn't see any reason to. Kyle made a request, I honored it."

I didn't answer.

Bedard said, "Please don't tell me something disgusting went on. I refuse to believe Kyle wouldn't have told me. Most kids don't talk to their parents. But with Kyle and me it was different. There was ab-solutely *no* sign of *anything* like that."

Milo said, "That's not what we're after but if you do suspect some-thing, now would be a—"

"I don't. And frankly I don't see what any of this has to do with Patty Bigelow and her daughter. I'm still confused about why you asked Kyle about Patty in the first place and why he's so concerned. Patty died of cancer, not under suspicious circumstances."

"What did Kyle tell you?"

"That you were going back and looking into her death and that possibly it was related to Lester's death."

"How'd you find out about Lester's death?"

"Kyle called me in Venice and told me."

"When?"

"Yesterday morning." Wry smile. "Quite *early* in the morning. Right after I arrived from a rather gourmandish night in Paris and was trying to sleep it off."

"What else did he tell you?"

"That's it," said Bedard. "The part about Patty didn't come up until the ride from the airport."

"Kyle's explanation for why he wanted to drive past Tanya's."

"Not that it clarified matters."

"Why'd you come back to L.A., sir?"

"Kyle asked me to."

"Just like that, with no explanation."

"You're not a father, Lieutenant. I heard the need in my son's voice and responded. I did try to get him to explain, but it made him more upset so I dropped it. I've learned to let Kyle proceed at his own pace—did you see how tough it was just getting him to leave the damn *room*?"

Milo said, "Why exactly did Kyle say he wanted to drive past Tanya's house?"

"To make sure she was okay. And then he blushed and got fidgety. From that I inferred that he was smitten by the girl. That surprised me but not unpleasantly. 'Kyle' and 'women' aren't two words often uttered in the same breath."

"Not a ladies' man."

"It wouldn't shock me if he was still a virgin." Dry chuckle. "Where did I go wrong?"

I said, "Why did Kyle drive by Mary Whitbread's duplex?"

"I had no idea he was going to do that. When he turned on Third instead of Beverly, I figured it was an alternative route, maybe something to do with traffic patterns—I haven't been in L.A. for months, the bastards at City Hall keep digging up the streets. Then he turned off at Orlando and before I knew it, we were idling in front of Mary's duplex. I asked him what the heck he was doing and he turned and gave me a strange look and began humming 'Auld Lang Syne.' "

"Doing it for old times' sake."

"But he didn't look amused. Quite the contrary, he was uptight and stayed that way, refused to explain."

Bedard swallowed the last of the bourbon. "The ride home was tense. I'd just left Venice for him and believe me, that city is gorgeous any time of year—if you haven't been there, trust me, you have to. Before the whole damn thing sinks into oblivion."

"You came home because Kyle sounded upset," I said, "but he wouldn't explain why."

"I tried to get it out of him. That's why we were sitting in the driveway when you pulled your little commando raid."

Running a finger under the knot of his ascot, he said, "Why can't you tell me what the hell's going on?"

"Let's go back a bit," I said. "How exactly did you meet Mary Whitbread?"

"Through my brother-in-law."

"Lester Jordan."

"The late, unlamented."

"How did he know her?"

"As I said, Mary's an exuberant gal. Do you know anything about her background?"

"In Chicago?"

"Her story—and I can't vouch for it—is that back in Chicago she hung around with Mafia types. She also said she knew Mayor Daley, the Kennedys. But isn't that the standard claim? Perhaps if you chat with her long enough she'll claim to have bedded Jimmy Hoffa and Amelia Earhart."

"Standard claim for who?"

"Aging bimbos. I'm not trying to be cruel, but let's face it, that's what Mary is. I'd take anything she says with more than a dash of *sel de mer*."

"You don't trust her but you did a real estate deal with her."

"Her cashier's check was genuine."

"How'd she know Lester Jordan?"

"Among her varied interests were musicians," said Bedard. "Les played sax in a traveling combo that had a gig at a club where Mary was ahem *dancing*." Wink wink. "I suppose push led to shove . . . so to speak. And wouldn't you know it, that's the one time Mary got careless. A one-night stand and it's time to buy diapers."

He shook his head. "Stupid."

Milo said, "Jordan was Peterson's father?"

"Perhaps that was what motivated her to get her tubes tied. Or perhaps it was just a convenience. Given her new occupation."

"Porn."

"Aha," said Bedard. "You know about all that. Have you ever seen Mary's work?"

"No, sir."

"High-quality, Lieutenant. For what it is."

"If she didn't want kids, why didn't she abort?"

"She considered it," said Bedard. "Told me so—pillow talk and all that. Her reason for not doing so was that she was dating a wealthy old man at the time. A wealthy *generous* old man, whom she thought she might be able to con into thinking the baby was his. Unfortunately, the plan backfired."

"Sugar Daddy wasn't overjoyed," said Milo.

"Sugar Daddy demanded a paternity test and when she procrastinated, he kicked her somewhat enlarged butt out into the street. By the time it happened, she was too far along to feel comfortable aborting."

"Scruples."

"I suppose she has a few. Poor Mary. She's blessed with vaginal muscles from heaven but her judgment sometimes falls short of the mark. She had the baby but from what I could tell, didn't do much in the way of raising it. In that way, she's not unlike my ex-wife." To me: "No, my seeing her was *not* an example of neurotic pattern. In crucial ways, there were *differences* between Mary and Iona."

Playing with his glass. "One hears about maternal instincts but I've run into quite a few women who seem to lack it."

"When's the last time you saw Mary?"

"I thought I answered that."

"You said she was too old."

"And has been for at least a decade. That's why I was surprised when Kyle pulled up in front of her place and started humming. I do my best to *forget* old acquaintances."

"Unpleasant memories?"

"Not at all, Doctor. I believe in moving on."

"So you met Mary through Lester Jordan."

"Ah, Lester," he said. "Lester was a cancer on my married life—rock-filled baggage that I was willing to tolerate when I still had feelings for Iona. But I never liked giving him money because I knew where it was going. I met Mary, when I came by to give Lester yet another check and she was there. The sight of a woman who looked like that associated with a dried-up scrotum like Lester caught my attention."

"Why was she there?"

"The two of them were having some kind of spat. Lester's mood didn't concern me but a beautiful woman so upset?" Touching a blue silk breast. "She ran out, I handed Lester his dole and went after her, gave her a shoulder to cry on." Adjusting his glasses. "One thing led to another."

"Why was she crying?"

"She wanted Lester to see Pete. Pete always asked to see his father but Lester rarely agreed. Par for the course."

"His being an addict," said Milo.

"Addiction's all about self-indulgence, right? That's what Patty told me. My sense was she was happy to be rid of him. That would be any rational person's reaction to Lester."

"Except his son's."

Bedard removed his glasses. "Sons can be like that."

"Attached," I said.

"Beyond the point of reason. I'm sure being rejected inflicted wounds on the kid's psyche, but believe me, Pete was better off not being exposed to Lester. The man was *dirt.*"

"And you had to support him."

"Like I said, baggage."

"Your ex thinks you killed him."

Bedard pulled out a foot of ascot and wiped his lenses. "That tells you about her judgment. I've been in Europe for two months."

"She says you wouldn't do it yourself, you'd hire someone."

"I'm sure I would. *If* killing Lester was my aim. Unfortunately for Iona, Lester had been out of my life for years. Why the hell would I waste money—not to mention put myself in jeopardy—to squash a roach in someone else's kitchen?"

I said, "What else did Patty tell you about Lester?"

"Nothing, he wasn't a topic of frequent conversation. Patty concentrated on caring for Father. And did a damn fine job of it. Iona was incensed when I took her from Lester. In her twisted view, Patty was obligated to stay with Lester forever and I was obligated to pay for it. By the time he'd flunked his third rehab, Iona and I were talking through lawyers. When we settled, she got less than she wanted and more than I wanted to give."

Big smile. "Marriage is all about compromise, right?"

I said, "She got the building on Cherokee. And Lester."

"That alone," said Bedard, "was worth the cost of the damn divorce." He yawned. "I haven't slept in two days. Will you be kind enough to see yourselves out?"

"Kyle will show us out," said Milo.

"Let the boy be."

"He's the one who drove by Tanya's."

"I told you. He's got a crush on the girl."

"That doesn't explain driving by Mary Whitbread's."

Bedard struggled to his feet, swayed, grabbed a side table for support. "I suppose it doesn't. I'm going to have a nightcap and then I'll be in dreamland. I'm sure you'll find Kyle in the library. Good night, gents. Tell my son I love him."

CHAPTER

32

Kyle Bedard sat on the library floor, ringed by piles of loose paper. Laptop at his fingertips, cell phone in hand.

He put the phone away. "Did Dad regale you with his sexual triumphs?"

I said, "He said to tell you he loves you."

"He gets that way when he drinks."

"Affectionate?"

"Mawkish."

"He drink often?"

"More than often."

Milo settled on a Chippendale chair too puny for his bulk. I got down beside Kyle and pointed to his phone. "Able to reach her?"

He started to say, "Who?" Cut it off before the vowel sound. "She's okay."

"Back home?"

"She just got in."

"Late-night study group," I said.

He flinched. "What do you need from me?"

I said, "It's okay to care about her."

He said, "I don't hear a question in there."

"How about this: What bothers you about Peterson Whitbread?"

"I haven't seen him in—since I was a kid."

"I don't hear an answer in there."

His left index finger tickled the keyboard of his laptop. The Einstein screensaver dissolved to an engraved portrait of a long-haired, mustachioed man. Frank Zappa look-alike.

I said, "Descartes. Smart guy but wrong about a few things."

"Such as?"

"The split between emotion and reason."

"Is that supposed to mean something to me?"

"It means you can have your feelings and still be smart. We know your father took you along when he visited Mary Whitbread. You hung out with Peterson Whitbread. He did something that bothered you. Enough for you to ask to stop going. Now you're worried Peterson had something to do with your uncle Lester's murder. But what really scares you is he could've been involved in what bothered Patty Bigelow."

Tap tap tap. Descartes gave way to Aristotle.

I said, "Your father's convinced you're a genius. Maybe you are. In the current context, being smart means quelling the instinct to mindlessly buck authority."

Rapid eyeblink. "Why would I know anything about what bothered Patty Bigelow?"

"Because Tanya told you everything. Even though she'd been asked not to."

"I wouldn't hurt her. *Ever.*"

Milo grunted.

"You don't believe me?"

"We might, son, if you cut the bullshit and answered our questions."

"I don't *know* anything. It's all *supposition.*"

"Kind of like scientific research," said Milo. "We can live with that."

Kyle reached for a Styrofoam cup, looked inside, frowned, tossed it. Spying an unopened can of Fresca, he popped the top, watched liquid foam through the aperture and drip onto his papers.

We waited as he drank.

He said, "You're convinced that what happened all those years ago is relevant?"

I said, "You're not?"

Dipping a finger into the soda spill, he shaped an amoeba on the rug, played with the blob until it saturated the wool. "It started when I was nine. Dad and Mom were still married and we had a house a few blocks away from Grandfather's on Muirfield, had just bought the place in Atherton. When Dad took me with him on his *dates*—it wasn't just with Mary—I felt like a traitor to Mom. But I didn't want to get him in trouble because he was the one who . . . shit, why am I meandering . . . right to the point: Yes, I asked to stop going because of Pete. He's a sociopath, or whatever you call it nowadays. At first he made me feel he wanted to hang out. He was four years older. That made me feel uncharacteristically cool."

Lowering his eyes. "It was also a distraction for what was going on in Mary's bedroom."

He passed the soda can from hand to hand. "At first we did normal things—shot hoops, tossed a football, watched TV. He was small for his age, not that much bigger than me, but he seemed a lot more experienced."

"About?"

"Just a general attitude, he was cocky. But he never talked down to me or treated me like the social outcast I was. So I liked hanging with him. Then he eased into the other stuff. Started showing me naked girls he'd cut out of *Penthouse* and *Hustler,* he had piles under his bed. When I didn't freak out, he began taking me into the garage where he kept his hard-core stuff. Not simple porn, this was over-the-top. Women gagged and tied up, bestiality, things I still find repellent. At that point, I *was* freaked out. Why I didn't tell Dad, I don't know. But I didn't and Pete moved on to the next step. A toolbox he kept hidden behind some luggage. Inside were movie stills."

Placing the soda can on the floor, he looked at Milo, then me. "Pictures from movies his *mother* had made. Piles of them. He wasn't embarrassed, just the opposite. Put them right in my face and made gross comments. 'Look how she takes it all in.' 'That's what she's doing to your dad, right now.' I *still* didn't want to let on that it bothered me."

I said, "He was an older kid spending time with you."

"I have no sibs, in school I wasn't exactly Mr. Popular. I guess the pictures were also . . . arousing. Though what that means at nine, who knows?"

"It had to be confusing."

"I used to go home feeling as if I'd been in a trance. Dad never noticed, after being with Mary he was always in a *great* mood. The next time we'd go she'd offer me milk and cookies, and I'd flash to her pictures, start feeling dizzy, sure I was giving something away. But no one noticed and the minute Pete and I were alone, out came the box and he'd start in again. Talking about his mother as if she were a piece of meat. What made it especially weird is she made it a point to be friendly to me. Big hug, milk and cookies, the works."

"Maternal."

"Like a TV mom—she *looked* like a TV mom. I'd see that and then minutes later I'd be watching her do three guys, then Pete licking his lips and rubbing himself. Looking back, it's obvious he enjoyed shocking me. But I kept following him out to the garage." Blinking. "One day he touched me while he showed me a picture. I jerked away and he laughed, said he was just kidding, he was no fag. Then he opened his own fly and started masturbating."

He scratched his head hard. "I've never told anyone. Maybe if I'd spoken up, Pete could've gotten some help."

I said, "From what I've heard about his mother, she couldn't have been counted on."

"I know, I know . . . Dad's choice in women . . . but still . . ."

"It wasn't your job to fix things, Kyle."

"No?" He laughed. "So why are we talking about it now? Don't bother answering, I get it . . . I guess my point is that whatever Pete's done, he never had a chance."

Milo said, "There are always choices."

"Are there? I can't even figure out my own calculations, let alone human nature."

I said, "Welcome to real life. What finally made you ask not to return?"

"Something else happened . . . oh, Jesus—fine, fine . . . It was a Sunday, a long weekend—Presidents' Day, something like that. As usual, Mom was off skiing and Dad and I were home. Off to Mary's we went, but this time Dad and Mary went to have brunch by themselves. I was nervous about being left alone with Pete but Dad wasn't paying attention. Pete picked up on my anxiety right away, said, 'Hey, man, sorry if I grossed you out but I've got something totally cool to show you. Something different.' "

His shoulders dropped. "I was relieved. He seemed so *jaunty*."

"You were never scared he'd hurt you?"

"I was scared the way you are when you're playing hide-and-seek and you know someone could be just around the corner. But no, apart from that one time, he never touched me and he was always friendly. I *was* upset about not spending time alone with Dad. Doing normal father-son things—don't tell him any of this, he's tried to the best of his capabilities. His dad mistreated him but he never did that to me." Deep breath.

I said, "So Pete was jaunty."

"Stay on topic, Kyle." Knuckling his brow. "Back to the garage. The 'different thing' was another box, full of audiotapes. He said they were bootlegs that he'd learned to splice together to make his own music . . . He showed me the razors he used to do it, pretty sloppy job. Then he played his homemade cassettes on a boom box. Dreadful, mostly static and white noise and bits of lyric that made no sense. But it was a lot better than looking at his pictures and I told him 'Cool.' That made him happy and we shot some hoops, went into the house, had a snack. Cap'N Crunch. Pete drank some wine and tried to get me to try it but I refused. He didn't push it, he never pushed anything. I trailed him to the garage again like a good little puppy, and he went straight to a refrigerator they kept back there. I'd always seen it bolted with a chain but now the chain was off. It looked as if it hadn't been cleaned for a while. The only thing inside was a large see-through plastic bag. Inside were what looked like chunks of raw meat. It smelled horrible, despite being sealed. I held my nose, started to gag. He laughed, spread a tarp on the floor—one of those bright blue things gardeners use—and dumped out the contents of the bag."

His face had gone white. His hand shot to his belly. "Even now, it's unbelievable . . . sometimes I still wonder if I dreamed it." Moments passed. He sucked in breath.

He said, "What he dumped out was animal matter, all right. But not beef or pork."

Another inhalation.

"Body parts. Guts, limbs, fur, bones, teeth. Heads, too. Squirrels and rats and I think I saw a cat. I just lost it, out came the Cap'N Crunch. Pete thought that was hilarious. Got up and grabbed a fork from a barbecue set they kept out there and used it to push gobs of the stuff around on the tarp. As if he were stir-frying. All the while, he's laughing. 'Time for dinner—no, it's breakfast—no it's brunch, hey dude, we can have our *own* brunch.' Then all of a sudden, he speared a forkful and jammed it right up against my face. I jumped up, still barfing. I tried to get out of the garage but couldn't. The door was shut, one of those metal rolling dealies, I had no idea how to open it. Pete kept waving the goop, offering it to me, making gross jokes. It reeked beyond *belief.*"

"Disgusting," said Milo. Meaning it.

Kyle placed his palms on the rug, braced himself, as if ready to levitate. "I'm screaming and barfing, begging him to let me out. He keeps advancing on me, then he stops, leans against the fridge. Opens his fly and whips it out and takes a gob and puts it *there*. And touches himself. It didn't take him long. He was turned on."

He excused himself to go to the bathroom, came back with damp hair and raw eyes.

"I don't want to talk about it anymore."

I said, "How'd you get out of the garage?"

"He finished, let me out, ignored me for the rest of the day."

"How much contact did you have with him after that?"

"None. I never saw him again."

"Family obligations never got in the way?"

"What are you talking about."

"You don't know?" I said. Wondering if he really didn't.

"Know what?"

"Lester Jordan—"

"Is his father, yeah, yeah, technically he's my cousin, but not functionally. There was absolutely no contact. And I didn't find out about the relationship until years later. Hell, with all of *Dad's* running around, I could have cousins all over the world."

"When and how did you find out Lester was Pete's father?"

"I was already living in Atherton, it was a couple of years later. I came down to spend time with Dad and he wanted to go see one of his girlfriends. This time I asserted myself and said if he didn't care about spending one-on-one time with me, I'd go to a museum. He got really apologetic, started beating himself up about being a shitty dad. So of course, I consoled him, told him he was a great dad. Somewhere in the midst of that, the subject of Lester and Pete came up. I believe he'd gone off on a speech about bloodlines, how any good genes I'd gotten were from his side because Mom's side was a bunch of losers. After the divorce, both of them were doing that to me—bad-mouthing each other."

I said, "He used Lester as an arguing point."

"Exactly. Then he dropped in the nugget about Lester being Pete's father. Made an apple-not-falling-far kind of comment."

"Sounds like he knew Pete had problems."

"I guess so."

"But he didn't ask if Pete had ever mistreated you."

"No," he said. "Dad's curiosity only extends so far."

I said, "How'd you find out about Pete's learning disabilities?"

His eyes widened. "What do you mean?"

I said, "You told Tanya you had a cousin who'd been put on medication to little avail. Or were you referring to someone else?"

"I . . . no, that was him. I guess I did call him that. But not because I really consider us kin. Tanya and I were having a theoretical discussion. I didn't think I was going to be *parsed*."

"How'd you find out Pete was on meds?"

"He showed me his pills. Mary let him keep the bottle on his nightstand and take them unsupervised. He told me he popped when he felt like having energy."

"Ritalin?"

"I never read the label, he just called them energy pills, said they'd been prescribed because his school was trying to control him. He said they made him feel good but he still wasn't going to do any work because school sucked."

Milo said, "Ever see him take any other drugs?"

"He had a Baggie of weed right out in the open, next to the pills. I saw him roll and smoke a few times. He was also into wine, whatever he'd steal from Mary's stash."

"All that and animal guts."

"Don't remind me."

"Why'd you contact Tanya?"

"When Dr. Delaware dropped in here and talked to me about Ms. Bigelow, it got me remembering."

"Remembering what?"

"That whole period of my life, Lieutenant."

I said, "Seeing Tanya in the garden."

"I wasn't spying, it was nothing weird, she was just there. Mom and Dad were still married but living apart and I was being shuttled back and forth from Atherton. Grandpa was pretty much vegetative. No one had time for me except Patty Bigelow. She'd ask me how I was doing, fix me a sandwich. Tanya and I never spoke a word. She says she noticed me but I couldn't tell. After you came here, I looked her up on Facebook, saw how pretty she'd become. I copied down her class schedule and pretended to bump into her on campus. I know it sounds like crazed stalking, but I was curious, that's all. I wasn't even planning to talk to her. I'm not exactly a player. As if you haven't guessed."

I said, "You managed to talk to her."

"She was eating a sandwich. By the inverted fountain—right where you found us. Right near the physics building, that seemed . . . providential. I brought my lunch out, we started talking, she was easy to talk to. I came right out and told her I'd looked her up. She remembered me, it didn't freak her out, she didn't make me feel like an utter dork. It's as if we've known each other for a long, long time. As friends—I have *not* touched her. I don't think she sees me that way."

Staring at us, craving contradiction.

I said, "Now you're worried about her."

"How could I not be? You go talk to Lester and the next day he's dead?"

Milo said, "Who do you think did it?"

"How would I know?"

"Make an educated guess."

"Pete."

"Why?"

"He hated his father."

"He told you that?"

"He never mentioned Lester by name but he always said his old man was a useless junkie and he couldn't stand him."

"It just came up in conversation?"

"This was years ago, Lieutenant."

"Try to remember."

"If I had to guess I'd say it came up as a comparison. 'Your dad's cool, mine's crap.'"

"What'd he like about your father?"

"That he was rich. That he was a 'stud.'"

"What else did he tell you about Jordan?"

"Nothing, it wasn't as if he was preoccupied. If he was obsessed with anyone it was his mother."

"How much contact did he have with Jordan?"

"What's that, a trick question? I already told you Lester wasn't a part of my life and once I stopped going to Mary's, I never saw Pete."

"You had no contact with Lester because your dad couldn't stand him."

"No one could. Mom's his sister and *she* would have nothing to do with him."

"Your dad gave him free rent and hired Patty Bigelow to look after him."

"So?"

"Nice treatment for someone you hate."

"Mom probably did that to keep Lester out of her hair. Back when they were married, Dad gave her anything she wanted and she looked the other way when he fooled around. Model family, huh?"

I said, "Why was Lester killed?"

"How would I know?"

"Think it was related to Patty Bigelow?"

Silence.

Milo said, "Tell us what you know, son. Now."

"Tanya told me what her mom said before she died. Please don't come down on her. She needed someone to talk to and I just happened to be there."

"What exactly did she tell you?"

"That her mom felt she'd done harm to a neighbor."

"Felt?"

"Neither Tanya nor I believe Patty was capable of actually hurting another human being. I'm sure her being terminal had something to do with it. At the worst, she was witness to something that she didn't report and felt guilty about."

"Something related to Pete Whitbread?" I said.

"That's the logical conclusion, right? He's a sociopath, Tanya and Patty lived a few houses away. Patty probably saw something."

"What have you told Tanya about Pete's proclivities?"

"Nothing. I've never told anyone." Sudden, harsh laughter. "Can we draw this to a close? I've got a ton of work."

"Why did you flinch when I mentioned Tanya's study groups?"

"I did?"

"Noticeably."

He hunched, scratched his head. "Please don't tell Tanya but I know for a *fact* that there *are* no study groups. When she claims to be hanging with other students, she's really sitting by herself in the library. When she's not in class, she's in the library doing work-study. She sticks around long after shift's over, goes into the stacks. Sometimes she's the last one to leave. She walks to her car alone, in the dark. It scares the hell out of me but I can't say anything because I don't want her to know that I follow her."

Milo said, "Ever think of detective work?"

"Don't tell her. *Please.*"

I said, "All these secrets, Kyle. Sometimes it's easier just to go straight from point A to point B."

"Great theory, but I haven't found it helpful in real life. I've been open with you, don't betray me. I can't risk having Tanya think I'm a weirdo."

"Fine, for the time being," said Milo, "as long as you continue to cooperate."

"What else is there to cooperate on? I've told you everything I know."

"What made you suspect there was no study group?"

"She never mentioned the names of any other students. I've never seen her with anyone on campus."

"Just like the old days," I said. "Playing under the trees."

He said, "Old days, but not necessarily *good* old days. I was lonely as hell and she was, too, but we never got together. Now we're friends. I'd like that to continue."

Milo showed him pictures of Robert Fisk and Moses Grant.

Head shake. "Who are they?"

"Friends of Pete Whitbread."

"This one looks nasty." Pointing to Fisk.

The Internet shot of Whitbread/De Paine evoked a nod. "He's

punked himself up, but that's him." Pointing to the pretty faces surrounding De Paine's narrow, bland countenance. "Looks like he does okay with women."

"No accounting," said Milo, rising.

"Are you confident you can keep Tanya safe?"

"We'll do our best, son. Here's my card, call if you think of anything else."

"I won't. My brain feels *leached*."

He walked us to the front doors. "What are the parameters, Lieutenant?"

"Of what?"

"The rules of engagement with Tanya. I don't want to get in the way but I do care about her. And *you* can't be everywhere all the time."

"You're planning to guard her?"

"At least I can be there."

"Be there, but don't do anything stupid and don't impede the investigation."

"Deal."

We stepped out in the warm, dark silence of Hudson Avenue.

Kyle called out, "So I can still see her."

"I just said that, son."

"I mean socially."

"Go do some calculations, Kyle."

33

We got back in the car, sat shadowed by the mansion's haughty face. I watched as a second-story light went off. Miserly moon; the rest of the block had receded into mist. An easterly breeze ruffled stately trees. Hudson Avenue smelled of oranges and wet cat and ozone.

Milo said, "Young love. So much for Tanya being discreet. Did I screw up by allowing Kyle to be Mr. Protective?"

"Could you have stopped him?"

He rubbed his face. "You trust him?"

"My gut says he's okay."

"And if he's telling it right, she could use a friend. Lying about having a social group. You wondered about that."

"Would've been nice to be wrong," I said.

"I can't even imagine going it alone at that age."

From the little he'd told me of his childhood, he'd felt alienated by age six, a big, fat Irish kid who looked and acted like his brothers but knew he was different. The few times he'd talked about his family, he could've been an anthropologist describing an exotic tribe.

I said, "Yeah, it's tough."

"But you think she's doing okay?"

"As well as can be expected."

He laughed. "Dr. Discreet. Anyway, be nice if we could clear all this up and watch the two of them waltz into the sunset . . . not that kids waltz, nowadays." Flash of teeth. "Not that *I* ever waltzed . . . so where do we stand on Cuzzin Petey?"

"Kyle's diagnosis seems right-on."

"Animal guts on his weenie goes beyond basic sociopath, Alex."

"Plus-four sociopath," I said. "He was giving out some serious danger signals early on and no one bothered to care."

"Glommin' Mommy's photos."

"His entire childhood was eroticized. Sex and violence could've gotten blended. That makes me wonder if Patty's 'terrible thing' was related to a lust crime. What if she really did kill someone—a bad guy she considered a threat to Tanya?"

"Some scuzzy pal of Pete's?"

I nodded.

He said, "Scary pedophile crosses Tanya's path and Mommy uses her little .22. Why tell Tanya now?"

"Maybe she was frightened because she hadn't finished the job."

"Sparing De Paine," he said. "Years later she runs into him at the E.R. and he makes a threatening comment. But if he'd collaborated with another lowlife on something unspeakable, why would Patty off his buddy and give him a pass?"

"Because he was young," I said. "Eighteen years old when Patty and Tanya lived on Fourth Street. He was also the son of a man she'd cared for. And possibly cared about."

"Everyone else despises Jordan but she had a soft spot for him?"

"She watched over him as if she did. It's also possible killing once traumatized her and she didn't have the stomach to repeat it. It can be like that for good folk."

The breeze blew harder.

"Okay," he said, "for whatever reason she doesn't shoot little Petey. Why not report him to the cops?"

"Because she'd eliminated his accomplice and didn't want any contact with the cops."

"Theoretical accomplice," he said. "Given your logic, someone older. Now all we have to do is conjure this phantom out of the ether. And unearth some unspeakable sex crime no one's ever heard about.

Also, if Patty was worried about De Paine hurting Tanya, why not come out and warn her explicitly?"

"I don't know. It's possible the disease *did* affect her thinking. Or she didn't want to terrify Tanya—or have Tanya go it alone. By being ambiguous and directing Tanya to me, she hoped Tanya would get help from both of us."

"I guess."

"It worked, didn't it?"

He put his hands behind his head. "Imaginative, I'll grant you that."

I said, "When Tanya told me she felt Patty was trying to protect her, I put it down to romanticizing her mother. But maybe she had it right."

He closed his eyes. The dash clock said one forty-six.

"It also fits Lester Jordan's murder, Milo. What if Jordan knew Patty had spared his son? We come by asking about her, he gets jumpy, wonders if Junior's finally going to pay. Or if Junior's into something new. He calls Junior, maybe warns him to stay away from Tanya. Or sends the warning through Mary. Either way, De Paine wonders if Jordan can be trusted to keep his mouth shut. That tops off the rage he's felt toward his father his entire life. He pays a social call on Dad in the guise of bringing over product. Jordan fixes up, nods out, De Paine lets in Robert Fisk."

"Oedipus wrecks," he said.

"You don't need to be Freud to see it in this family. One of De Paine's earliest sexual charges was looking at his mother's movie stills. Feeding his father's habit put him in the power chair."

"Do sociopaths dig irony?"

"They process it differently than the rest of us."

"Meaning?"

"Shark-eats-minnow is good!"

"How does Moses Grant fit in?"

"Nothing we've heard about him so far indicates criminality, so maybe he was an oversized minnow. He gave up his day job and his apartment to run with De Paine because he believed De Paine would help his deejay career. Along the way, he saw too much, reacted with fear or revulsion. That kind of weakness would be a danger sign to De Paine and Fisk."

"Cleaning house," he said. "You're figuring Grant was also there when they did Jordan."

"Fortuno called him a lackey and whatever else he is, Fortuno's perceptive. We know Grant drove the Hummer so maybe that night he was the wheelman, waiting somewhere up the block."

Another long silence.

"You do have a flair for the dark side," he said, looking past me at the mansion. "Start the car, Jeeves. This zip code's raising my blood sugar."

Two twenty-three a.m., lights off at my house. When I stepped in, sounds from a corner of the living room made me jump.

Robin said, "Hi, honey."

As my eyes habituated, I made out her form. Curled on a sofa, concealed by a blanket but for curls raining on a silk pillow. Blanche nestled in the triangle defined between Robin's belly and arm. The TV remote sat on the floor.

She switched on a low-voltage lamp, squinted, sat up knuckling her eyes and pushing hair out of her face. Blanche curled a tongue and smiled.

I turned the light off, sat down on the edge of the sofa, kissed her hair. Her breath was the sweet-sour of lemon yogurt.

"I was watching a show, guess I conked out."

"Must've been fascinating."

"People looking for new houses. Thrilling."

"Real estate," I said. "It's the new sex."

"The old sex ain't out of commission, yet . . . in principle . . . what time is it?"

I told her.

"Oh, wow. Big night?"

"Nothing dramatic," I said. "Sorry for not calling."

"S'okay, I had my home-girl here, we had plenty to talk about."

"Such as?"

"Girl stuff; *you'll* never know. Help me up, *Caballero.* I need to stretch out in a real bed. Blanchie can stay with us if you want."

"She snores."

"So do you, darling."

"I do?"

"Just once in a while."

"Is it disruptive?"

She pecked my cheek and got to her feet. I walked her, still wrapped in the blanket, up the hall.

"Do I keep you up, Rob?"

"I have a technique."

"What?"

"I kick your butt, you roll over, you're fine."

"Any excuse," I said.

She laughed. "Who needs one? By the way, I'm still asking around about De Paine. No one in the biz takes him seriously and no one's seen him for a while. One other person had that same rumor about the house in the hills but you've already dealt with that."

I kissed her. "Thanks for trying."

"My middle name."

I called Tanya at eight thirty the next morning.

She said, "I just got off the phone with Kyle. I know you think I was stupid for confiding in him, but I *really* know him. He thinks whatever Mommy remembered could've had something to do with Pete Whitbread and that sounds logical to me."

"What do you remember about Pete?"

"Not much. I used to see him on the block but we had nothing to do with each other."

"Did he hang with anyone in particular?"

"Never saw anyone. What I do recall is that Mommy didn't like Mary Whitbread."

"Why not?"

"I don't know, but I could tell from the way she acted when Mary dropped by to collect the rent. It embarrassed me a little because Mary was nice to me, sometimes she'd bring me candy. I admired the way she looked. By then I was out of my Barbie stage but I thought Mary looked like a Barbie Mom—glamorous, ultra-feminine. The times she came by, I sensed that she wanted to socialize, but Mommy never invited her to stay. Just the opposite, she seemed to want her out as quickly as possible. One time Mommy had just brewed fresh coffee and Mary remarked how great it smelled. Mommy said, 'It's old, I was just going to dump it.' It was such an obvious lie. Mary left with a look on her face as if she'd been slapped—oops, look what time it is, I've got to get going, Dr. Delaware."

"Another study group?"

"No, that's later. Ten o'clock lab. I don't know if any of that was helpful, but it's all I remember. Thanks for not being mad about Kyle."

"How're you doing with the self-hypnosis?"

"Great, excellent, I practiced yesterday. Ran through it a dozen times."

"Ah," I said.

Nervous laughter. "Was that too intense?"

"Practice is great, but you may not need that much."

"You think I'm hopeless."

"Just the opposite."

"What do you mean?"

"I have high hopes for you."

"Thank you, Dr. Delaware. I needed that."

At ten twenty-eight, Detective Raul Biro phoned to ask if I could make a one p.m. meeting at Hollywood Division.

"Progress?"

"Nothing I've heard about. Petra just said she wanted a sit-down. She's over in Records, figures to be clear by one."

"I'll be there. How's the Whitbread surveillance going?"

"I'm a block up from her place right now. So far, it's real quiet."

"Thanks for calling, Raul. See you at one."

"I won't be there," he said. "I'm sticking to Whitbread like Krazy Glue."

The conference room at Hollywood Division smelled like a catering truck.

On the wall was a poster of Bin Laden wearing a cartoonishly dirty diaper. The caption said, *Someone get me out of this dump.*

Milo wrestled with a sumo-sized double chili-cheeseburger, Petra nibbled on curly fries and a Mexican salad, Dave Saunders and Kevin Bouleau chopsticked pork lo mein from paper plates.

A wrapped parcel sat in front of an empty chair.

Petra said, "Got you a steak sandwich but I can't vouch for the quality."

"Or the species," said Saunders, twirling a stick.

I thanked her and sat down.

She said, "It's been a good morning, thanks to our Central brethren." Flourishing a hand at Saunders and Bouleau.

Saunders's mouth was full. Bouleau said, "We found Grant's kill-spot, abandoned building on Santee. A homeless guy who crashes nearby remembers seeing a Hummer pull up and some guys getting out. He isn't sure if it was two or three and doesn't know when they left because he was stewed on Night Train. To be honest, this isn't a person who's totally sane. But the fact that he spotted the Hummer's decent evidence, not too many of those cruising that neighborhood."

Saunders swallowed. "They left blood on the floor and the walls, but took the casings. Initial scrapings are O-positive, which is Grant's type and common, but I'll lay odds with anyone who wants to bet against the DNA."

I said, "Leaving a Hummer in full sight says they were confident about not being discovered."

Saunders said, "No one's around there at night and guys who'd shoot their own compadre in cold blood probably figured they could handle a car-booster."

I thought the topic merited more discussion but kept silent.

Milo said, "Excellent work."

Bouleau grinned. "It's what we do."

Saunders said, "No luck finding any of Grant's relatives, yet. But we're relentless."

"We roar like lions but we dig like moles," said Bouleau. "And wait, kids, there's more, little surprise at the autopsy. Mr. Grant was shot to death but first they tried to strangle him. Coroner found a ligature mark around his neck. Grant being so big, it was obscured by fat folds when the C.I. looked him over. No rupture of the hyoid, but there was some bruising and petechial hemorrhaging in the eyes—in the corners, you'd have to be looking for it."

Saunders said, "Like you said, they tried to choke him out, dude was too big, so they shot him."

Petra said, "Any sign of a struggle?"

"Nope. And given Grant's size, a frontal attack would have produced upwardly angling pathways. The tracks in Grant say he was probably prone when he got drilled. The room was basically an empty shell, big cold place, some discarded rusty engine parts in a corner, it used to be a machine shop or something."

Milo said, "Big guy like that just lies back and takes it?"

"Coroner wonders if he was tranquilized, let's see what the tox screen says."

I said, "Choking's more personal. More of a thrill."

"My thought exactly, Doc," said Bouleau. "But his neck was too thick so practicality won out."

Petra said, "Attempted strangulation could also mean two people. Meaning Fisk's car left near Lindbergh Field could've been a ruse."

"He drives down there, comes back some other way?" said Saunders. "If he knows he's being looked for, why would he return?"

"Because De Paine needed him," I said.

"Dude must pay well," said Bouleau.

Milo said, "Dude has income, from trucking heroin, dirty pictures, anything else people lust for. He does well enough with dope to leave behind a grand worth of H at Lester Jordan's. We know he used speed and booze as a kid, but with that kind of self-control, he probably doesn't shoot smack. But maybe Moses Grant was into H and that incapacitated him same as Jordan. When's the tox coming back?"

Saunders said, "Couple of days, three, four. We were lucky to get the autopsy prioritized."

Petra said, "How'd you pull that off?"

"To be honest, we had nothing to do with it. Coroner saw lig marks in addition to bullet holes, got curious, put Grant at the top of the pile."

I unwrapped my steak sandwich, revealed a three-ounce sliver of something oily corrupting two halves of crumbly French roll. Closer inspection revealed curling cutlet verging on cinder, lettuce in need of Viagra.

Petra said, "Ooh. Sorry—share my salad."

"No, I'm fine."

"Oh, man," said Saunders, "whatever that is could turn a carnivore into a vegan. Want some Chinese, Doc?"

"No, thanks."

Milo hoisted his burger. "I'm not offering."

I said, "This is when you find out who your friends are."

"I'm watching out for your cholesterol." He put down the sand-wich. "Westside can't compete in the evidence department, folks, but there's more to hear about Mr. Whitbread/De Paine than dope, and it ain't pretty."

Three pairs of eyes sparked with curiosity. Milo told the story.

CHAPTER

34

Petra said, "Animal guts. That is one sick Chihuahua." She shoved her salad aside.

Kevin Bouleau said, "It's nasty but if Grant really was a solid citizen who just happened to hang with two bad guys, I'm not seeing any connection to our case."

"So far we haven't learned anything to the contrary, Kev."

"Damn shame. I like it better when bad guys meet an untimely end. More leads and you don't have to feel as sorry unless they've got nice relatives."

"Weeping mothers, the worst," said Dave Saunders. "So where do we go from here?"

Petra said, "We all have the same goal: find these two sweethearts. Robert Fisk is a gym rat and a martial arts freak plus he likes to dance. But all my inquiries in those directions have gotten nowhere. Blaise De Paine visited his mommy right before Jordan's murder, so we know he's on speaking terms with her. Raul's watching her house as we speak. No luck subpoenaing her phone records, her only crime is giving birth to the little bastard and he hasn't been formally identified as a suspect. On top of that, everything's tightened up on data searches because of Fortuno. If you guys learn something that connects Grant to De Paine, I'll try again."

"We will sharpen our claws and dig," said Bouleau. "If Grant is a citizen he left tracks. So you got a face-to-face with Fortuno, huh? We Downtown folk never get to meet celebrities."

"Not an impressive piece of humanity, Kev. You didn't miss anything."

"Maybe so, but I'm still looking for stories to tell my grandkids when I'm drooling on the front porch." Bouleau turned serious. "Given the Fortuno link and De Paine being a music guy, you see any showbiz connections to any of this?"

Petra said, "I've asked around and so has Dr. Delaware's girlfriend—she works with musicians, helped I.D. De Paine in the first place. Guy's not a player, just dabbles on the fringes."

"Sounds like ninety-nine percent of the mopes in Hollywood," said Saunders. To Petra: "No offense, but doesn't your captain have a SAG card?"

"He does, but he's done real work for it."

Bouleau said, "Like what?"

"Technical advising." Not mentioning Stu Bishop's minor acting roles.

"Really?" said Bouleau. "Can he get me a card? I'll advise anyone about anything."

Saunders said, "De Paine lives on the fringe but has expensive wheels registered to a bogus corporation. Dude like that isn't likely to be crashing in a studio apartment in the middle of the LAX flight path."

I said, "Maybe he's living in a house his mother owns."

Petra said, "I've already looked into that. Mary's total holdings are the four Mid-Wilshire duplexes Myron sold her and a six-unit in Encino. De Paine isn't staying at any of them."

"Those are the properties in her name," I said.

"She's got a shadow corporation? I guess anything's possible."

Dave Saunders said, "Time to check the DBA files, Detective Connor."

Kevin Bouleau said, "Narcotics have anything to say about De Paine?"

Petra said, "They don't know him."

Saunders said, "He's dealing all these years and never got busted for anything?"

"Apparently."

"Lucky boy," said Bouleau. "Or he's connected. Fortuno knows lots of criminal lawyers." Slow smile. "Which is a redundancy, right?"

Saunders said, "Back to the world of showbiz?"

"If only, partner."

To us: "Kevin wants to be Will Smith."

Bouleau said, "Why not? Have you seen *Mrs.* Smith? But hey, am I off the mark? Fortuno's a fixer and it sounds like this boy may have gotten fixed."

Petra said, "It's possible something was stifled before it got to the arrest stage, but if charges were never filed, good luck finding out. Good luck finding anyone who'll admit *thinking* about Fortuno."

Saunders dabbed his lips with a napkin.

Kevin Bouleau said, "So we've got a Class A whodunit. Guess we were due . . . okay, so Dave and I just continue working Grant and you do your thing on Lester Jordan, and if the high road meets the low road, we confer. Any psychological issues to consider here, Doctor?"

I said, "The neighborhood where Grant was shot wasn't populated but it was still brazen for Fisk and De Paine to cruise around in a Hummer at night. Ditching Fisk's car in San Diego and returning here to kill Grant was also high-risk, considering they had easy access to the Mexican border or could've headed east for Nevada."

"L.A.'s their comfort zone?" said Petra.

"I think there's more to it than that. Lester Jordan's murder was accomplished with guile, but Fisk left his print on Jordan's window. If you're right about Grant being tranquilized, that was more guile. But Grant was big and strong and resisted so they shot him point-blank. They took the shell casings but didn't bother cleaning up his blood. Then they dumped him where he was sure to be found."

Milo said, "Mix of evasive and brazen."

I said, "There's an amateurish quality to all of it—playing at clever while being blatant and exhibitionistic. That fits with De Paine's theatrical demeanor and with Fisk's body-consciousness. It also points to a thrill motive. Jordan and Grant may have been eliminated to cover something up, but the killings took on their own meaning."

"Once you off your daddy, the rest gets easier," said Saunders.

"I've interviewed serial murderers. Several have told me after they pull off a few killings they start to feel invisible. The good part is it leads them to get careless and I can see these two headed in that direction."

Petra said, "What's the bad part?"

"Given De Paine's sexual kinks, they could be gearing up for something really unpleasant."

Petra said, "I've hand-checked the files. No one got brutalized on or near Fourth Street five years before or after the time Patty and Tanya lived there. I guess it's possible something didn't get reported but maybe we shouldn't limit ourselves to Patty's old neighborhoods because of some ambiguous message about the guy being 'close by.'"

"I'm not wedded to geography," I said, "but I'd at least canvass Fourth Street to find out if anyone's still around from back then."

"I agree," said Milo. "It would need to be done without tipping off Mary Whitbread, and she knows my face and yours."

Dave Saunders said, "A couple of tall, handsome African American gentlemen sauntering door-to-door isn't exactly inconspicuous. Plus we need to concentrate on Grant."

Petra played with black strands of hair and laughed. "Leaving guess-who. You really think it's worth it, Alex?"

I said, "It might not help you find De Paine, but it could lead back to the original motive."

She closed her eyes, massaged the lids. Opened them and aimed clear brown irises at each of us in turn. "Nothing else seems to be panning out. If Raul spots Mary leaving her house, I'll give it a try. Maybe I'll buy a Girl Scout uniform and sell cookies."

She stood and gathered her files. "Talk about self-delusion."

Milo said, "Hey, do the pigtail thing, you could pull it off."

"My hair's too short and you lie shamelessly," she said. "For which I thank you."

Robin's note said she'd taken Blanche to her studio in Venice, would be back around six. I called Tanya and told her I needed to see her as soon as possible.

"I've got lab until four thirty and work-study at six."

"Four thirty it is. I'll come to campus."

"Is everything okay, Dr. Delaware?"

"No emergency, but I need to touch base with you."

"You're worried about me," she said. "My OCD."

First time she'd put a name on it.

I said, "If that's on your mind we can deal with it, too. But I'm talking about the investigation."

"You caught someone?"

"Not yet—let's talk in person, Tanya."

Telling, not asking.

She said, "If you say so. Where?"

"Do you eat dinner before work?"

"Not a meal. Sometimes I buy junk from a machine and sit outside if the weather's nice."

"The weather looks fine. How about the inverted fountain?"

"Sure," she said. "I like that spot."

I hadn't run for a few days and decided to walk the three miles to the U.

Before I left, I phoned Robin. She said, "Think you'll be back by dinner?"

"Planning to."

"Takeout okay?"

"Fine."

"Any particular ethnicity?"

"I'm a pluralist."

"I'm thinking Mexican. The place on Barrington that delivers."

"Fine."

"You're preoccupied," she said. "I could've said deep-fried cardboard."

"I'll try to be focused by six. Let me run something by you, babe. The more I learn about De Paine, the more concerned I am about Tanya's safety. How do you feel about her staying with us, temporarily? She really has no one else."

"Sure," she said. "Even if she doesn't make her own bed."

"This one makes her bed. She might make ours if we don't move quickly enough."

"Hmm," she said. "Anything else I should know about her?"

"She's under a lot of stress but she's a good kid."

"Bring her over."

"You're a doll."

"So they say."

"Who's they?"

"Mostly you say it. But every so often I have been known to evoke admiration from others. Back in high school I nearly made it in with the *popular* girls."

Thinking about Blaise De Paine avoiding a police record got me thinking about Mario Fortuno. He'd said his ex-wife would be calling soon but she hadn't. Had Fortuno ever intended to follow through? Or was the negotiation in his hotel room a pathetic distraction from the joys of protective custody?

Not my problem; Santa Barbara was a beautiful town but I had plenty to keep me busy in L.A.

I arrived at the fountain five minutes early but Tanya was already there. So was Kyle.

The two of them sat thigh-to-thigh, his arm around her shoulder, her hand on his knee. Book bags on the ground, talking earnestly. Tanya listened to something Kyle said, smiled, tilted her head back. He touched her chin, her cheek, played with her hair. They rubbed noses. Kissed lightly. Got lost in each other's eyes. Lip-locked for a good thirty seconds.

I stood back until they came up for breath. Waited as they dove into a grinding kiss.

When they broke for air, I said, "Afternoon, guys."

They both stiffened. Two hand-in-the-cookie-jar stares.

I sat down next to Kyle. He wore his Princeton sweatshirt, grubby jeans with non-intentional rips, the shameful yellow running shoes. Sparse black stubble dotted his chin. His fingernails were gnawed ragged.

Tanya's jeans were pressed. Her pale blue sweater was spotless. Tiny seed pearls glinted from her ears.

I said, "What I've learned about Blaise De Paine and Robert Fisk makes me concerned about your safety, Tanya. If De Paine suspects your mother told you something incriminating, he could come after you. That's far from certainty, but we are talking about someone who murdered his own father. I know you're careful but I don't like the idea of your living alone and it's time to be flexible. Moving's a hassle but it wouldn't be long-term, what do you think?"

Tanya looked at Kyle.

He said, "We're way past that. Tanya's moving in with me."

"It's the optimal solution," she said. "Hancock Park is an extremely safe neighborhood, Kyle's got a premium security system, and I'd never be alone because someone's always in the house. It wouldn't even be a major change. I used to live there."

Smiling at Kyle.

He said, "Every single door and window is alarmed and the system is maintained regularly."

He tightened his grip on Tanya's arm. She shifted closer, put one hand on the back of his neck, kept the other drumming his knee.

He said, "I'm talking alarm screens and infrared motion detectors that can be switched on in multiple zones and motion-triggered perimeter lighting all around the property."

"Sounds like state-of-the-art," I said.

"Grandpa was always safety-conscious but he upgraded years ago after a neighbor—a diamond dealer on June Street—was murdered. We've never come remotely close to being broken into."

"Wilfred Hong," I said.

"Who's that?"

"The diamond dealer."

"The police investigated that as a link to Ms. Bigelow?"

"They looked into every unsolved homicide that occurred near any of Tanya and her mom's residences."

"And?"

"Nothing, so far. For the moment, we're going to narrow it to the Fourth Street area, possibly a crime that wasn't reported. Do you recall anything new, Tanya?"

She shook her head.

Kyle said, "You're concentrating on Fourth because Pete lived there."

"Yes."

"You might want to consider a computerized database, some kind of algorithm that could classify crimes based on multifactorial indexes. Give me access to the data and I could set it up reasonably quickly."

"We've got that."

"Oh," he said. "And still nothing?"

"Afraid not."

"So Pete got away with something . . . why do you think you can get him now?"

"We're drawing the net tighter," I said. "It's just a matter of time."

"Well," he said, "until that bright shiny day, Tanya stays with me."

Not asking, telling.

I said, "Sounds like a plan."

"It's a great plan. I've also got weapons. Grandpa had a huge gun collection, there's a special room in the basement for them."

"Do you shoot?" I said.

"No, but how hard can it be?"

Tanya said, "There are seven bedrooms, I'll have my own space." Blushing.

Like a chameleon on a leaf, Kyle's face soaked up her color. "She'll be safe, I'll see to it."

I said, "Tanya, do your best to be reachable. And when you're on campus, be especially careful."

Kyle cleared his throat. "As in walking to and from the library."

Tanya lifted her hand from his knee. "We've been through that. I need to work."

"I don't see why you can't take a temporary leave—"

"Kyle—"

"—fine, fine. Just be careful."

"I always am."

He grazed the ends of her hair with his fingers. "Sorry. I don't mean to patronize."

She patted his thigh.

He sighed.

I said, "Do you remember what De Paine and Fisk look like?"

Reaching into her book bag, she withdrew a thin, glossy magazine. *National Insider.* Garish colors, suggestive headlines, the cover attraction a close-up of a starlet's derriere insured for ten million bucks. Above the prized mounds, the actress looked over her shoulder and come-hithered the camera.

A yellow Post-it tagged a page toward the rear. Tanya flipped.

Group shots taken at various night spots in L.A. and New York, accompanied by snarky captions.

Tanya jabbed a photo in the lower left corner. Late-night party at the Roxbury. The paparazzi targets were a washed-up rock drummer

and the pneumatic slattern with whom he'd sired six kids; the supporting players, a coke-eyed clothing designer and a NASCAR driver who
should've known better.

Behind that quartet, just right of the designer's rusty dreadlocks,
was a thin, boyish face. Eye-shadowed and mascaraed.

Black hair spiked with yellow, elfin grin, chipmunk teeth. Hint of
scarlet, gold-collared tunic.

Tension around the neck as Pete Whitbread aka Blaise De Paine
strained to get in the picture. He'd succeeded but hadn't made the caption.

I said, "This was in the pile you took from the hospital?"

Tanya nodded. "Mommy must've seen it." Pointing to a sharp
white diagonal crease, oily remnants of fingerprint. "I decided to throw
them out, was carrying a stack out to the garbage when I broke down
and started crying on the back steps. All of a sudden, I was going
through them. This page had been folded, it caught my attention."

I looked at the picture again.

She said, "Seeing him like that—knowing what a terrible person he
was and here he was partying with celebrities. *That's* what made her tell
me. I'm certain she was trying to protect me."

I said, "This may have been the tipping point but De Paine was already on her mind." I told her about Moses Grant's E.R. visit.

"You think he threatened her?" said Tanya.

"Subtly or otherwise. Maybe something to do with you."

Tears filled her eyes. "She must've been so worried. And then she
got sick and couldn't do anything about it. And then she saw *this.* Poor
Mommy."

She wept. Kyle held her.

When the tears stopped, he said, "My question, honey, is why didn't
she just come out and warn you to watch out for De Paine?"

"Maybe she planned to, then she . . ."

More crying. "She did what she could to *protect* me, Kyle."

"I know, I know."

I said, "I think she wasn't satisfied with warning you, Tanya. If De
Paine threatened you, she wanted him caught and directed you to people who could pull that off."

"If that's what she intended," said Kyle, "it was borderline brilliant."

Tanya didn't answer.

He said, "Totally brilliant," took her hand, laced his fingers through hers.

She didn't move.

Kyle said, "Protecting you gave her meaning, honey. And she succeeded. You've got a whole army behind you."

And you'd like to be the general.

35

R obin fed *arroz con pollo* to Blanche. "And here I was all prepared to nurture a member of my own species. I just finished
setting up the guest room."

I said, "Sorry. The two of them came up with their own plan."

"This boy can be trusted?"

"He seems madly in love with her."

"Seems?"

"He loves her."

"Listen to me," she said. "I've never met the girl and I'm med-
dling."

The reflexive response never made it out of my mouth: *maternal instinct.*

Robin and I used to talk about having children. Years ago, after our
first breakup, she got pregnant by a man she barely liked and termi-
nated at six weeks. Since then, the topic hadn't come up.

During that time I'd healed hundreds of other people's children,
considered the possibility that I might never be a father. Sometimes I
was able to appreciate the irony. When that didn't work I busied myself
with the pathologies of strangers.

Blanche panted for more rice and Robin obliged. When the next
gulp was followed by begging, she said, "We don't want to stress your

tummy, cutie," and began clearing the dishes. Standing at the sink, she said, "Her staying with him is probably for the best. We'd do our best to be cool hosts but being under our roof would've stifled her."

I got up and placed my hands on her shoulders.

She said, "Let's take a drive."

When we have nowhere to go, we usually end up somewhere on Pacific Coast Highway. This time, Robin said, "How about bright lights, big quasi-city?"

I drove Sunset east through Hollywood and the Los Feliz district, crossed into Silver Lake where she'd heard about a new jazz club.

The Gas Station turned out to be a former Union 76 outlet that still sported blue paint and smelled of motor oil. Inside were antique gravity pumps, mismatched plastic chairs and tables, photo blowups of musical geniuses.

Five other customers in a room that held forty. We sat close to the stage, under the piercing glare of Miles Davis.

A quartet of guys in their sixties was pushing lightweight bebop. Robin had worked on the guitarist's Gibson archtop and he acknowledged her with a smile and a spirited solo on Monk's "Well You Needn't." When the set was over, he and the drummer sat down with us and made thin, alcoholic conversation. Somewhere along the line, Robin worked in the topic of Blaise De Paine. Neither of the musicians had heard of him. When Robin told them about his mixes, they cursed viciously, apologized, and went out for air.

We stuck around through the next set, made it home by eleven forty-five, put on pajamas, fell asleep holding hands.

Just after three a.m., I was sitting up in bed, wrenched awake by a pounding heart and throbbing temples. Gnawing pain below my rib cage felt like mice clawing my diaphragm. I deep-breathed some of that away.

Then the tape loop began:

Was Tanya really safe with Kyle?

He'd found her on Facebook. What would stop De Paine from doing the same thing?

Plenty of guns in Kyle's house but he had no clue how to use them. Despite his hero fantasies, he couldn't be everywhere.

Tanya was a stubborn girl.

I pictured her leaving the library alone, late at night.

Small girl, huge campus.

So easy to—Stop.

Would Tanya really be safe with Kyle—STOP!

Fine, fine, but would Tanya really be safe—

Robin stirred.

I sank back down.

Facebook.

What would stop De Paine. Big campus.

Gunsstubborngirl—

One hundred, ninety-nine, ninety-eight—there you go, this stuff works.

Seconds of respite.

Stubborn girl . . . what would stop . . .

The next morning I pretended to be rested.

When Robin got out of the shower, she said, "Did you have a rough night?"

"I was playing the sinus-tuba?"

"No, but you moved around a lot."

"Maybe that's the cure," I said.

"Being restless?"

"Symptom substitution."

"I'd rather you be peaceful."

"I'm fine, babe."

We dressed in silence. "Breakfast, Alex?"

"No, thanks, not hungry."

"What's on your mind, sweetie?"

"Nothing, really."

She took my hand. "You've done what you can for her. With all those detectives looking, those creeps will be found."

"I'm sure you're right."

"Let's at least have coffee before I go."

After she left for work, I drove to the U., parked in a pay lot on the south end, and walked to the science quad. Hordes of students and faculty crossed the square. No sign of Robert Fisk or Blaise De Paine. Or Tanya.

I drifted north to the inverted fountain, walked through the physics building. Exited at the back and continued along a tree-shaded pathway. Foot traffic was heavy for the summer. Seconds later I spotted a small, muscular, shaved-head guy among the students. Wearing all black; perfect fit to Fisk's stats.

Sauntering along the outer edge of the crowded pathway.

I got closer, trailed him until the front steps of the anthropology building, where two young women in tight jeans ran up to greet him.

As he turned toward them, I caught a glimpse of his face. Mid-forties, clean-shaven.

One of the women said, "Hi, Professor Loewenthal. Could we talk to you about the exam?"

I bought coffee at a kiosk, strolled to the library, was just about to enter when my phone beeped.

Milo said, "Ballistics just came back on the bullets that killed Moses Grant. Perfect match to the slugs dug out of Leland Armbruster. Little Petey was *real* precocious. Lord knows what else he's done that we haven't uncovered. Talk to Tanya yet?"

"She's moving in with Kyle."

"Girl in a big house," he said. "So now it's Gothic. Think it's a good idea?"

"It's what they've decided."

"Kyle playing Lord Protector. A few more years of living and he might conceivably be minimally qualified."

"He's green but motivated. The larger problem is he can't be with her every second. What do you think about faxing the photos of De Paine and Fisk over to the unicops?"

"Sure, but don't expect too much. First thing outta those guys' mouths is always how understaffed they are. Let's talk later about beefing up security for her. Meanwhile, we just might be getting a little closer to whatever happened ten years ago. Mary Whitbread left her house at nine thirty and Biro followed her. She's still out, trying on designer duds at Neiman Marcus. Petra got to the neighborhood by ten fifteen, found someone on Blackburn who remembered the bad old days. Lives right behind Mary. He wouldn't talk at his house or the station but Petra convinced him to meet over in Encino where his office is. One p.m." He read off the address.

"Nervous fellow," I said.

"Seems to be. Maybe he should practice what he preaches. He's one of you guys."

Before setting out for the Valley, I pulled Dr. Byron Stark's stats from the psychology licensing board Web site. Twenty-eight years old, B.A., Cornell, Ph.D., University of Oregon, postdoc at the Portland V.A., freshly certified.

His building was a six-story mirrored cube on Ventura and Balboa that had all the charm of a head cold. The door said *Advent Behavioral Group*. Stark's was the last of fourteen names. Six psychiatrists, eight psychologists, specialties in eating disorders, substance abuse, strategic management, career guidance, "life coaching."

Stark's single-window office and hard beige furniture fit his status.

He was midsized and narrow-shouldered, wore a blue minicheck buttondown shirt, maroon tie, and pressed khakis. A round, pink baby-face was topped by a beige crew cut. A fuzzy goatee looked glued on. Beneath the wisps, his small mouth seemed permanently pursed; the resulting look of disapproval wouldn't serve him well with patients.

When I'd started out, I'd tried to ward off the *Doctor, how* old *are you?*s with facial hair. I have a heavy beard and sometimes it worked. Stark would need another source of gravitas.

Petra, Milo, and I crowded in front of his desk.

She said, "Thanks for meeting with us, Doctor."

Stark said, "Byron's fine."

Boyish voice. *Use the title, kid. Harness every bit of placebo.*

"I didn't expect a symposium, Detective Connor."

Petra said, "It's an important case. We brought our psychological consultant." She introduced me.

He said, "What do you do for them, profiling?"

I shook my head. "Formal profiling's pretty much useless when it comes to solving crimes. I weigh in on a case-by-case basis."

"I considered a forensics fellowship until I read up on profiling and found it basically without merit. Talk about restricted sampling."

We traded jargon for a while. Stark relaxed. When he broke to take a phone call—something about billing for inpatient services—Petra gave me a go-ahead nudge.

"Sorry," he said, hanging up. "Still learning the system."

I said, "We appreciate your talking to us about Peterson Whitbread."

"It's funny to hear you say that. I never thought this day would come."

"Why's that?"

"Right after the girls disappeared, my father called the police. They were totally unresponsive."

"The girls . . ."

Stark's mouth compressed to a pink bud. "You're not here about that."

Milo said, "We're here to listen, Doctor."

Stark laughed. "I agreed to this because I thought someone was finally going to investigate, like one of those cold cases on TV." To Petra: "That was the clear implication you gave me, Detective Connor."

"What I told you was the truth, Dr. Stark. We're looking into Peterson Whitbread's background. Our immediate focus is on several crimes he's suspected of committing recently, but we're certainly interested in anything he might've done in the past. If you have knowledge of a crime, you need to tell us."

"Unbelievable," said Stark. "So he's suspected of something new. No big revelation, his tendencies were obvious even to me."

"Even?"

"I was a senior in high school."

I said, "You're the same age as Pete."

"I am, but we didn't hang out. My parents were teachers who took out loans so my brother and I could attend Burton Academy and Harvard-Westlake. All my spare time was spent studying. Pete always seemed to be out on the street. I'm not sure he even attended high school."

"What tendencies did you notice?"

"Antisocial personality," said Stark. "He lurked around the neighborhood at all hours, with no clear purpose. Smiled a lot but there was no warmth to it. He was blithe to the point of recklessness—would smoke dope openly, just amble up my block toking away, not even trying to hide it. Other times, he'd walk around with a bottle of Jack Daniel's in his rear pocket."

"Not much parental supervision."

"None that I ever saw. My mother said his mother was an airhead more concerned with fashion than child-rearing. I was fifteen when we moved in, my brother a year younger. Mom sized up the situation pretty quickly and forbade both of us from having anything to do with him."

I said, "Some teens would rebel at that kind of restriction."

"Some would, *I* didn't," said Stark. "He was clearly someone who wouldn't be good for me. And that was buttressed by what happened a few months after we moved in. There were a bunch of burglaries in the neighborhood. Nighttime break-ins, while people were sleeping. My parents were convinced Pete had something to do with it. My dad, in particular, was certain he had criminal tendencies."

"Why?"

"Pete sassed him a couple of times. And I wouldn't discount Dad's opinion. He worked as a high school counselor, had experience with acting-out adolescents."

Milo said, "Tell us about the girls."

"There were two of them, the summer before my senior year they lived above Mrs. Whitbread and Pete. Older than me, maybe twenty-one, twenty-two. A few months later—after I took my SATs but before I went on a college tour, so it would have to be late September or early October—they disappeared. Dad tried to spur some police interest but couldn't get anyone to take him seriously."

Petra said, "Where can I reach your father?"

"Eugene, Oregon. His and my mom's pensions stretch a lot further up there, so after I graduated they sold me their place and got a house with acreage."

"Names and number, please."

"Herbert and Myra Stark. I can't guarantee they'll cooperate. When the police didn't get back to Dad about the girls, he got so irate he complained to his councilman. But no help there, either. No one cared."

Petra said, "What were the girls' names?"

"I never knew their surnames, their first names were Roxy and Brandy. We knew that because they'd shout to each other, didn't matter what time of day. Bran-deee, Rox-eee."

"What did they do for a living?"

"My parents said those were stripper names, they had to be strippers, but I had my doubts."

"Why?"

"Strippers would work at night, right? But those two had irregular hours. Sometimes they'd be gone during the day, other times, at night. They always left together, arrived together. Weekends they'd sleep in, never show themselves. During the week they'd be out, working and partying."

"Tell us about the partying."

"I don't know for a fact, I'm using logic. They'd drive up three, four a.m., race the engine, slam the car door, and if that hadn't woken us, their laughter and chattering did the trick. They were extremely raucous and from the way they slurred their words, high on something."

"Your parents ever complain?"

"Never, not their style. Instead, they fumed and gossiped and regaled Galen and me with morality tales using the girls as negative examples. Of course, the end result was to get Galen and me interested. A couple of wild girls living right across the backyard? But we never tried to talk to them, even if we'd had the guts there was no opportunity. When they were home, we were at school, and when we were home they were sleeping or out."

Milo said, "They'd come and go together in the same car?"

"Every time I saw."

"Remember the make and model?"

"Sure do. White Corvette, red interior. Dad called it the Bimbomobile."

Petra said, "Tell us about the disappearance and why you suspect Pete."

"Right before I took the SATs I was up in my room and got distracted by loud music. The way my bedroom's situated, I have an angled view of Mrs. Whitbread's yard. The girls were out there sunbathing and blasting a tape deck—dance music. I was about to close the window but got even more distracted by what was going on. They were rubbing lotion on each other, giggling, playing with each other's hair, slapping each other's butts." Stark tightened his tie. "Totally naked, it was kind of hard not to notice."

Milo said, "Good-looking girls."

"Of that type," said Stark. "Long blond hair, long legs, sunlamp tan, big chests. They looked alike, for all I know they were sisters."

"Roxy and Brandy," said Milo. "What year Corvette?"

"Sorry, I'm not a car guy."

"Who'd they hang out with?"

"I never saw them hang with anyone, but that doesn't mean much. Except for that week of SAT prep, I barely saw them during the day. What I *can* tell you is that Pete Whitbread was aware of them. Midway through the week, when I was cramming advanced vocab, really trying to concentrate, the music started blasting again. Same deal, naked girls, lots of merriment. But good little grind that I was, I actually intended to ignore it. Then I noticed Pete sidling down the driveway and sneaking around toward the back. I say sneak because his head was darting all around, obviously furtive. And he'd pressed himself against the wall, found himself a vantage spot where the girls wouldn't notice him. He stood there watching them for a while, then he unzipped his fly and did the predictable. But not normally—he was yanking at himself so hard I thought he'd rip it off. With a bizarre *smile* on his face."

I said, "Bizarre in what way?"

"Teeth bared, like a . . . coyote. Pleasuring himself but he looked angry. Enraged. Or maybe it was just sexual intensity. Whatever it was, it grossed me out and I moved away from the window and never went back. Even when the music blasted the next day and the next."

"The girls had no idea they were being watched?"

"Were they putting on a show for him? I've wondered about that."

"Did you ever see Pete with them?"

"No, but as I said, I wouldn't have. What you *should* be concerned about is a few weeks later, they were gone. Just like that." Snapping his fingers. "No moving van, no truck being loaded. And when they moved in, they did use a van, had tons of stuff. I knew they weren't sleeping in because (A) it wasn't the weekend, (B) the lights never went on for two consecutive days, and (C) on the second day my mother took a walk by and the door to the upstairs apartment was open and a cleaning crew was working full-guns. Plus, the Corvette was still there. Parked in back next to the garage, the girls always parked in the driveway. It sat there for an entire week, then one night I heard it start up and looked out. Someone was easing it out the driveway. Driving extremely slowly, with the headlights off. I told my father and that's when he called the police."

Milo said, "Two days of dark windows."

Byron Stark said, "If you want to believe they just moved to Kansas, be my guest. But maybe you should reserve judgment until I tell you the rest. The night after the car was moved, my father was walking the dog over on Fourth, I'm talking one in the morning."

"Kind of late for a dog-walk."

Stark smiled. "I could tell you the dog had a bladder problem but sure, Dad was curious, we all were. And it paid off. A van was pulled up to Mrs. Whitbread's building and two guys were loading stuff. When Dad got closer he could see it was Pete and his friend and what they were hauling were garbage bags. Lots of them. When they saw Dad, they jumped in the van and slammed the door shut. Didn't drive away, just sat there. Dad kept walking, circled the block again, stood at the corner. The van was still there but a second later it took off full-speed."

"Did the dog react?" I said.

"Are you asking if he smelled something? Chester wasn't a bloodhound. He was a fourteen-year-old mostly blind, deaf, senile chow mix. It was all Dad could do to get him to exercise. Anyway, Dad came home, told my mom about the van, the two of them decided something horrible had taken place, they had to persist with the police. Frankly, Galen and I thought they were overreacting. But a few weeks later, when Pete's friend showed up dead, we started to believe them. Unfortunately, *you* guys didn't."

Petra said, "Let's back up a bit, Dr. Stark. Who was Pete's friend and how did he die?"

"An older guy, thirty or so. Tall, thin, long hair, unruly beard, kind of bummy. He drove a motorcycle but not a chopper. A Honda, not huge. I had a 350 in grad school and this one was definitely smaller. Noisy little contraption. He'd pick Pete up on it and they'd zoom off. My parents said his name was Roger but I can't tell you where they got that and they never mentioned a last name. More like 'that bum Roger.' Or 'Here's Roger again on that stupid rattletrap.' Their theory was he and Pete were selling dope around the neighborhood, doing the break-ins, as well. It wouldn't surprise me, Roger looked like a doper. Emaciated, spacy, unsteady walk."

Stark ruffled his crew cut. "I know it sounds as if Mom and Dad were obsessed but they weren't. Granted, both of them are huge murder mystery fans and they're into puzzles, but they're also insightful and completely sane. My mother taught in the inner city for twenty years, so she's not naive. And on top of his counseling background, my father was a military policeman in Vietnam and served as a reserve officer in Bakersfield before we moved to L.A. That made it especially irritating when the police here shined him on."

Milo said, "Exactly what did he report?"

"You'd have to talk to him but my recollection is he reported the disappearance as well as the car being moved a week later, plus the van and the garbage bags."

"Not the part about Pete masturbating near the girls?"

Stark colored. "No, I never mentioned that to anyone but my brother. Are you trying to say that would've made a difference? I can tell you it wouldn't. The police were unresponsive."

"What did the police tell your father?" said Petra.

"That Roger's death was an overdose, case closed."

"Please tell us about the death, Doctor."

"From what I understand, the body was found in the gutter, right on Fourth, not far from Pete's building. It happened in the middle of the night and by the time I was awake, the scene was clear."

"How'd you find out?"

"My father heard from a neighbor who didn't know whose corpse it was. Dad called the police for details and of course they didn't want to give any out. Finally, he pried out the fact that it was Roger. That got him to try again to stir up interest in the girls. But whoever he talked to kept insisting there was no evidence of any crime, the girls were adults, a missing person case hadn't been filed, and Roger's death was ruled accidental."

Petra hid her frown behind one hand as she wrote with the other. "After that, did Pete cause any other problems?"

"Not that I heard. But by December I had a girlfriend, wasn't interested in anything at home. Then I went to China as a volunteer with Operation Smile, then to Cornell. This is the first time I've been back in ten years."

"Have you seen Pete recently?"

"No. What's he done?"

She stood. "When we can tell you we will, Dr. Stark. Thanks for your time." Flashing a smile. "Maybe you can call your parents and tell them we're paying attention."

"That might not help. They're strong-willed people."

I said, "Despite their suspicions, they didn't move from the neighborhood."

"No way," said Stark. "They finally owned their own home."

"Hard to beat that," said Milo.

"You bet, Detective. It's all about equity."

CHAPTER

36

Byron Stark's narrowing of time and place made the search easy.

A coroner's file on Roger "Kimo" Bandini was unearthed in the archives at Mission Road and the fax came through to Petra by four p.m.

White male, twenty-nine, six two, one forty. A multitude of old needle tracks, fresh puncture wounds, and a tox screen that shot back a generous amount of speed and a monumental dose of diazepam had all screamed overdose, no need to autopsy. Missing was any record of where Bandini had been buried, or even if his body had been claimed.

By five thirty, Petra had gotten a Wilshire Division detective to unearth the corresponding police file, a slim affair, most of which was a photocopy of the coroner's findings. Sergeant J. Rahab, the coordinator at the scene, noted that an anonymous call at 3:15 a.m. had prompted the call to Fourth Street.

Embedded in Rahab's clumsy prose was mention of a "burglar's kit" found under Bandini's corpse.

Searches of national databases revealed a ten-year police record and several brief incarcerations for Pete Whitbread's friend, stretching from California to Utah: three breaking and enterings, a DUI, two arrests for possession of marijuana, three for methamphetamine, an intent-to-sell crank bust dismissed on procedural grounds the year before Bandini's death.

Neither Peterson Whitbread nor Blaise De Paine showed up on Bandini's buddy list, but Leland Armbruster and Lester Jordan did.

Petra said, "All of them into the Hollywood dope scene. But no cross-reference to Armbruster's homicide file so Isaac never picked it up. Boys, we are still living in the Dark Ages."

Milo said, "Little Petey doesn't respect his elders. They let him in the game and end up dead."

I re-read the coroner's report. My breath caught and jammed up in my chest. I let air out slowly.

Milo said, "Something we missed?"

"The anonymous call was never followed up on. Someone just happening upon a body at that hour is unlikely. Wouldn't you be curious?"

"I'd follow it up," said Petra.

Milo said, "Bandini being a low-life crank-head, no one cared who spotted him. Why do you?"

"Bear with me," I said. "With a passerby being unlikely, the logical assumption would be a neighbor. Bandini's body was found one building east of Patty's duplex. Patty wouldn't want Tanya waking up and seeing that."

Petra said, "And Patty would know a body was lying out on the street because . . ."

I said, " 'Killed a man close by.' "

Milo and Petra looked at each other.

He said, "The terrible thing."

"Hot-shotting Bandini would qualify," I said. "Think about it: His blood was swimming with speed and Valium. He'd been shooting crank for years but there's no mention of downers anywhere in his jacket. Valium *is* a common hospital drug."

Milo rubbed his face.

I said, "Something else Isaac's data search wouldn't pull up because it was classified as an accidental death."

Petra said, "What would be Patty's motive? And how are you suggesting it happened?"

"Unless we find De Paine and he talks, we may never know the details. My guess is he and Bandini were pressuring Patty for prescription drugs. He knew she was a nurse from when she cared for his father and now that she was his mother's tenant, he tried to exploit that. He could've started off wheedling, met resistance, and turned up the pressure. The most effective way would've been a threat against Tanya, veiled or otherwise."

"Patty would give in to that?"

"She might've, out of fear," I said. "She could've developed some serious suspicions—just like the Starks."

Petra rubbed her temples. "She wondered about the missing girls?"

"If De Paine silenced Jordan because he knew about the girls, where would Jordan have found out in the first place? Patty talking to him about his wayward son."

"It's starting to shape up like a whole bunch of people knew about the girls."

Milo said, "When the Starks complained, the department flipped them off, why would anyone else come forward? Jesus."

Petra looked as if she'd swallowed a grub. "Makes me proud to be a sworn law enforcement specialist . . . Alex, you really think Patty could've overdosed someone premeditatedly? And same question: How'd it go down?"

"Let's say Bandini and Pete were behind the hot-prowl break-ins and that Bandini tried the same thing with Patty. Brought his kit late one night, picked her lock, started searching for drugs. Patty woke up, confronted him, used her gun to back him down. She didn't call the police because that wouldn't solve the problem permanently. Bandini would be out eventually, maybe return to get even. So she defused the situation by making a peace offering Bandini couldn't refuse."

Milo said, "I'll dose you up now, and if you behave yourself there's more in the future. But don't come creeping around my place at night. . . yeah, a hungry crank fiend might go for that. He sits in the kitchen, she fixes a needle, Bandini's expecting a jolt of speed, but instead she cocktails him."

"With no extensive downer experience, that much Valium could've stopped his heart cold."

Milo said, "Valium I can see her having, easy to swipe from the hospital. Where would she get meth?"

"The tox screen said amphetamine, unspecified. Any number of prescription stimulants could produce that result. Secondary tests could've teased out the specifics but no one saw any need for that."

"I'm still picturing it," said Petra. "She doses him, sits there, watches him die?"

"Bandini broke in," said Milo.

"That's still cold. And if she had uppers and downers ready, well planned." The room grew silent.

Milo said, "Patty came right out and told Tanya she killed a guy. We were the ones pretending she meant something symbolic. And hell, if Alex is right about what led up to it—hot-prowl break-ins, missing girls, maybe threats to Tanya—I'm happy calling it justifiable."

Petra said, "Whatever happened, the lady's long gone, no sense judging . . . back to the scene for a sec. Bandini croaks, Patty's got a DB to deal with, she drags him out to the street, waits awhile, calls it in . . . guess it fits."

Milo said, "It sure doesn't *not* fit."

She smiled faintly. "You and your grammar, Mr. English Major."

"Lieutenant English Major."

The two of them bantering, so as not to think about Patty.

I said, "Here's something else that fits: Bandini's break-in tools were found under his body, which is consistent with someone wanting to make it look like a bad guy O.D.'ing. But there was no mention of a needle on his person in either the coroner's or the police file. Or anyone looking for a needle."

Petra scanned both reports. Shook her head. "Fresh needle mark in the guy's arm and no one checks it out. Oh, man, this is law enforcement at its finest." To Milo: "You know this Rahab guy?"

"Nope."

"Maybe Stu does . . . not that it's worth churning dust over . . . another question, Alex: If Patty killed Bandini, I can see her leaving his tools in order to show he was a bad guy, maybe set up a little additional distraction. But why wouldn't she do the same for the needle?"

"Her prints were on it," I said. "She might've worried they wouldn't clean off totally, or there'd be some way to trace it back to Cedars and her. Or maybe she simply forgot. She was an amateur in over her head."

"Protecting her kid . . . Mama bears do get aggressive," said Petra.

Her own mother had died birthing her.

Milo said, "Let's get back to the logic of killing Bandini in the first place. If she was out to protect Tanya, why leave Petey alive?"

"He was young and he wasn't directly involved in the break-in," I said. "Having someone else do his dirty work is consistent with everything else we know about him. Maybe Patty got that, figured he wouldn't hassle her on his own."

"Plus," said Petra, "the personal connection to him through his father."

Milo said, "The old mayhem hierarchy. It's okay to shoot a coyote but your neighbor's poodle gets nasty, you have second thoughts."

"Or one killing took everything out of her," said Petra.

Milo said, "Watching a guy fade out could dampen your enthusiasm."

I said, "And prey on your mind forever. Shortly after Bandini's death, she moved to Culver Boulevard, a big comedown. Right after, Tanya came to me for the second time. She talked about Patty being nervous, cleaning compulsively in the middle of the night."

"Anxiety," said Petra.

"Part of the move could've been moving away from Pete's sphere of operations but maybe there was an element of self-punishment, as well. Eventually, she made some kind of peace with it. Then a decade later, Pete reincarnated as Blaise De Paine shows up in her E.R., recognizes her, tells her something that frightens her. I've been assuming verbal menacing of Tanya but what if De Paine threatened to expose her for Bandini's murder?"

" 'I know what you did that summer'?" said Petra. "But De Paine and Patty were the only two people aware of what happened and self-preservation shut both their mouths. So why would De Paine shake that up?"

"He's gotten away with crimes his entire life, is impulsive and egotistical enough to think he's invulnerable. Coming face-to-face with Patty triggered his mouth, he couldn't resist harassing her. It brought back all those memories she'd fought hard to bury. And terrified her. If De Paine chose to incriminate her, her life would fall apart. Everything she'd worked for would be history. Or even worse, it's possible De Paine decided to take revenge by coming after her and Tanya. Maybe she tried to ward him off with a counterthreat. 'I know what *you* did that summer—the missing girls'—and he laughed it off. She realized he was a total sociopath, couldn't be counted on to be careful."

"Risky move bringing up the girls," said Milo. "Be easier just to shoot him."

"But when De Paine showed up in the E.R., he wasn't alone. Patty may have eliminated a hungry speed freak but stalking and murdering three apparent bad guys was way out of her league. Maybe she even contemplated ways to do it. But then she got sick. As a nurse, she knew she had very little time left, had to prioritize getting Tanya's future in order. Once she did that—when her strength had waned to almost nothing—she tried to warn Tanya. Refused her pain meds so she could cling to consciousness. She managed to direct Tanya to me, but I was a stop along the way. It was you she wanted involved."

"Aw, shucks," said Milo, grimacing. "Getting terminally ill right after being reminded of your big sin, a religious person could see that as divine retribution. What was Patty's take on faith?"

"We never discussed it," I said. "But whatever views she started off with, knowing death is imminent changes everything. She had so much to do in so little time, struggled to sort out what to tell Tanya. Whatever her cognitive state, her worries stayed with her because she was obsessive. Pinpricks in a fading brain."

He winced at the image.

Petra said, "As she's trying to figure it out, Tanya brings her those magazines, she leafs through, spots De Paine hobnobbing. *That* could've been seen as Cosmic Fate. She decides to tell Tanya about the terrible thing with an eye to warning her, but is too sick to get it all out?"

"That and she didn't want Tanya handling it alone."

"She sows, we reap."

Milo said, "Let's talk about Brandy and Roxy. Two girls vanish from a nice neighborhood without being missed?"

Petra said, "I put a call in to Stark's father, haven't heard back. Stark Junior does seem to be right about no MP report being filed. So what do we do now, put an ad out about two strippers who haven't been seen for a decade? Girls in that business can lead transient lives. Maybe they did move out in the middle of the night—escaping debt. Left the Vette behind for the same reason. For all we know, the car was days from the repo man."

"Maybe they weren't strippers," I said. "Became Mary Whitbread's tenants through a work connection."

"Porn actresses."

"It would explain the irregular hours."

"Daytime shoots," said Milo, "and nighttime's the right time for some extra-cash escorting. Being a Hollywood person, you know anyone in the biz, kiddo?"

Petra said, "Hey, that's Valley stuff."

"If the two of them made films ten years ago," I said, "they might be listed on some video Web site."

"Ah," said Milo. "The rigors of research."

Petra said, "I don't think I should do that on the department computer. Things are so jumpy around here since Fortuno went into protective that even a righteous porn search is going to look sleazy."

I said, "Speaking of which, Fortuno might remember the girls."

Petra pulled out S.A. Wanamaker's card, punched the number. Hung up. "Disconnected. If I have time, I'll try his superiors and if that doesn't work, I'll talk to Stu. But my gut says the Feebies have cooperated as much as they're going to. You guys mind surfing a few dirty sites?"

"I'd do it," said Milo, "but my delicate constitution and all that. Also, there's actual detecto-stuff I'd like to try, like harassing various Vice personnel around town to find out if Brandy and Roxy ever got busted on their turf."

They both looked at me.

"Sure," I said.

"Hey," said Milo, "if you enjoy it, all the better."

At seven thirty, I took Robin out to a quiet dinner at the Pacific Dining Car in Santa Monica. By nine, we were back.

She said, "Want to play Scrabble or something?"

I said, "Sorry, got to look at filthy pictures."

Vivacious Videos' Web site had logged five million viewers during the last three months. Videos and DVDs on sale, special offers if I acted *NOW!*

User-friendly site, just plug in the names and catch an eyeful.

Brandee Vixen and *Rocksi Roll* had co-starred in eleven movies, all girl-on-girl, filmed during a one-year period.

Ten years ago.

The films were classified as "old-school classics." The director and producer were proud enough to list their names.

Darrel Dollar and Benjamin Baranelli, respectively. Maybe Baranelli wasn't a pseudonym.

His name pulled up twelve hits and three images. Little knob-nosed, white-haired man in his seventies, presenting the award for best oral scene at the Adult Film Convention in Las Vegas to a six-foot blonde in pigtails.

She was topless. Baranelli wore an amethyst velvet dinner jacket, tomato-red turtleneck, chest medallion the size of a dessert plate, and grotesquely wide denture smile.

I switched to various yellow-page sites. No business listing under Baranelli's name. I tried 818 information on a lark, was stunned to get a residential hit.

Baranelli, Benjamin A., Tarzana, no address.

A wheezy, dry old man's voice answered, "Yeah?"

I rattled off a fast, ambiguous introduction, threw in Brandee and Rocksi's names.

Baranelli said, "Finally you idiots do something."

"Which—"

"You cops. They were gorgeous girls, what, they just walked off the face of the earth? I called, over and over, got nowhere. Because of jobism."

"Jobism?"

"Discrimination cause by what they did for a living. This was some so-called straight actress who sucked cock and did weekly bukkake to get her sitcom job and then pretended she was born without a pussy, the SWAT team woulda come out in force. You guys are fucking puritan hypocrites."

"What can you tell me about—"

"I can tell you those girls had a bright career. No way—no *fuck*ing way—would they just boogie off and not tell me. We did a film a month, each one doubled the gross of the last, they were making good money. Because of the E-factor. Know what that is?"

"No—"

"*Enthusiasm.* Every girl who walks in has the hair, the tits, the tongue. Some of them even fake you out at the audition. Then you put 'em in a scene and they generate as much enthusiasm as Hillary doing it with Bill. What I'm telling you is *those* two didn't have to fake it. They were *into* each other. They were in *love.*"

"Do you know their real names?"

"*Now* you're asking?"

"Better late than never."

"Not when it comes to a money-shot, heh, heh . . . their real names? Brandee—with the two *ee*'s, that was my idea, to set her apart from the *y*'s and the *i*'s—Brandee was Brenda something. Rocksi was Renée something . . . don't recall the last names. They were from Iowa. Or Idaho, something like that. One of those religious nut things."

"A cult?"

"They told me they had to pray all day and dress up like Amishes or nuns. Which gave me the idea for the fourth picture we made— *Nasty Habits.*"

"Do you remember the name of the cult?"

"I don't remember what I never knew. Why would I give a shit?"

"How old were they?"

"Legal. Don't try to—"

"I'm just trying to get as many details as I can. What else did they tell you about their backgrounds?"

"That's it," said Baranelli. "That's what happen when you exploit kids."

"What do you mean?"

"Religious nuts, always pressuring. So what do the kids do? They rebel, right? Those two got off the bus from Iowa, a few weeks later they had fake tits and tongue-pierces and were ready to go."

"Who paid for the surgery?"

"Listen to me carefully: They were of age and it's no crime helping someone improve their self-esteem. That's all I'm going to say. Good night, I'm turning off the phone, don't bother me again."

CHAPTER

37

Next day: division of labor.

Raul Biro continued to watch Mary Whitbread's duplex. She shopped in the morning, lunched alone at Il Pastaio in Beverly Hills, seemed to know the waiters quite well. Arriving home at three, she stayed in. No sign of her son or Robert Fisk.

Petra's fourth application for a subpoena of Mary's phone records went through and she began the paperwork. Several tips had come in on the alerts for Blaise De Paine and Robert Fisk but each dead-ended. By seven p.m., she was ready for a sit-down with Captain Stu Bishop.

Milo drove to Tarzana and did a face-to-face with Benjamin Baranelli. The retired pornographer was a cranky eighty-year-old with poor hygiene who walked with two canes and refused to cooperate. Milo did a lot of listening and eventually Baranelli turned over a box of photo stills of Brandee Vixen and Rocksi Roll. By six, Milo was at his recalcitrant computer at the West L.A. station logging onto missing person databases and researching religious cults in Iowa and Idaho.

Dave Saunders and Kevin Bouleau's search for Moses Grant's kin bore fruit when a trace on Grant's disability checks led to a Long Beach address. There the Central detectives found a great-aunt of Grant's who'd been saving her nephew's money. She collapsed when told of his demise.

I walked Blanche and fed the fish and bothered Robin at her shop a couple of times and thought about Patty Bigelow watching a man die. I phoned Tanya at noon, then at five. She assured me everything was fine and asked if I'd learned anything new.

I said no. The lie slid out of my mouth as easy as breath.

Petra called a nighttime sit-down at ten p.m. My attendance was optional. I exercised the option and drove to Hollywood.

Same conference room. Saunders and Bouleau wore gray suits, white shirts, and crisp ties undaunted by double shifts. Petra had on a black pantsuit and looked preoccupied. Milo wore a mud-colored mock turtle over navy poly slacks and desert boots. Fire in his green eyes but it was hard to figure out what that meant.

I was the last to arrive and this time, they'd started without me.

Petra said, "Welcome to show-and-tell. Dave and Kevin were just showing us what master sleuths they are."

Bouleau said, "Just back from Grant's great-aunt." Pronouncing it "awnt." "Maybelle Lemoyne. She didn't take the news well, we actually called the paramedics but she's okay."

"Salt of the earth," said Saunders. "Widow, raised seven kids of her own, churchgoing, the whole deal. Moses was her oldest sister's son, both she and Moses' father died a few years ago. The family has roots in Louisiana—Baton Rouge and Nawlins. Moses played football in high school, was thinking about Tulane, then the diabetes killed that."

"Hence," said Bouleau, "the disability checks."

"The family house went down in Katrina," said Saunders. "Moses' brother and sister went to live in Texas but he came out here to make it as a deejay. He was living with his aunt part-time, got some party gigs with that broker, rented a dump single in the Valley, and drove back and forth in an old Toyota. Car's still at the aunt's, dead battery, hasn't been started for months."

Bouleau said, "Not since Moses quit the broker and started hanging with some people he told Aunt Maybelle were 'big-time.' He gave her check-cashing authority on the disability money, told her to keep it, he was going to make it big in the music biz. She cashed the checks, started a bank account in his name."

"Salt of the earth," Saunders repeated. "She says Moses was always a nice boy, went to church, obeyed his mama when she was alive. His appearance would scare people, then they'd talk to him, see he was soft."

I recalled Grant exiting the Hummer, standing near Mary Whitbread as she waved to us. Hesitating, then lifting his own huge hand.

Bouleau said, "Maybelle's never seen or heard of Blaise De Paine but she did I.D. Robert Fisk. He came by with Moses a couple of months ago, stayed in the car when Moses went in and got some clothes. Auntie thought that was unfriendly, especially after she waved to come in. Fisk just sat there, pretended not to notice. Auntie asked Moses why he was associating with impolite people. Moses said Robert—he used the name—was okay, just a little quiet. In terms of motive, Auntie says Moses was a law-abider who definitely would've freaked out after witnessing or getting involved in a murder."

Saunders said, "Everyone thinks their kin is angelic. I've heard Crips' mommies insisting no way Latif could've shot those five people, meanwhile we've got Latif at the scene with the Uzi in his hand. But this lady I believe. We got some phone numbers in New Orleans from her—Moses' pastor, an ex-girlfriend, a teacher. Everyone says the guy looked like trouble but was a lamb chop."

"Also," said Bouleau, "no genius. De Paine spins him some yarn about making it big in music, he would've bought it." Sitting back. "And that's the whole deal, folks."

Petra said, "Thanks, guys," told them about the missing girls and Roger Bandini's death.

Bouleau said, "So if anyone did this Bandini it was Patty. Right after De Paine and Roger did the girls."

"That's the working theory, assuming anyone did anyone. We don't even have names for the girls."

Milo said, "Ahem," opened his attaché case, and spread three photos in the center of the table.

The largest was an eight-by-ten still from *Busty Babes Vol. XI,* copyright Vivacious Videos. A pair of blondes reclining poolside, naked, splayed, flaunting inflated chests. Matching gigantic hairdos and tans suggested a twin fantasy. Brandee Vixen and Rocksi Roll grinned, fondled, and tongue-dueled.

The other two pictures were color faxes of what looked to be school photos.

A brown-haired girl around sixteen, wearing a white blouse with a starched Peter Pan collar, and a strawberry blonde in long braids, dressed identically. Braces and spots of acne on the brunette. Soft blue eyes and pretty features yearned to get past all that. The other girl was freckled and pug-nosed and brown-eyed, with pixie ears, a wide-open smile, and perfect dentition.

In the white space at the bottom of both photos, a cross of thorny vines was wreathed by a gold ribbon imprinted *Faith Triumphant Academy, Curney, North Dakota.*

Under each picture, Milo's handwriting:

Brenda Hochlbeier.

Renée Mittle.

He said, "Best friends according to their parents. Their classmates knew it was more than that. They came from seriously fundamentalist families, not a cult, but close. The school was all girls, skirts down to the ankles. These two started rebelling in their junior year of high school. A month before graduation, they ran away. Brenda was seventeen and a half, Renée barely seventeen. They confided in some pals that they were going to New York to be Rockettes. The pals spilled and the search concentrated on the East Coast, poor parents tramping all over, hiring P.I.'s, including a couple of "apostolic investigators" who ripped them off gloriously. Whether or not the girls did go east is unclear. So is what they did between the time they split and when they started making movies out here a year later."

I said, "Byron Stark thought they were older but they were eighteen . . . they look older."

"Hair and makeup and surgery can do that."

"So can attitude," said Petra, eyeing the film still. "Here they look like hardened pros. From high school to that in a year. Whoa."

Dave Saunders said, "You got all this from their parents, Milo?"

"No, from the sheriff in Curney, guy named Doug Brenner. Second-generation lawman, his dad was in charge when the girls ran away. Doug was one year ahead of the girls in the church boys' school, says all the kids knew it was a runaway because Brenda and Renée couldn't be themselves in that environment."

"You or he going to notify the families?"

"I told him to hold off until we learn more."

Kevin Bouleau said, "The good news is your daughters were lesbian porn stars. The bad news is we don't have a clue where they are."

"I'd say they were in garbage bags, ten years ago," said Saunders, flicking a corner of Brenda Hochlbeier's photo. "Man, that is gross . . . you're a little scumbag animal-parts-loving dope-dealer psycho killer like De Paine, Peter Pan, whatever you want to call him, where do you dump the body parts?"

Looking at me.

I said, "A lot of those guys want to revisit."

Milo said, "We know he liked to revisit Mommy's film escapades."

Petra said, "So somewhere relatively close to home . . . Stark's dad didn't see the van being loaded until eight days after the girls were gone. Petey probably kept the bodies in the garage, along with his other toys."

Saunders said, "Probably cut them up there."

Petra didn't blink. "That, too. But he couldn't leave them there forever. Or bury them in the yard, too risky. So he and Bandini trucked them off. But *where*?"

Milo said, "If that's how it happened, it tells us about Mary. Her son hiding some animal parts, I can see, maybe she rarely used the fridge. But two human bodies?"

"Mama love," she said. "Good God."

I said, "What if the bags were taken to another property she owned?"

"Her name doesn't cross-reference to DBAs in the business files."

"That's her stage name," I said. "What about the one she was given at birth?"

"She changed it legally. Why would she continue to do real estate deals as Maria Baker?"

"She could've done them before the name change. Myron Bedard told us she owned a home in Carthay Circle. Which is a ten-minute ride to Fourth Street, tops."

Milo said, "The way Carthay's designed, no access from main avenues. Be a nice hidey-hole."

Petra waited for additional comment. When none came, she said, "Worth a try," and left the room.

Five minutes later she strode in fast, waving a scrap of papers, eyes ablaze. "Two Maria Baker properties for the price of one. Commodore Sloat and Del Valle, and she still owns them *both*."

She headed for the door.

"Another nice neighborhood," said Milo, following.

Saunders and Bouleau were the last to rise. Saunders said, "All this premium real estate, Kev and I are starting to feel West*side*."

38

Carthay Circle is a few square blocks of residential charm combined with denial of urban reality. Bordered by the high-rises on Wilshire to the north and the din of Olympic to the south, the enclave is a mix of beautifully kept Spanish, English, Mediterranean, and Cape Cod houses. Toward the center of the district, just off San Vicente, is an office complex where the Carthay Circle Theater once stood. *Gone with the Wind* premiered at the Carthay. The glamour and drama have given way to the ambient chatter of lawyers and such.

At night, the streets of Carthay are dark and still; a motorcade of detectives would stand out like objective reporting. Petra signed a Crown Victoria out of the Hollywood Division lot and the five of us piled in. She drove and Milo rode shotgun. Dave Saunders and Kevin Bouleau sat in back with me sandwiched between.

The car smelled of wet metal and old vinyl. Bouleau shifted his shoulders and tried to get comfortable. "Hope everyone's on friendly terms with their deodorant."

Milo said, "Let's see after the trip."

Mary Whitbread's rental property on Del Valle was a cream stucco, neatly kept Spanish with a tiny, faux-bell-tower over the entry and a small courtyard that hosted a trickling fountain. Low-watt lighting turned the fountain spray to amber mist. A kiddie play-set stood near the basin. Mazda RX7 in the driveway in front of a RAV4. On the SUV's bumper: *My child's an honor student at Carthay Circle Magnet School.*

Bouleau said, "And my little psychopath kicks his ass—looks like the porn lady got herself some nice, wholesome tenants."

Milo said, "Wonder how they'd feel about a cadaver dog sniffing around."

"Wouldn't that be fun," said Petra, "but we're a long way off. For all we know, the dump site's in Coachella."

No longer entertaining the possibility that there was no dump. As the facts had settled in, everyone was assuming two dead girls.

Petra drove to Commodore Sloat Drive. Another Spanish, white-washed, slightly larger than the first. No courtyard, different window style, stained-glass insets. In this driveway sat a pair of BMWs, a gray Z3 and a black 325i. Lights flickered in a side window. Petra parked two houses up, got out, tiptoed around toward the light, lingered a bit, got back in the driver's seat.

"Filmy drapes in the bedroom, cute couple in their thirties. The TV's on, she's doing a crossword puzzle, he's plugged into an iPod."

Dave Saunders said, "Happy family for A, yuppies for B. Conspicuous absence of psycho killers." He yawned. "I need to get home."

As the Central detectives drove their cars out of the division lot, Petra said, "Well, that was a whole lot of nothing . . . Alex, would you do me a favor and try Stark's dad tomorrow morning? I left three messages, no answer. No doubt he detests the department, can't say I blame him. Seeing as he's got a counseling degree maybe he'd relate better to you."

"I'll do my best rendition of professional courtesy."

"Thanks, you're a peach." Stifling her own yawn. "Why is that contagious, Doctor?"

"I have no idea."

"The mysteries of science," she said. "Guess I should do a little domestic duty. Eric just finished a monthlong job. Defense contractor in Arizona, industrial spy thing that turned out to be paranoia. He's been shuttling back and forth, we haven't seen each other much. If this thing ever cooks up, it'll be more of the same."

"Go for it, kid," said Milo. "Eric have an iPod?"

"Ha. Eric only listens to music when I switch it on. The man can sit and do nothing like I've never seen." She smiled but didn't budge. "So . . . eventually these bastards are going to have to show themselves, right?" Putting her palms together prayerfully. "I'm hoping to get Mary's phone records sometime tomorrow. Meanwhile, I'll catch Raul up on everything. He's doing great . . . I should tell him so."

Lowering her volume with each sentence so that by the end she was muttering.

Her shoulders rounded and her head dipped an inch. She looked older and tired, but just for the seconds it took to draw herself up and shake her hair loose. "Well, let's hope they get stupid—one more thing, guys, confidential. James Rahab—the sergeant who wrote up Roger Bandini's death—comes up on a list of Fortuno's possible sources in the department."

"How'd you find that out?" said Milo.

"Stu found out from his fed buddy. Who also informed him we will have no more access to Marvelous Mario."

I said, "Bandini wasn't looked into because Fortuno fixed the investigation for Mary?"

"If she thought a serious investigation into Bandini would've put Petey in danger, she'd have a motive to call in a favor. On the other hand, it may simply be coincidence. Rahab was righteously on patrol that night—training a rookie. And on the surface, Bandini's death *did* present as an overdose. The whole deal's moot anyway because Rahab died of a heart attack three years ago."

"Where's the rookie he was training?" said Milo.

"I don't even have a name. Only reason the Feebie told Stu was as a consolation prize—as in, This is the last thing you're getting."

"Or because he's getting us to work for him. We uncover something, he can add to the indictment against Fortuno."

Petra thought about that. "Could be . . . anyway, no reason to do the History Channel when I can't get anything done on a current homicide. Nighty-night, fellas."

At ten the following morning, I phoned Herbert Stark.

A woman singsonged, "You've reached Myra and *Herb.* We could be *fishing, hiking,* or just plain *loafing.* Leave a message and if it's *interesting,* we *might* get back to you."

"Mr. Stark, this is Dr. Alex Delaware, I'll do my best to make this fascinating. Years ago you did your civic duty only to run up against some incredible police incompetence. If you can find it in yourself to reopen your mind—"

A deep male voice broke in: "So that my brains fall out? Fascinating? Not quite. Minimally thought-provoking? Possibly."

"Thanks for—"

"Byron said you seemed quote unquote thoughtful. That's high praise from my son. I almost became a psychologist. No money and too many family obligations got in the way. So the cops have finally decided to take a look at that little sociopath. What'd he do, now?"

"Killed several people," I said.

"Oh, what a shock," said Herbert Stark. "It's always that way, isn't it? I just finished reading a book about serial killers—not pulpy crap, a professional textbook by a former investigator who got drummed out because he spoke his mind. His thesis is that ninety-five percent of the time the guilty party is interviewed early on in the investigation and the police have a name right there in front of them. You believe that?"

"Could be."

"I believe it. Byron said you don't put much stock in profiling."

"Not much."

"They give you grief for that in the department?"

"Not at all."

Stark grunted. "What do you think I can tell you that I already didn't try to tell those Einsteins in blue?"

I wanted to ask him to go over everything, but that would provoke a tirade. "When you came to believe those two girls had been killed, did you share your suspicions with anyone other than the police and your wife?"

"Of course I did," said Stark. "After the cops sat on their hands, I told a few people in the neighborhood. I figured if enough people got riled up, we might be able to stimulate some action."

"How many people did you tell?"

"After all these years you expect a count? I limited it to people I had a good sense about. Didn't matter, no one cared."

"Was one of the people a woman named Patricia Bigelow?"

"Yes," he said. "She was the first."

"Because—"

"First of all, I knew her. Second, I trusted her. Shortly after she moved in, my younger son, Galen, fell skateboarding and we worried he'd broken his leg. But he had an exam to study for, we didn't want to bother with the emergency room if it wasn't a break. My wife had talked to Patty a few times, knew she was a nurse, so she went around the corner and asked her to look at Galen's leg. Patty came by, inspected it, said she wasn't a physician, but it was a sprain. She iced it and wrapped it and we took Galen to the pediatrician the next morning, and she'd done everything perfectly. I also told her about the girls because she had a girl of her own—a child, nine, ten years old. I felt it was my obligation to let her know that her landlady's spawn was a menace. Why are you asking about her?"

"She died recently of natural causes and alluded to some terrible things that had happened while she lived on Fourth Street. That's what got the current investigation going."

"She believed me," said Herbert Stark. "My God . . . couldn't tell from her reaction."

"What'd she say?"

"Nothing, that's my point. She nodded and thanked me for informing her and asked me how Galen was doing, then she ushered me out. I thought it was ungrateful and a bit rude. I was trying to help. But she did move out soon after."

"Did she ever say why she was moving?"

"We didn't talk after that."

"Did your wife talk to her?"

"I doubt it and she's not here to ask, up in Seattle, some kind of knitting convention."

"When you warned Patty did you mention both Pete Whitbread and Roger Bandini by name?"

"Of course, there was no doubt who loaded that van. Have you found the bodies?"

"Not yet."

"What are the chances?" said Stark. "After all these years. Which is no one's fault but the vaunted LAPD. Holmes and Marlowe are laughing."

Click.

I tried Milo and Petra, got voice mail all around. While I brewed coffee, my service called. Herbert Stark recalling another detail?

The operator said, "Doctor, I've got a Kyle Bernard on the line."

Kyle's barely audible voice said, "Dr. Delaware? Sorry to bother you but is there any way we can get together? Tanya has a two-hour seminar right now, so on the off chance you've got an opening . . ."

"Is there a problem, Kyle?"

"It's . . . I'd just like to toss some things around with you."

"I can't discuss Tanya, Kyle."

"Yes, yes, I know, confidentiality. But there's no rule against listening, is there?"

"What's on your mind?"

"I'd really rather meet in person, Dr. Delaware. Here in the lab it's near impossible to find a quiet place, that's why I'm whispering. Outside reception's not too great—the psych building blocks everything out. Tanya said your office is in Beverly Glen. I could be there in ten minutes."

"Okay," I said.

"Really? Fantastic."

Where I live in the Glen, high above an old dormant bridle trail, even a mediocre day appears glorious. People who visit the first time are often compelled to comment on the green-blanketed hills, the sliver of Pacific peekabooing above the Palisades, the caramel light.

Since we've had Blanche, no one's been able to resist petting her.

When I opened the door for Kyle Bedard, he tramped past her, pumped my hand too hard, and said, "I appreciate this."

His hair was wind-tunnel wild and the flannel shirt he wore over a frayed red T-shirt and rumpled khakis was misbuttoned. Blanche rubbed herself against his cuff. He muttered, "French bulldog," as if answering a pop quiz.

Then: "Speaking of which, my father left for the Loire Valley."

I took him to my office. Blanche trotted after him, trolling for eye contact she didn't receive. Hopping up on my lap, she fell asleep.

"Dad had enough of L.A.?"

"L.A., the house—he despises it because it's Grandfather's domain. Having convinced himself he fulfilled his paternal duty, it was time to resume living." Rolling his shoulders, he tugged at his shirtfront, realized he'd misaligned and unbuttoned hastily. "There was also a bit of the old wink and nod. Three's a crowd, son, don't want to get in your way. I *told* him this wasn't about romance, it was about keeping Tanya safe. Dad can't conceive anyone being alone with an attractive female and not wanting to immediately get into her pants."

Sudden blush. "Of course I'm attracted to her, I'm a guy. But that's *not* the issue. I wanted to speak to you because Tanya's not sleeping."

"Not at all?"

"Not to any significant degree. The room where she's staying is directly above the library and when I'm working I can hear her pace. Incessantly, she can do it for hours."

"Sounds like you're not sleeping, either?"

"I'm fine. I work when I want because I don't have formal hours. Sometimes I even bunk down in the lab, there's a futon all the grad students use. But it's different for Tanya. Her life is structured, she has a schedule. I don't know how long she can keep going like this."

"Have you talked to her about it?"

"No, because I know what she'd say."

"'I'm doing fine, Kyle.'"

"Exactly. More than the insomnia, it's the pacing that concerns me. Back and forth, as if she's . . . I don't know . . . caught *up* in something. Is it something to be worried about?"

I sat there.

"You can't tell me *that*?"

"Why don't you stick to statements rather than questions and we'll try to make sense of things."

"That's basically it—no, I'm lying. It's not just the pacing. It's what it means—all her anxiety. It's a stress reaction, right?—sorry, no questions. Stupid question, anyway, of course it's anxiety. She's probably scared out of her mind. Not to mention the grief over her mother—she doesn't talk about that, either."

"People talk when they're ready."

"Like that old joke?" he said. "How many shrinks to change a lightbulb, but the bulb has to want to change? But it's hard when it's someone . . . On top of all that, America—our housekeeper—told me about some other routines Tanya has. She happened to walk in while Tanya was . . . granted, she's nosy, kind of a pain in the ass, actually, I liked Cecilia—her sister—a lot better. America's extremely moralistic, since

Tanya moved in she's been walking around with this lemon-sucking self-righteous expression. No doubt she thinks something's going on between Tanya and me, so maybe she walked into Tanya's bedroom accidentally on purpose. But still, she did see it."

"What did she see?"

He rebuttoned his shirt, bottom to top. Checked the order. "Maybe I'm making too big a deal out of this . . . there's a dressing room behind Tanya's bedroom and beyond that, a walk-in closet. The dressing room's mirrored and the walls are angled at such a way that if you're at the head of the bed you can see part of the closet. America claims she wasn't spying, just fluffing Tanya's pillows . . . She saw Tanya walking around the closet touching things. There's tons of stuff in bags, mostly my dad's overflow, stuff he hasn't worn in years, he never gets rid of anything, keeps hoping I'll eventually dig it. Like I'd do the whole smoking jacket and *ascot* thing—okay, okay, I'm getting off the topic. America says Tanya touched every single bag three times, then went back and repeated it four times, then five, then six, then seven."

"America watched and counted," I said.

"Told you she's a snoop. She says Tanya stopped at seven, then started doing the same thing with Dad's shoes. She asked me if seven was a magical number, had this look in her eyes like Tanya was some kind of devil-worshipper. She's unsophisticated, what the hell would she know about stress reactions?"

"Did you explain anything to her?"

"I probably should've but I just got pissed. Told her Tanya was my friend, whatever she does is fine, don't come finking to me. She didn't like that but I don't give a shit. She's only been working at the house for five years and I find her annoying."

"But you're concerned about Tanya's routines."

"Tanya told me about her OCD, how you cured her."

I kept silent.

"So that was also denial," he said. "Is it incurable?"

"People have tendencies," I said. "Stress brings them out. Habits can be unlearned."

"So I'm expecting too much of Tanya right now—that's the *last* thing I wanted to do."

"I'm hearing concern, not expectation."

"I'm not concerned about a few behaviors, Dr. Delaware. It's the root cause that bothers me. How much stress she must be under, not being able to talk about it. How can I help her?"

"You've given her friendship and shelter."

"That's obviously insufficient."

"Because she's not happy all the time?"

His jaw tightened. He closed his eyes and massaged the lids. "I'm thinking about *my* worries rather than hers. Jesus, why can't I focus on what needs focusing?"

"You're doing a good job, Kyle."

He waved that off. "Should I bring anything up with her? Would venting help?"

"Right now, no."

"Why not?"

"Lightbulb wisdom."

He stared at me. "So what, I just let her pace around and never sleep and pretend she's fine?" Pummeling his temple. "Listen to me. '*Let* her.' Like I'm the parent, where the hell did *that* come from?"

"Deep caring."

His mouth hung open. Bending down sharply, he yanked a shoelace loose, retied a sneaker. "Deep caring . . . you've got that right. I frickin' *love* her."

"I know you do."

Several moments passed. When he spoke next, his voice was low and indistinct. "Is there any chance it's reciprocal?"

"She accepted your shelter."

"But that could be desperation—oh, shit, here we go again, ego ego ego . . . so you're saying I do nothing?"

"I'm saying let her lead, be there to listen."

"And the pacing, the routines—it's temporary because of crapola hitting the fan?"

I didn't answer.

He said, "Yeah, yeah," and scratched his chin. "Next topic: Any progress in the detection department?"

"Nothing earth-shattering but good people are working on it."

"Pete killed his own father," he said. "That's beyond the frickin' pale . . . okay, I'm going, thanks for your time."

On his way out, he stooped and petted Blanche and said, "Sorry for ignoring you. You really are as cute as my girlfriend said."

I rested my hand on his shoulder. His muscles twitched.

"You really are doing okay, Kyle."

"Yeah, yeah, thanks for the plug, bye."

At two p.m. Milo came by and we sat in the kitchen eating cold Mexican food.

"No other properties are registered to Maria Baker or Mary Whitbread in six surrounding counties. If she used a third name, tough breaks. Petra finally got the phone records. Most of Whitbread's calls are to stores in B.H. and Brentwood. The exception is a cell that keeps coming up three or four times a day. Unfortunately, the account traces back to her."

"She bought a phone for Junior."

"Or he had her do it as cover. Once we find him, maybe we can get Mommy Dearest as an accessory. While I was in the assessor's office I saw some interesting aerial maps—some new contract they've got with a global positioning service, plug in the address of the plot plan and you get a nice, sharp photo. The citizen in me says Orwell was right. The gendarme in me says fantastic, let's get some shots of Mary's real estate, see if there's any sign of burial."

"Any burial took place ten years ago."

"Gee, thanks, now I'm back to being depressed," he said. "Ever think of working for the IRS?"

I said, "Here's some insight that might make you feel better: Patty definitely knew about the girls, the bags, the van." I repeated everything I'd heard from Herbert Stark.

"And that will make me happy because—"

"It clarifies the situation. When Bandini tried to break into Patty's place, she knew what he was and had prepared herself."

"Pistol-packing mama," he said. "No time for chitchat with Tanya sleeping a few feet away. She planned a way to control the situation, managed to jam him with a hot-shot."

I said, "The puncture wound wasn't in the back of his head or any other unusual spot. Right in the crook, where you'd expect it to be. He'd need to be completely subdued for that."

"Premeditation in service of maternal duty," he said. "Make it look nice and natural. I'm picturing it and feeling sorry for *her*. Having to work fast, hoping Tanya doesn't wake up. Dragging the body out to the street praying no neighbor happens to notice. But she had the presence of mind to leave Bandini's burglar kit under his body."

"Patty was all about focus."

"When she's done, she's focusing on escape. Waits a while so no one'll make a connection to Bandini, and tells Whitbread she can't afford the rent. Lives ten years with the secret, telling no one."

"Except Lester Jordan."

"Tattling to Petey's daddy. Why would she do that?"

"Maybe initially she wanted to hear that Herbert Stark's suspicions about the missing girls were unfounded. Maybe instead of calming her down, Jordan heightened her anxiety by telling her about Pete's other felonies."

"Lowball Armbruster."

"Jordan and Armbruster were known associates from the drug world. Jordan had to know, or at least suspect, that his son had murdered Armbruster."

"Precocious criminal," he said. "Jordan says no telling what my boy's capable of. That spurs Patty to load her .22 and sit up at night. But why would Jordan let on to her?"

"Patty saved Jordan's life more than once. They had a deep enough relationship for Jordan to write that angry letter after Patty left Cherokee. Patty saved the letter and a picture of the two of them, meaning on some level it was mutual."

"Despite that, Jordan knows his kid's dangerous but never turns him in. Even dope-filled blood can run thick."

"Then years later, we come around, bring up Patty, Jordan suspects it has to do with Pete. Jordan calls Pete, maybe to warn him, maybe to I-told-you-so. Or even to say if the pressure mounts, I'm not backing you up. Pete has hated his daddy for years, now Daddy becomes a direct threat—the last straw. He has Fisk strangle his father while he watches. The twin payoffs are keeping Jordan quiet and Oedipal joy."

"Lovely," he said, cupping one ear with his free hand. "Is that a Greek chorus I hear in the background?"

CHAPTER

39

For the next three days, Raul Biro followed Mary Whitbread as she shopped. Her pattern was to buy armloads of designer clothing, return everything the next day, run up another charge on her platinum Amex.

Petra got hold of charge account records and Southwest Airlines Visa bills. Mary paid her bills on time, she hadn't cashed in on the mileage, and nothing in a year's worth of purchases tipped off the whereabouts of her son or Robert Fisk.

The cellular number assumed to be Pete Whitbread's remained inactive until four p.m. on the third day, when Mary called it. Retracing the path of the towers revealed southward movement originating east of the downtown Civic Center. When the conversation ended, the recipient was somewhere north of Chinatown.

Minutes from the 110 ramp where Moses Grant's body had been dumped.

That sent Dave Saunders and Kevin Bouleau back to the abandoned auto shop where Grant had been shot. Recanvassing produced three more transients claiming to have seen a black Hummer cruising the industrial streets east of Los Angeles Street late at night. No details about the driver, passengers, or destination. Saunders drove to the dump site and canvassed Chinatown.

Milo stayed at home, playing with databases. Even Face of America produced nothing on Pete Whitbread/Blaise De Paine or Robert Fisk. Neither had filed any Social Security claims or paid income tax. Aerial photos of Mary Whitbread's property revealed no recent disturbances. A records clerk at the assessor's office opined that a sonar scan might be helpful. When Milo asked where to go for that, the clerk said, "Saw it on Forensics File, or something."

I phoned Tanya twice, was reassured both times that she was doing great, had a couple of big exams she needed to concentrate on. She sounded tired and faded, but maybe my opinion had been colored by Kyle's account of insomnia and compulsive routines.

Kyle didn't try to contact me again.

With nothing to do, I picked up two more consults from family court and prepared for another nosedive into the cesspool known as child custody conflict.

At nine p.m., Robin was reading in bed. I'd just finished an evening meeting with a man who hated his ex-wife so much that mention of her name caused his eyes to bulge and his neck veins to throb. She'd sat in the same chair earlier that day; her pet name for him was "Fucking Asshole." They had two kids who wet the bed and were failing in school. Both parents claimed they were determined to do "what's best for Amy and Whitley."

As the door closed on the husband, I headed to the dining room liquor cabinet, figuring this was an occasion to break open an old gift bottle of Chivas Century.

The phone rang. Milo's voice was tight. "Robert Fisk just showed up at Mary's. Petra called for the flak-jacket squad. I'm on my way, would invite you to attend but with all that artillery—"

"Figure out a way," I said.

"To what?"

"Let them know I'm persona grata."

The SWAT team had tucked its vehicles around the corner.

Keeping as low a profile as possible, given a squadron of sharp-jawed men in full assault regalia. The night nourished concealment, but the air was charged.

The team leader was a tall, rangy lieutenant named A. M. Holzman with a gray brush cut and mustache, and mirror-shard eyes one shade lighter. Milo called him Allen and Holzman acknowledged him with a brief smile. Recognition didn't mean small talk. Everyone was focused on Mary Whitbread's duplex, where Robert Fisk had entered thirty-three minutes ago.

Fisk had approached on foot, walking east from La Cienega, dressed in a black shirt, matching sweatpants, and sandals. As he knocked on the door, he'd stepped under the porch light. Raul Biro had seen his face clearly and called for backup.

Now Biro went over it for Holzman. "Guy was empty-handed, looked relaxed. I got a close enough look at his clothes to tell you there was definitely no firearm. As far as a knife, I can't say for sure, but she opened the door and let him in, no resistance."

Allen Holzman said, "He knocks, entrez-vous?"

"You got it, Lieutenant."

Petra said, "We're sure she's aware of at least some of her son's crimes. At the very least, accessory after the fact."

Holzman said, "So maybe this guy Fisk was sent by the son to get money, provisions, whatever."

"That would make sense."

"Or," said Holzman, "he got in using guile and did something bad to Mommy. We're talking a known associate of someone who already killed his own daddy."

He smiled. "Probably going to ask for clemency 'cause he's an orphan."

Petra: "If that's the case, we're too late, aren't we?"

"Unless he's in the process of torturing her."

Milo said, "You're a font of good cheer, Al."

"This is happy times compared to the anti-terrorism squad." To Petra: "You know Eric Stahl, right?"

Petra smiled. "A bit."

"I didn't make the trip to Tel Aviv where he stopped that suicide asshole, which is a shame, I've got cousins in Jerusalem. But we were together in Jakarta, went to Bali, saw the damage. Anyway, enough b.s., what's your wish-list?"

"In a perfect world," said Petra, "you go in and get them both out alive."

"In a perfect world, I'm squeezing blood out of Osama's liver while he sits in a tub of acid and watches . . . okay, let's see if we can get the rear neighbors to allow us visual access to the back of the place. Depending on what we see or hear, we'll figure out a plan. I don't see any time exigency here. If she's alive, they're pals. If she's not, it's time for the mop-and-tweezers squad."

Petra said, "The neighbor on top is a doctor named Stark, owns the building and he's already cooperated."

"Excellent," said Holzman. "Community involvement and all, huh, Milo? Remember those P. C. seminars we had to do?"

Milo nodded.

"Total horseshit, this is better," said Holzman. "Okay, find Dr. Stark and involve him some more."

Byron Stark looked on as a laser scope aimed from his bedroom revealed that the rear door to Mary Whitbread's ground-floor unit had been left ajar.

An inch.

Allen Holzman said, "If she's in the shower, doesn't hear the front door, he can let himself in? That make sense, Milo?"

"As good a theory as any, Al."

"Or she's just careless."

Stark said, "She leaves it open all the time."

Blushing.

Holzman said, "Guess we've got a relaxed lady. Okay, let's go in fast."

No crash-bang like on TV. The SWAT team entered silently and took control of the apartment within seconds.

Mary Whitbread and Robert Fisk were sleeping in bed. A fake fireplace glowed orange, a tape loop simulated crackling flames. New-age music piped in through wall speakers added another layer of mellow. A tray on the floor beside Mary's side of the bed held honey-macadamia muffins, Godiva chocolates, sliced kiwi, champagne flutes filled with what turned out to be organic mango-lychee nectar.

Whitbread and Fisk were naked and entwined. By the time they reached full awareness, both had been flipped on their bellies and cuffed.

Mary Whitbread screamed, then whimpered, then started to hyper-ventilate. Fisk thrashed like a fresh-caught cod on a slimy deck. The prod of a rifle barrel stopped all that.

"Silicone Tits and Mr. Macho Tattoo Kickboxer," one of the SWAT guys reminisced as the squad peeled off armor and drank Gatorade.

"Silicone Tits and Thimble-Weenie," said another.

A third chimed in: "Miniature Vienna sausage dehydrated, com-pressed, and extruded through a pinhole. No excuses, dude, the room was *warm*."

"We *shriveled* him, man. Mr. Macho Asshole *Kickboxer* Killer, we got you righteous and you dropped like a wet *turd*."

"Mini-mini-mini, dude, even accounting for the shrivel factor. Bad career choice, Pencil-Dick."

"Uh, uh, uh—" Exaggerated falsetto. "—is there something *in* there, Bronco?"

Allen Holzman said, "Good job, guys. Now shut the hell up and someone volunteer for the paperwork."

The career the cops had mocked was porn actor. Videos found in Mary Whitbread's apartment documented Robert Fisk's audition, two years ago, for a Canoga Park outfit called Righteous & Raw Productions.

Financial documents in Mary's attic showed her to be a shareholder in the company, which had folded thirteen months after incorporation.

No sign Fisk had ever worked for her or anyone else.

Plenty of tapes and CDs from Righteous & Raw's backlog in a small half basement, but no souvenirs of Mary's career.

No evidence of excavation there, or in the backyard.

Mary's terror had left her thighs urine-stained, but she calmed down quickly and asked for a robe while flaunting her body.

Petra found a kimono and helped her slip into it. "Where's Peter-son?"

Mary said, "That little shit? Why would I know? Or care?"

"Robert Fisk is a—"

"No, no, no, *no*! Stop talking to *me*, I want my *lawyer*."

CHAPTER

40

Robert Fisk didn't ask for an attorney.

Thanking Petra for getting him the bottled water, he sat Buddha-placid.

The menacing skinhead of his mug shot had been replaced by a neat cap of dark hair. The pallid wicket framing his mouth memorialized a recently shaved mustache. Smallish mouth, delicate like the rest of him. But for the brocade of body ink extending from under his cuffs and snaking above his collar, a nondescript man.

Ramrod posture suggested a dance instructor or personal trainer. So many of those in L.A.

Picking him out on a dark street with only the mug shot as reference spoke volumes about Raul Biro's skills. Biro sat near Petra, both of them watching Fisk across the table. Milo and I were on the other side of the glass.

Fisk drank his water, put the cup down, smiled. An instant of sharp, wolfish teeth caused Petra to inch back. Fisk might've sensed that he'd given something away. He shut his mouth, sat low to make himself smaller.

"Anything else I can get you, Robert?"

"No, I'm fine, Detective Connor. Thanks very much."

"You know why you're here."

"Not really, Detective Connor."

"Care to take a guess?"

"I wouldn't know where to start."

Petra shuffled papers and watched him.

Fisk didn't move.

"Does the name Lester Jordan ring a bell?"

"Of course," said Fisk. "He was Blaise's father. Blaise killed him."

"And you know that because . . ."

"I was there, Detective Connor."

"At the murder."

"Blaise asked me to be there, but what happened took me by surprise."

"Why'd Blaise ask you to be there?"

"Moral support," said Fisk. "That's what I assumed."

"Why would Blaise need moral support?"

"Lester had hit him before."

"You saw that?"

"Blaise told me. Lester was an addict. That means unpredictable."

"How well did you know Lester?"

"I saw him a few times. Always with Blaise."

"Father-son business transactions."

"I had nothing to do with that part of it."

"What part?"

"Narcotics. Never touched dope in my life. Never tasted alcohol, my parents drank, I saw what it did."

"Clean living."

"You can do any tests you want," said Fisk. "My blood is clean. I don't eat red meat or refined sugars, either. If people didn't eat meat there'd be no global warming."

"Really?" said Petra.

"Cows fart and mess up the atmosphere."

Raul Biro said, "Why don't we just give 'em Beano?"

Petra smiled. Fisk didn't.

She said, "Let's get back to Blaise and Lester. You were there when Blaise went to sell his father drugs."

Long silence.

"Robert?"

"Blaise didn't tell me."

"You went along for protection."

"Moral support."

"When you went to Lester's apartment, you just walked in through the front door with Blaise."

"Yes, ma'am," said Fisk.

"Hmm," said Petra. "Then it's kind of funny, your fingerprints showing up on Lester Jordan's outer windowsill, by the side of his building."

Fisk's wrists rotated. His new smile was tight-lipped. "That's weird."

"Weird but true, Robert." She slid the AFIS match over to him.

Fisk barely glanced at it. "I'm not picturing this sill."

"Outside Lester Jordan's bedroom window."

"Whoa," said Fisk. "That's bizarre."

"You didn't enter through the window?"

Fisk gazed at the ceiling. A minute passed, then another. Petra crossed her legs. Raul Biro stared at Fisk.

Fisk said, "Let me ask you something, Detective Connor. Theoretically."

"Sure, Robert."

"If a window is already open and you climb in, is that breaking and entering?"

Milo muttered, "Idiot's up for a murder bust and he's worried about B and E."

"Hmm, interesting question," said Petra, turning to Raul.

Raul said, "Never thought about that."

"That's what happened, Robert? The window was left open?"

"Let's just say."

"Well," she said, "I guess it *wouldn't* be breaking and entering, because there was no breaking."

"That's what I'm thinking," said Robert Fisk.

"Who left the window open?"

"Blaise."

"Why'd he do that, Robert?"

"Tactical," said Fisk. "Like I said, he was scared of Lester, used to get beat by him."

"And having you come in through the back window helped because . . ."

"Element of surprise."

"For when . . ."

"If something happened."

"Which it did," said Petra. "Something definitely happened."

"I didn't know that, Detective."

"Tell me about it, Robert."

"I came in like Blaise asked me to, stopped and listened, made sure there was no problem."

"Blaise had reason to think there might be a problem."

Long silence. "Lester called Blaise to come over, said Blaise was in trouble."

"What kind of trouble?"

"Don't know, but it made Blaise angry." Fisk's eyes shifted to the left. Petra didn't push him. Any undue pressure could evoke the dreaded lawyer request. Mary Whitbread had already been released with no charges filed, an assistant D.A. opining that at most she was vulnerable for obstruction and even that was doubtful.

Petra said, "So you went in and listened. Then what?"

"It was quiet," said Fisk. "I figure everything's mellow. Blaise says, 'I'm in the crapper, Robert.' I go over, the door's open, Blaise is stand-ing next to Lester, Lester's on the can, his spike and spoon and the rest of his works is on the sink, he's fixed up, totally nodded off."

"With stuff Blaise brought him."

"I guess."

"Then what?"

"Blaise laughs, that crazy bird laugh he does, gives Lester's cheek a little slap, Lester doesn't wake up. Blaise slaps him harder, laughs again, says, 'I fixed him a nuclear-hit, he's so gone, I could do anything.'"

"Anything," said Petra.

"I didn't figure he meant *that*," said Fisk.

"What did you think he meant?"

Fisk's eyes drifted left again. "Actually, that's not exactly what he said."

Petra waited.

Fisk said, "It's kind of gross."

"I can handle it, Robert. What did Blaise say?"

"'I could put my dick in his mouth, he wouldn't know.'"

"Talking about his father like that?"

"I told you it's gross. They're not like father and son. More like . . . Blaise sells him dope, hates him. Blaise hates everyone. He's insane."

"That comment," said Raul. "Is he gay?"

"Dunno."

"You've been hanging with the guy for months."

"I never saw him with a man," said Fisk. "Or a woman. Mostly, he likes to look and . . . I don't want to talk disgusting in front of you, Detective Connor."

"Appreciate that, Robert, but anything you can tell us would help."

"What he likes is to look at stuff and touch himself. Like the only person that turns him on is himself. He did it that night."

"In the bathroom?"

"Yes," said Fisk. "Laughing about Lester being out of it, he starts touching himself."

"Lester's still alive at this point."

"But out of it."

"Blaise is getting a charge out of masturbating in front of his father."

"Insane," said Fisk.

"Then what happened?"

"Then Blaise says go into the kitchen and get me a Coke. I got a can and came back. By that time, Blaise put a rope around Lester's neck and strangled him."

"How long were you gone?"

"Long enough."

"Could you be a bit more specific, Robert?"

"Hmm," said Fisk. "Maybe a few minutes."

"You come back and Lester's dead."

"Yup."

"You check if he was dead?"

"He looked dead."

"You didn't try to revive him."

"Blaise said he was dead, he looked dead, I didn't want to touch him. Blaise laughed about it, we went out through the back window."

"How'd you feel, walking into that, Robert?"

"Bad," said Fisk without inflection. "Surprised, I guess." Rapid eye drift. "Blaise never told me he was going to do that."

"Why did Blaise murder Lester Jordan?"

"Because he hated him," said Fisk. "Blaise hates *everyone.*"

"What did you do with the soda can?"

"Gave it to Blaise."

"What did he do with it?"

"Drank it."

"Then what?"

"Pardon?" said Fisk.

"Did he take the Coke with him?"

"I . . . no, I don't think so."

"We didn't find any Coke in the apartment," said Petra, lying smoothly. Jordan's kitchen had been a jumble of take-out boxes, bottles, and cans.

"Then maybe he took it, I don't remember," said Fisk.

Petra wrote in her pad. "You go with Blaise for moral support because he's worried about some kind of trouble with Lester. Blaise waits until Lester shoots up, nods off, tells you to get him a drink, and by the time you get back, Lester's dead."

"Yes."

Petra looked at Raul. He shrugged. Fisk said, "That's what happened."

Petra said, "The problem is, Robert, we're talking multiple homicides and you're the guy who left prints at the scene of one of them."

"Multiple?"

"Moses Grant."

Fisk's jaws knotted. "That was . . . not me." He slumped, straightened.

"Why did Moses die, Robert?"

"Oh, man," said Fisk. "Can I please have some juice? Apple's best, but I'll take orange if you've got it, pulp's okay."

"What we've got in the machines here is soda and Snapple, Robert."

"Forget it, then."

"Robert," said Petra, "you want kickapoo-coconut-pago-pago juice, we can probably score it. But if you want to nourish your soul, you need to be totally honest."

Fisk considered that for a while. "I never killed anyone. Please write down that I'm being fully cooperative."

Talking softly as his wrists rotated and his fingers clawed the table-top.

"You're talking, Robert, but I'm not sure you're *communicating*." To Raul: "What do you think, Detective Biro?"

"I think he tells a good story."

"Make a nice movie," said Petra.

"With an all-star cast," said Raul.

Robert Fisk said, "I'm telling the truth."

No argument or assent from the detectives.

"Okay," said Fisk, flashing sharp teeth. "Get me apple-guava juice and I'll tell you *everything*. A PowerBar, too."

Leaving suspects alone sometimes gives up the best information. People who forget they're being taped, or are too stupid to know it in the first place, talk to themselves, display anxiety they were able to mask during the interrogation. Sometimes detectives leave suspects' cell phones in the room and monitor calls. The Motorola paid for by Mary Whitbread sat on the table.

During the half hour Robert Fisk was alone, he never touched it. Closed his eyes five minutes in, and went to sleep.

Raul Biro returned from the all-night market, glanced through the glass, and said, "Zen felon."

Petra said, "You need a conscience for insomnia."

She and Milo and I had been reviewing Fisk's story. Unanimous conclusion: His strength and assaultive nature said he'd strangled Lester Jordan at Blaise De Paine's behest, probably Moses Grant, as well. All the rest was the typical criminal dance-away.

Clumsy dance; he'd given away enough to be vulnerable on a dozen felony charges.

When Petra and Raul reentered the room, Fisk sat up, took the juice and the granola bar. Thanking both detectives by name and title, he drank, munched, folded the wrapper into a neat little square.

"That do the trick, Robert?" said Petra.

"Yes, thank you."

"My pleasure, Robert. So why'd you strangle Lester Jordan?"

"I didn't, *he* did."

"Peterson Whitbread."

"To me he was always Blaise."

"What does his mother call him?"

Fisk smiled. "Mostly, 'the little shit.'"

Raul Biro said, "Papa beats him and Mama doesn't care."

"He's been giving her stress since day one," said Fisk. "That's how I met him, she wanted me to babysit him."

Petra said, "Mary paid you to watch over Blaise?"

"Yes."

"How much?"

"Hundred here, hundred there."

"Cash?"

"Yes."

"How'd you and Mary meet?"

Fisk rolled his shoulders. "I was working out five times a week at The Steel Mill, Santa Monica and La Cienega. Guys there were always talking about how much money they were making doing adult-genre films. Directors like guys with cut bodies."

Stroking his own forearm.

"Adult genre," said Petra.

Fisk nodded. "I was between teaching jobs, some guy at the gym says they're auditioning out in the Valley, I figured why not? Mary was there."

"Mary was auditioning also?"

"No, running the audition. With some other guys."

Petra checked her notes. "Was the company Righteous and Raw Productions?"

"Yes."

"What kind of teaching jobs were you in between?"

"Yoga, aerobics, tae kwon do, kendo, Javanese spear, judo, you name it. My ultimate goal is to be a fight coordinator."

Milo said, "Idiot's still talking in the present tense."

Petra said, "A fight coordinator like for the movies?"

"Fights don't just happen," said Fisk. "You've got to set them up."

"Choreography."

"Kind of."

"So," said Petra, "you auditioned for Mary. Get the job?"

Color seeped up Fisk's neck, made its way to flat, static cheeks. "I changed my mind."

"Adult genre wasn't for you."

"Not really."

Petra said, "But you hooked up with Mary."

Fisk said, "It started off as a training thing. I got her into advanced stretching, light weights, balance and posture. Cardio she already did on her treadmill. She's in great shape for forty-seven."

Mary Whitbread's stats put her at fifty-three.

Petra said, "She is a very attractive woman, Robert. So the two of you developed a sexual relationship."

"Not really," said Fisk.

"Robert, we found you guys in bed."

"There was sex but it wasn't *primarily* sexual."

"What was it?"

"Intimacy. Being friendly."

"But that did include a sexual relationship."

"Depends on what you mean by relationship."

Milo muttered, "This guy should run for president."

Raul Biro said, "We're defining it as you fucked her."

Long pause. "That happened. Occasionally."

Biro leaned in. "Is there some reason you're ashamed of that, dude?"

"No, she's . . . no, I'm okay with it."

"What?" pressed Biro.

Fisk didn't answer.

"Something go wrong in that department?"

"No, no, nothing like that," said Fisk. "She's older, that's all."

"Hey," said Petra, "age is arbitrary."

"That's what she said."

"You and Mary became intimate and you came to see her tonight."

"We didn't see each other in a while, she said she was making a vegan dinner, tempeh and tofu. I got her into vegan, sometimes we went to Real Food Daily."

Milo said, "Ah, the pitfalls of tragic love."

Petra said, "Mary had you hang with Blaise so . . ."

"He wouldn't do anything stupid."

"It wasn't dope Mary was worried about, was it, Robert? She was concerned about some really bad stuff. She knew about other crimes Blaise had committed."

Silence.

"Robert, we got you the juice and the PowerBar and we even bought some extra bottles, which are right outside if you get thirsty again. But you've got to hold up your end. Let's not forget: Those were your prints on Lester Jordan's windowsill. If Blaise tells another story, that makes it your word against his and we've got to follow the evidence. But if we knew Blaise had a history of violence, that would change things."

"Let me ask you," said Fisk. "Again, theoretically."

"Sure."

"Knowing about something isn't a crime, right?"

"Not if you had nothing to do with the crime."

"That fingerprint, Detective Connor, it could happen any kind of way. Maybe I walked by there another time and touched it. Maybe Blaise got one of my prints and stuck it there. Or someone made a mistake, that happens, right?"

Petra smiled. "Anything's possible, Robert. But even flawed evidence is better than none."

Fisk said, "I can tell you more important stuff than what happened to Lester. But all I *know* is what Blaise said. I was never there."

"What kind of important stuff?"

"Mary knew, too. You're right, that's why she hired me."

Milo said, "Intimacy goes the way of all bullshit."

Petra said, "Anything you can say to help us—and yourself—would be appreciated, Robert."

Fisk sucked in his breath. Stared at the empty wax cup he'd drained five times. "I'm thirsty again."

Petra sat back, crossed her legs.

"Detective Connor, all I know is what Mary told me. She said Blaise killed some guys over dope, they tried to cheat him because he was young, fifteen, sixteen. They figured he'd be too scared to fight back, so he shot them."

"Names?"

"She said one was Lester's friend and Lester didn't like that, woulda slapped Blaise around but he got scared Blaise would shoot him, too."

"Bunch of anonymous dope guys," said Raul.

"Don't know any names. She said he also killed some *girls*," said

Fisk. "Two girls, used to live on top of them. Mary knew Blaise did it, probably with some guy he used to run with, but she couldn't prove it."

"Yet another anonymous guy," said Petra.

"Some tweaker," said Fisk. "Sold smack for Blaise and Blaise gave him speed."

"Why'd Mary figure the two of them were involved?"

"The guy showed up in a van one night, late, packed stuff with Blaise."

"Stuff," said Petra.

"Garbage bags. Mary thought maybe bodies, she was scared," said Fisk.

"But she never told anyone except you."

"Scared," Fisk repeated.

"Where's this pal of Blaise's?"

"Dead, O.D.'d. Right on their street, Mary figured he came by to score from Blaise, shot up and dropped."

Raul said, "Another anonymous addict bites the dust."

Fisk squirmed in his chair. "Don't you want to hear about those *girls*?"

Petra said, "Sure, why not."

"Actresses," said Fisk. "Adult genre."

"Why did Blaise kill them?"

"Because he's insane."

Petra scrawled in her pad. "No-name dope guys, no-name porn actresses, no-name tweaker. Quite a list." She looked up. "Anything else?"

"That's all I know—heard about."

"How many years ago did these girls supposedly get killed?"

"Way before I met Mary. Ten, fifteen years, I don't know."

"Mary never told anyone."

"She's scared of him," said Fisk. "He used to look at those girls and yank himself. She caught him, out in the garage. Instead of apologizing, he tells her she doesn't stop bugging his privacy, he'll hurt her."

"He threatens his mommy—your intimate friend," said Petra. "You hang with him anyway?"

"With me, he's respectful."

Milo said, "This guy's *brain*-dead."

Petra said, "Must've been fun hanging with someone like that."

"No, ma'am, it wasn't."

"Blaise ever talk to you directly about any of these alleged murders?"

"Never," said Fisk, too quickly. "He bragged about other stuff. Being a big-time music producer."

Petra said, "Mary knew he'd murdered two girls a long time ago, waits years later to hire you to watch over him? Why would she do that unless she knew about other murders he'd done in the interim?"

Fisk didn't answer.

"Robert, what else has Blaise De Paine done?"

"Never seen or heard anything. I swear."

"Okay, let's talk about Moses Grant."

"Can I have more juice?"

"First tell us about Grant."

"The night Blaise killed Lester, Mosey drove, he was waiting on the street, in the car. Blaise had him park it around the corner."

"The Hummer."

Nod. "Blaise gets back in, brags to Mosey about what he just did. Mosey thinks Blaise is kidding. Blaise screams at him, I'm serious, asshole. Mosey looks at me like, No way, right? I don't answer. Mosey's hands start shaking, he starts driving, goes through a stop sign, we almost crash into another car. Blaise is screaming, Pay attention, asshole. Mosey makes himself calm down but he's different after that."

"How so?"

"Watching out the side of his eye, not eating so much, not sleeping great."

"Despite that, he kept hanging with you and Blaise."

"He thought Blaise was going to hook him up with Puffy, Dr. Dre, Russell Simmons."

"Blaise has those kinds of connections?"

"Mosey believed he did."

"Blaise was stringing Mosey along," said Petra.

Nod. "So Mosey'd drive and do stuff for Blaise and Blaise didn't have to pay him. Blaise liked having a big black guy being his slave, Get my shirts from the laundry, dude, buy me this, buy me that, dude. Everyone thought Moses was a bodyguard but he's soft."

"You were the muscle."

"I was looking after Blaise for *Mary*."

Milo said, "Did a great job, Bozo."

Biro said, "Blaise wanted an entourage."

"Yes, sir."

"Who were the other members?"

"That's it."

"You and Moses."

Nod.

"Why'd Blaise reduce his entourage by killing Mosey?"

"Mosey kept *saying* he was cool with it but you could tell he was lying."

"Blaise figured he might talk about Lester," said Petra.

"Guy was *soft,*" said Fisk.

"Why'd Blaise kill Lester?"

"Lester called Blaise, said you guys were looking into the girls, other old stuff Blaise did, Blaise should get out of town. Blaise said fuck that, there's an easier way."

I said, "He just admitted knowing Blaise intended to murder Lester."

Milo's grin lit up the observation room. "Thank you, Lord, for stupid criminals."

Petra said, "So that's Blaise's pattern. He kills people to keep them quiet."

"Yes." Loud and definite.

"What about the girls?"

"That," said Fisk, "he just hated them. I guess."

"He never talked about it?"

"No, Mary told me."

"Okay. Robert, this is good, we appreciate your cooperation. Let's get back for a sec to Mosey Grant. How and where did he die?"

"*Where* was this building we were crashing in, used to be a car mechanics or something, then it was a club, then it got empty. *How,* I didn't see. Blaise sent me out to buy food, I went to the Grand Central Market—that big place, where the Mexicans sell stuff cheap?" Quick glance at Biro.

Biro said, "You get any of those hand-folded tamales?"

"I bought junk and crap for the two of them, fresh vegetables for me," said Fisk. "I like those edamame beans. I get back, Mosey's lying there, Blaise is fooling with his ProTools, doing a mix like nothing happened. I say what's up, Blaise says he slipped roofies in Moses' milk. Moses drank a lot of milk, liked butter, cheese, anything dairy. All the high fat, that's why he looked like that."

Shaping a convex abdomen and frowning.

Petra said, "How'd Blaise kill Moses?"

"Shot him."

"With what?"

"This .22 he carries around. He's got other stuff, but he carries that."

"What other stuff?"

"Shotgun, .44, bunch of knives. The .22 fits in his pocket."

"What make?"

"Cheap gun, Czechoslovakian or Romanian or something. He calls it his best friend, he got it on the street when he started dealing dope at thirteen. That's what he killed those dope guys with."

"Those nameless guys."

"He just called them dope-fiend dead guys."

"So you come back from the market and find Mosey dead. That would be the second time you walked into one of Blaise's nasty scenes, but you stuck with him."

"I was pretty frustrated," said Fisk. "That's what I was doing at Mary's tonight. Came to tell her I had enough."

"Instead you ended up getting intimate."

"It's what happens with us," said Fisk. "We've got chemistry."

"So your plan was to . . ."

"Turn Blaise in to you. You want him, go to 13466 Hillside View up in Mount Washington, it's this house he's been crashing in."

"*He?*"

"He found it. I was going to leave tomorrow."

Petra copied down the address, exited the room.

Milo was already on his phone, dialing SWAT. As he called in for a raiding party, Petra returned to Fisk, stayed on her feet, looking down at him. "Mary own that house?"

"No, it belongs to some deejay, got a karaoke machine, Blaise knows him from clubs."

"Name?"

"The mail says Perry Moore."

"Where is he?"

"Away," said Fisk. "Playing on some cruise ship, Blaise said."

"Does Mr. Moore know you've been staying at his house?"

Eye shift. "According to Blaise."

"Blaise have a key?"

"He said he lost it."

"How'd you gain entry?"

Fisk shifted in his chair. "He broke a window."

"After he broke, you entered."

"He said it was okay." Fisk clicked his teeth together. Began rocking a leg.

"Something bothering you, Robert?"

"Still thirsty," said Fisk. "Can I have that juice, now? Also an attorney?"

CHAPTER

41

Petra's heavy foot and two a.m. quiet made Hollywood to Mount Washington a quick drive.

Blaise De Paine's hideout was a little gray frame house atop a short, obscure street, just up the freeway from Chinatown where Moses Grant had been dumped. SWAT vehicles clogged the block. The altitude offered a misty, pine-interrupted view of a black damask sky.

An open garage door framed the bulk of the Hummer. Inside the house, clothing, food, and body odor clogged four slovenly rooms, but no sign of De Paine.

The second SWAT team was more subdued than the jocks who'd busted Fisk, everyone let down by big buildup, no action. A deputy commander had showed up to stage-direct, a thickset, bowlegged bald man named Lionel Harger, with meaty furrows sausaging his forehead and a multicrushed nose that sniffed the air with canine intensity.

He charged out of the house now, bounded across the porch, planted himself in front of Petra, folded his arms across a pigeon-chest. "Two in one night? We should charge you desk-folk by the hour."

Milo said, "Be grateful you don't get paid by the suspect."

Harger's chin jerked upward as if he'd been jabbed. "You're that West L.A. so-called ace, does things . . . uniquely." Corkscrew smile on the last word.

Milo said, "Beats administrative meetings and other random bull-shit," and made the most of his height.

Harger's eyes bugged and his thorax swelled. "Concentrate on your clearance rate, Lieutenant. For comedy, stick with Robin Williams."

He stomped away, began gathering his troops. The crime techs were swarming the property like picnic ants, examining the Hummer, flashlighting oil stains in the driveway, searching for tire tracks. The five-year-old Mazda Miata registered to Perry Moore was nowhere in sight. Petra had put an alert on it five minutes ago.

Lionel Harger strutted to an armored Ford Expedition, stopped to glare, got in, roared off.

Petra said, "Making friends and influencing people, Lieutenant Sturgis."

Milo said, "Meathead doesn't recall but he was one year ahead of me at the academy. Assorted sneaky individuals used to leave hostile printed matter in my locker. Ol' Lionel could always be counted on to snicker when he just happened to pass by as I was unearthing some treasure."

His turn to stomp away, over to the house, where he ducked under the yellow tape.

Petra said, "Everyone's fading from sleep deprivation," but her eyes were on high-beam. "Blaise is one lucky little monster, keeps slipping away."

I said, "When he didn't hear from Fisk, he probably got jumpy."

"Any guess about where he's gone?"

I shook my head.

"Reach Tanya?" she said.

"Left messages at her cell and Kyle's."

"This hour, they're probably snoozing. Though when I was in college, I seem to recall three o'clock being midafternoon. Try again?"

I did. Same result.

She said, "At least that mansion's got a good security system."

Her cell beeped. Raul Biro informing her Robert Fisk had been taken to County Jail. She filled Biro in, turned back to me. "We'll get Blaise eventually. Until we do, Tanya should take a semester off and go far away."

Before I could answer, a tall, mustachioed tech came out to show her a rumpled red velvet jacket with gold-braid lapels. *Hollywood Elite*

Custom Tailors label inside, low-rent address on the east end of the Boulevard, *BDP* monogram above that.

"That's our boy," she said.

"Snappy dresser," said the tech. "He walks around like that, who knows, you might even find him."

She pointed a finger. "Go dig, mole." The tech laughed and returned to the house. "Think you can convince the kid to leave town until we find Blaise?"

"She's got nowhere else to go," I said.

"No other family?"

"Not that I know of."

"Maybe we can come up with a plan—well, look who's back walking jauntily."

Milo took several long steps, waved us over to the house. When we got there, he said, "Out back."

One of the techs had spotted soil disturbance at the rear of the skimpy yard, what looked to be recent excavation along a shaded strip created by a mock-orange hedge. Except for the hedge, the property was mostly dry dirt, landscaping not Perry Moore's thing.

The hand-dig took awhile, several sets of hands scooping inch by inch.

At three forty-seven a.m., Coroner's Investigator Judy Sheinblum nudged something soft two feet below the surface. A minute later, she was staring into a face wrapped in clear plastic.

Caucasian male, midthirties, brown hair, orange soul patch. Black-green sludge around the lips and eye sockets advertised the early signs of decomposition. Some fluid condensation on the surface of the plastic, but no maggots; the sheeting was industrial-strength and bound with drapery cord. Cool dry nights would slow things down.

Everyone from Mission Road agreed this was days, not weeks.

Further search of the house produced a cheap blue nylon wallet under a pile of dirty underwear. The photo on Perry Moore's lapsed driver's license matched the corpse. Five years ago, Moore's hair and patch had been tomato red.

The body was lifted out, examined. A protuberance on the left side of Moore's forehead looked like blunt-force injury. Then the hole in the back of Moore's skull put the lie to that.

"Bullet's still in there," said Judy Sheinblum. "No exit because not enough force."

"Twenty-two," said Milo.

"That's what I'd double-down on." Sheinblum returned to the corpse.

Other techs continued to search for additional earth movement, found nothing. Petra ordered a cadaver dog, anyway, learned it would take a couple of days.

We returned to her car. She leaned against the door and yawned. "Blaise is getting careless. Putting Moore in a shallow grave like that, leaving Moore's and his own personal effects behind."

I said, "He didn't expect to be found."

Milo said, "Fisk blew it for him. Speaking of which, Fisk had to know about Moore but he directed us right here."

"He probably figured it was just a matter of time. If he ingratiated himself, things would go easier for him."

"I fed that delusion," said Petra. "The whole time we're dancing around the murder thing, I'm pretending to buy his bull so he won't lawyer up. Then I bring up breaking and entering again and he ends it."

"Idiot focuses on the small stuff," said Milo. "Knows we're looking for him but visits Mary for a quick screw and walks right into it, anyway."

"Thank God for criminal brain damage, huh? Maybe Blaise will screw up big-time, now that he's *sans* entourage. Meanwhile, I'm going to sleep." She opened her car door, rubbed her eyes. Stared at something over my shoulder.

Perry Moore's body, wrapped in official crypt plastic, was being rolled into a white van. The sheath not that different from the one he'd been buried in.

"Kill you so I can get your house," said Petra.

Milo said, "Location, location, location."

42

I picked up the Seville at the Hollywood station and drove home with Milo sleeping in the passenger seat.

At Wilton and Melrose, eyes still closed, he said, "What's the chance Blaise will pull a psycho and go for Tanya, as opposed to doing the rational thing and disappearing?"

"Don't know."

"There's no logical reason for him to get rid of her to cover up old crimes. Perry Moore's body is enough to put him away for life. He's got to figure Fisk either got busted, or decided to bail on him. Either way, he'd know Fisk might talk about Lester and Moses Grant, tossing in a couple more life sentences, maybe even the needle."

I said, "If I was out to make you feel better, I'd say sure. But cover-up's only a small part of it. He's been killing people since before he could shave and getting away with it. It's always been about the thrill."

He grunted, turned toward the window, lapsed into genuine slumber, and breathed through his mouth.

Five-minute nap; he jerked upright, rubbed his eyes. "You need to have a serious talk with Tanya, Alex. Kyle's useless in a serious confrontation. Until Blaise is in custody, she needs to *go* somewhere."

"Same thing Petra said."

"Great minds," he said. "When do you want to do it?"

"Tomorrow morning."

"Let's hit the mansion tomorrow before the two of them leave for school, say seven."

"Okay," I said. "Maybe you should do the scary talk."

"Why?"

"More your line of work than mine."

"Fine," he said. "Make me the bad guy, I look like one anyway."

Shifting position again, he slapped his pocket, muttering, "Damn thing's on vibrator, feels like a ferret scurrying around in there," yanked out his phone, barked, "*Sturgis* . . . oh, hey . . . what . . . that's all you *know*? Okay, sure, sure, we're close, anyway."

Clicking off, he said, "That was Biro, guy doesn't seem to need food or sleep or any other kind of human sustenance. Monitoring calls, one just came in from Hudson Avenue. Guess we hit the mansion, now."

Iona Bedard, drunk, glassy-eyed, gunmetal sharkskin Prada suit twisted so severely that it corkscrewed her torso, screamed, "Get your greaser hands off me!"

The officer looking into the cruiser was a white man named Kenney, big and muscular and amused. His partner, a black woman named Doulton, stood on the front landing of the mansion listening as Detective Raul Biro spoke to America. The housekeeper wore a long pink robe, kept cinching the belt tighter and pointing at the cruiser that held Iona.

Amber flickers from a few neighboring houses, but most of Hudson Avenue remained dim and quiet but for the sound of Iona's ire.

Lots of lights on in the Bedard mansion. The green Bentley occupied its usual place in the driveway. No sign of the white Mercedes.

"Greaser!"

Iona slouched in the backseat of the police car, hands cuffed in front of her as a courtesy, black hair stiff and mussed, runny mascara evoking a grade D sad-clown painting. Skinny legs were spread apart, revealing a crescent of black panty under panty hose.

I could smell the booze from a yard away.

Iona pummeled the seat with cuffed fists. "Let me out let me *out*!"

Officer Kenney said, "You've been arrested for creating a public disturbance, ma'am. Now you need to calm down before you get your-self in any additional trouble."

Iona's mandible protruded. "That is *my* fucking house and you're a fucking *service* employee! I *order* you to let me *out*!"

Kenney's "Ma'am—" was met by a flood of invective. He shut the cruiser's door.

A ratatattat sounded and the car's window shuddered. Iona had sprawled on her back, raised her legs, and was bicycle-pumping the glass with stiletto heels.

Kenney said, "She doesn't stop that, I'm going to have to hog-tie her."

Milo said, "Be my guest."

"She's no one important?"

"In her own mind."

Kenney smiled. "Lots of that going around."

As the cruiser drove away, Raul Biro finished with America and let her return to the mansion. His hair was combed back smoothly above an unlined face. No wrinkles in his blue suit, either. His white shirt was snowy, gold tie knotted in a perfect half Windsor.

Milo's hand drifted to his own limp ribbon of polyester as Biro talked. "According to Ms. Frias—the maid—here's what happened. Mrs. Bedard showed up this evening around seven p.m., unannounced. She insisted on coming in, which put Frias in a tough spot because Mr. Bedard's instructions are that she never be allowed in."

"Domestic bliss," said Milo.

"Frias says Mrs. Bedard has tried it before, but always when Mr. Bedard is here. Mr. Bedard handles it, trying not to provoke confronta-tion. This time, when Frias tried to close the door, Mrs. Bedard shoved her aside so hard she nearly fell, forced her way in, and started looking around the house for Kyle and 'that girl.' Apparently Kyle spoke to her earlier in the day and told her about Tanya and she didn't approve."

"Cuing Mommy in," said Milo. "Wonder why?"

Biro shrugged. "Anyway, Mrs. Bedard found Kyle and Tanya up in one of the bedrooms and went off on them. A big argument ensued, Kyle and Mrs. Bedard screaming, Mrs. Bedard throwing stuff, there was some breakage. At approximately seven fifteen, Kyle and Tanya left the house with Mrs. Bedard trying to restrain Kyle physically. She's yanking on his jacket sleeve, he slips out of the jacket, this time it's her turn to fall. She lands on her butt, screams for Kyle to help her up. Tanya starts to help but Mrs. Bedard screams at her—'Not *you!*' Kyle gets p.o.'d, leaves with Tanya."

"They take the Mercedes?"

"Yup," said Biro. "Haven't been heard from since. Mrs. Bedard punched Kyle's cell number a hundred times according to Frias. Finally, she gives up, goes to the wet bar, and gets to work on Mr. Bedard's private stash of single-malt whiskey. By eight, she's stone-blasted, starts dumping on the maid—how could she let this shameful thing happen, 'that girl doesn't belong,' can't Frias even be trusted with running a house, and so on. Apparently, some racial comments ensued and Frias went to her room and locked herself in. Mrs. Bedard goes after her, bangs the door, starts yelling, finally gives up and leaves. Then the doorbell rings at three a.m., Frias answers it because she's worried it's Kyle, he's in some kind of trouble. Instead, it's Mrs. Bedard again, even drunker, a taxi's driving away and she's got a suitcase, says she checked out of the Hilton, is moving in until order is restored. Frias tries to bar Bedard's entry. A struggle ensues, and both women end up on their butts. Frias runs to her room again, dials 911. Wilshire cruiser shows up three minutes later, the front door's wide open and Mrs. Bedard marches out and orders the patrol officers to arrest 'that taco-bending greaser bitch, deport her back to taco-land.'"

Lights went off serially in the mansion. Biro studied the Tudor facade. "Maybe it really is true, money doesn't bring happiness." Small smile. "Though I don't imagine being poor would be much comfort if you're crazy to begin with."

The three of us returned to our cars. Biro's civilian drive was an eighties Datsun ZX, chocolate brown, custom wheels, immaculately maintained.

"What next, Lieutenant?"

"I'd better find the kids, get 'em safe until De Paine's in custody."

"What about Mrs. Bedard? Once she sobers up, she'll be out."

"I don't see her as any big criminal risk but if someone loses the paperwork for a day or so, no one's crying."

Biro smiled.

"That could happen. What else do you want me to do?"

"Go home and get some sleep."

No reaction.

Milo said, "You don't believe in sleep?"

"Spent some time in Afghanistan, my whole bio clock got disrupted. Since then I'm okay with three, four hours."

"Listening for snipers."

"Among other things," said Biro. "You ex-military?"

"Way before your time," said Milo.

"Asia?" said Biro. "My dad did that. He drives a catering truck now. Tacos and all that good stuff."

Biro drove off. As the sound of his souped-up engine died, silence returned to Hudson Avenue.

Milo said, "Maybe Iona's ugly scene's for the best. Romeo and Juliet get upset, hightail it for parts unknown."

I said, "You see those two cruising to Vegas?"

"If I had a mama like that, I'd elope, change my area code, maybe my country code."

"Nice fantasy, but way too adventurous."

"Where do *you* see them heading?"

"Everything's been taken from Tanya. Kyle was a bright spot but Iona just polluted that. Tanya's a creature of habit. I can't see her heading anywhere but the home Patty created for her."

"Exactly what we told her to avoid?"

"She's got a hypermature facade, Milo, but that's just playing grown-up. Think '*You're* not the boss over *me*.'"

"Yeah, she has been disregarding our wisdom, hooking up with Kyle in the first place . . . Okay, let's check, maybe you're wrong."

"I hope I am."

"Takes a *big* man to say that."

"Not in this case."

◆

Half a block from the duplex on Canfield, Milo crushed his unlit panatela in the Seville's ashtray and cursed. "Right there in the open, might as well hang up a sign."

The white Mercedes ragtop blocked the mouth of the driveway. Tanya's van sat in front of it.

Lights off in the building.

Milo said, "Stupid smart kids. I should wake 'em up right now, give 'em Uncle Milo's scariest speech." He squinted at his Timex. "Couple of hours until daybreak—let's keep to the same schedule. Seven a.m., we're back here, in their faces big-time. Meanwhile, I'll check 'round back, make sure everything's kosher. So *I* can sleep."

He got out of the car. "If I don't—"

"Yeah, yeah the pencil box."

"Would my Flash Gordon lunch pail be more enticing?"

"You had one of those?"

"Nope. Everyone else lies, why not me?"

I cut the motor and sat at the wheel, watched him stride up the driveway and slip in front of the van. His right hand tickled the holster under his jacket. Probably a smart move, keeping the weapon under wraps. At his level of fatigue, blowing off a toe by accident was a serious risk.

Seconds after he'd rounded the building, the gunshot sounded.

Not the face-slap of a handgun.

Full-bodied roar; a shotgun.

I jumped out, began running back, ready to protect my friend.

With what?

I stopped, groped for my phone. Punched 911 so hard my fingertips burned.

Blast number two, then snap-crackle of a small-arms fusillade, at this distance no more ominous than a frog song.

Ring ring ring ring ring ring—"911 Emergency—"

I fought not to lose patience with the mechanical, just-be-calm-sir approach of the operator.

She said, "Sir, you need to answer my questions."

I raised my voice. Maybe *"Officer down!"* broke through her training-manual straitjacket. Or she could hear the third shotgun blast answered by a full-on ballistic chorus. In what seemed like seconds, sirens bansheed from the south. Four sets of headlights.

When the quartet of Westside units roared up the duplex, I was out of the Seville, standing on the street side of the car, hands up, feeling cowardly, useless.

Listening to a new, sick silence.

Eight officers advanced, guns drawn. I spoke my piece and they left one officer behind to watch me.

I said, "My friend's back there. Lieutenant Sturgis."

She said, "We'll just wait sir."

It took way too long for a sergeant to return. "You can go back, Doctor."

"Is he okay?"

Two more cops emerged, looking grave. I repeated the question.

The sergeant said, "He's alive—Officer Bernelli, double-check what's taking the EMTs so long. And ask for two ambulances."

Milo sat on the bottom step of the rear landing, knees drawn almost to his chin, head down. Pressing something to his arm—his jacket, wadded up. His white sleeve had turned red and his color was bad.

He looked up. "Forget the lunch pail, this doesn't count."

"Are you—"

"Just a flesh wound, Kimo Sabe." Big grin. "Always wanted to say that."

"Let me do that." I sat down next to him and pressed evenly on the jacket.

"We'll do it together." Another grin. "Like that *Sesame Street* song—'Co-Operation.' Most of those rag dolls are simps, but Oscar's got it going on."

"He does have his moments." The things you talk about when your friend's breathing turns raspy and his blood keeps seeping.

I pushed harder. He winced.

"Sorry."

"Hey," he said. "Nothing that can't be replaced." His eyes fluttered. I felt him shiver through his sleeve.

I put my arm around his shoulder, pressed tighter.

He said, "How cozy."

We sat there. All the cops were out front except for one officer standing near the top of Tanya's back steps.

Milo shivered again. What the hell was taking the ambulances so long?

The rear door to Tanya's unit was shredded but the window remained in place.

Milo said, "How it happened was the bastard was crouched up there, I walked into it like a total rookie jackass, my goddamn gun's still in the holster. Why the hell do I bother looking for trouble if I'm not *ready* for trouble? He opened up but I was out of range so I just caught a sprinkle. I jumped back in time to avoid the second blast and the third. Finally got hold of my trusty peashooter."

"A sprinkle," I said.

"It's no big deal, pal. When I was a kid I caught some quail-shot in the butt when my brother Patrick got stupid. This feels a little heavier-duty but nothing humongous—maybe deer."

"Okay, quiet—"

"Only a few pellets made their way to my manly biceps—"

"Great. No more talking."

The patrolman at the top of the landing said, "Deershot? Gotta hurt like a bitch."

Milo said, "No worse than root canal."

The cop said, "I had *that* last year. Hurt like a bitch."

"Thanks for the empathy." To me: "Press as hard as you want. And don't *worry*, okay? Everything's copacetic. Not for him." Laughter.

"He's—"

"Go take a look. Do some advanced *psycho*-therapy."

"I'll stay here."

"No, no, check it out, Alex. Maybe you can get one of those deathbed confessions." Cracking up and leaking blood. "Tomorrow we get drunk and laugh about it."

I sat there.

He said, "*Go*. Could be our last chance."

Making sure his hand was secure on the jacket, I stood and approached the stairs.

The cop said, "Where you going, sir?"

Milo said, "I told him to."

"Not a good idea, Lieutenant. This guy's in no—"

"Don't be a by-the-book lamebrain, Officer, and give the doctor a looky-loo. He's family, won't piss on the evidence."

"Whose family?"

"Mine."

The cop hesitated.

"Did you hear what I said?"

"Is that a direct order?"

"As direct as it gets. Give me any more lip and I'm coming up and bleeding all over you."

The cop laughed uneasily and moved aside. I climbed the stairs.

Peterson Whitbread/Blaise De Paine was stretched on his back, head to one side, whitewashed in profile by the overhead bulb.

He'd shaved his head shiny, wore a two-carat diamond in his ear, a pair of chunky diamond rings on his left hand, three on his right. The gem-clogged bracelet of his Rolex Perpetual had been styled for a football tackle's wrist and hung halfway down a narrow, pale hand.

Polished nails, blue-silver.

Slender young man, puny shoulders, bland baby-face, boy-sized wrists. Small frame diminished further by an oversized sweat suit, black and yellow and white velour, Sean John logo. Black patent-leather running shoes with curled-up toes sported a yellow cushion doodad on the side that resembled a carpenter's bubble. Crisp soles.

New shoes for a big night out.

Lettering on the back of the sweat jacket read *La Familia. Havana.* Below that: *The Good Life.*

Black, yellow, white. A little crushed bumblebee.

A clean black-cherry hole freckled one of his hands. Fabric puffed where bullets had entered his belly.

Eyes closed, mouth agape, no movement. Too late for any sort of confession.

Then I saw it: shallow up-and-down heaving of the bloodied torso.

The cop said, "He breathes once in a while but forget it. They shoulda called for a meat wagon."

I stood there and watched Blaise De Paine fade away. A walnut-grip shotgun lay a foot from his right ankle. Three ejected pellet casings formed a rough triangle behind his body, inches from the shattered door.

Light behind the door, splinters on kitchen tile.

I said, "Anyone inside?"

The cop said, "The residents."

"Girl and a boy?"

"Yup."

"They okay?"

"She's the one blew this loser away—you'd best be going back down now, coroner will need to certify the—"

Milo called, "You been watching too much TV, Officer."

The cop gnawed his lower lip. "I were you, Lieutenant, I'd avoid too much exertion. Keep the metabolism as low as possible so you don't bleed unnecessarily."

"As opposed to all those necessary bleeds?"

"Sir—"

Milo's obscene retort was obscured by the clank of a gurney on wheels, human voices, bright lights.

EMTs charging in with that bright-eyed, adrenalized look the good ones have.

The cop at the top of the stairs said, "Lieutenant's right down there."

Milo said, "Like it's a mystery? *Jee*-sus." Standing and removing his jacket and dripping blood. Shouting, "O-positive, in case anyone's remotely interested," as they rushed him.

I started to descend the stairs, was halted by a strange whistling noise behind me.

Blaise De Paine's eyes had opened.

His lips quivered. Another whistle, higher-pitched, just a teapot-squeak, emerged from between his lips.

Final air seeping out.

The lips formed a smile.

Nothing intentional, he had to be way past volition.

Then his eyes shifted quickly.

Toward me.

Fixed on me.

His head from the ground. Dropped down hard.

A seizure? Some terminal neurological burst—too much intention. He repeated the movement.

Watching me?

A third rise and fall of his head.

I hurried to his side, leaned in close.

His lips moved. Formed a smile.

I kneeled down next to him.

He croaked. Made eye contact. Laughed gutturally, or something awfully close to it.

I looked into his eyes.

He reared up.

Spat blood in my face.

Died.

As I wiped my face with my jacket, movement behind the door caught my eye. Tanya, standing behind the shattered panels, gazing out through the window that had, miraculously, remained intact.

The scene came together in my head.

De Paine blasting away at Milo, hearing something behind him, wheeling, shooting low.

Getting off one last round through the door before the opening he created allowed return fire and sudden pain burned through his hand and belly and the shotgun.

I waved at Tanya.

Maybe she didn't see me. Or she did and it didn't matter. She remained motionless. Staring at the corpse.

Kyle Bedard materialized behind her.

The cop who'd been at the top of the stairs returned and climbed halfway up.

"How's he—"

"Gone."

"You need to go, sir. Right now."

"She's my patient—"

"I don't care, sir."

"I'm stepping over him," I said, still tasting blood.

And I did.

CHAPTER

44

Eruption, then excavation.

　　The way I saw it, Law Enforcement ended up with the light shovels.

A key found in the mess Blaise De Paine had left in Perry Moore's house was traced to a rental storage bin in East Hollywood. Double unit, complete with fluorescent lighting, a sleeper sofa, and electrical hookup.

　　The refrigerator at the rear hummed nicely. Next to the cooler was a sealed box of heroin packets, a host of over-the-counter painkillers, and thirty-five soap-bar-sized chunks of hashish. Inside the fridge were six-packs of Jolt Cola, a nice variety of microbrewed beers, and a trash bag filled with human bones, some still dusted with desiccated flesh. The bones offered up four distinct DNA patterns, all female. Mitochondrial matches were eventually made to Brenda Hochlbeier and Renée Mittle, aka Brandee Vixen and Rocksi Roll. Those remains were sent back to Curney, North Dakota, where the girls' families offered thanks for the chance to provide a proper Christian burial.

　　The other two samples remained Jane Does.

　　Benjamin Baranelli ran an ad in *Adult Film News* announcing the reconstitution of Vivacious Videos, initiated by a "re-release tribute five-CD set featuring our beloved Brandee and Rocksi."

Robert Fisk's public defender offered to plead his client to obstruction of justice. The D.A.'s office proclaimed its "unalterable" intention to charge Fisk with multiple first-degree murders. The compromise reached four days later had Fisk plead to two counts of voluntary manslaughter with a fifteen-year sentence. The nugget Fisk offered up was the fact that De Paine had bragged about killing "two bitches from Compton."

Further work on the unidentified bones confirmed likely African American heritage. Attempts to identify the sources continued.

Mary Whitbread was charged with nothing. Within a week of her son's death, her ground-floor unit on Fourth Avenue was up for lease and she'd moved to parts unknown.

Whispers around town had Mario Fortuno incriminating a horde of Hollywood notables in illegal wiretapping, with indictments to come. East Coast papers covered the rumors with greater enthusiasm than the *L.A. Times.*

Petra, Raul Biro, David Saunders, and Kevin Bouleau all received departmental commendations. Biro nudged up against a fast-track promotion to Detective II.

When Milo was wheeled into the Cedars E.R., Rick was there to greet him. The surgeon broke his own rule about treating relatives and dug the pellets out of Milo's arm personally. The procedure turned out to be more complex than expected, with several small blood vessels requiring repair. Milo insisted on nothing stronger than local anesthesia. Conscious sedation made him loopy and he peppered the operating room with a barrage of obnoxious comments.

Days later, he claimed to be healed and threw away his sling, against medical advice. Rick was on call and not there to argue. I didn't enter the debate, even after I caught Milo wincing when lifting a coffee cup.

My shovel weighed a ton.

I met with Tanya daily, sometimes for hours at a time. When called for, Kyle attended.

Getting therapy off on the right foot meant starting with a lie: Patty had never killed anyone, had merely been referring to the death of a drug-dealing friend of De Paine, at De Paine's hand. The "terrible thing" was her guilt at not reporting the crime.

I built up Patty's justification for keeping quiet. Others had already notified the police, with poor results; she'd felt compelled to escape so she could ensure Tanya's safety. Years later, she'd run into De Paine and he'd smirked, threatened Tanya. Before Patty could do anything about it, she'd fallen ill, had been forced to "get her ducks in a row."

The deathbed pronouncement, muddled by terminal disease, had been aimed at warning Tanya.

"I'm sure," I said, "that had she lived she would've tried to fill in more details."

Tanya sat there.

"She loved you so much," I said. "It all traces back to that."

"Yes," she said, "I know. Thank you."

Next topic: the fact that *she'd* killed a man.

The crime reconstruction confirmed the scene I'd imagined.

De Paine's first blast at Milo had been taken from the top of the stairs. Milo, hit, had run backward into darkness, clutching his arm and groping for his service gun.

De Paine had descended several stairs, straining to locate his prey. He'd heard something behind him, or imagined he had. Wheeling, he'd shot through the door from a now-lowered vantage point, destroying wood but leaving the upper window intact.

Tanya, hearing the noise, grabbed up the nine-shot Walther semiautomatic she'd borrowed from Colonel Bedard's gun room and, ignoring Kyle's pleas, ran into the kitchen.

Hearing De Paine's third blast and Milo's return fire, she'd aimed wobbily through the shattered door and squeezed off all nine shots.

One bullet embedded in the doorjamb and was dug out by the reconstruction crew. Five others sailed clear of De Paine, hit concrete steps, and rolled, defaced, to the bottom of the stairway.

One hit De Paine in his left hand, a nonfatal flesh wound.

Two pierced his gut, demolished his spleen and liver.

Clear case of self-defense. Tanya said she was fine with what she'd done. Maybe she'd eventually believe that.

Kyle Bedard moved into the duplex on Canfield. Iona Bedard protested and was ignored. Myron Bedard remained in Europe but called twice to "make sure Kyle was okay." When informed of his exwife's resentment of "that girl," Myron wired Kyle fifty thousand dollars and instructed him to "take your cutie on a nice vacation and don't tell your mother where you're going."

Kyle banked the money and returned to work on his doctoral dissertation.

Tanya told me she loved him, but it took a bit of adjustment to have someone in her bed. Since the shooting, Kyle dozed restlessly.

"He sits up, asleep, but looking terrified, Dr. Delaware. I hug him and tell him everything's okay and the next morning he doesn't remember a thing. What is that, a deep-stage night terror?"

"Could be," I said.

"If it doesn't clear up, maybe he can come to you."

"How're you sleeping, Tanya?"

"Me? Great."

Further questioning revealed she completed at least an hour of compulsive ritual before bedtime. Sometimes the routine stretched to ninety minutes.

"But that was an exception, Dr. Delaware. Mostly I clock in at sixty or just below."

"You time yourself."

"To get a handle on it," she said. "Of course it's possible that the timing itself has become part of the routine. But I can live with that—oh, by the way did I tell you I changed my mind about psychiatry? Too ambiguous, I'm thinking about E.R. medicine."

Over the next month, her compulsive habits intensified. I concentrated on the big issues until, three weeks later, she was ready to work on the symptoms. Hypnosis and cognitive behavior therapy proved useful, but not completely. I contemplated medication. Perhaps she sensed that because she devoted half of one session to a paper she'd written on the side effects of selective serotonin reuptake inhibitors. Opining that she'd never "mess with my brain, unless I was truly psychotic."

I said, "In the end, it's up to you."

"Because I'm an adult?"

I smiled.

She said, "Adulthood's kind of a foolish concept, isn't it? People grow up in all kinds of different ways."

CHAPTER

45

Just about the time Milo's arm returned to full function, a woman named Barb Smith called my service and asked for an appointment for her child. I take very few therapy cases and because of Tanya, half a dozen court consults, and my desire to spend more time with Robin, I'd instructed the service to deliver that message routinely.

Lorraine, the operator, said, "I tried, Doctor. She wouldn't take no for an answer—called back three times."

"Pushy?"

"No, she was actually kind of nice."

"Meaning I should stop being a hard case and return her call."

"You're the doctor, Doctor."

"Give me the number."

"I'm proud of you," said Lorraine.

One of those meaningless cellular prefixes. Barb Smith picked up on the first ring. Young voice, radio-sultry. "Thanks so much for calling, Dr. Delaware."

I gave my little speech.

She said, "I appreciate all that, but maybe you'll change your mind when I tell you my former married name."

"What's that?"

"Fortuno."

"Oh," I said. "Philip."

"Felipe," she said. "That's his legal name but Mario won't use it, just to needle me. You've met Mario."

"Dominant."

"Tries to be," she said, softly. "He ordered me to call you months ago. I think Felipe's a wonderful boy, the problem's all in Mario's—let's talk about that in person. I know you get paid for your time, and I don't want to mooch. Would it be okay if I came by myself, without Felipe? Then, if you think there's a problem, you can see Felipe?"

"Sure. You live in Santa Barbara."

Hesitation. "I used to."

"Moving around," I said.

Another pause. "This call—you don't record anything, right?"

"Not to my knowledge."

"Well," she said, "that's not always relevant—what people think they know. How about we meet halfway. Between L.A. and Santa Barbara."

"Sure. Where?"

"Oxnard," she said. "There's a winery there, away from the beach, in an industrial park off Rice Avenue. Nice little café and they make a great Zinfandel, if wine's your thing."

"Not when I work."

"You can always take some home. I probably will."

I met her the next day at noon.

The winery was a two-story mock-adobe structure set on a couple acres of landscaped lawns and spotless parking lot fifteen miles above the upper reaches of Malibu. Grapes trucked in from Napa and Sonoma and the Alexander Valley, pressed and bottled in an antiseptic setting, freeway-close for shipping. Far cry from the fragrant earth of Wine Country, but the tasting room was busy, as was the ten-table restaurant near the back.

Barb Smith had reserved a corner booth. She was young and bronze—maybe thirty—with long, wavy black hair, searching brown Eurasian eyes, a wide soft mouth. A baby-blue pantsuit covered skin but couldn't conceal curves. Brown Kate Spade bag, high-heeled sandals to match, discreet emerald earrings, delicate gold-link necklace.

A glass of red wine sat in front of her. Her handshake was firm, moist around the edges.

She thanked me for coming, handed me a check for three times my usual fee, and took a wallet-sized photo out of the bag.

Dark-haired little boy, shy smile. Lots of his mother in him; the only trace of Mario Fortuno, a slightly undersized chin.

"Handsome," I said.

"And good. Inside—where it counts."

A waitress came over. Barb Smith said, "The cod cakes are unbelievable, if you don't mind fish. That's what I'm having."

"Sounds good."

The waitress nodded approvingly and left.

"Not when you're working," said Barb Smith. "I respect that. My only job is taking care of Felipe and he's in school until three."

Meaning Oxnard was driving distance from home.

My Coke arrived. Barb Smith sipped her wine. "This isn't the Zin, it's a Cab-Merlot blend, like they do in France. Mario doesn't like Merlot, calls it Cabernet for girls. I drink what I want—if I'd have hugged you when you walked in you'd have thought I was forward, right?"

"Hugs can be Hollywood handshakes," I said.

She laughed. "I love you, baby, now change completely? Once upon a time I thought I wanted to be part of that. The reason I brought up hugging is it would've had nothing to do with friendliness. That's how Mario taught me to check for wires."

"Ah."

"But the way you're dressed—polo shirt and slacks—it would be pretty hard to conceal something. Unless you were up on the latest technology."

"To me that means stereo."

"Just a simple guy, huh? Somehow I doubt it, but I'm convinced you're not wired. Why would you be, I called you. At Mario's behest—that's a good word, isn't it? I work on my vocabulary, always trying to better myself. Felipe has a great vocabulary. Everyone tells me he's gifted."

She drank some more, glanced off to the side. "I didn't want to do this but Mario—you're probably wondering what I saw in him. Sometimes I wonder myself. But he is the father of my child and I do know he's going through some incredibly rough times. Did you know he's got a bad heart—two bypasses years ago but there was damage they couldn't repair? That part never gets in the papers."

The corners of her eyes moistened and she swiped them with her napkin.

"Oh, look at this," she said. "I hate him and still I feel sorry for him."

"They say he's got charisma."

"Are you interested in how I got involved with him? Or is that too egotistical of me?"

"Tell me," I said.

"It all goes back to what I just told you before. Wanting to be part of the scene. I thought I was an actress, did some community college back in . . . majored in theater, everyone said I had talent. So I came out here, did a string of temp jobs while trying to break in. One of them was working for a caterer, doing high-end industry parties. I met Mario at one of those, he was the only person who bothered to look at me when I came by with the plate of curried shrimp. Terrible food, if I told you what went on behind the scenes, you'd never eat at an industry party again."

"Again?" I smiled.

"Sorry," she said. "I'm coming across so pretentioso. One of Mario's made-up words. He despises the people who pay him . . . anyway, that's where I met Mario and later, after the party, he took me out for drinks and drove me around in his Cadillac. I ended up telling him my life story—Mario has a talent for listening—and he told me what he did. He got a kick out of the fact that I had no idea who he was. I hear P.I., I'm figuring some small-time guy with an office over a Mexican restaurant, like on TV, I mean anyone can drive a Caddy, right? He never touched me, perfect gentleman, drove me home and asked me out again. Kind of nervous, like a teenage boy. Later, of course, I found out he'd been faking it, Mario can make you think whatever you want. He acts better than any of those stars he works for . . . anyway, he tells me he could use my talents, P.I.'s hire aspiring actors all the time, there's lots of crossover. So I went to work for him. And he was right, acting skills are a big part of it."

"Undercover work?" I said.

"I did some of that, but mostly it was pretending to be something I wasn't. Going to a cocktail lounge and getting the target to flirt with me so Mario could take pictures. Process serving—it's amazing how easy it is to gain entry into someone's house or office when you lift the hemline of your skirt."

She finished her wine. "I'm making myself sound like some kind of hooker, aren't I?"

"More like a decoy."

"Nice of you to say, but I was selling sex appeal. Not that I ever did anything sleazy, it was all false advertising. Meanwhile, I'm falling in love with Mario and he's claiming to feel the same way."

She shook her head. "Old enough to be my father and he'd been married four times before. File that under 'What was I thinking?' Meanwhile, I'm pregnant. Which turned out to be the best thing that ever happened to me. Felipe's an angel, so sweet, couldn't ask for a more perfect little boy."

"Yet Mario's concerned about him."

"Mario thinks he's gay."

"Because he's quiet," I said.

She laughed. "Meaning Felipe doesn't argue, doesn't like to fight or play sports. He's got his nose in books all the time, is kind of small for his age. My side of the family, my mom's Chinese—oh, here's our food."

We ate in silence until she said, "Maybe Felipe is a bit overly gentle. Yes, he has a pretty face, when he was a baby everyone thought he was a girl. But does that make him gay?"

"Not at all."

"Exactly, Dr. Delaware. That's what I keep telling Mario but he kept wanting me to push Felipe into things he hates."

"Sports?"

"Sports, karate." She put down her fork. "I tell you, if he got involved in something rough and injured that cute little nose of his, I'd be shattered. I said so to Mario. He told me I was crazy, a few scars are what every guy needs—do you have scars, Dr. Delaware?"

I smiled.

She said, "Sorry, that was nosy. Mario has scars. Plenty of them, from when he was growing up in Chicago. To me, that is not masculine. Masculine is being secure and not having to prove yourself."

"You're not concerned about Felipe and you know him best."

"Exactly."

"But you're here . . ."

"To fulfill my obligation to Mario. Kind of like a final kiss, you know? Because he's going away—not to prison, not if he gives up what I think he's going to give up. But when the you-know-what hits the fan, it's going to be huge, Dr. Delaware. People you won't believe are going to tumble."

"The A list."

"The A-*plus* list," she said. "I'm talking red-carpet faces, people who run major studios, corporate emperors. Mario's big thing was that he'd never tell. But with what they've got against him, his bad heart, most of his money gone, he's going to spill everything. And then he'll have to go somewhere and I won't ever see him again and neither will Felipe. So I figured, why not be a good person. Even though I know Felipe's not gay."

"Do Mario and Felipe have a good relationship?"

"Mario didn't spend much time with Felipe but Felipe likes him. And the funny thing is, with all Mario's talk about getting Felipe into rough stuff, he was gentle with him. They'd play cards, just sit around. The truth is, Mario's not much of an athlete himself—you met him, he's a little guy."

"Little guy with big-guy charisma."

"Another Napoleon," she said. "For some reason I fall for them. Maybe it's because my father—that doesn't matter, this isn't about me, it's about Felipe. Do you agree he's okay?"

"Nothing you've told me says he's not. And if he is gay, there'd be nothing I could or would want to do about it."

She wiped her mouth. "You're not gay, yourself?"

"No," I said. *But some of my best friends . . .* "Sexual therapy reorientation isn't something I'd generally recommend."

"I agree, totally. But Felipe's *not* gay. He's *absolutely* well adjusted."

"Mario did mention some teasing at school and some toilet problems."

"No big deal," she said. "Felipe's small and he doesn't play sports so some older boys ribbed him. I told him to stand up to them, say mind your own business. That worked. As far as the toilet problems, my pediatrician said Felipe was holding in and getting impacted. I talked to Felipe and he said he didn't like to use the bathroom at school because it was too dirty. I went and checked and he's right, the place is filthy, I wouldn't let my dog go there. But I didn't want Felipe all clogged up so I started giving him a little mineral oil, woke him up a little earlier for breakfast and then thirty minutes later, ten minutes before he had to go to school, he was able to go and wouldn't need to go in school. For number one, I did tell him to use the urinals, just stand back so his body didn't touch anything dirty."

"Sounds like you handled everything."

"I thought I did. Thank you for agreeing." Big smile. "So now I've fulfilled my obligation to Mario and we can enjoy our lunch."

She spent the rest of the time recounting cases she'd worked on. Dropping names, then pledging me to confidentiality, then declaring that since she'd paid me and this was a professional meeting, the law said *anything* she told me was confidential.

When we finished, she insisted on paying but we split the check.

I walked her to her car. Gray Ford Taurus with an Avis sticker.

Careful woman.

"Thanks for meeting with me, Dr. Delaware. I feel a whole lot better."

"My pleasure. Regards to Mario."

"I doubt I'll be talking to him. By the way, do you want to know the real reason I think Mario wanted me to see you? It has nothing to do with Felipe, Felipe's obviously fine."

"What's the real reason?" I said.

"Guilt, Dr. Delaware. Mario may be a sociopath but he still has the capacity for guilt. And maybe I'm the only one he could show that side to."

"What does he feel guilty about?"

"Not his work," she said. "Not all those lives he ruined with his wiretaps and his extortion, that he's proud of. But as a father . . . he knows he failed. He told me so. He's got three daughters from three different mothers, four other sons, and they're all a mess, two have been in prison. Plus, there was a son who he never acknowledged, who turned *really* bad. Mario said he was into dope and crime, all sorts of heavy-duty stuff. Mostly, he blamed the mother—someone he never married, the whole thing was a one-night stand. But the last time I spoke to him—when he ordered me to see you—he admitted maybe he had some blame for saving the boy's butt so he never learned to take responsibility. Even though he insisted it was *mostly* the mother's fault, because of who she was."

"What was she?"

"Porn actress, a real lowlife, according to Mario. He said she re-invented herself as some kind of investor, but she was the same old amoral slut he'd made the mistake of knocking up and look at the re-sults."

I said, "Mario had no contact with this son?"

"None, the boy has no idea who his father is because Mario paid the woman off big-time so she'd lie and say it was someone else. She used the money to buy real estate, Mario used to say the Mafia had nothing on L.A. real estate people. I asked Mario why he never stepped up to the plate, because shirking wasn't like him, he was all about pa-ternal duty, paid child support for the other kids and Felipe. He got a look on his face and didn't answer. Only time I've ever seen a hint of fear in Mario's eyes. Anyway, nice knowing you, Dr. Delaware. I'd say till we meet again, but that's not going to happen."

I watched her drive away.

Stood there breathing in ocean air and a hint of fermented grapes, thought about calling Milo and finding out if Mario Fortuno's arrest process had included taking blood.

Changed my mind.

I had six court cases pending, a nineteen-year-old patient who'd need me indefinitely. A woman who loved me.

A dog that smiled.

What else mattered?

ABOUT THE AUTHOR

JONATHAN KELLERMAN is one of the world's most popular authors. He has brought his expertise as a clinical psychologist to more than two dozen bestselling crime novels, including the Alex Delaware series, *The Butcher's Theater, Billy Straight, The Conspiracy Club,* and *Twisted.* With his wife, the novelist Faye Kellerman, he co-authored the bestsellers *Double Homicide* and *Capital Crimes.* He is the author of numerous essays, short stories, scientific articles, two children's books, and three volumes of psychology, including *Savage Spawn: Reflections on Violent Children.* He has won the Goldwyn, Edgar, and Anthony awards, and has been nominated for a Shamus Award. Jonathan and Faye Kellerman live in California and New Mexico. Their four children include the novelist Jesse Kellerman. Visit the author's website at www.jonathankellerman.com.

ABOUT THE TYPE

This book was set in Simoncini Garamond, a typeface designed by Francesco Simoncini based on the style of Garamond that was created by the French printer Jean Jannon after the original models of Claude Garamond.